Istanbul Passage

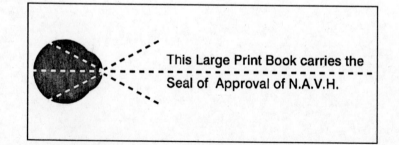

This Large Print Book carries the
Seal of Approval of N.A.V.H.

ISTANBUL PASSAGE

JOSEPH KANON

THORNDIKE PRESS
A part of Gale, Cengage Learning

GALE
CENGAGE Learning·

Detroit • New York • San Francisco • New Haven, Conn • Waterville, Maine • London

LP

KAN

GALE
CENGAGE Learning®

Copyright © 2012 by Joseph Kanon.
Thorndike Press, a part of Gale, Cengage Learning.

ALL RIGHTS RESERVED

Thorndike Press® Large Print Basic.
The text of this Large Print edition is unabridged.
Other aspects of the book may vary from the original edition.
Set in 16 pt. Plantin.

LIBRARY OF CONGRESS CATALOGING-IN-PUBLICATION DATA

Kanon, Joseph.
    Istanbul passage / by Joseph Kanon.
      pages ; cm. — (Thorndike Press large print basic)
      ISBN 978-1-4104-4813-2 (hardcover) — ISBN 1-4104-4813-4 (hardcover)
    1. Intelligence agents—Fiction. 2. Americans—Turkey—Istanbul—Fiction.
    3. Cold War—Fiction. 4. Istanbul (Turkey)—Fiction. 5. Large type books. I.
    Title.
    PS3561.A476I88 2012b
    813'.54—dc23
                          2012003652

Published in 2012 by arrangement with Atria Books, a division of Simon & Schuster, Inc.

Printed in Mexico
2 3 4 5 6 7 16 15 14 13 12

For
David Kanon
My Istanbul Companion
&
Michael Kanon
My Music Maker

1
BEBEK

The first attempt had to be called off. It had taken days to arrange the boat and the safe house and then, just a few hours before the pickup, the wind started, a *poyraz,* howling down from the northeast, scooping up water as it swept across the Black Sea. The Bosphorus waves, usually no higher than boat wakes by the time they reached the shuttered *yalis* along the shore, now churned and smashed against the landing docks. From the quay, Leon could barely make out the Asian side, strings of faint lights hidden behind a scrim of driving rain. Who would risk it? Even the workhorse ferries would be thrown off schedule, never mind a bribed fishing boat. He imagined the fisherman calculating his chances: a violent sea, sightless, hoping the sudden shape forty meters away wasn't a lumbering freighter, impossible to dodge. Or another day safe in port, securing ropes and drinking plum brandy by the cast-iron stove. Who could blame him? Only a fool went to sea in a storm. The passenger could wait. Days of planning. Called by the weather.

"How much longer?" Mihai said, pulling his coat tighter.

They were parked just below Rumeli Hisari, watching the moored boats tossing, pulling against their ties.

"Give it another half hour. If he's late and I'm not here —"

"He's not late," Mihai said, dismissive. He glanced over. "He's that important?"

"I don't know. I'm just the delivery boy."

"It's freezing," Mihai said, turning on the motor. "This time of year."

Leon smiled. In Istanbul's dream of itself it was always summer, ladies eating sherbets in garden pavilions, caïques floating by. The city shivered through winters with braziers and sweaters, somehow surprised that it had turned cold at all.

Mihai ran the heater for a few minutes then switched it off, burrowing, turtlelike, into his coat. "So come with me but no questions."

Leon rubbed his hand across the window condensation, clearing it. "There's no risk to you."

"Wonderful. Something new. You couldn't

10

do this yourself?"

"He's coming out of Constancia. For all I know, he only speaks Romanian. Then what? Sign language? But you —"

Mihai waved this off. "He'll be German. One of your new friends."

"You don't have to do this."

"It's a small favor. I'll get it back."

He lit a cigarette, so that for a second Leon could see his grizzled face and the wiry salt-and-pepper hair on his head. Now more salt than pepper. When they had met, it had been dark and wavy, styled like the Bucharest dandy he'd once been, known in all the cafés on the Calea Victoriei.

"Besides, to see the rats leaving —" he said, brooding. "They wouldn't let us out. Now look at them."

"You did what you could." A Palestinian passport, free to come and go in Bucharest, to beg for funds, leasing creaky boats, a last lifeline, until that was taken away too.

Mihai drew on the cigarette, staring at the water running down the windshield. "So how is it with you?" he said finally. "You look tired."

Leon shrugged, not answering.

"Why are you doing this?" Mihai turned to face him. "The war's over."

"Yes? Nobody told me."

11

"No, they want to start another one."

"Nobody I know."

"Be careful you don't get to like it. You start enjoying it —" His voice trailed off, rough with smoke, the accent still Balkan, even now. "Then it's not about anything anymore. A habit. Like these," he said, holding out his cigarette. "You get a taste for it."

Leon looked at him. "And you?"

"Nothing changes for us. We're still saving Jews." He made a wry face. "Now from our friends. No visas for Palestine. Where should they go, Poland? And I'm helping you talk to a Nazi. A wonderful world."

"Why a Nazi?"

"Why all this? Some poor refugee? No, someone who knows the Russians, I think. And who knows better?"

"You're guessing."

"It doesn't matter to you? What you deliver?"

Leon looked away, then down at his watch. "Well, he's not coming tonight. Whoever he is. I'd better call. Make sure. There's a café."

Mihai leaned forward to start the car again. "I'll pull around."

"No, stay here. I don't want the car —"

"I see. You run across the road in the rain. Get wet. Then you run back. Again, wet. To

12

a waiting car. That will be less suspicious. If anyone is watching." He put the car in gear.

"It's your car," Leon said. "That's all."

"You think they haven't seen it by now?"

"Have they? You'd know," he said, a question.

"Always assume yes." He made a turn across the road, pulling up in front of the café. "So do the expected thing. Stay dry. Tell me something. If he had come, your package, was I going to drive him to — wherever he's staying?"

"No."

Mihai nodded. "Better." He motioned his head to the side window. "Make the call. Before they wonder."

There were four men playing dominoes and sipping tea from tulip glasses. When they looked up, Leon became what he wanted them to see — a *ferengi* caught in the rain, shaking water from his hat, needing a phone — and he flushed, a little pulse of excitement. A taste for it. Had Mihai seen it somehow, the way it felt, getting away with something. The planning, the slipping away. Tonight he'd taken the tram to the last stop in Bebek and walked up to the clinic. A trip he'd made over and over. If he'd been followed, they'd stay parked a block away from the clinic gates and wait,

13

relieved to be snug, out of the rain, knowing where he was. But just past the big oleander bushes, he'd headed for the garden side gate, doubling back to the Bosphorus road where Mihai was waiting, feeling suddenly free, almost exhilarated. No one would have seen him in the dark. If they were there, they'd be smoking, bored, thinking he was inside. This other life, just walking to the car, was all his own.

The phone was on the wall near the WC. No sounds in the room but the click of tiles and the hiss of boiling water, so the token seemed to clang going in. A *ferengi* speaking English, the men would say. If anyone asked.

"Tommy?" At home, luckily, not out to dinner.

"Ah, I was hoping you'd call," he said, a genial club voice with the clink of ice at the back of it. "You're after that report — I know, I know — and my steno never showed. Trouble with the boats. Typical, isn't it? First hint of weather and the ferries —" Leon imagined his round face at the other end, the jawline filling in, fleshy. "I can have it for you tomorrow, all right? I mean, the contract's all right. We're just waiting for the quotas. I've had American Tobacco on the phone half the day, so you're all in the same boat on this one. All we need now are the signatures." At Commercial Corp., the wartime agency that was Tommy's cover at the consulate.

"That's all right. I'm stuck here at the clinic anyway. Just wanted to check. If it was on its way."

"No. Tomorrow now. Sorry about this. Let me make it up to you. Buy you a drink at the Park." An off note. This late?

"I'm in Bebek."

"I'll get a head start." An order, then. "Don't worry, I'll roll you home." Their standard joke, Leon's apartment building just down the hill from the Park Hotel, before Aya Paşa made its wide curve.

"Give me an hour."

"From Bebek?" Surprised, an edge now.

"Take a look outside. It'll be a crawl in this. Just save me a stool."

The domino players were looking down, pretending not to listen. But what would they have made of it anyway? Leon ordered a tea, a way of thanking the barman for the phone. The glass was warm in his hand, and he realized he was cold everywhere else, the wet beginning to seep through his shoes. And now the Park, everyone looking and not looking, Tommy's old-boy voice getting louder with each drink.

15

"Rain check," he said to Mihai, getting into the car. "You free tomorrow?"

Mihai nodded.

"Something's up. We're having a drink at the Park."

"Very exciting, the tobacco business."

Leon smiled. "It used to be."

In fact, it had been sleepy, as routine and predictable as a Book of Hours. Agents bought the cured Latakia leaf, and he arranged the shipments, then took the train to Ankara to get the export permits. Leave Haydarpaşa at six, arrive the next morning at ten. That's how it had started, carrying things on the train for Tommy, papers they couldn't put in the diplomatic pouch, something for the war effort. No money involved then. An American helping out, not just standing around at the club getting drunk with Socony and Liggett & Myers and Western Electric, the men interchangeable, lucky businessmen sitting out the war. Tommy asked him to help Commercial Corp. buy up chromium, so the Germans wouldn't get it, and suddenly he was in the war after all, the peculiar one that played out over dinner at Abdullah's or those consulate receptions where the sides lined up on either end of the room, cocktail wars. What surprised him later, when he knew more, was how many others were in it too. Tracking shipping through the straits. Collecting gossip. Turning a commercial attaché who needed the money. Everyone spinning webs, watching one another, the Turkish Emniyet watching them. Nothing sleepy anymore.

"I'll drop you home. You'll want to change."

"No, just back to the village. I want to go to the clinic. Look in."

Mihai waited until they were almost there. "How is she?"

"The same," Leon said, his voice neutral.

And then there was nothing to say. Still, he'd asked. Anna was still alive to him, a presence, not just someone in Obstbaum's clinic who had retreated into herself, gone somewhere behind her own eyes. People used to ask all the time — painful questions at the club, an awkward concern at the office — but gradually they began to forget she was still there. Out of sight, out of mind. Except Leon's, a wound that wouldn't close. Any day she might come back, just as quickly as she had gone away. Someone had to be there waiting.

"You know what I think?" Mihai said.

"What?"

"Sometimes I think you do this for her.

17

To prove something. I don't know what."

Leon was quiet, not answering.

"Do you still talk to her?" Mihai said finally.

"Yes."

"Tell her we got a boat out. She'll like that."

"Past the British patrols?"

"So far. Otherwise we'd be in Cyprus. Tell her three hundred. We saved three hundred."

He took the same side street back, the same garden entrance. He'd expected to have to ring, but the door was unlocked and he frowned, annoyed the staff had been so careless. But no one was trying to get out and who would want to get in? The clinic was really a kind of nursing home, a place to be out of the way. Dr. Obstbaum had been one of the German refugees welcomed by Atatürk in the thirties to help the new republic get up on its feet. The ones who could afford it had moved to Bebek or, closer in, Ortaköy, where hillsides covered in fir trees and lindens may have reminded them of home. Or maybe, lemminglike, they had simply followed the first settler. Most of the clinic's medical staff was still German, which Leon had thought might help, her own language something she would understand, if she was still listening. But of course the nurses, the people who bathed her and fed her and chattered around her, were Turkish, so in the end he realized it didn't matter and now he worried that she was more isolated than ever. Dr. Obstbaum himself encouraged Leon to talk.

"We have no idea what she hears. This form of melancholia — it may be a matter of responding, not awareness. Her brain hasn't shut down. Otherwise she wouldn't be breathing, or have any motor functions. The idea is to keep up the level of activity. Over time maybe it grows. So, music. Does she hear it? I don't know. But the brain does, somewhere. Something functions."

Not disturbing music, but things she knew, had played at home. Lovely notes to fill the silence in her. If she heard them.

"Most of the time I think I'm talking to myself," Leon had said.

"Everyone here talks to himself," Obstbaum had said, a puckish joke. "One of life's great pleasures, evidently. You at least are being asked."

"It's late," the nurse said in Turkish, a hushed whisper, her eyes glancing down to the water dripping from his coat.

"Is she asleep? I'll just say good-night. I'm sorry about —"

19

But the nurse was already opening the door, brusque, the client's whims no business of hers. He'd sit and talk, the way he always did, and she'd have to check back again, another round, but it was a private clinic and he was paying.

Anna was lying in bed, the room shadowy, only a dim night-light on. When he touched her hand, she opened her eyes, but looked at him without recognition. It was the disconcerting thing, the way she took in what was happening around her without responding. Having her hair brushed, people moving across the room — things happened far away, just little blurs of movement.

"How are you feeling?" he said. "Warm enough? There's a terrible storm." He nodded toward the French windows, the sound of rain on the glass.

She didn't say anything, but he no longer expected her to. Even her hand didn't touch back. When he talked, he answered for her, silent responses to keep things going. Sometimes, sitting next to her, he'd actually hear her voice in his head, a ghost conversation, even worse than talking to himself.

"But this is nice, isn't it?" he said, indicating the room. "Cozy. *Gemütlich.*" As if a change of language would matter.

He let her hand go and sat down in the chair.

When they first met, she'd never seemed to stop talking, bubbling over, switching from German to English as if one language couldn't contain it, everything she had to say. And her eyes had been everywhere, ahead of the words sometimes, waiting for them to catch up, lighting her face. The odd thing was that the face was still her own, stopped in time, the wonderful skin, the soft line of her cheek, everything just the way it always had been, aging itself put off while she was away. Only the eyes were different, vacant.

"I saw Mihai tonight. He sends his love. He said they got a boat through. People are getting out again." Something that might register, what she cared about. Don't try to startle her, Obstbaum had said, just ordinary things, domestic matters. But how did Obstbaum know? Had he been to where she lived now? Did it matter to her that Fatma had been ill, sent her sister to do the cleaning? "Three hundred," he said. "So they must be operating again. Mossad. Who else could it be? A boat that big."

He stopped. The last thing he should have said, a reminder. Obstbaum thought it had happened then, when the *Bratianu* sank.

21

Corpses bobbing in the water. Children. Her brain turning away from it, drawing a curtain. Obstbaum had even suggested she be put in a garden room, not a front one facing the Bosphorus, where ships passed all day, each one a possible reminder. Leon had gone along with him. Everyone in Istanbul wanted to see the water — in Ottoman times there had been laws about builders blocking the view — so a garden room was cheaper. And it was pleasant, looking toward the hillside, cypresses and umbrella pines and a Judas tree that dropped pink blossoms in the spring. A fortune back home but something he could manage here. And not a boat in sight.

"I thought I might need Romanian. They bring someone out but they don't tell you who. They want me to babysit. I got Georg's old landlord to find me a room. Out near Aksaray. They'll never think to look in a Muslim neighborhood. And then the weather started up —"

He caught himself, hearing the sound of his voice saying names out loud, telling her what he didn't want anyone to know, all the slipping away and double-backing for nothing. It occurred to him, one more irony, that since she had gone away they could finally talk to each other. All the things they couldn't say before, other people's secrets, now safe to talk about. Some things, anyway. Now there were other drawers you didn't open, things you didn't say. Your parents are dead. We haven't heard, but they must be. They're not on any lists. You can't imagine what it was like, how many. The pictures. I see a woman. Just for the sex. It used to feel — wrong — and now I wait for it. Not like us. Something different. I don't think you're ever coming back. I can't say it — can't say it to you — but I think it's true. I don't know why this happened to us. What I did. What you did. Better to keep those drawers closed.

"I ran into Gus Hoover. Socony's sending him home. You still can't get a boat, though, so what do you think? They're putting him on the clipper. Hell of a lot of money, but I guess they've got it to spend. Can you see Reynolds doing it for me? Not that I want to go. But you always wanted to, didn't you? See New York." He paused, leaving time for an answer. "Maybe when you're better. We can't really move you now. Like this. And I can take care of you here." He motioned his hand to the room. "You could get better here." He paused again. "Maybe if you'd try. Obstbaum says it isn't a question of that. But what if it is? You could try. Every-

23

thing could be the way it was. Better. The war's over. All the terrible things." Knowing as he said it that they weren't over — people still in camps, boats still being turned around, everything she had gone away to escape still happening. What was there to come back for? Him? The drawer he shouldn't open. Was it my fault? Another casualty of the war, Obstbaum had said, but what if she had left the world to leave him? Something only she knew and wasn't coming back to answer. Not ever. Gus would fly home, all the others, and he would still be here, talking to himself while she stared at the garden. "You have to be patient," Obstbaum had said. "The mind is like an eggshell. It can withstand tremendous pressure. But if it cracks it's not so easy to put it back together." A Humpty Dumpty explanation, as good as any other, but it was Leon who was sitting here, his world that had been cracked open.

"I have to go soon. Tommy wants to have a drink at the Park. On a night like this. Not that rain ever kept Tommy from a drink. Still. You know what occurred to me? He wants to bring me inside. Run my own operation. I mean, a job like this tonight, it's not messenger work anymore. There'd be money in it. It's about time he —" Babbling, filling time. "Do you have everything you need?"

He got up and went over to the bed, putting his hand on the dark hair fanning out beneath her. Lightly, just grazing it, because there was something unreal about physical contact now, touching someone who wasn't there. And there was always a moment when he flinched, apprehensive, expecting her to reach up and snatch at his hand, finally mad. He passed the back of his hand over her forehead, a soothing motion, and she closed her eyes to it, looking for a second the way she used to after they made love, drifting.

"Get some sleep," he said quietly. "I'll be back."

But not tomorrow. In the beginning he'd come every night, a kind of vigil, but then days slid by, filled with other things. Because the worst part was that, without even wanting to, he'd begun to leave her too.

Outside, he walked through the village to the shore road, glancing at parked cars. But he wouldn't see them, would he? Not if they were any good. After a while you developed an instinct. The Turkish police had been clumsy when Anna worked with Mihai. They'd park someone in the lobby of the Continental, where Mossad had its office, a bored policeman in a business suit who must have thought himself invisible behind the cigarette smoke. The work had been open — arranging visas for the weekly train to Baghdad, the overland route to Palestine. Just a trickle of refugees, but legal. The police watched Anna go to the Red Crescent offices, watched her check the manifest lists at Sirkeci, watched the transfer to Haydarpaşa, a pattern so familiar they never thought to look anywhere else. When the illegal work began, Mihai's boats, they were still following Anna to Sirkeci, still smoking in the lobby.

Later, her work became a cover for Leon too. It was the Jewish wife working for Mossad who needed watching, not her American husband. Once he'd been playing tennis at the Sümer Palas in Tarabya when a man he assumed to be police wanted a quiet word. His wife. No doubt well meaning, but her activities were attracting attention. Turkey was a neutral country. They were its guests. It was a husband's duty to watch over his household. Nobody wanted to be embarrassed. Not the R.J. Reynolds Company. Not the Turkish government. Leon remembered standing speechless in front of the old hotel, staring at the famous hydrangea bushes, trying not to smile, to savor the unexpected gift. Anna suspect, not him.

But that had been the locals. The Emniyet, the security police, were something else, never obvious, part of the air everyone breathed. Playing the home advantage. When Macfarland had been station head he was convinced they'd planted somebody inside, which would mean they might know about Leon too. Even unofficial, off the books. Tommy didn't just pull the money out of his pocket. Where would they find him? Miscellaneous expenses? Jobs Tommy wanted to freelance out, like tonight.

The square was empty, no tram in sight, just two women huddled under umbrellas waiting for a *dolmus*. And then, improbably, there was a single taxi, maybe out here on a run from Taksim. Leon stopped it, glancing over his shoulder as he got in, half expecting to see headlights turning on, a car starting up. But no one followed. He looked out back. Only a thin line of traffic, everyone chased inside by the rain. In Arnavutköy a car pulled in behind, then went off again, leaving them alone. No one. Unless the taxi was Emniyet. But then the driver started to complain about something, the details lost in the *swoosh* of the windshield wipers, and Leon gave that up too. So much for instinct. Maybe he hadn't had to do any of it —

sneak out of the clinic, meet Mihai in the road. Maybe no one watched anymore. Maybe Mihai was right. It had become a habit.

Tommy had already had a few by the time Leon got to the Park, his face red, cheeks shining with it. His broad shoulders still had the strong lines of someone who'd once played for Penn, but the rest of him had gone slack, pudgy from years of sitting and extra helpings.

"Christ, you're soaking. What'd you do, walk? Here, take the chill off. Mehmet, how about two more of the same? We'll have them over there," he said, lifting himself off the stool with a little grunt and heading for a small table against the wood-paneled wall.

There were more people than Leon had expected, probably hotel guests who didn't want to go out, but still plenty of empty tables. The long outside terrace, with its view of the Stamboul headland, had been closed for weeks. Leon remembered it full, waiters with trays darting in and out like birds, people talking over each other, looking around to see who was there. What the Stork must be like.

"Sorry about tonight," Tommy said. "Didn't know myself till I got the message.

There won't be any problem about the place, will there?"

"No, I've got it for the month. I didn't know how long he'd —"

"The month? How much is that going to run us?"

"It's in Laleli. Cheap. You can afford it."

"Laleli. Where the fuck's that? On the Asian side?"

Leon smiled. "How long have you been here?"

Tommy shrugged this off. "And what do we do with it after we move him?"

"You could take your women there. Nice and private."

"Yeah, just us and the fleas. Ah, here we are," he said as the drinks arrived. "Thank you, Mehmet." He raised his glass. "Blue skies and clear sailing."

Leon raised his glass and took a sip. Cold and crisp, a whiff of juniper. Mehmet put down a silver bowl of pistachios and backed away.

"Christ, imagine what he's heard," Tommy said, watching him go. "All these years."

"Maybe he doesn't listen."

"They all listen. The question is, who for?"

"Besides us?"

Tommy ignored this. "They used to say every waiter in this room got paid twice.

And sometimes more. At the same time. Remember the one used to send little love notes to von Papen, then turn around and feed the same thing to the Brits?" He shook his head, amused. "Six months he pulls this off. You have to hand it to him."

"What good did it do? Anybody ever say anything at the Park that you wanted to know?"

Tommy smiled. "You live in hope. You live in hope. Anyway, that wasn't the point, was it? Point was to know. What they were saying, what they weren't saying. Might be useful to somebody. Who could put the pieces together."

"You think there was somebody like that?"

"Christ, I hope so. Otherwise —" He let it go. "I'll tell you something, though. It was fun too, this place. Goddam three-ring circus. Everybody. Same room. Packy Macfarland over there and that Kraut who kept pretending he was in the navy right next to him. Navy. And the Jap, Tashima, remember him, with the glasses, a spit of fucking Tojo. At first I thought it *was* him. And Mehmet's listening to all of them."

"The good old days."

Tommy looked up, caught by his tone.

"Come on, Tommy. It's a little early for last rites at the Park. Mehmet's still listen-

30

ing. God knows who else. For what it's worth."

Tommy shook his head. "It's finished, this place."

Leon looked around, feeling the drink a little. "Well, the Germans are gone. And Tojo. That's what we wanted to happen, right?"

"I mean the whole place. Neutral city in a war — everybody's got an interest. Turks coming in? Staying out? What's everybody up to? Now what? Now it's just going to be Turks."

"You've still got me meeting boats," Leon said, finishing his glass. "We're still here."

"Not for long."

"What do you mean?"

Tommy looked away, then raised his hand to signal for another round.

"You're going home?" Leon guessed.

"We need to talk."

"That's why we're having the drink?" Not a new job.

Tommy nodded. "They're rolling up the operation."

Don't react. "Which operation?"

"Here. All of us. Well, most."

"You?"

"Washington. You know, September they handed us over to the War Department.

31

Couldn't get rid of Bill fast enough, I guess. What G-2 wanted all along. R&A went to State. Whole unit. Now they're Research Intelligence. Office of. But the field? What's the War Department going to do with field officers? War's over."

"Tell that to the Russians," Leon said.

"That's Europe. Not here. Christ, Leon, you didn't think we'd just keep going here forever, did you? After the war?" he said, his tone slightly defensive. "Ah, Mehmet." Making room for the new drinks, some banter Leon didn't hear as he watched Tommy's face, the red cheeks moving as he talked. Knowing it was coming, arranging his own transfer, taking care of business. A desk at the War Department? Or something closer to the Mayflower bar? He looked down at the fresh drink, his stomach queasy. Now what? Back to the desk at Reynolds, days without edge.

"When does this happen?"

"End of the month."

Just like that.

"What about me?"

"You? I thought you'd be glad it's over. You never wanted — I had to talk you into it, remember? Though I have to say you took right to it. Best I had. You know that, don't you? That I always thought that." He moved

32

his hand, as if he were about to put it on Leon's, but stopped. "I could put in a word for you — I mean, knowing Turkish, that's something. But they're closing the shop here. Everything back to G-2 and you don't want to join the army, do you?" He looked over the brim of his glass. "It's time to go home, Leon. OWI's already packed up. Everybody's going home."

"I haven't been back to the States in — what? Ten years now."

"You don't want to stay here. What's here?"

My life.

"Get Reynolds to transfer you back. Be a big shot in the tobacco business."

Would they? An office in a long corridor of offices, sharing a secretary, not his own corner overlooking Taksim. A house in Raleigh with a small yard, not the flat on Aya Paşa looking all the way to the Sea of Marmara. Anna where?

He shook his head. "I don't want to move Anna. She's doing so well now. Real progress. A move now —" The lie effortless, one of the reasons he'd been the best.

"She'd do even better in the States, if you ask me. They could do something for her there. Hospitals here —" He stopped. "You look all funny. What is it? The money?"

33

"The money?" Leon snorted. "What you pay? That's not enough to notice." Just enough to make a difference. "It's the drink, I guess," he said, pushing it away. "I'm beat. All the waiting around." He looked up, feeling Tommy staring at him, alert behind the glassy eyes. "I never did it for money, you know."

"I know. I appreciate that."

"I'm surprised we're pulling out, that's all. Be a little dull. Pushing paper at the office."

"Want to push some more? They're going to need somebody at Western Electric. Middle East account — the whole territory. Guy in charge now is leaving."

"For Washington?"

"So I hear."

"You had someone at Western too?"

"Now, now."

"Like to keep your bets all over the table, don't you?" Separate drawers, separate secrets.

"Safer that way."

"You'll be running out of covers soon. No more Lend-Lease. No more OWI. Western Electric. Even the guy in the tobacco business."

"What guy?"

Leon smiled. "I'm going to miss you. I

guess. When do you go?"

"As soon as we can arrange air transport. For our friend. The one who got seasick tonight."

"You're going with him?"

"We don't want him to travel alone. He might get lost. We just need to park him here for a day or so. Then all your troubles are over. But while you've got him — well, I don't have to tell you. It's not as if you've never done this before. Just be careful."

"Always."

"With this one, I mean. Lots of people want to talk to him. So all the old rules. He doesn't go out. He doesn't —"

"I know the rules, Tommy. If you're that nervous, why don't you pick him up yourself?"

"Spread the bets, Leon. This time, I'm not even at the table. Nothing to see, nothing to connect me. I just pack up my bags and leave. You run into people on the plane, that's all. But I can't put him there. The board would light up. I'm not invisible here."

"And I am."

"You're freelance. They won't be expecting that. Not for him."

"What's he got, that you have to take him to Washington yourself?"

"Leon."

"You owe me that much."

Tommy looked at him for a minute, then downed the rest of his drink. "Lots," he said finally, nodding. "Up here." He touched his temple. "Also a very nice photo album."

"Of?"

"Mother Russia. Aerial recon. The Germans photographed everything, when they still could. Valuable snaps now."

"And he got these how?"

"That I couldn't say. Fell off a truck, maybe. Things do. Want another?"

Leon shook his head. "I'd better go. Start being invisible. Here, finish this."

"Well, since I'm paying —"

Leon stood up. "Some evening."

"Tomorrow then. One more and you're a free man."

Leon looked at him, disconcerted by the phrase. "Who is he, Tommy?"

"He'll answer to John."

"As in Johann? German?"

"As in John Doe." He glanced up. "No funny business, okay? Let Washington ask the questions. Just do your piece. There'll be a bonus in it, if I can talk them into it."

"I don't care about that."

"That's right. Good of the country. Still. Think of it as — I don't know, for old times' sake." He turned his head to the room.

"You coming?"

"I'll just finish this. Give the place one last look. Goddam three-ring circus, wasn't it?" he said, his voice drooping, like his eyes, maudlin.

Leon picked up his damp coat.

"By the way," Tommy said, sharp again. "Separate pieces, but where the hell's Laleli?"

"Past the university. Before you get to Aksaray."

"Christ, who goes out there?"

"That's the idea."

It was still raining hard enough to get wet again and he was shivering when he got home. The Cihangir Apartments, just down Aya Paşa from the Park, had been put up in the twenties and still had a few moderne touches in the lobby, but the plaster had begun to chip, a sign of larger decay to come. Reynolds had bought a company flat here because it had central heating, a luxury, but fuel shortages had kept the radiators tepid all during the war, and now Leon relied on space heaters, a few rows of toaster coils barely strong enough to warm your hands. The elevator was sporadic. Hot water came through the geyser in a trickle,

37

so that it was cool by the time the tub had filled.

None of it mattered. The first time he and Anna had come to the flat, a ritual handing over of keys, all they saw was the window with its view across the rooftops of Cihangir, past the mosques at Kabataş and Findikli to the open mouth of the Bosphorus, alive with boats. On a clear day you could see Leander's Tower, the green park at Topkapi. That first year they'd sit with a drink after work and watch the ferries crossing to Asia, the freighters passing up the strait. There was no balcony, just the window, a private movie screen.

"You'll like it here," Perkins had said, a little wistful. "Of course, it helps if you're handy yourself. Mr. Cicek, that's the building — well, manager, I suppose. Not much with a wrench. With anything, really. So if you need something —"

"Oh, it's wonderful. Just the way it is," Anna had said, eyes fixed on the view. "How can you bear to leave it?"

But that was when everything was new, Istanbul something almost magical after Germany, somewhere you could breathe. Leon remembered the very first day, stepping out of Sirkeci station into a swarm of motorbikes, the smell of frying fish, trays piled with *simits* balanced on vendors' heads, boats crowding the Eminönü piers, everything noisy and sunlit. In the taxi crossing Galata Bridge he had turned back to look at Sinan's graceful minarets pricking the sky, and at that moment a flock of birds rose up, swooping around the dome of the Yeni Mosque, then diving back to the water, rippling with light, and Leon thought it was the most wonderful place he had ever seen.

During those first weeks they didn't see the old wooden houses, listing and creaking from neglect, the backstreets with clumps of garbage and mud, cracked fountains seeping moss. They saw color, heaps of spices, everything that wasn't Germany, and water everywhere, a city where you took ferries just to be out on it, looking at domes and spires, not the crooked dirty streets. Anna wanted to see everything, the famous sights, then things she found in books, the Camondo Stairs, twisting down Galata Hill, the cast-iron Bulgarian church, the Byzantine mosaics out near the old city walls where they could eat picnics on the yellow grass, looking up at giant stork nests in the ruins. Their building had been fronted with sunny lemon plaster then, a confection, the plane trees in the median shading Aya Paşa.

That was before the grime had settled in the edges, the white trim faded, before anything had happened to them.

There was a small pile of mail on the floor just inside the door, pushed through the slot by Cicek. Did he glance at them first, report anything interesting? But these days not much came. No air letters from home, no thick envelopes with consular seals. When he and Anna had been a new couple in town, invitations fell in clumps through the door — tennis parties, drinks parties, receptions, the endless social life of the European community. Then, after she got sick, he noticed the thinning out, events one could attend alone, sometimes just bills or nothing at all. He picked up the mail — at least one invitation, a thick envelope — then shivered again, a chill that didn't stop at the door. He went over and switched on the space heater, stood next to it, and opened the envelope. A party at Lily's, something to look forward to. Piles of food and the *yali* warm even this time of year, fuel never a problem for the rich. A woman who had actually been in the sultan's harem, something out of the last century, now serving cocktails to modern Turks who still left their wives home, one more Istanbul paradox.

He looked down. As usual, the coils were

glowing without producing any heat. At least get out of the wet clothes. He went to the bathroom, stripping on the way, the clothes sticking to him. When he reached for his bathrobe, he shuddered with cold, almost a spasm. Chilled to the bone, not just an expression. He threw the clothes over the shower rod to dry, then wrapped the robe tighter and went back out to the drinks table to pour a brandy. You don't want to get sick, not before a job. Which Tommy could easily have done himself, putting John Doe up at the consulate, safe, out of sight, until the plane was ready. Why involve Leon at all? A bonus in it for you, if you do your piece. The brandy burned as it went down, the only heat in the room. But why do it in pieces anyway? Unless he didn't want anybody at the consulate to know, didn't even want his own office to know. I'm not invisible. No connection until they were on the plane together. A German with photographs. Important enough, maybe, to get Tommy a bigger desk in Washington. Planning it. You were the best I had. A cheap compliment, while he looked out for himself and Leon went back to buying tobacco.

He went through the rest of the mail. A utility bill, a circular for made-to-order suits, and a card from Georg Ritter, a namesake knight on the front. On the back, a pen drawing of a chessboard. "A game this week? Thursday?" Tomorrow. Well, not Thursday. He'd have to call. Which Georg could have done. Why send a card when you could just pick up the phone? But a call was an intrusion. You could ignore a card, just not respond if you'd rather not, the formal manners part of Georg's way of dealing with the world, as if the past fifty years had never happened. Calling cards, notes, a *pneumatique* if they still existed, even his flat with its heavy furniture and Meissen figurines a relic of old Europe. He'd been fond of Anna, a kind of substitute father, and now like an aging parent was becoming easy to neglect. He shouldn't have to be sending cards, gentle reminders. A game once a week, some gossip, just being company — it wasn't a lot to ask. Call tomorrow and set a date.

He put the invitation on the piano, the upright Georg had found for them. Keys dusted, in tune, ready for her to play again. During the war it had been Mendelssohn because you couldn't play him in Germany, *jüdische Musik,* Anna thumbing her nose at the Nazis with *lieder.* Along the piano top was the row of framed photographs Leon had come to think of as his war memorial. Anna's parents, dressed for a walk in the Tiergarten, the last picture they'd sent before they were taken away. Anna herself, mouth open in laughter, when she still had words. Phil kneeling with the ground crew on an airstrip somewhere in the Pacific, the propellers just behind their heads. His unexpected baby brother, so many years between them that they had never been friends and then suddenly were the only family each of them had. The telegram had come to him, the only one left. Missing in action over New Guinea. Then, months later, a letter from an officer who'd survived the Japanese camp, who wanted Leon to know that Phil had been brave to the end. Whatever that meant. Maybe a samurai sword to the back of the neck, maybe dysentery, anyway gone, Leon's last tie to America. And yet, oddly, losing Phil had pulled him closer to it, wanting to be part of it, even carrying papers for Tommy, as if that would help somehow, like a ground mechanic who checked the oil and waited for the others to come back.

He draped an afghan over his shoulders and sat next to the electric fire. One of your new friends, Mihai had guessed. Now on a VIP ticket to Washington. What would Anna have said? Who else would have reconnaissance pictures? A Nazi or a thief. Your new friends. Not what he imagined doing when it had started. An innocent train to Ankara, then dinner at Karpić's to leave the papers. No need to go to the Embassy, just in town on business. And then Tommy had other things for him.

"You have a gift for languages," he'd said. "Who picks up Turkish? *And* Kraut." Leon's grandfather's legacy — English at school, German at home. "You should be proud — the language of Schiller." But of course he wasn't, hiding it from his friends, an embarrassment, until one day it got him a job, not Paris, where he wanted to go, but still overseas and paid in dollars. One job to another, Hamburg then Berlin, where he met Anna.

After that the trips home became less frequent and then, when his mother died, there was no reason to go. They stayed in Berlin until Kristallnacht when Anna's parents, in a panic, pleaded with him to take her to New York. They would follow, as soon as things could be arranged. But when would that be? An ocean between them, something final. And then, almost a fluke, the Reynolds job came up, somewhere safe but still close enough to help get them out.

44

You could take a train there, Vienna-Sofia-Istanbul, twice a week.

But they never did, delaying until no one got out unless they were rescued, unless Anna and Mihai somehow got them on one of their boats. Anna never stopped trying, even after they couldn't be found, two more who had disappeared. And Leon had started working for Tommy, his own way of helping. Fighting Nazis. And now he was hiding them.

He looked at the window, still blurry with water. What if it hadn't rained tonight? What if John Doe had made it through? Would Tommy have told him about the pictures? Any of it? Just do your piece. While I make plans. It wasn't the money, there were always ways to get more money, but the end of things. Just like that. He shivered again, now a chill that wouldn't go away, but something else too, an uneasiness. About what? Maybe just the quiet. With the windows closed, there were no sounds — no foghorns on the water or even cars grinding up the steep streets below. When he struck a match he could hear it, a loud rasp. He pulled the afghan tighter, an old man huddling in front of the fire. But not exactly a fire, and not really old yet, either. Too old to be asked back to Washington? Tommy was going. Nagging at him. Take a pill and get into bed, under Anna's old duvet, always warm.

He went into the bathroom, about to open the medicine chest, and stopped. The same mirror he used every morning, but someone else in it. When had that happened? It wasn't the gray hair or the tired eyes. He looked the same, more or less. Something worse, a sense of time running out. Why hadn't Tommy ordered a backup? That was one of the rules. Not even ask for the safe house address? Careless, his mind already on the plane, leaving Leon behind to mop up. I'm not invisible here. Then why have a drink in the most visible place in Istanbul? To tell Leon he was leaving? But he could have done that after. Why even make contact before the job was finished? To be in Mehmet's report. Somebody's. Tommy King spent the evening getting soused with a business colleague at the Park, not waiting for a boat in the rain. Covering himself, the way he did. One step ahead.

He was restless all morning, moving papers and fidgeting with pens, sending Osman out twice for coffee. He glanced at the telephone. Tommy wouldn't call today, he'd keep his distance until after the pickup.

46

Outside, Taksim Square, scrubbed almost clean by the storm, was sunny. Perfect sailing weather. There was nothing to do now but wait out the day. But the clock barely moved.

He was always anxious before a job. Simple, but you never knew. And today was Thursday, his afternoon with Marina, and that anticipation had already begun, a prickling all over his skin, his mind filled with how it would be — the afternoon sun through the curtains, catching the dust, the thin silk wrapper she called a kimono, loosely belted so that it came apart at a touch, his breath getting shorter on the stairs, almost there, not wanting her to see how eager he was, but already hard when she opened the door. The way it always was. And then, afterward, the sudden deflation, embarrassed at wanting it so much, something he shouldn't be doing. Only once a week, so that it wouldn't feel like cheating, more like a medical appointment, just a time you set aside. An affair would have meant one of the European wives, unpredictable emotions, a betrayal. This was a simpler transaction — if you paid, it didn't mean anything.

He had never bought sex before, but what other choices were there in Istanbul? The houses in the alleys on the water side of Galata Hill, waiting downstairs with sailors and stevedores for ten minutes upstairs and months of disease? The apartments over the clubs near Taksim, fading red wallpaper and businessmen, the risk of meeting someone you knew? Then he had overheard a man talking about her in the bar at the Pera Palas, a girl with her own place, and he had gone once, nervous, almost drugged with the thought, his first woman in a year, and then it was every week.

What he hadn't expected was that sex itself would be different, not what he had known with Anna, but something furtive and heady, the way it had been in adolescence. He knew that if he saw her more often everything would change, that strings would begin to attach themselves, guilt, the afternoons no longer just physical, just pleasure. He thought she felt it too, a kind of relief that he only wanted her body, leaving the rest of her to herself. They had sex, that was all. They didn't want to touch anything else.

Once he offered to keep her, pay for the room.

"No, I don't want that. Just pay me like always."

"Why not? It would make things easier for you."

"Oh, for me. And why would you do that? So I wouldn't see anybody else. That's what it means. Just you. But I would, and then I'd lie to you. Let's just stay as we are."

"How many do you see?"

"You're jealous? If you want a virgin, go somewhere else."

"I don't want to go anywhere else."

"You know when I was a virgin? When I was twelve. So it's too late to be jealous."

"You like them, the others?"

"Everyone wants to know that. Now you. Some yes, some no. I like it with you — that's what you want to know, yes? Nobody really cares about the others, just 'how is it with me?' But they ask anyway. What are they like, the men who see you? They want to hear stories."

"Do you tell them stories about me?"

She shook her head. "What could I tell them? Thursday afternoon — that's all I know about you. Somebody who doesn't ask me questions. Until today. And now what? Pay for the room. I pay for it. I told myself, if you ever get out of that place, you'll have your own room, just yours, not in some house with people walking around. It's mine," she said, looking at the room. "I pay for it."

"But this is how you pay for it," he said, nodding at the bed, the tangled sheets.

"Yes."

"Then I'm paying anyway."

"Not for the room."

Which is when he realized someone else was keeping her, their Thursday afternoons just extra cash, something to tuck away under the mattress. All the others just pin money too. Did the man know about him? The afternoons, the most private thing he had, seemed suddenly invaded, no longer safe. It became important to know. He even watched the building for a while, curious to see the others. Europeans, always in the afternoon, like him. Only one at night, a Turk who showed up at odd times, as if he never knew when he could manage to get away. Someone she kept her evenings free for, just in case.

"Why do you want to know?" she said when he pressed her.

"Does he know about me?"

"No. I told you that."

"Or the others?"

"You think there are so many?"

He waited. "Does he know?"

She belted her robe tightly, reaching for a

cigarette. "No. Why? Do you want to tell him?"

"You said you didn't want to lie to me. But you lie to him."

"Maybe I have feelings for you."

"Now you are lying to me."

She glanced over at him, then smiled wryly, and drew on the cigarette. "I'm a whore. That's what we do. You're surprised?"

"Tell me."

"Oh, tell what? Leave me alone. He's rescuing me. That's how he sees things, a fairy story. He gives me this room. So I'm like a princess, somebody in a window. In a drawing."

"And he's the prince?"

She smiled again. "The pasha. He stole the building. An Armenian owned it. Remember the *Varlik Vergisi,* how they taxed the Jews and the Armenians and when they couldn't pay they sent them to camps and took what was left? He got the building. So he gives me this room. No rent. But I pay for it with him. Is that what you want to know?"

"And he thinks you've given it up? The others?"

"He thinks I'm grateful. I am grateful. But I have to think of the future too. He gets tired of me. Anything can happen. He's a simple man. A business in Şişhane. He never thought he could have anything like this, a girl in a room, waiting for him. But now he's a big landlord. Rents. So it was the tax, maybe, that got me out of that place. Strange how things work."

"Why strange?"

"I'm Armenian. He steals from an Armenian and he gives the room to another. I don't think he knows. A woman — it's all the same to him. So I lie to him. I don't lie to you."

"Why not?"

"I know who he is. A man who steals. You — I'm not so sure. You never tell me anything."

He touched her wrist. "I don't come here to talk."

"Everyone else — I think that's why they come, to tell me their troubles."

"Maybe I don't have any troubles."

She raised her eyes, meeting his, and held them for a second, a sudden connection, not saying anything, not having to.

He met Ed Burke for lunch in one of the restaurants in the Flower Passage, a table out in the arcade, under the belle époque globes. Ed had ordered wine and drank most of it himself, Leon sipping a little for show, barely touching the stuffed mussels, his mind somewhere else.

"So when are you going home?" Ed said.

"What's the hurry?"

"You don't want to wait too long. The import business is finished. Where are they going to get the hard currency? Another year, it'll be strictly domestic here. You should get out now."

"I'm buying, not selling. They're still open for business."

"Until the fucking Russians get their hands on the place. What they always wanted." He looked down the arcade to the Istiklal Caddesi, busy with trams and old cars. "Be a hell of a thing, won't it, to see all this go." He looked again to the street. "You know when I first got here, they still had the women in veils."

Had Marina worn one, as a girl? But she was Armenian, so a Christian, something he hadn't known before, another piece, like filling in an outline. What did she look like when she went out? He had never seen her in anything but her silk kimono, a swishing sound as she moved, smooth to the touch, like the soft flesh of her inner thigh. He looked up, aware again that Ed was talking.

"You hear about Tommy? It's all over the

53

consulate. Back to Washington."

"Really?" Leon said, noncommittal.

"I thought you two were thick as thieves."

Leon shook his head. "I helped him out with a deal once, that's all."

"What kind of deal?" Ed said, suddenly curious.

"Chromium. I knew some people in Ankara."

"Well, that always helps, doesn't it?"

"Always," Leon said, looking more closely for something behind the words. But Ed's face was the same, long and droopy, like Fred Allen's, pouches now under the eyes.

"Board of Economic Warfare. That's where he's going. Except there's no more warfare," Ed said.

"So they change the name. It's the government. You're in the government."

"Not where he's going."

"What do you mean?"

"Come on, you never thought Tommy might be doing something extra on the q.t.?"

"Like what?"

"Hush-hush stuff. You never suspected?"

"Tommy? Who'd trust him with a secret? Just hand him a drink."

"You worked with him. Who knows, maybe you —"

"Worked. I put him in touch with some people in Ankara. That's it. What's this all about?"

"War's over. What does it matter now? I'd just like to know. Was I right?"

"Ask him. How the hell would I know?"

"Of course, that's what you'd have to say, isn't it?"

Leon looked at him, then forced a laugh. "I guess it is. If I didn't have a foreign wife. German, for Christ's sake. I'm the last person they'd ask." The Anna cover, still useful. "And I'll bet they didn't ask Tommy, either. With his big mouth. What you're talking about — I thought all that was over at OWI. And I hear they packed up. So maybe we'll never know."

"OWI," Ed said, nodding, not letting it go. "And the college. Remember early 'forty-two, all of a sudden Robert College gets a whole new group of teachers? You'd meet them at parties, they'd never talk about their classes."

Leon smiled. "Maybe they came for the view." A hilltop looking down at Bebek and the Bosphorus. Cocktail parties on the terrace in the evening light. Not what the founding missionaries had had in mind. "Come on, Ed. You see those guys doing parachute drops? Four-eyes? With Tommy?

I never saw him open a book. I'll bet he doesn't even know where the college is."

Ed smiled, a cat licking cream. "He's giving a party there."

"A party?"

"He didn't ask you?"

Leon shrugged. "I told you, we're not that close. What kind of party?"

"Just some drinks. Say good-bye to his friends there." He looked over. "Those guys he doesn't know."

"Well, Tommy. Any excuse. When's this?"

"Tonight. Why don't you come? The more the merrier. That's what he said to me. Wants to fill the place."

With witnesses. Distancing himself.

"I can't tonight."

"Hot date?"

"I'm going to see my wife."

"Sorry," Ed said, genuinely embarrassed. "Well, try to drop in late. You're right there. She's in Bebek, right?"

Leon nodded. Near the college. But not as far up the coast road as the boat landing. Tommy making a diversion. If anyone followed him, they'd never go farther than Bebek, waiting for him to come down the hill. Hosting a party, not meeting boats.

"I'll see what I can do," he said, signaling for the bill. "You find out who's who first so

I don't say anything I shouldn't."

"You think I'm kidding."

"I think the place is getting to you. Here, let me get that."

"Tell me one thing then."

"What's that?" Leon said, dropping some lira notes on the bill.

"Remember that secretary of von Papen's? Switched sides?"

"The one asked for asylum. Sure."

"I was at the consulate that day. And where do they send him? To Tommy. Now why would they do that?"

A flustered attaché, an instinctive reaction, forgetting the rules.

"I don't know, Ed."

"Think about it," Ed said, taking another sip of the wine and leaning back, settling in. Leon imagined another hour of this, Ed probing, a meaningless cat-and-mouse game. To learn what, exactly?

"I have to run," Leon said, glancing at his watch. "End-of-the-month figures." He got up. "Watch yourself tonight. With the professors. Loose lips."

"Very funny. But I'll bet you I'm right."

"I'll try to make it later," Leon said, a lie they both accepted.

He left by the side exit to the fish market, the narrow street slippery with melted ice

57

and old frying grease, then turned through the covered vegetable stalls and out to Mesrutiyet, a long street of apartment buildings looking west to the Golden Horn. What did Ed want, anyway? Imagining Tommy lurking in alleys, missing the real sleight of hand. Follow me to a party while my freelancer does the work up the road.

The street curved, hugging the steep hill, opening up to the water view below. Once there would have been hundreds of sails. A dip in the road, past the Pera Palas and then up, threading through the narrow streets to the Tünel station. Marina's building was just behind, a gray apartment block grimy with neglect. Some of the windows looked toward the square where commuters poured off the funicular, but Marina's faced down to the Şişhane shipyards, the flat waters of the Horn beyond.

"I can see my whole life from here," she said once, smoking by the window, her body wrapped again in her kimono. "That's my childhood." She nodded toward the streets squeezed behind the docks. "Then, if you lean out this way — well, maybe it's better, you can't see that house. But the same hill. A few streets, what a difference. Another life."

"And now what," Leon said idly.

"Now here. I like it here. I like looking down on it."

He checked his watch. A little early, driven away by Ed's prying, but Marina wouldn't mind. Thursdays were his. "You couldn't wait?" she'd say, teasing, opening the robe to her breasts, waiting for him to take them in his hands, lean down.

He had just left the square when he saw the man coming out of the building. Stopping for a minute to adjust to the sunlight, then straightening his hat. A western suit, not the workers' overalls or *jellabas* you usually saw in the building. Leon turned, almost a pivot, and stepped toward the station newsstand, looking at a newspaper, waiting for a presence behind him, then turning again. The man was heading to the Istiklal tram. High cheekbones, thin nose, dark but not necessarily a Turk, anybody. Who went to her building in the middle of the afternoon. Now walking past the tram into the crowd. He felt suddenly warm. Of course she saw others, he'd always known that. But not on his day. That was the point. Not to be somebody waiting in line, like a sailor in a Galata house. The illusion of something more, the whole day paid for. Unless the man had been somewhere else, visiting one of the other flats. Except he

59

hadn't. Sometimes you knew, just by instinct.

"You're early," she said, opening the door, the air golden, blinds half shut against the light.

"I know. I just missed your friend."

She hesitated for a second. "What friend?" she said, not sure, trying to find a tone.

"I saw him coming out."

"Oh, and I'm the only one who lives here," she said quickly.

"Who was he?"

"No one. What a little boy you are. Pretending to be jealous." She tugged a little at his belt. "Close the door. Did you see the pail? On the landing? Another leak."

"You should complain."

"Oh, to the *kapici*. In a building like this."

"To the owner. Was that him?"

She moved closer to him. "Look at me. My eyes. So you know it's true. I haven't been with anyone today. You know you can smell that, when there's somebody. On the skin. Do you smell anyone?"

"Just perfume."

"That's right. The one you like." She stared at him again. "I haven't been with anyone today. All right?" She put her hand on his crotch, rubbing him. "I always save today for you. You know that." Stroking him,

60

the lie like another hand on him, so that he was hard instantly, excited by both, unable to separate them.

He took a *dolmus* taxi to Bebek this time, making conversation with the other passengers so that he'd be remembered, a foreigner who spoke some Turkish. Anna had already been fed and changed for bed, a soft nightgown she seemed not to notice. "I'll just sit with her until she falls asleep," he told the nurse, holding up the magazine he'd brought to read. An open-ended visit, no need to check back. Fifteen minutes later he was through the garden entrance, back on the road where Mihai was waiting.

"Anybody around?"

"Busy night. Egyptians are giving a party," Mihai said, looking out the windshield toward the old khedive's summer palace.

"Anybody else?"

"Hard to see. No moon."

Outside the village the night was black, only a few yellow windows visible through the cypresses and umbrella pines. On the Bosphorus a passing freighter's lights reflected on the water, then were swallowed up again by the dark.

"Let's see if we have company," Leon said,

turning to look out back as Mihai started the car.

But no one else pulled into the line of cars, moving quickly tonight, winter traffic, not the usual jam.

"We'll be early," Leon said.

"It's not exact, the time. Like a train."

"No rain tonight anyway. I checked the reports. It's clear all up along the coast."

He looked again at the black water. Where Jason had once sailed the *Argo*.

"Did you see Anna? Tell her about the boat?"

Leon nodded. "If she heard."

"They say hearing is the last sense to go. When you have a stroke."

"She didn't have a stroke."

Mihai said nothing. It had been his boat, the one he and Anna had organized, also out of Constancia, as it happened. Overcrowded and listing, stuck in Istanbul for repairs, then waiting for sailing permits, two hundred people taking turns on deck. They'd run tenders out with food and water, medicine that Anna had somehow rounded up out of nonexistent supplies. Black market drugs. And still no permits, then panic, everyone seeing a repeat of the *Struma,* the ship sent back, then torpedoed in the Black Sea, everyone down with it.

One survivor, they'd heard.

So the decision was made, a desperate run through the Marmara, a moonless night like this one that made them hope they could slip through. Mihai's decision. No, both; Anna's too. Worth the risk. What could the Turks do? Tow them back to Istanbul, where they were anyway, rotting? Better to make a run for it.

Later it was said the engines would never have made it, not at that speed, that weight. They were bound to overheat. But no one really knew how the fire had started. Some sort of explosion, probably, flames suddenly leaping up into the night. The ship had been just off Yedikule, close enough for the fire to be seen, but even so the rescue boats were late. The *Bratianu* had begun to break up by then, people screaming in the water, going under, later washing up, the shore littered with them, like driftwood. Anna had managed to save a few, swimmers strong enough to stay afloat, grab onto paddles, but the children were gone. It must have been then, watching the debris and corpses float toward her in the ship's lights that something had broken in her too, another overheated engine.

"There's the chance of another one," Mihai said. "A boat. The British are watching

Brindisi now, so we're trying to get one here."

"Should I know this?"

"Why not? We have no secrets from each other. Except the ones you don't tell me."

Leon looked over at him. "I don't know who he is."

"So you said. Well, a surprise for both of us. *Eine kleine Überraschung.*"

"You're so sure he's German."

"Who else comes out this way? The Americans. First they put them on trial. Now they take them home. A change of heart, very useful."

"You can't put everyone on trial."

"Why not? They wanted all of us dead. No exceptions."

"Anna's German."

"A Jew. It's different."

"That's what they wanted everyone to think."

"In that they succeeded. Now we know who we are."

"Where are you getting the ship?" Leon said, changing the subject.

"Trabzon. Of course a wreck. But if it can make it this far, why not Palestine?"

"A freighter?"

"Maybe for your tobacco. From Trabzon. Tobacco and hazelnuts."

Leon pointed out the windshield. "Pull up here."

"I don't see anyone."

"They'll see us."

They parked in the drop-off area by the quay. A few boats bobbed against their mooring posts, launches you could hire, their owners probably keeping warm in the café on the other side of the road. No one else around.

Mihai put on a knitted sailor's hat, pulling it over his ears. "Let's hope they're not late. It's freezing."

They walked over to the edge of the pavement, looking out at the black water. Any minute now, unless the boat had had to dodge a patrol around Garipçe.

"The money's already arranged?" Mihai said. "You don't want to hang around bargaining."

Leon tapped his breast pocket. "On delivery." He looked over at Mihai, clamping his ears for warmth. Two men standing in the cold, outlined by the café lights behind them. Up to what? They'd have to move soon.

"Hear that?" A boat being put in gear, the noise moving toward them, their shadowy figures spotted from the water.

"Right," Mihai said, "one, two, three. Let's

go. You pay, I'll get Johnny in the car."

The fishing boat, still without lights, now swung toward the quay, throwing out a rope.

"John?" Leon said, feeling foolish, as if it were a password.

The passenger nodded. Thin, smaller than Leon had expected, about Mihai's height. A heavy woolen jacket. He shoved a step box against the gunwale.

Mihai pulled him up out of the boat, gripping his hand. "Come on. Car's over there. Get in the back," Mihai said in a rush, then stopped, his eyes on the passenger's face, reading it.

Below them the fisherman started talking in Turkish, Leon answering before he got louder.

"My bag," John said, nodding to a duffel bag in the boat. "I have a bag."

For a second Mihai didn't move, still staring, until John looked back at him, a question mark. "I'll get it," Mihai said finally, breaking his own trance. "The car. Over there. Hurry."

"It's all right?" John said to Leon, suddenly anxious, a what's-wrong expression.

Leon made a shooing motion. "Fine. Get in the car."

"And my money? What about my money?"

Leon took an envelope out of his pocket

66

and handed it down. The fisherman started to count the bills.

"It's all there. Throw us the bag and get out of here." Behind him, he heard the car door slam. "Before anyone sees."

"Ha. Before anyone sees *you.*"

"Just throw up the goddam bag," Mihai said, edgy, putting one foot on the boat, reaching out.

"First I count," the fisherman said. "Who are you anyway? Nobody said two. One man."

"Count it, then," Leon said, impatient now, watching him thumb through the notes. Unshaven, face surly.

"Nothing extra for the extra day?"

Leon could feel Mihai tense up next to him, coiled. "Not here," he said quickly, improvising. "After you're back. And we know no one's seen you." Something Tommy could easily arrange. Pocket change.

"The bag," Mihai said, his voice low, almost threatening, so that the fisherman picked it up without question, heaving it across the gap. Mihai swung it onto his shoulder.

"No lights till you're past the landing," Leon said, reminded by a sweep of headlights from the road.

Mihai tossed back the rope.

67

"Did he say anything? You had two days."

The fisherman shook his head. "No Turkish. We play dominoes."

"The money will be there when you get back," Leon said. "The extra."

The fisherman smiled, an uneven row of teeth with gaps. *"Inshallah,"* he said, a hand on his chest. He went over to the controls, pushing the handle forward. The boat choked, then started moving, the engine grinding, swinging out again toward the dark, the sputtering still audible even after it was out of sight.

"They're lucky they made it. In that," Mihai said.

"Come on, let's get out of here."

Mihai turned to him. "You know what you're doing?"

"What do you mean?"

A crunch of tires, a car door slamming. Mihai turned to it, then suddenly swiveled, the air near him exploding, his body jerking back, as if he'd been punched. He let out a sharp cry, hit somewhere. Leon saw the duffel bag falling, then Mihai pitching forward, rocking.

"Get down!" A hoarse grunt as he dropped onto the duffel, scraping the pavement to get behind it.

Another shot, hitting the concrete near

the edge of the bag, Mihai rolling away from it. Leon ducked, then threw himself down, flattening his body on the concrete. Out of the light but still exposed, his mind a minute behind what was happening, trying to catch up. What soldiers must feel, everything around them moving too fast. Getting killed. Afraid they'd pee.

He lifted his head a little, looking across the quay. The shots had been so loud that everyone must have heard. He expected people rushing out of the café. But nobody appeared, even the café lights now hidden behind the dark bulk of the car where the shots had come from.

"Mihai," he said, a hiss.

"Keep down." He was reaching into his pocket, pulling out a gun, crouching farther behind the duffel for cover. "Roll away!" Mihai said, still hoarse. "Keep moving."

But the next bullet went to the duffel again, a locator shot for Mihai, who now aimed at the point in the dark where it had been fired. Leon watched him steady the gun. Nothing but dim reflected light on the road. But he found the spot. Another explosion, louder than the others, almost in his ear, and then a grunt from the other car, a surprised scream, a shadow forming, trying to stand then falling down again. For a second, silence, so quiet he could hear the boats creak against their ropes.

"Mihai?" he whispered, crawling over on his belly, still trying to keep his head down.

"I hit him."

Now close enough to see Mihai's hand, covered in blood. "Jesus."

"We have to get to the car. We don't know how many —"

Mihai pushed himself up, knees, then a low crouch, moving, his eyes fixed on the other car. Leon scrambled up, following, then saw the shadow take shape, on its knees, hand extended.

"Watch out!" he shouted, flattening himself again.

"My hand. It's stiff," Mihai said, sliding the gun to Leon. "Get him."

For a second, less, Leon stared at the gun, reaching for it as if it might snap at him, a gray lizard flecked with blood, alive.

"Quick!"

Then, a pure reflex, he was aiming the gun, firing, hearing another grunt, this time the crack of bone as a head hit the pavement. Mihai was up and running, bent over, dragging the duffel.

"Get in the car," Leon said, taking the bag from him, risking a half-standing sprint, an easy target now. But moving, racing.

70

He slammed back against the car when he reached it, hearing his own breath, then yanked the door handle to get in. He reached across the seat to open the other door for Mihai, who slid in, a writhing movement, still low.

"Here," he said, handing over the keys.

Leon jammed them into the ignition, turning them at the same time.

"Keep down."

Leon put the car in gear and felt it jump beneath him, wheels squealing as he pressed the accelerator, shooting out of the parking area and left onto the road, past the café. No one outside. Hadn't anybody heard? Gunshots were startling, always recognizable, not cars backfiring. Or maybe they were huddled inside, cowering behind windows. Or maybe it had all never happened, a fever dream. But there was Mihai's hand, bleeding. And his own, shaking, his whole body trembling, adrenaline still surging, shocked. Someone shooting at him.

"They said there wouldn't be any trouble," John said from the backseat, his voice apprehensive.

Leon looked in the rearview mirror, somehow surprised that he was there, an afterthought.

"You're safe," Mihai said.

71

"Did you see them?" Leon said over his shoulder. "How many?"

John shook his head. "They thought you were me," he said to Mihai. "You had the bag."

Leon looked in the mirror again, taking him in for the first time. Short gray hair, receding at the temples so that he seemed almost bald, a thin face pulled tight over high cheekbones, sharp eyes peering back at him in the mirror.

"How's your hand?" he said to Mihai.

"I can move it."

"There's a shirt in the bag," John said. "You can wrap it in that. Stop the bleeding."

"I don't need your shirt," Mihai said to the mirror, pulling a handkerchief out of his back pocket.

"Anyone behind?" Leon said.

"There will be. Would they send just one?"

"They?"

"Whoever they are, who'd want to put a bullet in your head," Mihai said to the mirror. "Who is that, do you think?"

John looked back, saying nothing.

"You brought a gun," Leon said, glancing down at the seat.

"In case."

"In case. There was no reason to think

72

—" Leon said, his voice still ragged, back at the quay.

"There's always a reason," Mihai said evenly. He looked up at the mirror. "Don't you think so?"

"Where are we going?" John said, not answering him.

"A safe place," Leon said. "Don't worry."

"Not the consulate?"

"How?" Mihai said. "In a diplomatic pouch? So the Turks don't see?"

Leon glanced over at him, surprised at his tone, still shooting back. "Don't worry," he said again to the mirror. He made a sharp right turn, into the village.

"What are you doing?" Mihai said.

"You can't lose anyone on the coast road. We'll take the back way," Leon said.

"What back way?"

"Just watch behind," Leon said, gesturing to the rear window.

They shot up the steep grade toward Nispetiye, Leon leaning forward to concentrate on the twisting road, dark with pines.

"Anyone?"

"No."

"It's hard to follow here." Suburbs with shady local roads circling the hills, easy to get lost in even during the day.

"So you're called John?" Mihai said, mak-

73

ing conversation, holding the bloody hand. "So many Johns. Ivan. Johann. Ion in Romania."

John looked into the mirror. "Alexei," he said. "John was for the fisherman."

Mihai continued to look back for a second, then turned to Leon. "Who knew about the pickup?"

"Here? Nobody. That's why they used me. Someone outside."

"So then, your end," Mihai said to Alexei, turning in his seat to face him. "Someone at your end."

Alexei just stared back at him.

"Any ideas?"

"No."

"Of course, there's always the fisherman. If someone pays more. But who? Who wants to kill you?"

Alexei looked at him, deliberate, moving a chess piece into place. "Everybody," he said. "Why do you think I'm coming to you? Do you have a cigarette?"

Leon reached into his pocket and handed back a pack.

"So thank you for that," Alexei said, lighting one. "Saving my life."

Mihai nodded. "That's right, isn't it? I did. And the bag saved mine. How things work."

"What if he isn't dead?" Leon said, taking a left at the intersection down toward Yildiz.

"Who? Our friend? Then he's as good as dead. He can't go to a hospital. What would he say?"

Leon looked over, his stomach suddenly light. Someone was dead, had to be. And he hadn't felt anything, just the blind panic of firing back, saving himself. It must be different for snipers, taking aim, knowing you're about to kill. Detached, not shaking later, gripping the wheel tighter, head filled with it.

"It was supposed to be a simple pickup," he said.

They drove for a while in silence, then skirted the dark border of Yildiz Park where Sultan Abdul Hamid had walled himself away, frightened of shadows. Leon glanced at the rearview mirror. Nobody behind.

"You know the pharmacy in Taksim? The late-night one? I should get some iodine for this."

Leon spotted the green pharmacy sign and double-parked in front of a *borek* stall, looking both ways as he stepped into the street. Maybe he would always do this now, listening for bullets. Inside he got the iodine and bandages and then, an afterthought, some aspirin so it would look like a general supplies run. When he got back to the car, he had a sense that something had happened, a change in the air, but neither Mihai nor Alexei said anything. Maybe the change was in him, a new churning uneasiness, as suspicious now as Abdul Hamid.

"Shit!" Mihai gasped as he applied the iodine.

Leon was heading downhill again toward Galata Bridge. "Can you drive home? With that?" he said, indicating the bandage.

"I'll be all right. Just worry about him." A hard look, Mihai somehow blaming Leon.

They crossed the Horn and went up into the old city, past the tourist monuments, then Beyazit. Laleli Caddesi turned downhill toward Yenikapi station in a stretch of small hotels and cheap textile dealers.

"We'll get out here," Leon said, stopping. "So they don't see the car."

"Who?"

Leon pointed to a light three doors down. "Hotel."

"It's safe?" Alexei said, looking out, suddenly vulnerable.

"Let's hope so." Leon turned to Mihai. "You sure you'll be all right?"

Another look, his eyes meeting Leon's, then letting it go, pushing the bag back to Alexei. "Here, keep it close. It might come in handy again." He slid over to the driver's seat, waiting for them to leave, then handed Leon the gun. "Better have this. Watch your back."

Leon touched it, feeling it alive again, then nodded.

"Keep the car off the street. In case anybody spotted it." He hesitated. "I'm sorry."

Mihai shrugged. "Don't be sorry. Just get him out of Istanbul."

"You were never there. You can trust me on that."

"And him?"

They moved to the curb, watching the car pull away. Down the hill three men appeared out of the shadows, probably on their way to a *mihanye*. The night belonged to men here, roaming the streets in bored groups, the women safely shuttered away. Except for the ones loitering near the station, hoping for a few hours in one of the hotels. Salesmen from Izmir, with suitcases of samples. Workers up from the country to see about a job. A neighborhood used to new faces, passing through.

Leon took out a folded paper and handed it to Alexei. "In case they ask. They might not."

"What?"

"Your *tezkere.* Internal passport. Foreigners have to carry them."

"Foreigners. What am I?"

"Bulgar. I didn't know what you could pass for. If you knew Turkish."

"No." He glanced at the passport. "It's real?"

Leon nodded. "A refugee I knew. He moved on."

"Your friend," Alexei said, motioning to where the car had been. "He's Romanian."

"Was. Why?"

"He spoke to me. In the car. To see if I knew Romanian."

"Why Romanian?"

"It's like that with us. Romanians recognize each other. Something in the voice, maybe." He looked in the passport. "Now Bulgar. Jakab?"

"A Bulgar Jew. That's why you left."

"A Jew," he said to himself, trying it on, like a hat.

But the night clerk didn't ask for a *tezkere.* A pale man with a beak nose and small eyes who might have been Bulgar himself, he took the money and handed Leon a key attached to a weight with a tassel. When Leon asked for glasses, he scowled but got up and went to the room behind and brought out two raki glasses, muttering in

Turkish, a weary put-upon monotone.

"What did he say?" Alexei asked on the stairs.

"Not to make too much noise," Leon said, holding up the glasses.

The hall light was on a timed switch, just long enough to get the key in the door before it snapped off again. The room was small, stained Liberty wallpaper and a curtain on a rod for a closet, not intended for long stays. A Turkish toilet and a shower, no tub. Alexei looked around.

"How long do I stay here?"

"About half an hour," Leon said, going over to the window, parting the curtain to take in the street. "Don't unpack."

"Ah. Then where?"

"Somewhere nicer." He looked at the lumpy bed. A chenille spread, pink, something a young girl would have. "Private."

"And the man downstairs?"

"There's a back way." He put the glasses on the table.

"So. You brought some raki?"

"No."

"Then why —"

"Anybody checks with him, he says we're up here having a party. Tomorrow we're sleeping it off. Buys us time to move."

"A game," Alexei said. "Hide-and-seek."

Leon didn't answer, lighting a cigarette and leaning back against the wall, giving Alexei the bed, the only seat.

"Two places. You expected trouble?" Alexei said.

Leon shook his head. "Just wanted to keep ahead of the Emniyet. If they're watching. You're not in the States yet. And illegal here. If they pick you up, there's nothing we could do."

"It was them? At the boat?"

"No. The Emniyet don't like people coming in, but they can send them back. They don't have to shoot them."

Alexei leaned back against the rickety headboard. "Who then? The Russians. Old friends, maybe. Not Turks. Not my new friends, either," he said, looking at Leon. "Not before we have our talks."

"The photographs are in the bag?" Leon said.

"What photographs?"

"German aerials. I thought you were bringing out —"

"Do you think I'm a messenger? I brought myself out. The photographs — that was arranged in Bucharest. Your embassy has them. Maybe already in the pouch. In Washington. Who knows? How efficient are you?"

"You're here, aren't you?"

Alexei smiled. "A lucky man. Nice hotel rooms. A trip to America. Everybody wants to go to America." He looked down. "Before the Russians get them. And now they know I'm here. In Istanbul."

"But not where."

Alexei looked at him. "That's right. Not where."

Leon turned, glancing down at the street.

"Anything?" Alexei said.

"No, it's quiet. We'll give it a few more minutes." When he turned back to face the bed, he saw that Alexei had closed his eyes. "Don't get too comfortable."

"Only resting. I get tired all the time now. Before I could go for days — now, always tired." He smiled to himself. "Age, maybe."

Leon looked at his face, softer with his eyes closed, but drained and spent, like someone winded after a race. He went to the window again, touching the gun in his coat pocket, still not real. The seedy hotel room, the empty raki glasses, the man lying dead on the quay — all part of someone else's life. He just took the Ankara train and passed along papers. And now there was a gun in his pocket.

"Okay," he said, eager to move, "better leave the light. Too early for bed."

81

"But no one's watching, you said."

"I didn't think there was anyone at the quay, either."

Alexei nodded. "You know, it's interesting. What saved me? We were early. A little later and I wouldn't have been in the car. I'd have been —"

"Where they thought you were. Getting off the boat with your bag."

"Who shot him? You or your friend?"

"We both did."

He held the door open, a sliver of light, until Alexei reached the back stairs, then followed, feeling his way, back against the wall. The stairs themselves were easier, shadowy but catching light from the ground floor. He could hear a radio in the desk clerk's office, loud enough to muffle any creaking steps. Alexei barely touched the banister, the duffel on his shoulder, not making a sound, someone used to going out the back. No one at the desk when they reached the ground floor. Audience laughter on the radio. Just the hallway now, past a utility room, then the back door, not even locked. In the street behind, no wider than an alley, Alexei stumbled into a trash bin but caught the lid before it could fall off, holding his breath for a second. Leon nodded toward the streetlight at the end. No one was out, all the *mihanye* customers farther down the hill.

"Which way?" Alexei said when they reached Ordu Caddesi, turning away as a half-empty tram passed.

"Just across. A few blocks."

Small, quiet streets, then a larger one looking down toward the Şehzade Mosque. A modern building with a buzzer entry system, not a courtyard with a nosy *kapici*. Leon opened the front door with a key. More timer switches on the stairs, but at least everything working, the lobby clean, smelling faintly of disinfectant.

"One more floor," Leon said when they reached the landing.

"Who lives here?"

"University people. It's nearby."

"Students?"

"No, they couldn't afford it."

"So I'm a professor?"

"You're not anything. You don't go out. You're not here."

The flat was no more than functional, but a pleasant step up from the hotel.

"I stocked the fridge," Leon said. "You should have everything you need. At least for the next few days."

"Few days?"

"Or sooner. Depending on the plane."

Alexei threw the duffel on the bed, then walked over to the bottle on a side chest. "So now the raki."

"Not for me. I have to go."

"We don't talk tonight?" Alexei said, surprised, thinking Leon was Tommy, not just the babysitter. "No questions?"

"Later."

"Well, join me anyway. A welcome toast." Alexei poured the drinks, then raised his. "To safe journeys."

"Safe journeys," Leon said, feeling the heat as it slipped down, finally something real.

"You don't stay here?" Alexei said. "The watchdog?"

"It's safe."

"Safe," Alexei said, his voice neutral.

"No one followed us here."

"I know. I worked in the field too. So, now the only risk is you."

"Me?"

"When you come back. Or is someone else coming tomorrow? Either way, a visitor leaves a trail. Like Hansel and the pebbles. So perhaps it's better to stay." Again trying to be light. He poured more raki in his glass. "I haven't talked to anybody in two days. Dominoes, it's not the same thing. A game for simpletons. You see them in the mountains. Every village. Sitting in the cafés, *click, clack.* Two days of that."

Leon smiled a little. "You'll be all right now. Just stay put."

"Where would I go?" He walked over to the window. "Where are we? What part?"

"The old city."

"Constantinople," Alexei said, playing with it for effect, a student reciting homework. "And that?" He pointed to a hulking shadow beyond the mosque.

"Valens Aqueduct."

"Aqueduct? From Romans?"

"Byzantine. Fourth century." A fact he'd picked up from Anna on one of their walks.

"Fourth?" Alexei said, genuinely impressed, a tourist. "They still use it?"

"Not anymore. Not for fifty years or so."

"So nothing is forever." He turned to Leon, a half smile. "But of course that's why we're here. The new order. Another one. Yours, this time."

Leon drained his glass. "I have to go."

"Let's hope this one lasts for a while," Alexei said, turning to glance again at the aqueduct. "I can't change sides again. You're the last."

Leon looked at him for a moment. Not what he expected, not a rescue, one of ours, someone buying his life with betrayal.

85

"I'll be back tomorrow. Do you need anything?"

"Something to read maybe," Alexei said, nodding to the empty shelf. "Not even dominoes now. What should I do? Think about my sins? That's what the priests used to recommend."

"When was this?"

"When I was young." He smiled. "Before I had any."

"Lock up behind me," Leon said, turning.

"One more thing? The gun?" He held out his hand.

"You're safe here."

"Then I'll be safer. A precaution," Alexei said, staring him down until Leon reached into his pocket and handed it over. "Thank you." He looked at the gun, then around the room. "Very trusting, Americans. No guard."

"You're not a prisoner. You came to us, remember?" Leon said, improvising, a guess.

"What if I changed my mind?"

"Changed it to what?"

Alexei made a wry smile. "Not so many choices left, you mean. No," he said to himself, then shrugged.

"I'll see you tomorrow then."

Alexei raised his head. "I'll look forward to that."

86

Outside, Leon crossed the street heading toward Süleyman's Mosque, then ducked suddenly into a doorway catty-corner from the building. A few minutes, just to be sure. No one in the streets. He felt the same tingling, the caffeine alertness he'd felt on the quay. He should have arranged for someone to watch the building. But there hadn't been any reason for that. Not a few hours ago. A simple pickup, just slipping someone in and out of the country, a kind of card trick. Not shoot-outs, someone lying in a pool of blood. Or carried away by now, tossed into the Bosphorus, another secret in the water.

Leon looked up at the lighted window, remembering Alexei's face, wary and then tired, gone to ground. But there must have been other times, eyes confident, standing tall in his uniform. Romanian, it turned out, not *Wehrmacht,* whatever that looked like. Probably the same peaked hat, padded shoulders. Fighting alongside the Germans, all the way to Stalingrad. And now in the Russians' crosshairs, Mihai taking the bullet instead. Luck just a matter of turning a few inches, a hand on the duffel where his head should have been. He thought of himself, flat on the damp concrete of the quay, waiting, afraid to breathe.

He moved away from the doorway, through the dark streets around the mosque, then the even darker ones below the Grand Bazaar, just an occasional light through shutters or a radio playing, streets as dark as they must have been when Valens was building his aqueduct. The timeless city, houses with bay overhangs, cobbles slick with peels and rinds. Leon had never been afraid on the streets in Istanbul, not even in the back alleys of neighborhoods like Fatih, full of headscarves and long stares, but tonight every movement, every faint rustling, put him on edge. In one street, two dogs raised their heads to watch him pass, some of Istanbul's roaming wild dogs, fed on scraps.

He kept going east, through Cağaloğlu, where all the newspaper offices were. Had they heard about the shooting yet? Pages being made up, lines of type. Murder in Bebek. Mysterious shooting on the Bosphorus. No witnesses. Never suspecting the witness was outside their windows right now. Not just a witness, the killer. And looking at the swirl of lights down at Sirkeci, he knew the sudden shortness of breath, doubling

88

over, was about this, not about Alexei or Mihai, how the job had gone wrong, but about this, killing a man, a line he'd never expected to cross. The sound of the shot was still in his head, an echo. Life gone in a minute, that easy.

He caught a taxi at the station and took it to the Park. A few minutes just to establish his presence, pretending to look for someone in the big art deco dining room, waving at Mehmet in the bar, then using the men's room off the lobby, spotted by regulars who would say, vaguely, that they'd seen him there that evening.

A few minutes later he was back out on Aya Paşa, past the now dark German Consulate, down to his building, sliding the key in the door, then freezing, the door already unlocked. He pushed at it gently, listening for sounds. No light, but the smell of tobacco, a cigarette burning, still here. He felt for the gun in his pocket, then remembered it wasn't there. He took another step, a faint creaking. Not a burglar, something he knew without knowing why. Someone waiting for him.

"Turn on the light, for god's sake." Mihai's voice in the living room. "It's only me."

Leon flicked on the hallway switch, then walked into the room. Mihai was sitting by

89

the window smoking, the only light the glow of his cigarette tip.

"How did you get in?" Leon said.

"A child could get in."

"What are you doing here?"

"Thinking."

"About what?" Leon said, turning on a table lamp.

Mihai winced at the sudden light. "What you know. What you don't know. Whether you're a fool. Or something else."

Leon nodded to his bandaged hand. "You think I knew? I wouldn't have asked you —"

"Not that," Mihai said, waving his hand toward the drinks tray. "Make yourself a drink."

"I just had one."

"Oh yes? With Alexei?" he said, his voice curling around the name. "A celebration?"

"Not exactly."

"And how did you find him? Good company?"

"Worried."

"Ah. Pour me one, will you?"

Leon poured two, handing one over.

"A natural reaction," Mihai said. "To being shot at. I don't feel so wonderful, either."

"Not just that. Worn out."

"A sympathetic figure. And now such a

helpful friend." He took a drink. "Who sent you? Tonight?"

"You know I can't tell you that."

"Scruples, at such a moment. If the bullet had got me, would you have told me then?"

"Does it make any difference, who? What's this all about?"

"Trading with the enemy. A drink with the devil," he said, holding up his glass.

"He's not the enemy anymore."

Mihai looked at him, then down at his glass. "So I wondered, is he a fool? Now I know. Sit down."

"You've got something on your mind?" Leon said, taking a chair.

"My mind, yes. Not on my conscience. Yet. I thought, he doesn't know. He should know."

"Know what?"

"Who he is. Your Alexei. Shall I guess what you think? The Romanians. Well, they sided with the Germans. How could they not? The expedient thing. Our friend too. What choice? Then Stalingrad, the Russians push back. And push. *Into* Romania. Now Germany's losing and who's coming? So why not make a deal with them? Throw out the fascists. Fight with the Russians instead. The new expedient thing. But meanwhile some people get caught in between. Our friend, for example. The Russians don't forgive him. They're going to put him on trial. Like Antonescu. So he runs. And he has something to sell. Things he knows. I'm right so far, yes?"

Leon nodded.

"Only one bidder in this deal. And better not to ask too many questions. The whole Romanian army was fascist, so, yes, he was a fascist, but now the Communists are after him, a recommendation in itself. In such a situation you take what you can. All right. An opportunist. But our opportunist. That's what you think, isn't it?"

"I haven't thought. I don't know."

"But I do. I recognized him. Before I took a bullet for him. You think he's someone — not so good, maybe, but Romanian politics were like that. Who can blame him for wanting to save himself?"

"You, it seems."

"Yes, me. I know what he is, Jianu. That's his name. A butcher. But you don't know, I think. So what do I do? Keep my mouth shut? Somebody this close to me? Anna I used to trust with my life. We killed a man tonight — you, me. And you don't even know."

"Tell me, then," Leon said quietly.

Mihai nodded to his hand. "Get me another. It hurts."

"It's not infected, is it?"

"Such concern. So where to start? King Carol with his hand in everybody's pockets? The wolf at the door. But still, thank God, the Jews to hate. So, the Legion of Archangel Michael. You know it? The Iron Guard."

"Yes."

"A wonderful group. Pouches with Romanian earth around their necks. Little ceremonies where they drink each other's blood. Like savages. My countrymen. Well, not by then. I'm in Palestine. My family said, how can you be a Zionist? Jassy is a Jewish city. Well, it was. So I'm in Palestine and things get worse for the Jews. Mossad sends me to Bucharest, to get them out. The Athénée Palace, everyone in the same place. You go to dinner at Capşa and bribe someone, then back to the Palace and bribe someone else. You could still do that then. But how many Jews listen? Then Carol runs away with Lupescu, the mistress — and the treasury. For them, at least, the happy ending. No one else. Now Michael is king, but really General Antonescu, the army. And meanwhile the Iron Guard are running wild. Killing people. Government people even. Pogroms naturally, what else? Terrible excesses. Finally, it's too much even for Antonescu. He sends the tanks out — the army fighting the Iron Guard, fascist against fascist. But Hitler prefers Antonescu. Not so crazy. He sides with him. And so does our friend Jianu. Your Alexei."

"He was in the Iron Guard?"

"But now he helps Antonescu break them. So Antonescu joins the Axis and the army goes off to invade Russia. A reign of terror in Odessa — that you know from the trials this summer. Deportations from Bessarabia. All the Jews. The Romanians set up extermination camps — the only ones the Germans didn't run themselves. They killed almost two hundred thousand, we think. Quite a record. My countrymen."

"And Alexei?"

"Now a right hand to Antonescu. Antonescu liked him. Someone who would betray the Guard? Who better for intelligence work? He knew how to get Russians to come over. The Romanians had good intelligence, right up to Stalingrad. But he had to know about the Jews too. The army carried out the deportations. It was the Guard all over again. Jassy they emptied out in 'forty-one."

"Your family."

"Everyone. Then bigger things. Until they started to lose. After Stalingrad, they knew.

Antonescu was so desperate he put out feelers — this time to save the Jews, help them get to Palestine. Sell them. I was here then. We bought some out. The Americans more. They had the money. Already Antonescu must have been thinking about the end, making some friends for after. He should have looked closer to home. When he was deposed, 'forty-four, where was loyal Alexei? Nowhere to be found." He paused. "Until you found him."

"So he knew. That's not the same as —"

"Who pulls the trigger? Is that what you mean?"

Leon looked away, flustered.

"Maybe I've been going too fast for you."

"I get the picture. He'd sell his mother. What am I supposed to do?"

"Not let him sell her again. Antonescu goes on trial soon. But not Alexei. Why not?"

"Because he made a deal." Leon looked up. "He didn't make it with me."

"So it's not your responsibility. Nobody's." He took a drink, letting the air settle a little. "Let the Communists have him. Put him on trial. With Antonescu."

"A show trial. They don't try people. They shoot them."

"In this case, well deserved."

"Maybe he's more valuable this way. I

don't know. I don't know what he knows."

"I know what he is. I said before a butcher. I didn't tell you why."

Leon held up his hand. "It doesn't matter. It's not up to me —"

"One more thing. Then you decide. The Guard. You remember I said there were excesses. But what's in a word? Excesses. You know Bucharest?"

"No."

"Dudeşti was the main Jewish district. Three days they went crazy there. First Strada Lipscani, a killing spree, looting. Then out in the Băneasa forest, making them dig pits before they shot them. The reason for this, by the way? No one said. Enough they were Jews. But the second day, before Antonescu decided to send the tanks, the Guard went even crazier. Maybe they drank each other's blood again, who knows. For courage. What courage? Who was fighting them? Terrified Jews, begging for their lives? That was the day they got two hundred of them — men, women — and took them to Străuleşti." He stopped, then tossed back the rest of the drink. "The slaughterhouse. South of town. An abattoir."

Leon waited, not moving.

"They put the Jews on the conveyor belts. Stripped, on all fours. They made them

96

bleat, like the animals. Crying, I suppose, maybe screaming, but also bleating like they were ordered. Then through the assembly line, the same treatment the animals got. Heads sliced off, then limbs, then hung up on hooks. Carcasses. And then they stamped them, the carcasses." He said something in Romanian, then translated. "Fit for human consumption. The inspector's stamp." He paused. "You decide."

Leon said nothing, staring, as if the belt were moving through the room before them, blood spurting, running into gutters.

"And Alexei was there?" Leon said, marking time, his stomach queasy.

"There were no witnesses. Among the Jews. Just the Guard. But he's still with the Guard then. He was seen. Ask him."

"He sold the Guard out, you said."

"When it was convenient. A fine point." He paused again. "You decide."

Leon was quiet. "I can't," he said finally. "It's not my decision."

"It's somebody's."

"Not yours, either."

"No, I just speak Romanian and drive the car. And keep my mouth shut. That was before. Help a man like this escape? I won't be part of that. Whoever sent you — maybe he doesn't know, either. He needs to know.

So somebody can decide."

"You're not part of it. They don't even know you were there."

"That's not so easy now. Maybe you didn't think about this, either, what it means for me, what this is now."

Leon looked at him, waiting.

"So more thinking. I had this time," he said, waving to the room, "while you were having your drink. Who were they tonight? Russians? All right. Who else would have such an interest? Stop him before — So they send a unit, three, four men. In which case they've already cleaned up the mess, got rid of the body. But no one followed us. It's more important to get Jianu than worry about the fallen comrade. But no one follows. So he must have been alone. Think what that means."

"I know what it means."

"Yes? You have thought about this too? No one moves the body. It lies there to be found. And it will be found. Now something for the police, even Emniyet. And what are they looking for? My gun. My car. Who protects me now? The boss you can't tell me about? Who wants me to help the butcher? I'm working for him now too. I have a right to know."

"I never meant —"

"It's too late for that. Do we want to tell the police it was self-defense? Then we have to tell them what we were doing there."

Leon stared at his drink for a minute. "Can they trace the car to you?"

"This is your response?"

"They can't, can they? Where is it?"

"The garage."

"Where it's been all night, as far as anyone knows. There's nothing special about the car, if they saw it from the café. Unless they got the plate number. It could be anybody's."

"So I have nothing to worry about."

"There's nothing to connect you to this."

Mihai looked over. "Except you."

"If it comes to that, we'll protect you. I promise you that. I'll talk to —"

"Protect me. A Palestinian helping the Americans, killing Russians. I'd be out of the country in a day."

"At least you wouldn't be in jail."

"Those are my choices. And my work here? Who does that?"

"You were never there," Leon said, his voice level. "Nobody knows except Alexei and he'll be gone."

"The butcher goes free. And we protect ourselves. So we protect him. That's what I'm doing now, protecting someone like

99

that. A knot," he said, twisting his fingers, "not so easy to pull apart."

"I didn't know."

"That's what the Germans say," Mihai said wryly. "Every one." He put down the glass, ready to go. "So, a good night's work. He's safe and so are we. Only the Turks have this problem. This body. One thing, though, still to think about. How did they know, the Russians? The arrangements? Where he'd be? Just you. No guns. So easy they could send one man. If they knew all that, what else do they know? So maybe we're not so safe. And neither is he," he said, getting up.

The phone rang, twice as loud this late, startling them, like an unexpected hand on the shoulder. Leon glanced at his watch, then looked at Mihai, who shook his head, a tic response. Another clang filling the room, waves of sound. He picked up the receiver, snatching it.

"Leon? I've been trying to reach you." Ed Burke. At this hour.

"I was at the Park." Accounting for himself to Ed Burke, already making alibis. "Do you know what time —"

"It's about Tommy," Ed said quickly. "I thought maybe you'd know something."

"Know something?"

"Since you were in Bebek. With your wife.

We couldn't get past the police."

"Police?" Just an echo.

"You haven't heard? He's dead. Killed."

"What?" A first wave of heat rushing through him. Tommy hit too, the one who was supposed to meet the boat, not a freelance. They'd known where he was. He looked over at Mihai, who was watching him.

"Leon, you there?"

Say something. "Killed? In a crash?" he said, trying to keep his voice steady.

"No, that's the thing. Shot. In Bebek. That's why I called. I thought you might have heard something before they blocked the whole place off. By the water, just down from that fort."

"Rumeli Hisari," Leon said, an automatic response, not hearing himself. "Shot?" His mind racing now, his blood seeming to travel in two directions. "By the water?"

"The boat landing. That's what I wondered too. Hell of a place to be, that hour. Tommy leaves his own party, I figure he must have something going on. But, Christ, you never know, do you. Maybe somebody saw the car and said, there's money there. So if he hadn't left then. But maybe something else."

"God," Leon said blankly. "Shot?"

"You don't expect that here."

"No," Leon said. "You don't." Fire into the dark and wait for a thud, the crack of a head on the pavement.

"Well, I didn't mean to bother you."

"No, no, I'm glad you called. Thanks." Police cars and lights, questioning people in the café. His head filling with blood, face hot.

"I'll let you know if I hear anything about the arrangements."

"Arrangements?"

"Well, Barbara will want to bury him here, don't you think? I mean, shipping a body home —"

"Barbara," Leon said vaguely. The widow, a bottle blonde who flirted after the second drink.

"She had to identify the body," Ed said, in the know. Who else had he called? "It's a hell of a thing. One minute you're at a party, the next you're —"

"I can't believe it," Leon said. What you were supposed to say.

"You never saw anything? They must have had half the force out."

"Not while I was there." He waited a second. "When did it happen?"

"Right after he left the party, I guess."

"I must have already gone. Jesus, shot."

"Well, I'll let you go," Ed said, slightly disappointed, hoping for details. "I still say, it's a funny place to be, that hour." Fishing.

"Thanks again, Ed," Leon said, not responding.

He put down the receiver, moving slowly, and turned to Mihai.

"What?" Mihai said, looking at his face.

"You have to think some more. It wasn't a Russian."

■ ■ ■ ■

2
LALELI

■ ■ ■ ■

He spent all morning waiting for a call —
somebody from Tommy's office at the consulate, maybe even the Consul himself. The
account in *Hürriyet* had been skimpy, a
businessman shot, but the details were
already racing through the foreign community. Why hadn't Barbara been invited to
the party at the college? Why had Tommy
left early? Heading away from town? Suspicions percolated up and down the phone
lines, but no one believed Tommy was seeing another woman, certainly not one who
would shoot him. Which left robbery. Except, according to Barbara, his wallet had
been in his pocket when the police found
him. His gun had been fired, so he must
have scared them off. But why was he carrying a gun?

A full morning of it, pacing, then staring
at the phone, expectant. Turhan, Leon's
secretary, one of the Atatürk new women

who didn't cover her head, but still went home to her family at night, gave up any pretense of working, answering calls in a breathless voice, eyes wide with interest. During a normal day not much happened at R.J. Reynolds; today the phone kept ringing. But not with the call he wanted.

By noon, standing at the window overlooking Taksim, he realized that no one was going to contact him, that he was alone. Nobody knew. Did his name even appear on any record, some payment voucher? Tommy spreading his bets over the table, the way he liked it. Using someone outside so he could distance himself, someone to blame if anything went wrong. But why should it? A job so routine it hadn't required the usual precautions. Tommy hadn't even asked where the safe house was, just the neighborhood.

Why not? But the answer was the same one he'd been getting all night, sitting up with it. The address didn't matter. Alexei was never supposed to get there. He was supposed to die on the quay. And Leon? Would he have been left there, Tommy squealing away in his car, not sure if he'd been recognized? Impossible to risk that. Of course he'd have to be killed too. An easy target, not expecting it, just picking up a package. Two people left dead. Who'd killed each other? How would Tommy have arranged it? Dressed the scene? He thought of his face at the Park bar, pink, reminiscing. Already planning it. And that always led back to why and the other answer he circled around, the one he wasn't ready to accept. He gripped the windowsill as if his body had caught the swirling in his head.

Meanwhile, he had to hand Alexei on to someone. Who? Tommy's people at OWI were already gone. The plants at Robert College, whoever they were? But Tommy hadn't used any of them; they didn't know. Nobody had called. His operation now. He had to find the next link in the chain. There must be a name, maybe in Ankara, maybe lying around Tommy's desk.

But when he got to the consulate he found it surrounded, small clusters of people drawn by the police cars in the street, patrolmen at the gate cadging cigarettes from the guards, the carved American eagle over the door staring down at them all. Not just a consulate matter anymore, a courier assignment. A crime. Police. Wanting answers. Tommy setting up his own man. Why would they believe it? Why would the Consul? The only story they'd hear was that he had killed Tommy. His word against a dead man's. What proof did he have besides Alexei himself, who wasn't here, not to the police.

He looked up, some movement at the door, the Consul shaking hands with a Turk in a bulky suit. Cigarettes doused, orders being given, a few policemen staying behind, everyone else moving toward the gate. They passed around Leon as if he were a stick in a stream. Nobody knew. Getting into cars, writing up reports, not one of them looking at him. He stood there for a minute feeling them all around him, unable to move, invisible. Nobody knew.

They had arranged to meet in the second-hand booksellers market, a narrow passage shaded by plane trees near the Beyazit Mosque. Mihai was waiting at an English-language stall near the end, flipping through a book.

"You're late. Anything on the car?"

Leon shook his head. "Nothing. If anybody saw it, they're not saying. No calls from the consulate, either. Nobody."

"You said there was a plane arranged."

"That was Tommy's job."

"Then now it's yours. You have to get him out. He starts to panic — Where'd you park him?"

Leon said nothing.

"They'll be checking the hotels. First thing they do."

"He's not there." He picked up a book, the cover a blur.

"As long as he's in Istanbul, we're — A man who'd sell out anybody. Cheap. He says what's good for him. Not us."

"But we didn't — I mean —"

"Which explanation do you think they'll believe? Let's say the real one, what we were doing there. Just for the sake of argument. Your new friend can vouch for it," he said, his voice suddenly hard. "A wonderful history of telling the truth. And then what? Your ambassador intervenes? An embarrassment for him. But let's say he does. A deal. No prison. They deport us instead. Resident permit? Revoked. If they believe us." He looked away. "We don't want to explain anything."

"We won't have to. I'm telling you, nobody knows. If I can get him to the consulate —"

"The consulate. It's police now. With a body. Murder. The Emniyet have to have at least one pair of ears over there. At least. Take him in and the police —" He let the thought finish itself. "And the Russians. If they're watching, you wouldn't even get him to the gate. Maybe what he deserves, but not the best thing now, an incident. More police."

"He has to talk to somebody eventually. Tell them."

Mihai made a wry face. "His American confessor. Discretion guaranteed." He lifted a finger from his book. "But not here. If he's gone, the Turks have nothing to use against us." He placed the book on the barrow. "Except each other." He looked at Leon, quiet for a second. "What are you going to do if there's no plane?"

"Tommy said there was."

"He said a lot of things. I know someone at the airport. I can have him check the manifests. Not a scheduled plane, I suppose, not for this passenger. Military?"

Leon shrugged his shoulders.

"Wonderful. All right, I'll check all of them."

"Look, you don't have to get involved in this. You weren't there, remember?"

"If everyone says so. But will they?" He looked over. "I'll let you know about the airport."

"You think there is a plane, then."

"Probably. Your Tommy was passing him along. He'd want his end covered. It's just that Jianu wasn't going to be on it. Thanks to you. Given that any thought?"

Leon met his glance. "All night."

"It's something to think about," Mihai said, turning to go, then put his hand on Leon's upper arm, a good-bye gesture. "How long have you known me?" he said quietly. "There's blood here. Like blood. We have to look out for each other." He squeezed the hand tighter. "Keep your head. Everything normal. Or they'll smell it. It's not just for us. You know what I'm doing here. What Anna did. These people, it's the last hope. For them I'd even help a pig like Jianu." He dropped his hand, still looking at him. "Since you want him alive. Your new American friend."

He got on the tram at Beyazit, preoccupied. It's something to think about. Shooting at Jianu, shooting at him. How long had Tommy been someone else? But how do you prove it? Make one thing lead to another, like the stations on the map over the door. Next to him two women in robes and headscarves were talking to each other, as cut off from the rest of the car as if they were still in the harem, the men barely noticing, staring out the windows, stubble and bushy moustaches. Not Europe. Outside, the old city jerked past. The Blue Mosque. The Hippodrome. Chariot races a thousand years ago. Old enough to have seen every-thing, Alexei's Iron Guard a modern ver-sion of an old story, infants impaled, blood smeared over doorways, bodies flung into the Golden Horn, staining the water. Every-thing. Not what Anna had seen, clutching her guidebook. The Iznik tiles. The delicate carvings on the *minbar*. A city of wonders to her, not the other one, no longer surprised by anything.

At Topkapi, a group of sailors fresh off the seraglio tour crowded into the car, and Leon had to turn, facing the back. At first there were just the same anonymous faces, then he felt a prickling on his skin. Someone he knew. Head down, reading a Turkish news-paper, the same man who'd come out of Marina's building. A coincidence? When had he got on — before Leon? with Leon? So good Leon hadn't noticed. Still not look-ing up from his paper.

Leon turned back. Or was it just his imagination, jumpy about everything now. A public tram, a man Marina said she didn't know. Don't turn to look again. The car was heading down the hill into the swirl of Sirkeci. He had begun to sweat.

When the doors opened, the crowd pushed in. For a second he felt out of breath, as if they had taken all the air out of

114

the car. The buzzer rang. He held back, waiting, then plunged through the door just as it was closing. Don't look back. A face at the window. Or maybe not. Something he'd never know. Keep moving. He took a gulp of air, heavy with diesel fumes and charcoal smoke, and headed over to the Eminönü piers. Out on the water you could think. Follow the logic, one thing leading to another. Tommy had used someone outside.

He took the ferry to Üsküdar, sitting in the open back of the boat with a glass of tea, something warm, his coat pulled tight. He went over it all again, each move like a step into open space with nothing to break the fall. He glanced over at the birds, circling, and tried to fix on landmarks, Galata Tower, the shipping offices in Karaköy, but they seemed insubstantial too, just something to graze with your fingers as you fell past. In over your head, a phrase he could actually picture now. Where Tommy had wanted him to be. Grab onto that, follow it.

Someone must still be expecting Alexei. There had been people in Bucharest, the fishing boat. Only Tommy's link had broken. And now they'd come looking. But not for Leon, not yet. It was the trap that folded in on itself: the minute he went to someone about Alexei he was putting himself on the pier. And Mihai. He watched the boat crunch against the rubber tire buffers on the dock, the gangplanks being slid into place. Everybody in one another's hands.

He changed boats for Beşiktaş, looking at people, half expecting to see the man from the train. Two places, a coincidence? But there were only clumps of men in woolen peacoats, smoking, indifferent. Didn't anything show in his face? A man dead. When they landed, he stood on the pier for a minute, at a loss. Commuters brushed past him as if he weren't there, like the police at the consulate. Nobody knew. Go back to the office. Everything normal. But nothing was normal.

Anna was sitting in a chair, and she lifted her head when he came in. She was aware of physical activity, knew when she was being dressed, helped into clothes, even though her face showed no expression. When he leaned down to kiss her forehead she didn't flinch, simply accepted it.

"Something's happened," he said, then hesitated. Too abrupt. "Are you warm enough?" he said, fidgeting. The nurse had opened the French windows, letting in a crack of air. He put a shawl around her shoulders. "I was thinking about you on the ferry. How you love the water." But he hadn't been. Her eyes stayed fixed on the garden. Just say it. "Tommy King's dead. Shot. In a robbery, they think —"

He stopped and sank into the other chair, falling again.

"Am I doing that? With you? It wasn't a robbery." And then he couldn't say anything more, not out loud. Instead he followed her gaze to the garden, the patch of sun on the bare Judas tree. "I was there," he said softly. "He tried to kill a man we're bringing out. He tried to kill me."

Anna stared ahead, not moving.

"There wasn't anything I could do. I had to." Still not finishing it. "It didn't feel like anything. Not at the time. It's only later you — But I can't explain what happened, to anybody, until I get him out, the man we're moving." He took a breath, looking away from her. "And I don't know if I can do it. Tommy was supposed to —" He stopped. "And then there he was, with a gun."

He heard her question in his head and nodded.

"I've been going over it. All night. It has to be. Why else would Tommy have to kill him? I keep coming back to that. Why he'd have to. But think what it means. Tommy. It turns everything upside down. All these years working for — Christ. I worked for him. How long was he —"

He stopped talking, the two of them sitting in silence.

"Nothing was supposed to happen. Just a babysitting job. And now I've got him. He'll be killed if I —" He looked down. "A man who would have killed you. Not even thinking twice."

He got up and walked over to the French window, careful not to step into her line of sight. A bed of late asters near the wall.

"But if I don't help him, the Turks'll get involved. Then it's murder. And Mihai —" He let the thought drift, his eyes following a bird fluttering between branches. "You know what I was thinking before? If I can do this, deliver him — it's the kind of thing people notice. In Washington. It would be a chance to show them I could —" He stopped. "And then I thought, maybe it would have been better if Tommy had got him. They'd both be gone. Nothing to explain. Easier if he were dead too. And what kind of person thinks that? What kind of person."

A reflection in the glass, someone standing in the doorway. Obstbaum.

"Doctor," he said, turning, his voice changing. "I've just been telling Anna —"

118

How long had he been listening?

"Don't let me interrupt." Obstbaum held out his clipboard, a visual excuse.

"No, no, please," Leon said, then glanced down at his watch. "Anyway, look at the time. I'm seeing Georg," he said to Anna. "I couldn't put him off again." Do all the normal things. "An old friend," he said to Obstbaum. "She was very fond of him. Weren't you? I'll give him your love." He leaned down and kissed her forehead, then looked back up at Obstbaum. What had he heard?

"I hope it's all right, talking like that," he said at the door.

"It's good, your coming. The activity. And two days now. Last night too, I hear."

From whom? Why?

"How is she?" Leon said, ignoring it.

"No worse." He caught Leon's expression. "It's something, you know, no worse. At least there's no deterioration. It's good, the talking."

"Sometimes I think it's for me. Just sitting here. It makes me feel calmer."

Obstbaum nodded. "An oasis. It can have that effect. You know the shooting last night? Up the road? It was in the papers. All the patients so upset, you know what it's like — just getting them to calm down. But for

119

Anna it never happened."

Leon looked away. But now it had, his voice registering somewhere in her brain.

"So that's one good thing," Obstbaum said.

Georg Ritter had come to Istanbul the week Hitler became chancellor. A job at the university barely paid for his room in an old wooden house in Fener, but he was free, and he'd brought the Lessing manuscript with him, his future. Years later, when Leon and Anna got there, he was still working on the book and by then had become an institution in the foreign community, the man who knew where to get residence permits, secondhand appliances, Turkish lessons. He and Anna shared a passion for the city, out-of-the-way fish restaurants, the best carpet seller in the Bazaar, and he became an ersatz father to her, as cranky as her own, full of convictions that everyone else had abandoned.

When the house in Fener was seized for the wealth tax — the owner, a Greek, sent to a work camp — he was rescued by a former student, a rich Turk who set him up in a building he owned in Nişantaşi. "The only Marxist in the neighborhood," Georg claimed. But the move suited him. He could now shock the bourgeoisie just by being among them, something he couldn't afford before, and Yildiz Park was nearby for his dog.

"You don't mind we take a walk? She's been in all day."

"I thought you wanted to play chess."

Georg waved his hand. "With you? No surprises. Move the knights out first. Keep the pawns back." He was snapping on the leash, locking the door. "Are you all right? You don't look —"

"Just tired."

"At your age. Wait till you see how it feels later." He sighed, the air seeming to wheeze out of his plump cheeks.

"How's the book?"

"Mendel wants to use the new chapter on *Nathan der Weise*. He thinks they'll be interested here, the comments on Saladin. As if the Turks will read it. A German journal in Istanbul. Well, where else? Germany? At least you keep something alive."

"Nathan?" Leon said, trying to remember the chronology. "Then how much more to go?"

Georg shrugged. "The last years. At Wolfenbüttel. Not so happy for him, but very productive. Several chapters at least. A pauper's grave, you know, in the end. Me too, by the time I'm finished. What about your friend?" he said, tacking. "Where are they going to bury him?"

"Who? Tommy? You heard about that?"

"Everybody's heard about it. Like a Western. Karl May. Shootouts in Istanbul," he said, shaking his head.

"I don't know. That's up to his wife. I knew him, I wouldn't say he was a friend."

"No? Just drinks at the Park." He caught Leon's reaction. "You hear things."

Leon looked at him, waiting, but Georg moved away from it. "You've seen Anna?"

"Yes, the same."

They were passing through the gates into the park, the wooded hills dotted with pavilions, the sultan's old compound.

"I wonder what she sees." Georg gestured to the trees. "A shame to miss these. But of course the mind — Abdul Hamid thought people listened in the trees. Everywhere. So it was very quiet here. Whispers. And that made him worse. Why are they whispering? The mind. You know he thought every week he would be killed. Every Friday, in the great *selamlik* down to Hamidiye Mosque. Hundreds, all lined up, the only time they could see him. So one of them must be an assassin. The whole time, all during prayers, waiting to be shot. You know there were five hundred slaves in Yildiz then? Not forty years ago, not even history yet. Slaves here. And people listening in trees." The kind of detail Anna loved.

"How did you hear about the drink at the Park?"

"Someone mentioned it. I don't even remember who. It's a great place for rumors here."

"A farewell drink," Leon said, answering what hadn't been asked. "He was going back to the States. They say it was a robbery."

"And no money taken. So now everyone has an idea."

"Like what?"

"You know, maybe a coincidence, but there's a man missing. So one theory, he was meeting your friend Tommy but shot him instead and ran away."

"Why?"

Georg shrugged. "A hundred reasons, who knows? An unreliable type, apparently."

"Unreliable," Leon said, marking time. "Who's missing him?"

"Russian friends," Georg said, looking at him. "He took something valuable, so they want to find him." He paused. "It would be worth a lot to them."

"Money, you mean?"

"Money, yes, certainly. Favors. Whatever is required."

"How much?" Leon said, going along.

"That would depend. A tip, some information, they would be grateful. But if someone knew where he was, could find him, that would be worth — I don't know a price. A good sum. And of course it would mean finding the man who shot your friend. So it's good that way too."

"Why are you telling me this?"

"So suspicious you are. Not just you. They want people to know how valuable this help would be."

"Like a reward. More Karl May. Why don't they just put up posters?"

"A joke. You don't think it's serious."

"I don't know, is it? They're your friends." He paused. "I didn't know you were still in touch with the comrades. Anna said you'd left the Party."

"Old ties, only. It's a serious matter. They have to use every channel."

"And not the police."

Georg looked away, watching the dog.

"What, Georg?" Leon said, then pointed to the trees. "Nobody's listening. Or is that why we came here? So we could talk. They asked you to approach me? Why?"

"You were a — business associate."

"Of Tommy's? We weren't in business together."

"An acquaintance then. Maybe you have an idea why he was shot. Maybe he told you something. A man who's drinking with him the night before. You understand, they have to ask."

"And get you to do it. Sorry. He never said a thing. Why do the comrades think he was shot?"

"That's something they'd like to ask their friend."

"And they're willing to cough up a reward to do it? Maybe they should just write him off."

"That's not possible."

"What did he take? Stalin's phone number?" He moved his head toward the main pavilion. "Another one. Like old Abdul. Assassins everywhere. So get rid of them. How many now? Millions? That's who you want to do business with?"

"It's a world of excesses."

"Isn't it just."

"He killed your friend. He's of no use to you. What do you care what happens to him? It's an old quarrel between them. Not with you."

"So why not make a little money while they work it out. Georg." He turned to go.

"What makes them think he shot Tommy anyway?"

"We know they were meeting. One's dead. Now the other one is gone. Why would he be unless —"

"How do you know they were meeting? Another rumor?"

"He's capable of this," Georg said, not answering. "A violent man. Unreliable."

"I'm surprised they want him back."

"They don't want him for long."

Leon looked at him, but Georg simply stared back.

"I'll keep my ears open," Leon said, about to leave. "As a favor to you." He stopped. "I didn't realize. All these years. Still with the comrades."

"A messenger only."

Leon nodded. "Delivered." He started to go, then turned to face Georg again. "Do you really think I would do this? If I did know? Shop a man?"

"This man? It would be the right thing to do."

Leon looked at him. "Then you wouldn't have to pay me."

He used the agreed-upon three knocks.

"I brought you some food," he said, handing over a bag, grease from the kebabs

126

already beginning to stain through. "Every-thing okay?"

He looked around the flat, as neat as the night before, no clothes draped over chairs, uninhabited. Alexei was sitting before the miniature board of a travel chess set, the only thing that seemed to have been removed from his duffel.

"The plane? We have a time?"

"Not yet. We're going to need to switch airfields. After last night." The all-purpose excuse, nothing safe now.

Alexei grunted and got up. "You want some tea? It's all I do, drink tea." He coughed. "And smoke." Puttering with spoons, lighting the kettle.

"I see you're a chess player."

"It passes the time."

"You play against yourself?"

"You make a move, then you turn the board. And you know what's interesting? When you're on the other side, it's completely different. You think you anticipate the move, but you turn and you see something different."

"I'll have to try it sometimes. Playing both sides."

Alexei looked up at him.

"You'd better eat. It gets messy."

"Did they find the body?" Alexei said, taking the food to the table.

"Yes."

"So he was alone. Maybe I'm not so important. And now someone's raising hell. Melnikov. Whose idea to send one? You'll pay for this. It never changes."

"You knew him?"

"Political officer," he said, eating. "You know what that means? At Stalingrad? The Nazis in front of you, Melnikov behind. No cowards there. No Stalin jokes. He shot them on the spot. Easier than sending them back to the gulags. Less paperwork." He crumpled up the bag. "But you have all that in Bucharest. His staff list. That was my deposit. You want to do that again? And then again with the tape recorder? Over and over until a slip, a name you forgot, or maybe didn't forget. Well, everyone does it."

"Save it, then. For the tape recorder. I'm not here to interrogate you."

"No? What, then?"

"Just get you on a plane."

"Ah, to be my friend. Easier to get them to talk. A little trust. So, you have a name? You never said." Familiar, somebody at a bar. He got up to pour the tea.

Leon looked over, trying to imagine it, the abattoir, putting bodies on hooks. An ordinary man, making tea. "Leon," he said.

"Leon?" Asking for the rest.

"Bauer."

Alexei handed him a glass, smiling a little. "A German name. Farmer," he said, translating. "Also pawn." He opened his hand to the little board. "In the game. So that's you, the pawn?"

"That's everybody."

Alexei looked up at him, pleased. "A philosopher. Something new. It's different with the Russians. No sandwiches, either. Just fists."

"When they interrogated you?"

"My friend, if they had done that you would see it," he said, putting a hand to his face. "The bones. You see the prisoners after, their faces are different. They take pictures for the files. If they're alive."

"So you were lucky."

He shrugged. "I ran. I knew what they were. That was my job, to know about them." He took a sip of tea. "But you know that. And you're not here to interrogate me."

Leon looked over. A conveyor belt. People bleating. Now calmly lighting a cigarette. But Tommy had talked about old times while he planned to kill him.

"You have a wife?" Alexei said, running a hand across the top of his head, hair cropped so short it seemed to have stopped growing.

"Yes."

"In America?"

"No, here. And you?" The obligatory response.

"Magda. Like Lupescu. But not so lucky. She was killed."

"In the war?"

Alexei nodded. "Partisans. In Bukovina. Three years now. It's a convenience, sometimes. To have nothing to lose." He drew on the cigarette. "That's what you wanted to know, isn't it? Can they use somebody? Keep me on a leash." He shook his head. "There's nobody. Just me. You didn't know this before?"

"Why would I?"

"That's right. Not the interrogator. What, then? A wife here. So there's a cover."

"Businessman."

"At Western Electric?"

Leon raised his eyes. How many of Tommy's people did they know? All? Even the freelancers?

"No."

"Where then?"

"Dried fruit. Apricots. Figs."

"Apricots," Alexei said. "It's a good business?"

"Now you're interrogating me."

Alexei smiled. "Just talking. Like you. We do it differently. Maybe better." He leaned his head to the side, still amused. "Yes, I think so."

"That's because you don't know what I'm after."

Alexei looked straight at him, no smile now at all. "No. So it's an advantage you have. What do you want to know?"

Leon hesitated, trying to frame it. "How it was, at Străuleşti."

A stillness, Alexei's eyes locked on Leon's, not blinking. After a minute he looked down at his hand, the cigarette burning to his finger. He rubbed it out, still quiet, a test of wills, his eyes neutral, sorting things out.

"We do that too," he said finally. "Tell them you know the worst thing. So they think you know everything."

Leon waited.

"Nobody asked me this before. Your people. So why now?"

"You were there."

Another silence, calculating. "Your Romanian friend. He told you."

Now it was Leon who was quiet.

"When did a Romanian not betray a Romanian? A national gift." He reached for another cigarette. "Well, I'm one to talk." He waited another second, then shook his head. "I had no part in that."

"Just the rest of the Guard."

He nodded. "That's when I decided —"

"What?"

"That they were crazy."

"They weren't crazy before? Blood oaths?"

"But this. It was bound to call attention. Make them turn against us."

"So you did."

"That's what you want to know? Why I turned against the Guard? That's easy. Because I could see what was coming. The future was Antonescu."

"For a while."

"Yes."

"And now he's going on trial. But not you."

"Trial for what?"

"You were there. That would be enough."

Alexei nodded. "They're not so interested now, what happened. They just want to shoot us. Then all these things can go away."

"So you made a deal."

"That's right," Alexei said, eyes on Leon. "With you." He got up, clearing his cup. "You know what it's like, a mob? Like water. You can't stop it. They were going to ruin everything and who could stop them?"

"Not you." Leon paused. "You knew what they were going to do."

132

"No," Alexei said, raising his voice. "Shoot them maybe. This was already happening. Dudeşti, all over the city. But this —" He stopped, his shoulders suddenly slumping. "Of course, you know in the end they were dead anyway."

He shuffled over to the window and stood there for a minute, lifting his hand to part the shade, then letting it rest there, staring.

"When you have blood on your hands, does it matter how it got there?" he said.

Carcasses dripping.

He turned. "Is that what you're asking? What's on my hands?" He held one out. "Not so clean. Are yours? In this business?" He lowered his hand. "Do you know how easy it can be? Something you never thought you could do. Easy. Later, it's harder. People forget, but you live with it, whatever you did." He turned. "We penetrated their military intelligence. That's all that should matter to you now. You want to put me on trial with Antonescu? For what? The Guard? The camps? All of it my fault. Maybe even the war. My fault too." He stopped. "Nobody cares about that anymore. Not them, not you. It's in the past." He looked up. "Except your Romanian friend maybe. So eager to tell you things. Maybe he'd like to tell someone else. A Romanian will sell anything. Maybe me."

Leon looked at him, intrigued. A life revealed in a phrase.

"He can't. He doesn't know where you are."

"Only you. If you weren't followed," he said, dismissive. "And what do we talk about? All these arrangements — the truck from Bucharest, the boat, this place — and now it's what happened to the Jews? They died." His voice final as a window being slammed shut.

He went to get more tea, refilling Leon's glass, Leon watching him, not saying anything. Alexei raised his eyebrows, waiting.

"All right," Leon said. "The American working for the Russians. Let's talk about him."

Alexei stared at him.

"I need to know."

Alexei held his gaze, sipping some tea, calculating, as if he were running his finger over a chess piece, not yet ready to move.

"How long have you been doing this?" he said finally. "This work. Maybe you're new to it. Maybe that's it. So let me explain something to you. If I knew such a thing, would I tell you? We talk in Bucharest — enough information so you know it's real. The rest? When I'm out, safe. If I tell you

134

here? You squeeze a lemon, what's left? So you throw it away."

"We don't do that."

"Everybody does that," he said flatly. "Everybody. So you can wait."

"Not anymore. I need to know. For your sake. If he had anyone else here."

"Here? An American here?" Alexei said, a little surprised, relieved. "Well, you wouldn't have to wait for that. It's not such a bargaining chip." He stopped. "I mean —"

Leon looked at him, turning this over. "Not worth a trip to the States. But someone in Washington would be."

Alexei met his glance. "Yes, he would be. But we're here. Wasting time. These questions. I don't know anyone here." He sipped more tea. "You're so sure there is such a person."

Leon nodded.

"How?"

"I shot him last night. On the pier."

At first there was only a flicker of movement in Alexei's face, the composure still fixed, then his eyes began darting, as if they were involuntarily following his thoughts, leaping from point to point.

"They identified the man," he said, leading. "Not a Russian."

"No. One of us. Who knew you were coming out. And who tried to kill you. Why would he do that? In the open? Take that chance. Unless you were someone he had to stop. He couldn't give you back to the Russians — he'd expose himself — so he'd have to kill you."

"Expose himself?"

"He was running this operation, getting you out. Which makes for some complications."

"Running —"

"This piece of it anyway. So the trip had to end here. Things go wrong, but he's safe, no one blames him, and the Russians get their rat. But then I shot him and I got you instead. So I need you to tell me. Are there others? Am I wrong?"

Alexei put the tips of his fingers together in a pyramid, pressing them against his lips, almost prayerlike, thinking. "No," he said finally, then hesitated, as if he were eliminating more possibilities. "They had a man in Ankara. Why not here."

"Ankara," Leon said dully, seeing himself at Karpić's, leaving an envelope on the banquette.

"During the war. Now I'm not sure. You understand, it's only GPU I know, not the other agencies. But you see what this means. The Russians know. The whole operation.

We have to leave this place. It's not safe."

"He never knew about the flat. So they don't know, either. We're back where we started."

"No. Everything is compromised now. The plane — that's still your plan?"

"I don't see why not — if there is one."

But Alexei was shaking his head. "They must know. If I show myself there they'll kill me. We have to start over. Everything. I'll help you. We'll work together."

Leon looked up, caught off guard. His new partner.

Alexei started coughing, a smoker's hack. "Amateurs. It's my life, and the man in charge is working for them."

"Was."

"And now it's you," Alexei said, peering at him. "The new *gazi*. And who else?"

Leon shook his head. "I only knew Tommy."

"So," Alexei said. "And you had no idea. What he was."

"Not until he shot you."

"Not even me. The Romanian. Amateurs." He started coughing again, his face getting paler. "Istanbul," he said, choking on the word, still trying to stop the cough. "Maybe it ends here. I always wondered, what would that be like. When they finally get you." He looked up. "So. We make a new plan."

"We," Leon said.

"You can't trust anybody now. Not here. Not in Ankara." He put his hand to his mouth, thinking. "But we have one piece of luck."

"What's that?"

"Nobody's looking for you. Or they'd already be here. They'll think I'm running, not hiding. Who would be hiding me?"

"Who would."

"And then they'll think I'm gone. We can do it." He paused. "If no one else knows. Just you."

"Do what?"

"Get me out. Istanbul — it's a trap now. We have to leave here."

Leon was quiet for a minute, then got up. "To save your skin."

"My skin? I saw your face, when I told you about Washington. A valuable chip, no? People will want to hear about him." He looked up. "Always have something to trade."

Leon stood still for a second, as if he were balancing himself, testing his footing. Alexei's eyes, gray and clear, insistent. Which hadn't seen anything at the abattoir. He said. Holding up his bargaining chip.

"Let's start with the gun then," Leon said.

Ashe County Public Library
Mon-Thur 9-7, Fri and Sat 9-5
To renew: 336-846-2041 x221
or visit www.arlibrary.org
Like us on Facebook!

---

1. Istanbul passage : [large print]
   Barcode:
   50503010909580 Due:
   05/07/2015 11:59 PM
   ****

   ****

   ****

"One less complication. I'd better have it back."

"The gun?" Alexei said, not expecting this. "What are you going to do with it?"

"Get rid of it," Leon said, picking up the empty food bag.

"And how do I protect myself here?"

"Use the one you brought with you," Leon said, looking at him. "You'd have to have one. You just wanted this for a little insurance. And maybe to see if I was dumb enough to give it to you." He held out his hand. "It's a murder weapon now. Evidence. You might use it to put me there. In Bebek. If things don't go well. Right?"

Alexei looked at the open hand, then reached into his pocket and took out the gun, smiling a little. "A quick learner." He handed it over.

"You're right about the plane," Leon said, putting the gun in the bag. "I'll arrange something else." He started for the door. "Just stay put. You're safe here."

"And that's my protection now," Alexei said, nodding to the lock. "A door." He looked at Leon. "And you."

Leon reached for the knob.

"By the way, it matters to you? What happened at Străulești? I wasn't part of that. What they did. If your friend says yes, he's lying." Making a case now, reassuring. "I wasn't part of that."

Leon turned. "That must be a comfort."

On the ferry back, Leon stayed out on the lower deck, dropping the bag over the side halfway across, even the sound of the small splash covered by the grind of the motors. Ibrahim the Sot had drowned his whole harem here, sewn into sacks. The gun was easier. Just another secret in the Bosphorus. Nothing to connect him now to the quay, nothing to connect Mihai. Not even Alexei once he could pass him along the chain Tommy had tried to break. His new partner. He looked down at the dark water, uneasy again. The gun would be settling on the bottom, lodging itself in the silt, too heavy for the current. Except there were two currents in the Bosphorus, he'd read somewhere, the surface current flowing south and a deep undercurrent *kanal* flowing north, dense and saline, strong enough to drag a fishing boat by its net, pull someone off course.

Inside the cabin, the tea man was handing a tulip glass to a man in a knit cap, the kind Mihai had worn. A dockworker? A thief? Who was anybody? Tommy ordering drinks at the Park, every second a betrayal. Years of it. You can't trust anybody now, Alexei had said, asking Leon to trust him.

3
PERA

The funeral was held at Christ Church, near the Galata Tower, with a reception to follow in one of the private rooms at the Pera Palas. It was the same service Tommy would have had however he had died — the same hymns, the same homily about a man taken too soon, the same teary handkerchiefs. But he hadn't just died, released from illness. He'd been killed, the violence of it disturbing, somehow shaming, as if he'd been complicit in his own death. So people said comforting things to Barbara and fidgeted in their seats, wondering.

Leon sat to the side, watching people take their places. Ed Burke was next to Barbara as chief mourner, with the staff of Commercial Corp. filling out the pew behind. The business community had come out and most of the consulate, an almost official gathering, except for a sprinkling of unknown faces, part of Tommy's wide social net. Near the back were a few Turks secular enough to risk being in a church and two burly men Leon assumed to be police, scanning the crowd, their faces expressionless.

Frank Bishop had come from the embassy in Ankara, stiff and formal in a black suit and owlish horn-rimmed glasses. He had brought his wife, a woman Leon hadn't met, his dealings with Frank usually a drink at the Ankara Palas or an early dinner at Karpić's, just long enough to leave papers. She kept her head half bowed, so Leon had to crane slightly to see her face, or the part of it not shadowed by her hat. Pale skin, just a hint of makeup, reddish hair, younger than Frank. Next to them, the Liggett & Myers rep was handing out candy to his restless children. A committee from the club had sent a wreath. Barbara wept during the reading of the Twenty-third Psalm. The minister spoke of Tommy's open heart and concern for others. No one in the solemn, drafty room, Leon realized, had known him at all.

Afterward, they clustered at the door, hugging or shaking hands, then started the steep climb up. A taxi had been ordered for Barbara, its width almost filling the narrow street, but everyone else went on foot, wives clinging to their husbands' arms, careful of their heels on the paving stones.

"Christ, I don't know how the *hamals* do it," Frank said, winded, when they reached the top.

"*Hamals?*" his wife said.

"You know, stevedores, whatever you call them. Who carry things. You see some of the loads, you don't know how they can stand up."

"It'd be mules this far up," Leon said.

"I don't think you know my wife, Katherine," Frank said.

"Kay," she said, almost fiercely, as if she were angry about something. She was wearing dark glasses against the winter sun, her eyes no more visible than they'd been in church.

"Nice of you to come," Leon said, taking out a cigarette. "It's a long trip, Ankara."

"Could I have one of those? Do you mind? Or isn't it all right? On the street, I mean. I never know what the right thing to do is in this country." Not anger, more a general impatience, waiting for everyone else to catch up.

"You're among friends," Leon said, lighting hers.

"Katherine, I wish you wouldn't," Frank said, her name some pointless tug-of-war between them.

"Oh, I know. Set an example. Just two puffs. Those *hymns*. Barbara carrying on. I never thought she cared two cents for him."

"Katherine —"

"All right. Not appropriate." She dropped the cigarette and ground it out. "Sorry," she said to Leon. "I didn't mean to waste it."

Leon smiled. "I've got plenty. I'm in the business."

"What business?"

"I buy tobacco. For export."

"I thought you were with the consulate. Like everyone else," she said, dipping her head toward the others.

"Only when I need a permit."

"There's Barbara," Frank said. Her taxi had now reached the square and was waiting for the tram to turn. "At least we'll get decent grub at the Pera. And it's right by the consulate."

"Convenient," his wife said.

"Mm. Tommy's second office. Funny to think of having his wake there."

The tram moved and they started across.

"Ted," Frank said to the man ahead of them. "Katherine, do you mind tagging along with the Kiernans? I need to have a word with Leon. We'll catch up."

She lifted her head, about to protest, but Ted had already taken her elbow, so she

146

settled for being annoyed, not bothering to say good-bye.

"Do you have another?" Frank said, nodding to Leon's pack. "We need to talk," he said while he lit it. "Walk with me." A self-satisfied boarding school voice, used to getting his way.

They started up the Istiklal Caddesi.

"This is a real mess," Frank said.

"Tommy, you mean."

Frank nodded. "And I don't have a lot of time. What did you do for Tommy? Besides the courier job, I mean."

"Just a few favors," Leon said, hesitant. "I know a lot of people in Istanbul."

"And speak Turkish, I know," he said, checking off some invisible list. "Tommy liked to work outside. Now it looks like he had his reasons, but it makes it hell with the books."

"What books?"

"Petty cash. Special funds. Tommy liked special funds. So, all right, informants, they don't want their names floating around on check stubs, but it makes things hard to trace."

"Are you asking if Tommy paid me? He bought me a meal once in a while," Leon said.

"I'll buy you more than that."

Leon stopped. "To do what?"

"To be Tommy."

"What?"

"You're a businessman. You can read books, can't you?"

Leon nodded, suddenly light-headed, a new mix of absurdity and caution.

"Maybe you can read Tommy's. A fucking mare's nest. Maybe you can make some sense of them."

"You've already been through them," Leon said, still stitching things together.

"We need to put somebody on his desk. Until we can get a new man. Nobody at the consulate knows you worked for him, do they? So they won't suspect."

"Suspect what?"

"That you're working for me," Frank said, a little surprised, as if Leon hadn't been following. "I can't use anybody inside. It's compromised."

The same word Alexei had used, the same world.

"You think somebody at the consulate killed him?" Leon said, his voice his own but coming from somewhere outside his body.

"Or set him up."

"And you want me to find him?" he said carefully, slowing things down, not trusting his voice now.

"I'll find him. But I need someone to help. From outside. You knew him, the way he worked."

"How do you know it wasn't me?" Trying it, irresistible.

"Because your movements are accounted for. Sorry about your wife, by the way. I never knew. Anyway, this operation, it had to be someone inside. He wouldn't have let you in on this. Nothing personal. Just the rules."

For a second Leon felt a rush of air in his throat, not a laugh, just an odd release of pressure. Of course they still trusted Tommy. By dying he'd become the only one they could trust.

"What operation," Leon said, testing.

"Look, you in this? I know you guys during the war — you did it for that. Now you think it's over. Believe me, it's not over." He paused. "Tommy always said you were good."

Leon turned, focusing on a tram approaching, keeping things straight.

"Reynolds doesn't have a problem with this. If that's what's bothering you."

"You've already talked to them," Leon said, surprised. He let a minute go by. "What operation?"

Frank dipped his head, plunging in. "He was bringing someone out."

"One of ours?"

"Theirs. Knows Russian Military Intelligence. The cast list. Lots. We were going to have a nice talk."

"And now?"

"Well, if Tommy's dead, I'd say he's back with the Russians, wouldn't you? Or dead. Let's hope so, anyway. Better for everybody now."

"If he's dead," Leon said quietly. Yesterday's friend.

Bishop nodded. "Now he knows us. Tommy wasn't the only one in this. So let's hope he's dead. We want to be sure of that," he said, almost casually, without menace, only the eyes steely. Leon looked at him. Same sandy hair, probably the same glasses he'd worn at Groton, but everything hardened now, years in the business.

"How can you do that?"

"Whoever sold out Tommy's in touch with the Russians. Let's start with him. Let's find him."

Leon took a breath, the air in his head clouding again, feeding on itself.

"Look, I know what you're thinking. Somebody killed Tommy. Maybe they'll try to take a shot at you."

"No, I wasn't thinking that. Really." An irony almost too complicated. Move away. "What do you want me to do?"

"Start with the people he ran. Who else knew?"

Leon nodded, buying time. Think how to do this. There were no explanations. Not plausible ones. Everyone would rather believe Tommy, whom they'd believed all along.

"I have to tell you, I wouldn't blame you, if you were thinking that," Frank said, leading them down to Mesrutiyet. "He'll want to protect himself."

"Yes."

"Nice you don't scare easy," Frank said, as if he were putting a note in the file.

They were passing the wrought-iron gates of the American Consulate. Tommy's office, he remembered, was in back, facing down to the Horn. Now his, as surreal as attending the funeral of a man you'd killed.

"What was the next link?" he said, thinking. "How were you getting the guy out of Istanbul?"

"Plane. Don't worry, we've canceled it," Frank said, the sound to Leon of a door closing.

The banquet room at the Pera was crowded,

spilling over with consulate staff and Turks who hadn't been to the church and were now lined up at the buffet table, plates in hand. The food was American, chicken and potato salad and cold roast beef, not even a stuffed grape leaf to remind them where they were. Barbara stood near the door, receiving, still blotchy from crying, cheeks puffy.

"Oh, Leon," she said, embracing him. "Thank you for coming. It still doesn't seem real, does it? One day everything's — And *shot.* I keep thinking, those last few minutes, what was that *like.*"

"Don't," Leon said, disconcerted. "Don't think about that."

"I know, I know, everyone says. And just when we were finally getting Washington. That's all he could talk about. Getting our things there. You know what the boats are like. And now — what do I do?"

"Don't do anything," Leon said. "Take some time. You don't want to rush into anything."

"I can't stay here."

"Where's home?"

"Boston, I guess," she said vaguely. "But that's years ago. You know what it's like overseas, you take home with you. I don't know anyone in Washington. That was for

Tommy's work. Frank," she said, touching his arm as he joined them. "All this way. Ankara."

"How are you holding up?"

"Everyone's been so kind," Barbara said, suddenly genteel, something she'd heard in the movies.

"Kay's staying over for a few days — I promised her a break — so if you need anything —"

She nodded. "I never realized how much *paper* — Now they want a form to take him home. His ashes. I mean, who else's would they be?"

"I'll get Ted Kiernan to take care of it for you. That's what he does, gets cargo out."

"Cargo —" Barbara began, but Frank, miming apologies, was being pulled away to meet someone.

"He certainly got here fast enough, didn't he?" Barbara said, watching them go. "Taking over the office. You'd think they could wait two minutes. Tommy's not even cold and here's Ankara —"

"Barbara."

"Well, he isn't. Oh, what does it matter? Office politics. We're not in the government anymore, are we? Now what? Would you come by, help me sort things out? I always felt I could talk to you," she said, looking up, oddly coquettish. "Tommy took care of everything and now —"

"Are you all right for money?"

She nodded. "Yes, fine, it's just all the paper —" she said, leaving it open-ended, and he saw that she was misinterpreting, responding with an unexpected intimacy. Tommy's wife.

"You should talk to Ed Burke," he said, pulling away. "He's a lawyer."

"Oh, Ed. He never said five words to me, and now every time I turn around there he is. Maybe he thinks I'm a rich widow. Ha, not that rich."

"But you'll need a lawyer. Did Tommy leave a will?"

She shook her head. "I haven't found one anyway. You don't expect — at his age —" She trailed off, beginning to tear up again.

"Here you go," Ed said, coming up from behind with a fresh drink, exchanging it for the empty glass in her hand.

"Thank you, Ed," she said, voice quavering, a new mood. "You've been so wonderful."

"Chin up," he said, raising his glass.

"Don't let me get tipsy. That's all I'd need."

"You won't," he said. A friend of the family, even more attentive now, wanting a seat at the table, a curiosity he couldn't contain.

"Excuse me, Mrs. King?" The hotel manager with a question about the champagne.

"Well, I thought I said with dessert, but if people are asking for it," she said, following him.

"You meet Frank Bishop?" Ed said.

"Just to shake hands. In Ankara."

"He's the sheriff, don't you think?" Ed said, leaning forward, confiding.

"How do you mean?"

"This must have set off some pretty loud bells. The minute they hear, he's on a plane."

"I'm not sure I'm following, Ed."

"For a desk holder at Commercial Corp." He raised his eyes, a knowing look.

"Who's that he's talking to?" Leon said, looking across. A man he recognized but didn't know, one of those people you saw at parties but somehow never met.

"Al Maynard. Western Electric. You don't know Al?"

Leon shook his head. Tommy's man.

"Too late now. He's going to Washington."

"Mm. Tommy mentioned it."

"He did? Why? I mean, if you don't know him."

"Well, not him, the job. He thought I might be interested in his job."

"Funny how things work. Al might get Tommy's now. The new one, in Washington. Somebody will. Look at him sucking up to Frank."

"What did you mean, he's the sheriff?"

"They don't trust the police here. They sent their own man. They know it wasn't a robbery."

"How do they know that?"

Ed nodded toward Frank. "Then why send him?"

"Ed."

"I'm just saying what everybody in this room is thinking. Everybody in the room."

Were they? Leon looked around. The indistinct hum of social conversation, but a tension too, people shooting side glances at Frank, lowering their voices when Barbara went by, speculating, buzzing with it, everybody with his own idea. But no one knew. Leon felt the tingling at the back of his neck again. No one knew.

Frank had moved on to someone else now. Another link in Tommy's network? Maybe you could follow him like a diagram around the room, point to undercover point. But what did they all do now? It had started with watching boats, the traffic in the Bosphorus. Drinking at the Park, hoping for an indiscretion. No one got shot. But that war

156

was over. In the new one you brought out murderers and kept them safe. So they could tell you about other murderers. With a job in Washington at the end. Now open again. Waiting for a new Tommy.

"Could I cadge one more?" Kay Bishop said, suddenly next to him. "Or don't they like it inside, either?"

He blinked, coming back.

"Smoking," she prompted.

He took out a pack and turned to introduce Ed, but Ed had gone. How long had he been standing here, watching the room?

"I think you can risk it," he said, putting on a party smile. "This crowd."

She had taken off her dark glasses and now he saw her eyes for the first time, shiny and alert, so bright they seemed to have drained the light from her pale skin, leaving a sprinkling of tiny freckles. They looked directly into his, steady, without fluttering movements to the side, and the effect was an easy familiarity, as if they already knew each other and were simply picking up the thread of an ongoing conversation. Then the eyebrows went up slightly, a question, and he realized he'd been staring.

"They're green," he said. "Your eyes. Like the song."

"Just flecks. They're really brown. It's a

157

trick of the light."

"Some trick."

"Is that a pass?"

"Sorry," he said, surprised, "did it sound like one?"

"How would I know anymore?" she said. "I'm in Ankara."

"They don't make passes in Ankara?"

"If they do, I missed it."

"What do they do?"

"The wives play cards. The men, I don't know. Try to stay awake, mostly. Anyway, no passes."

"Government town. It's always like that. Saves trouble later."

"And the Turks —"

"Ah."

"No, worse. They just look. Like you're something in a candy store."

"It's new for them, men and women mixing. They're not used to it."

"But they're married. Don't they talk to their wives?"

He smiled. "Maybe that's why they don't talk to you."

She raised her glass in a touché gesture.

He smiled again, feeling suddenly buoyant, the first time since Bebek that he felt himself, his mind clear, not twisting around anything. Then she tilted her head, "what?"

and he shook his in reply, "nothing", embarrassed now. Flirting. Here, of all places. With Frank's wife. Not even especially pretty. Except for the eyes. Aware of her perfume.

"There's one, for instance. He's been staring at me for five minutes."

Leon followed her gaze, then froze. Not staring at her, staring at him. The man in Marina's building, on the tram, only one coincidence allowed. A thin moustache, something Leon hadn't noticed before.

"How do you know he's a Turk?" he said, quickly turning back. "He could be anybody." Making conversation. The buoyancy gone, weighted down again with uneasiness. A flicker toward the man. Still there.

"The way he looks. Like you're a specimen. But he'll just look. So I guess that leaves you. Let's see. Eyes. Anything else you like?"

"Everything," Leon said, looking at her for a second. "But Frank probably does too."

She stopped, a ball suspended in midair, then looked down. "Don't get the wrong idea. I was just — passing the time. You get to learn how to do that."

"In Ankara," he finished for her.

She took a sip from her glass. "People

don't talk like this there."

"Like what?"

"Back and forth."

"Tell Frank to take a furlough. Stay for a while."

"He has to go back. But I'm here for a few days. Right here, in fact." She looked up, as if they could see through the ceiling into her room.

"Your first trip?"

"One day when we got here. Right off the train. We saw Topkapi. The big church."

"Haghia Sophia."

"Then another train. Then Ankara. So what should I see?"

"Süleyman's Mosque. Start with that."

"What else? Not in the guidebooks. What do you like?"

"Me? Everything. The water. All the boats. The food."

"The food?"

"Not this stuff. Their food."

"Eggplant," she said.

"But look what they do with it. The sultans had a chef just for eggplant."

"You like it here," she said, her eyes appraising him.

The man was moving away from the wall, heading toward the buffet table, but still keeping them in sight. Why not just come

160

over? But he wouldn't, not while they were talking. He'd wait for an opening.

"It's the layers," Leon said. "Take here, where we're standing. The Orient Express built it. So their passengers would have somewhere to stay. Somewhere grand. With all the latest."

"Here?" she said, taking in the faded room.

"The height of elegance then. Like the train. The dining room at Sirkeci has the same look. This was Pera in those days, the European quarter. All the embassies, until they moved to Ankara. Just across the bridge from the Ottoman city. Except all of it was Ottoman, really. For five hundred years. Before that, the hill was Genoese, a trading concession from the Byzantines. They built the tower. The Byzantines lasted a thousand years. You can probably see their shipyards from your room. All along the Horn. Istanbul is like that. You're always standing on layers."

"What about this layer? Now," she said, interested.

"Now? The war was a hard time for Turkey."

"But they were neutral."

"They kept a standing army. Just in case. A lot of money for a poor country. Now

161

they're broke. The house needs a paint job, but they have to put it off to next year. So everything looks a little shabby. But I guess that's true everywhere, since the war."

"Except home."

He stopped, then dipped his head, ceding the point. "Except there."

"But you want to stay here," she said, almost to herself, trying to read his face. "You don't give much away, do you? Before, when you were standing here, just looking, I had no idea what you were thinking. The others, yes, but you, no idea."

"I didn't know I was so mysterious," he said lightly. "Most people don't think so."

"Well, most people aren't, are they? Themselves. So they don't see it. They don't see the layers, either." She looked away, over his shoulder. "My god, who's that?"

He turned. "That's Lily. Nadir."

"But who is she?"

"Her husband took over Vassilakos Shipping. When the Greeks were thrown out. Widow. In Washington she's what they'd call a hostess. She gives parties."

"She's not shabby."

She was dressed for a funeral, a high-necked, black silk dress with padded shoulders and only a few jewels, day diamonds, a thin bracelet, and one giant pin that glittered, starlike, on the dark fabric. Her hair, wheat blond streaked with gray, was covered by a black cloth with silver thread, something between a snood and a head scarf, a soft Ottoman wrap that made all the hats in the room look dowdy.

"You don't see jewels like that in Ankara."

"You don't see them here much, either. Lily's a special case."

She had been standing at the doorway, scanning the room, and now saw Barbara and headed toward her, people stepping aside as she moved across, a kind of social choreography. She took Barbara's hands in hers, a regal moment, and said something, then as Barbara teared up, gripped the hands harder for emphasis, a gesture more dramatic than hugging. Everyone in the room had turned to watch.

"Another Istanbul layer," Leon said. "She was in Abdul Hamid's harem."

"His harem? How old is she?"

"It's not that long since they abolished it. Forty years, less. She was a child."

"A child?"

"They were often sent early. For training," he said, then saw her expression. "Not that kind of training. Household things. Manners. Not everybody got to sleep with the sultan. Certainly not children. It was sup-

163

posed to be a privilege, to be a *gözde*. One of the noticed."

"And was she? Noticed?"

"No, she was too young. After, she was lucky. She found a protector."

"I'll say," Kay said, still looking at the pin.

Lily was moving away from Barbara now, respects paid, and passing the man with the moustache. A glance, almost too quick to be noticed, not stopping, but aware of him.

"Would you like to meet her?"

"You know her?"

"Everybody knows Lily. She has one of the great *yalis*. On the Bosphorus. You come in on the train and see the houses, the ones that look like they're falling down, and you think that's Istanbul. But you don't see the *yalis*. The old gardens. The khedive used to stay in hers, when he came to Istanbul. Then her husband bought it. So now it's hers. A great friend of Atatürk's, by the way. From the early days. So don't say anything anti-Turk."

"First Frank, now you. I have been let out from time to time."

"I just meant —"

"I know what you meant. I'm an embassy wife. It's funny, though, she doesn't look Turkish. The light hair, I mean. You don't usually see —"

164

"Circassian. Originally."

She cocked her head. "And now you're not going to tell me where that is and I'm not going to ask because I don't want you to know I don't know, so I'll never know."

He smiled. "Part of Russia now. East of the Black Sea. Very popular with the sultans. For slaves."

"Gentlemen prefer blondes," she said.

"Even then."

Lily was surrounded by people but turned, a social instinct, as if she had actually felt Leon approach. "Leon," she said, the French pronunciation. "How nice. I was hoping." She extended her hand to be kissed, playful.

"I didn't know you knew Barbara."

Her eyes lit up, a naughty child caught out. "Hardly at all. But, darling, I couldn't resist. No one's talking about anything else. Imagine. Like a *roman policier*. In Istanbul. I had to come."

"But a robbery —"

"*Ouf.* With no money. A Turkish thief would take money, no? The Bosphorus at night? An *assignation*, it has to be. The fatal meeting. But who?" She looked around the room. "So maybe the jealous wife. She could do it. Very strong hands, that one, you should feel them. A gun would be noth-

165

ing for her."

Leon smiled. "Behave yourself. Meet Kay Bishop. She's here from Ankara."

"With the embassy?" she said warmly, taking her hand.

Kay nodded. "My husband. Does it show?"

"Everybody in Ankara is with an embassy. Why else would they go? The dust. My god, such a lot of dust. Of course, Kemal wanted a Turkish city, and that's right, but you lose something too, I think. Poor Istanbul, too decadent for him he said, he's just a soldier, barracks are fine, but you know he meant there were too many foreigners. In those days all the shop signs — Armenian, Greek, Hebrew. Now just Turkish. Even here. A Turkish city now."

"It's Kay's first visit."

"Yes? Then you have the perfect guide. No one knows the city like Leon. It's always the foreigners — we're the true Istanbullus."

"You? You haven't been a foreigner since —"

She raised a finger. "No ages. *Ça n'est pas gentil.*" She turned to Kay. "But then you must come to my party. It's so difficult to find women. It's new to them still, leaving the house. The husbands say they'll bring

166

them and then they don't. Leon, you'll bring her?" She paused. "And your husband, of course."

"He can't stay. It'd just be me, I'm afraid."

"Ah," Lily said, glancing at Leon. "So much the better. An extra woman in Istanbul. More precious than rubies. Oh dear, hysterics." On the other side of the room, Barbara had begun to weep loudly. "Perhaps not enough attention."

"Lily —"

"No, it's true. It's a day for the widow. And all these distractions —"

"You're the distraction," Leon said.

"I hope that's not true," she said, enjoying herself. "At such a time. Maybe I should leave."

"*That* would be a distraction. You just got here."

She arched an eyebrow at him, but said to Kay, "And what do you think? About the murder. You have an idea?"

"I didn't know it was. They said —"

"Oh, the thief in the night," Lily said, waving this off. "But so much more interesting, don't you think? It's selfish to say this, I know, but it'll be good for the party, a little *frisson.* During the war it was easy, invite a German, invite a Russian, and then watch. Same room? Will they look at each other?

And of course serious questions — will Turkey stay out? But always something. And since a little boring, I think."

"Just what you needed then," Leon said.

"You're making fun of me, but it's true, so why not say it? And of course so implausible. A man like that. A great love? How can you imagine it? So maybe a local woman and he's leaving her? Or an American friend. Just a *cinq à sept,* but now jealous. But someone."

"You're a romantic, Lily," Leon said.

"And you're not? Everyone, I think, if they're lucky. But this time, unlucky. I admit, to think of Tommy King as a lover —"

"Maybe it wasn't about him. Maybe he just got in the way," Kay said.

Leon looked at her, surprised, his mind's eye suddenly back on the landing, tracking bullets, positions, playing it out again. If you see a chessboard from the other side, Alexei said. But nothing changed. It had only happened one way.

"You're always reading things like that in books," Kay said. "People see something they shouldn't. Or they just happen to be —"

"But it's terrible, no? A murder by accident. Not even interesting enough to be a victim. Just someone — in the way. Better, I think, the widow. Those hands."

"He was shot, Lily."

"The trigger, then. No problem, *je t'assure*. Listen. Again."

A new arrival, Barbara in tears.

"Only the guilty cry like that."

"Don't have too much fun with this," Leon said.

Lily lowered her head, reprimanded. "It's true. Still a death." She looked up at Kay. "But you'll come to my party?"

"Of course. Thank you."

"Maybe he'll be there. Whoever it is."

"What an idea," Leon said.

"Why not? Maybe here too. Someone he knew. Not a stranger. It has to be."

"Why?"

"Who goes to a place like that to meet a stranger? Someone he knew. And the shot was close."

"How do you know that?" Leon said, alert.

Lily shrugged. "People talk."

"People in the police?"

"People. I told you, nobody talks of anything else. Except here, maybe. Where you all want to think it's a thief."

Involuntarily Leon looked across the room. Frank had reached the drinks table, then made a half turn as the man with the

169

moustache introduced himself. Polite, formal, maybe innocuous. Lily was asking Kay about her plans, a background noise as Leon fixed on the other conversation, too far away to hear. Coming out of Marina's building. A client? Why Frank? Then Frank looked over, a nod in Leon's direction, as if he were pointing him out.

"The hotel can arrange for a guide," Lily was saying to Kay. "Of course, if Leon's free — he knows it so well. Not the shopping, though. It was Anna who knew the shops."

"Anna?"

"My wife," Leon said.

"Oh," Kay said, not expecting this. But she must have seen the ring. "She's not here?"

"She's been ill."

"I'm sorry. Something serious?"

"Une maladie des nerfs," Lily said. "A terrible thing. A long time now. But perhaps soon —"

"That's the hope," Leon said, cutting her off. "Frank has my number, if you'd like to see anything," he said as Frank joined them.

Kay raised her head to say more, then nodded, letting it go.

"I'm sure you'll be busy at the office," Frank said. "She can use Cook's. Nice if you could spot her a meal though."

Kay shot him a quick, irritated glance.

Leon made a little half bow. "I'll look forward to it," he said, taking her hand.

"Yes," she said, polite again. "And to the party," she said to Lily.

"So —" Frank said, impatient now to go.

But Kay waited another second, looking at Leon. "Thanks. For the layers."

He watched them say good-bye to Barbara.

"You're interested in that girl?" Lily said.

"I just met her."

"That's your answer? To that question?"

"No," he said, a formal answer. "Don't play cupid. I'm too old."

"Oh, old. She's interested in you."

"I'm married."

Lily sighed. "Your faithfulness. So American. A Turk —"

"Would go to a teahouse and play cards."

Lily laughed. "Yes, perhaps. Only up here." She touched her head. "But you watched her. I saw. And she likes you."

"You could tell all this in five minutes."

"Two. And that husband. *Ouf.*"

"Well, that's her problem." He looked at her. "I'm married. So were you. Devoted. Everyone says so."

"Of course," she said easily. "He was the love of my life. And Anna was yours. But that's not all there is in life. It's unnatural, your faithfulness."

"Not to me."

She looked up at him, then put her hand on his arm, smiling a little. "As you like. But she's interested. She wants to know you."

"Know me."

"Women like to know. Detectives."

"And do you find out?"

"Eventually." She patted his arm. "That's the disappointing part. Oh no, more water-works." She nodded toward Barbara. "I should go. A mercy for both of us, I think."

"She's just had too much to drink. It's a hard day for her."

"You think so?" She turned to him. "It's an odd thing, men. We know you, and you don't know anything about us. She's not upset. Why would she be? Oh, the inconvenience maybe."

"Then so much for your *crime passionnel.*"

"Well, it's amusing to think that. A man like that. With a woman. But of course it was political," she said, matter of fact. "You know he was with the American — what do they call it, secret service, like the British, I suppose."

"What?"

"Well, everybody was a little, weren't they? During the war," she said, waiting for Leon to respond to this.

"Not everybody."

"No? All right. But Tommy — Hans Beckman always said so. You remember him, in the German consulate? He knew because he was in *theirs.* How, I don't know. The most indiscreet man. Of course, they lost the war, so maybe that's why."

"Lily," he said, drawing out the sound.

"Well, but it's interesting, no? Spies. Spying on what? Each other. But now Hans is gone, all the Germans. Tommy goes home, with the faithful Barbara. So why now? That's the question, *n'est-ce pas?* Some episode during the war maybe. And now it comes back. The Germans remember things. So maybe somebody's still fighting. I don't know."

"You sound as if it doesn't matter."

"This business? Oh, during the war, yes, everything matters then. Now maybe not so much. One death. How important, really? In the scheme of things." She paused. "Such a look. You think I'm terrible. It matters to you so much, this death?"

He turned his head, at a loss. Barbara crying across the room, maybe more upset than Lily imagined. Something you didn't replace. Taken away with the pull of a trigger. His.

"I know," she said, "we're supposed to feel that. But in a month or two? Already something in the past. Time — it's different here. You know I came to Istanbul as a slave. A slave. I had no idea then. It was just the way things were. They gave us new names, all the girls. Poetical names. Youthful Grace. Ever Young. I was Dilruba, Captor of Hearts. Well, so they hoped. Dili, my friends called me. Then after, I changed again. Lily. Then Refik's name. And you think, well, life, all these things that happen, it feels like yesterday. But really, a long time ago. A slave. Imagine how long ago that was. Another time."

He was quiet for a second, then smiled. "Captor of Hearts."

"Yes, but not the one they expected. So who knows? Maybe something unexpected here too. A *crime passionnel* after all." She looked toward Barbara. "Well, I'll say good-bye and leave Niobe to her grief."

As she dropped her hand, the man against the wall started moving through the crowd.

"What Hans told me, that's just for you," she said. "Not that it matters now. Everyone will know soon."

"Why?"

174

"It's bound to come out. When they find who did it. Unless they keep it quiet. They always try, don't they? Still, there'll be something. Now don't forget. Bring your friend to the party," she said quickly, already moving away.

The man from the wall was making eye contact now. As he got closer, oddly, the moustache disappeared, another trick of the light. His face was dark with stubble, someone who shaved twice a day, but no moustache, the man on the tram again.

"Mr. Bauer?" he said, there at last. "May I introduce myself? Colonel Altan."

Leon nodded.

"I thought perhaps we might have a cigarette together. Would you mind?"

"Outside, you mean?"

Altan moved his arm, after you, expecting Leon to move.

"Are you with the police?"

"No. Please." Extending the arm again, now more than a suggestion.

They moved to the door, weaving through the crowd.

"A sad occasion," Altan said. "A very popular man."

Leon said nothing, waiting until they reached the street, then offered him a

175

cigarette. "Colonel in what?" he said, lighting it.

"Emniyet," Altan said simply.

"I thought you never announced yourselves."

"A courtesy. To foreign guests."

"To put us at ease. Talking to State Security."

"Mr. Bauer, we are not Gestapo."

"No, but not just police, either. Is this an official visit?"

"Not yet."

Leon looked at him, trying to stay calm. Emniyet could do anything, detain you indefinitely, revoke a visa. Not Gestapo, no knocks on the door in the night, but just as privileged.

"How can I help you?"

"You had drinks with Mr. King the night before he died. What did you talk about?"

"His going home, mostly. He was looking forward to that."

"He didn't like Turkey?"

"No, not that. His job here was over. Now he had a new one, that's all."

"His job here. You worked with him?"

"No, Reynolds has had its licenses in place for years. Commercial Corp. — that was Tommy — was part of the war effort. Buy chromium. Embargo companies if they were selling to the Axis. Things like that. But now the war's over, so's the job."

"I meant his other work."

"His other work."

"Mr. Bauer, it's better to be candid in these matters. We know Mr. King's work. We know you were sometimes — what, an irregular? It's our business to know these things. We have to be the ears of Turkey."

"Listening to Tommy King."

"To many."

"And now you want to know who killed him."

"Not precisely. That's a matter for the police."

"Then why are you —"

"The police concern themselves with crime. Witnesses. What kind of bullet. Alibis. They do things in their way. Methodical. They will want to know about your talk at the Park too. Your movements the night of the crime. Bebek, so convenient, just down the road. A coincidence? The night before, drinks. That night, close by. They'll be suspicious of that. They'll think he might have been meeting you. They'll ask when you came to the clinic, when you left. Police."

"You think I shot Tommy?"

"I don't care."

Leon looked up at him.

"I'm not police. I'm not concerned with justice. My job is to protect the Republic. If you did, the police will find out. Or maybe not. They are not always successful, our police. Overwork, perhaps. I don't care one way or the other. No Turks have been killed. If the *ferengi* want to kill each other, that's their affair. Until it's ours."

"And when's that?"

Altan bowed his head, a silent "now."

"But you don't want to know who killed him?"

"For the record, of course. But what I want, Mr. Bauer, is the Romanian."

They had been walking back up to Tünel and now stopped at the wall near Nergis Sok, looking down toward the Horn. A haze was forming over the shipyards, blocking the pale winter sun.

"What Romanian?"

"More candor. A Romanian Mr. King arranged to meet. Of great interest to you. To the Russians too. A prize of war, so to speak."

"And you think he killed Tommy?"

Altan shrugged. "It's not important. What's important is where he is."

"Maybe he's with the Russians."

"No."

"How do you know?"

178

"Because I do."

Leon looked at him. "The ears of Turkey?" Another tip of his head.

"Everywhere." A new thought. "With us too. That's how you know Tommy was meeting someone."

Altan stared at him, not saying anything.

"Did Tommy ever suspect?" Leon said.

Altan rubbed out his cigarette. "We can't be everywhere. We have to choose carefully. Where there is likely to be mischief."

"Mischief."

"Look down there," Altan said, nodding to the Horn. "Once the hinge of the world. Now all we can do is listen. To protect ourselves. The Russian bear would swallow us so we don't offend. America is rich." He turned to Leon. "They embargo industries. Their war, our industries. So we don't offend them, either. A balancing act. Do you know what it was like for us, this war? The first one was a catastrophe. The Ottomans finished. Istanbul occupied. Greece invades. Only Atatürk saved us. Well, and the Greek soldiers being — Greek. Then a new one. Both sides say, come in. Maybe another catastrophe. So we walked a tightrope. One step, another step, always watching to see if someone might push, trip us. And now we're still watching. A man is shot in our streets. The police have a crime. But we may have an incident, something that gets worse. Both of you pulling at us. So we want this man. Before you tear us apart to get him."

"You mean the Russians have asked for him? They're accusing —"

Altan shook his head. "They can't do that. Officially such a man can't exist." He looked over. "For either of you. There is no Romanian. But what will you both do to get him? Already a man here from Ankara. The Russians offering money. Battle lines. And who's in the middle?"

Russians offering. Ears everywhere.

"But if everybody's still looking, then nobody has him."

"That point has not escaped me."

"What would you do if you got him?"

Altan smiled to himself. "A valuable thing to have."

"You mean you'd sell him to the highest bidder."

"No. We would advance our interests. Of course, it's not for me to decide how to do that. Only to find him." He paused. "It would be a good thing for Turkey, to stop this. Move the war somewhere else. We would be grateful for that, someone who helps."

Leon looked at him. "I'm an American."

"With interests here. A good life, I think. Your wife — you're satisfied with her care?"

"I can't help you, even if I wanted to. I never heard of your Romanian."

"No? I'm sorry to hear it." He reached for cigarettes, then stopped as Leon offered his again.

"And if you really know as much as you say you do, you know that I was nothing to Tommy. An errand boy when I happened to be going to the right place."

Altan nodded. "Karpić's."

Leon said nothing, taking this in. How long had they been watching?

"You could have been deported for that, you know."

"We were fighting Germany, not Turkey."

"In Turkey."

"I'm just a businessman. You've got some-body inside, from the sound of it. Ask him. I wasn't part of anything."

"Just an irregular. But that's what makes you so interesting. We don't know you."

"That's what this talk is all about?"

"No, I would say it's to warn you. Not to get involved." He turned. "Unless of course you are. This is excellent," he said, looking at the cigarette. "It's superior, American tobacco? And yet you're in Turkey."

"It's the blend. Virginia Bright is cheaper.

181

But Turkish Latakia has a stronger flavor. It brings the blend up. And there's a certain cachet to Turkish. People associate it with the rich. Custom blends."

"Then it's lucky for us."

"Your real competition is Kentucky Burley Leaf. You can flue cure and flavor it."

Altan drew on the cigarette. "So you know tobacco."

Leon looked at him. "It's my business. That's what I do here."

"Yes. You know," Altan said, as if something had just occurred to him, "you see people and you think you've seen them before but you can't remember where. And then it comes to you. I think I saw you yesterday on a tram. Maybe not. The hat, it's hard to tell."

"Where was this?"

"Beyazit. Was it you?" Not really a question.

"It may have been. I went to see a friend. At the university."

"Yes? Who?"

"Georg Ritter."

"Ah, our Marxist philosopher. There? I thought he was in Nişantaşi now."

"His office. He still keeps one there."

"He's well?" The rhythm of conversation, eyes watching carefully.

182

"Actually, he wasn't in. Stupid, I suppose, just stopping by like that but it gave me an excuse to go to the book market. You know, by Beyazit Camii."

"You pronounce it correctly. The *c,* it's tricky for foreigners. A valuable skill. So few Americans know the language. I'm surprised they didn't call upon you more, on a regular basis. Not errands."

"I prefer the tobacco business."

Altan raised his eyebrows. "On that we agree. We prefer you in it too." He began to walk, Leon following. "The book market. We had some dealings there once. You know the German bookseller? The corner with the old tree? Not just selling books. The Germans denied it, of course, but they stopped. It's always better that way, to arrange things quietly."

"Quite a coincidence, you being on the tram."

"Yes. Oh, I see, you think on purpose? What would be the reason for that?"

"None."

"No, I was out in Laleli. A hotel. The police, you know, it's routine with them to check hotels. After a crime. So we wanted to know, is the Romanian somewhere. Maybe an assumed name, but a *ferengi,* that's usually remembered."

"And was he?"

"Two men at this one. On a drunk, the clerk said. Sailors, he thought."

"But he could identify them if he saw them again?"

"Oh, easily, I think. Both," he said, looking at Leon. "Of course, the clerk, sometimes these types are not reliable. An unusual drinking party. The room was clean."

"Sailors are usually neat."

"Mr. Bauer, have you ever been drunk? Look at your room the next morning."

"The police could show him a picture. Of the Romanian. Then you'd know for sure."

"If they had one."

"Don't you?"

"Mr. Bauer," he said, not answering, "the police have their own methods. We don't interfere."

"Interfere? Emniyet? You can do —"

"I don't think you understand. The police must do their work, but it would be better if they don't solve this crime."

Leon looked at him, waiting.

"The men are gone, whoever they were. Whatever they did. If the police find who killed Mr. King, friends are likely to be embarrassed. Someone will be put on trial. The Russians are an excitable people. Quick to take offense. We could lose our balance, trip. Much better to deal with this quietly, out of the public eye."

"What if the Romanian shot him? Would you want to solve it then?"

"Even more quietly," Altan said, his own voice lower. "After we find him." He turned, making a formal good-bye nod. "Thank you for the cigarettes. The Turkish tobacco, it comes mostly from the north coast, I think."

"That's right."

"Your business, it must take you to the Black Sea ports then."

"Once in a while."

"Your wife too, I think."

Leon said nothing.

"A woman with Jewish interests."

"She is Jewish."

"Yes, I understand. Terrible things during the war. One can't help but be sympathetic. To save people, it's heroic. What is illegal when a life is at stake? Now, of course, a different time."

"What makes you think their lives aren't still at stake? Every day you hear stories —"

"And now another friend to balance. The Americans want this, the Russians want that, and the British — the British want us to stop ships. You say refugees, they say human contraband."

"You were the safety valve. All during the

war. The only people who got out, got out through here."

"But now a flood. And the British turning them back. To where? For myself, I don't —" He paused. "Your wife, I know, is ill. You don't share her interests, the old work?"

"No."

"Good. It's a difficulty for Turkey."

"Why do you ask?"

"No reason. Just to know your sympathies. Times change. The Black Sea — a very troubled place now. We think the Romanian came that way. Now all the Jews. A place that needs more ears. Familiar with the ports."

Leon took this in. An invitation? A warning? But Altan's face remained blank.

"Have you seen the human contraband? What they look like?" Leon said.

"Yes. Skeletons, some of them." They had reached the top of the rise, the Sea of Marmara a distant glimpse of blue between rooftops. "To think, when Jason sailed through there," Altan said, looking down at the water, "the Black Sea was a new place. A treasure house — hides, amber, maybe gold. Now it sends corpses. Europe's war. And the survivors float to us."

"They're just passing through."

"To where? America? No. Another war.

The British took Palestine from us. Now they ask us to help them keep peace there. And we have to do it. Keep our balance." He stopped. "You wouldn't want to help anyone pass through. Make difficulties."

"There seem to be a lot of things you don't want me to do. But I'm not doing any of them. I buy tobacco, that's all. And now the Emniyet is accusing me of — I don't know what exactly. Am I suspected of something?"

Altan looked over at him, taking a second. "Of not being candid, Mr. Bauer, that's all." He raised two fingers to his forehead in a salute. *"Hoşça kalin,"* he said and turned away, melting into the crowd of people at the funicular station.

Leon stood for a minute, watching, then went back to the end of the square and lit a cigarette, unnerved. What everyone dreaded, a talk with the Emniyet, but what had actually been said? Not said? Everything elusive, like the moustache that came and went with the light. But only one coincidence allowed, not two, and now the tram seemed to be the coincidence. He looked left, down the hill toward Marina's building. Maybe visiting someone else. But that would make two coincidences. He imagined them suddenly in her room, Altan slipping off the kimono, running his hands along her shoulders. Or talking, cigarette smoke drifting out the window, a notebook of talk, maybe weekly, his Thursdays too.

He tossed the cigarette and started down the street, trying to remember everything he had ever said to her. Did Altan pay her? Something more valuable than her body, a peephole into someone's secret life. How many, or just him? Everything they said afterward, lying on twisted sheets, Altan listening.

The vestibule smelled of damp plaster, something he hadn't noticed before, his senses usually overwhelmed by anticipation. And after, the smell of sex, his fingers heavy with it. Quiet on the stairs, a drip somewhere down the hall, gray light through the translucent landing window, his breath shorter now, anxious. Would she lie? A new lie to keep the other one going. The knock sounded loud, not the standard gentle tap, knowing she was waiting on the other side.

It took her a few minutes to answer, Leon straining to hear, listening for footsteps. She'd be surprised, clutching the kimono tighter, belting it. When she opened the door, hesitant, her face was exactly what he expected, puzzled, a little put out. What are you doing here, without her saying it. A silk wrapper, but not the kimono, the bedroom door closed behind her.

"What did you tell Altan?" he said.

She said nothing, looking at him, deciding how to react. "Murat?" she said finally. "How do you know about him?"

"We just had a chat."

"You're in some trouble?"

Leon shook his head. "He just wanted to scare me a little. Let me know he's there."

She stared for another second, then opened the door wider. "So come in. He told you he comes here?"

"No. He doesn't know I know."

"How do you?" she said, lighting a cigarette.

"I saw him coming out of your building. A client?"

She shook her head.

"Just information? He doesn't take a little something out in trade?"

She looked up, a small flash of anger. "What do you want?"

"He's Emniyet. What does *he* want?"

"To talk."

"About me?"

"About everyone."

"And you tell him."

"He's Emniyet," she said, the anger a little

189

weary now. "I'm a whore. What choices do you think I have?"

"What does he want to know?"

"The man who owns the building. They want to know about him. I don't know why. Do you think I would ask?"

"Know what about him? What happens in bed?"

Another flash of anger. "You think that's so interesting, what happens there?" She took in some smoke, calming herself. "What he says. His business. Does he talk about Inönü? Things like that."

"And me? What do you tell him about me?"

"Nothing. I said when you come here, it's only for what we do. That's all. It's true enough. What do you ever say to me?"

He saw them lying in bed, idle talk, drifting with the smoke.

She put out the cigarette. "Who are your friends? Who in the consulate. Do you have enough money? You know what I tell him? You have enough for me. That's all I care about." She stopped and came over to him. "You don't have to worry," she said, touching him. "I don't say anything to him. It's Bayar he wants to know about. You only come here to sleep with me. It's true, isn't it? That's why you come." Stroking his arm.

"You enjoy it."

"Why didn't you tell me?"

"Why. Because you'd tell me to stop and how could I stop? So then maybe you'd stop coming."

"And who knows? I might say something one day you could use. In a weak moment."

"You think I would do that?" she said.

"Maybe. Isn't that why they came to you? You make a good recruit. People tell you things all the time."

She turned to him, stung. "That's right. All the time. Wonderful things. Do you want to hear? Do this. More. Let me see you like that. Yes, open your legs," she said, everything in a rush, spilling over with it, louder. "Oh, you don't want to hear? Why not? Wonderful things. All my life. Just to have this," she said, her hand to the room. "Emniyet doesn't want to hear, either. Tell us what he says. What do they think men say to a whore?"

The bedroom door opened. Just a head, face unshaven, and the top of an undershirt. A quick exchange in a language Leon didn't understand, Marina telling him to go back inside. Glowering at Leon, unsure, then closing the door. Marina looked over at him, saying nothing, the mood now slightly deflated, interrupted.

"What was that? The language."

"Armenian," she said.

"A specialty?"

"He likes it, yes," she said, defiant now. "It makes it better for him. His language. Would you like to know what he tells me in it?"

Leon turned away, then caught his reflection, someone unfamiliar, as tarnished as the mirror itself, mottled with age, brown spots spreading around the edges. Wearing out. A place he'd found erotic, dust in the window light, a sheen of sweat, now just a tired room, a surly Armenian behind the door, a thin girl in a wrapper, waiting to please him, what her life was really like. He stared at himself for another minute, unable to move, the same hollowing out he sometimes felt after sex, the man in the mirror looking straight back, undeceived.

Marina came over to him, touching his arm, tentative, sensing his withdrawal. When he looked down he saw her differently too, more rouge brushed over the cheekbones, maybe the way the Armenian liked it. For a second he had the feeling, a strange jarring, that he had made her up, that all the visits here, those afternoons he'd waited for, had really taken place in his head.

"Come Thursday. Altan, it's nothing. I tell

him nothing. He wants to know about Bayar, not you." She paused. "And I wouldn't, you know? I wouldn't tell him. It's just — he likes to know who comes here. Come Thursday." A half smile, squeezing his arm. "We don't have to talk at all. If you don't want."

She moved her hand higher, to draw his head down, but stopped, both of them aware that something had happened, had broken whatever spell the room used to cast, like a crack in the mirror.

"Would you do something for me?" he said.

She raised her eyes, waiting.

"Don't tell him I know he comes here."

"Why not?"

"Maybe someday I will tell you something. That he'd want to know."

"And he'd believe it. Because I told him. You'd use me for that."

"It wouldn't be a lie."

"No? Then tell him yourself. You're alike, you two. You want to do what he does."

He moved to the door.

"I don't sleep with him," she said, as if it made a difference.

"Yet," he said.

He took the Istiklal tram to the office and

went through messages with Turhan, then got a *dolmus* taxi out to Aksaray, waiting until the other passengers found their buses, then waiting a little while longer to make sure he was alone. The Emniyet wanted you to think they knew everything, watched everywhere — wasn't that the point of Altan's meeting? — but no one could watch all the time. Only one man at the station seemed fixed in place, a possible plant, but then he got on a bus headed to the airport and Leon started back toward Laleli, twisting first down to the aqueduct, then up the hill.

Alexei opened the door, a half-filled chessboard behind him. "Nothing hot?" he said, looking into the bag Leon had brought. He was clean shaven, his shirt pressed, military crisp. Leon thought of the grizzled Armenian.

"Heat up a can of soup."

Alexei opened the cigarette carton, tearing the cellophane off a pack. "The food isn't much, but your cigarettes are excellent. They're easy to get here, American cigarettes? In Bucharest, like gold."

"I have a good source."

"So," Alexei said, taking a puff. "Why the face? There's trouble?"

"I've just been to a funeral."

"Ah, your friend? How did that feel?" he said, almost amused.

"Then I had a visit from the Emniyet."

"Why you?"

"They're seeing everybody who knew Tommy."

"And?"

"They'd like to find you. So they can play us off against the Russians. Odds on the Russians this time. You'd be a kind of peace offering."

"Feeding the beast to keep him quiet. And my new friends?"

"You're Topic A with them too. The embassy just sent a man from Ankara. The name Bishop mean anything to you? If it does, I need to know."

"To protect me?" Alexei said, smiling a little, then shook his head no.

"He canceled your plane." Alexei looked up. "There are a few ways to think about that. Depends whether you feel like trusting him."

Alexei waved this off, not worth answering. "And your Tommy? No one suspects?"

"They still think he died in the line of duty. Keeping you from the Russians."

"Who now have me?"

"Except they're offering money for you, which Frank's bound to hear. I did. So, no."

"Then it's as before."

"Not exactly. He wants to bring me inside to take over Tommy's desk. Find out who shot him."

Alexei raised his eyebrows at this, then looked over to the chess game. "A complicated board now. Every move." He stood up. "Every time you take your fingers off a piece. Very dangerous for pawns. Would you like some tea?" He moved over to the stove. "So now we're careful. That's how you survive. There's a leak in Turkey. Somebody told the Russians I was here."

"Well, Tommy would have."

"But that's the interesting thing," Alexei said, sitting down, sipping tea. "I don't think he did."

"What?" Leon said, a delayed reaction.

"There were no Russians there that night. Just him. One man. Not even a good shot. The Russians don't work that way."

"Go on," Leon said quietly.

"You leave me here alone all day, so what is there to do but think? Turn things over. Your Tommy was the Istanbul link? Think how this works." He took another sip. "He knows the fishing boat is bringing me to Istanbul. He keeps me here, he puts me on a plane. Nothing before, nothing after, so the chain is secure. Everyone works this way. But why shoot me in Istanbul? So public. Always a risk of being seen. Why not the coast? Not one night there, two. A delay in the weather. If they wanted to kill me, or take me away, why not there? He knew where we were. He called to see if we were coming. How easy to make another call. Have his Russian friends take care of things then. When everyone is inside, keeping out of the rain. But he waits for Istanbul. An odd decision, no?"

"But he came. With a gun."

"Alone. You can believe me, the Russians aren't known for restraint. So what does it mean?"

Leon waited, silent.

"They didn't know. They never would have handled it that way."

"But you agreed he must —"

"Yes, so I thought about it. Prisoners have time to think. Why here? The fishing village, a perfect moment. Bebek, still possible, but not as good. And not alone."

"Then why pick it?"

"Because he wasn't alone. He had you. No suspicions attach to him. If they attack at the fishing village, the leak might be traced. But here he's protected. He had you."

Leon said nothing.

"We were there to kill each other. That's what would have been found. And Tommy's still safe. He wasn't there. Just us."

The setup Leon had already imagined. He nodded.

"You were the only one who knew where the actual landing would be," Alexei said. "That's correct?"

"That's what he said."

"So think some more. He goes to an outsider. Someone he trusts. For such a job."

"Maybe he didn't want to lose one of his own men," Leon said, his voice sour.

"No, who gets killed — you, someone else, what does it matter? Not a time for niceties. The trust is the point."

"He didn't trust his own people?"

Alexei opened his hand. "So he doesn't tell them. Then how do the Russians know I'm here? They didn't know Bebek or they would have been there. But now they're offering money. So how do they know?"

"Someone else told them."

Alexei nodded.

"But only Tommy knew when you were coming. And me."

"But the operation itself — others must have known about that. Not when, but the fact of it, that Tommy would be alerted, that he would pass me on. And then, when he's killed, the obvious conclusion — I must be here, in Istanbul. Maybe running. Maybe snatched by someone else. But not by them." He looked across at Leon. "I'm safe in the next link. The problem is here. I knew this from the first, even before I thought things through." He walked over to the board and put his fingers on one of the pieces. "So, the next move. The Russians are looking, now the Turks, you say, so we have to get out of Turkey. You have people in Greece. It's not far, Edirne. But we'll need papers." He leaned over to his duffel and pulled out a passport. "It's a risk now, using this name." He opened it. "The picture's still good, only a little of the seal. Not hard to remove. Turkish this time, I think. Anyway, not Romanian." He handed it to Leon. "You can do it?"

Leon nodded.

"Then a contact name in Athens. For later. After we're there. Not before. No one knows, not here, not there. A surprise visit. You understand?"

"I'll need a day or two. For the papers."

"No more," Alexei said, the officer in charge.

"You have enough food? I don't want to come back here."

"Yes," Alexei said, then froze, lifting his hand up, a traffic cop. He crossed to the door in two steps, silent, leaning back against the wall, listening, drawing a gun from his pocket in what seemed to be slow motion, holding it up. Leon didn't breathe, staring at the gun. A sound outside he hadn't heard. Alexei listened for a few seconds more then lowered the gun, moving away from the door.

"The couple at the end," he said quietly. "They stopped in the hall. Maybe carrying something."

"You heard them."

"You learn to listen. Living like this."

"I see you found your gun."

Alexei nodded. "It's not much. Two would be better. You never know how many of them would come."

Leon said nothing. What it was like, day to day, waiting.

"And another gun would make a difference?" he said finally. "In that kind of shoot-out?"

"No, it's better to escape. But not always possible. So you listen. No surprises."

"Escape how?" Leon said, looking around the room.

"The bathroom window drops to the courtyard. But there's only one way out to

200

the street, and they'd have someone there. You have to assume that. Utility stairs to the roof — they might not expect that — and it's easy over to the next."

"How do you know?"

"I tried it. A test."

"You went out? You're supposed to stay here. I told you to stay here."

"Without a plan. Playing chess all day." He shook his head. "How do you think I'm still alive? Listening to people like you? Who knows? Maybe waiting for you to bring them."

"Trust nobody," Leon said, still imagining his life. "Then what do you do? Sit on a roof or walk around Istanbul? It would be a matter of time."

"A map would help. Also your phone number." He fixed his eyes on Leon, a kind of challenge. "If we're going to help each other."

Leon hesitated, then pulled out his wallet and handed him a business card.

"Your home?" Alexei said, glancing at the telephone number. "Or the dried fruit?"

"Office," Leon said. "Someone would be there, if I'm not."

Alexei held the card for another minute, memorizing it, then handed it back.

"Keep it."

"If they kill me and they find it, it leads them to you. Don't worry, it's here now." He tapped his temple.

Leon started for the door, then turned.

"If someone else told them, there must have been two inside. Tommy didn't know?"

Alexei smiled faintly. "The Russians did that sometimes, put two in. More. You don't want them to know each other — if one gets caught, it's only one. He can't lead to the others. Washington's like that. They don't know each other there."

Said casually, sure of it.

"Sometimes it backfires. In Bucharest there was a case, they were watching each other. As the most suspect. Which was right, as it turned out. A typical Bucharest situation." He snorted, the corners of his mouth creasing up. "I didn't make the world. Someone else's joke."

"But Tommy shot you without telling them."

"Yes," Alexei said, nodding as if he were appreciating a move Leon had made. "I'm still thinking about that. Heroics, maybe. He liked to act alone? Of course they would want me dead. So he hands them a fait accompli. With you to protect his cover. Or something else. I don't know — all we know is that he did. Maybe you can help. When you become him. Find out why he did it."

"Maybe he thought you deserved it."

"Maybe," Alexei said, looking at him. "He also shot you."

Leon left by the back, checking the courtyard to see if Alexei had been right. One exit. He imagined him racing up the utility stairs, across the roof, like a cat burglar. On his eighth life. Near the bottom of the hill, he turned into a side street and waited to see if anyone had been behind, but no one passed except two Turkish women in ankle-length coats, carrying string bags. He stood for a minute, making a list. New papers.

At the landing there were boats for hire to cross the Horn, the handful that hadn't been put out of business by the bridges. Once the whole shore here had been lined with slips for caïques, Istanbul's gondolas, slim and graceful in the old watercolor prints, the boatmen in turbans, ladies in veils on mysterious errands. Layers.

This caïque was a rowboat with a small outboard motor, the turbaned oarsman an overweight old man who smelled of raki and complained all the way across about the price of gas. How was an honest man to make a living? Or a dishonest one for that matter, Leon thought, then raised his head, remembering the boatman in Bebek. Who'd been promised more money, a loose end. But that request would end up on Tommy's desk and now he was Tommy.

He got off near the Koç shipyards in Hasköy and walked the few blocks to Mihai's office, an old industrial building given to Mossad by its Jewish owner before it could be seized for the wealth tax. During the war, Mossad had worked out of the Hotel Continental, and some of the staff still preferred it for the convenience, but Mihai had moved his unit down to the waterfront. Aliyah Bet, the illegal immigration, was like Noah's ark, he'd said. It should have a water view.

Only a few of the top story windows had one, though, a scummy stretch near the repair docks. The rest of the office looked like the sewing factory it had been, now divided by plywood partitions. Mihai's desk, an old cutting table, was covered with what looked like passports stacked in piles and a clipboard of lists.

"Sorry I'm late," Leon said, loud enough to be overheard.

Mihai looked up, surprised.

"Anna won't mind. We can take a taxi. You really don't have to do this, you know."

"Yes, I know," Mihai said, his eyes question marks.

Leon cocked his head toward the door.

"Give me a second," Mihai said, a normal tone now. "I have to put these away. Destination visas. Gold." He started to shelve them in a safe.

Leon picked one up. "Honduras? That's new."

"A generous host. No quotas."

Leon opened the passport. "Josef Zula, born Lodz. Going to Honduras. They buy that?"

"The Romanians don't care where he ends up, as long as he doesn't stay there. The visas are official. Cuba's drying up and we've got people ready to sail. Beggars can't be choosers. How many would you like to take? The land of the free. Jews? All full."

Leon put the passport down. "Wouldn't they be surprised in Honduras. If you did come. This must have cost you."

"What price would be too much for you?" He closed the safe's door and twirled the dial. "So. Let's not keep Anna waiting," he said, raising his voice, then told the secretary he'd be at the clinic. Bases covered.

"What's so urgent?" he said outside. "Now I have to go to Bebek. And on a day there's so much to do."

"I couldn't think of anything else. They

know you visit Anna. Why else would I come see you?"

"My conversation? What's wrong?"

"I had a talk with the Emniyet."

"Welcome to the club. What's so remarkable?"

"At Tommy's funeral. They want to know what happened. They know Alexei is here."

"So they talked to you?"

"Not only me. A little warning, I think. They also warned me not to get involved with you. Aliyah operations. They thought because of Anna —"

"That you might actually help, instead of making difficulties? How little they know you."

"You don't seem very concerned."

"The Emniyet and I are old friends. Sometimes they take an interest, sometimes not. Right now they're taking an interest. The English insist. So Istanbul is becoming difficult. We have to send the convoys to Italy. Then all we have to do is get past the Mediterranean Fleet and the Coastal Water Blockade. A piece of cake — RAF expression," he said wryly. "During the war it was easier. They had other things to do. Now they can turn all their attention to stopping the Jews. Let the Poles finish them off. But not these four hundred."

"With Honduran visas."

"Most. Some others. All good."

"You don't happen to have a spare."

Mihai looked at him. "They're already made out."

"I need another. A fresh passport."

"For him? The butcher? You're asking me that?" He leaned against a chain link fence enclosing the scrap metal yard behind them, dull gray and rust. "A killer of Jews."

"It's more complicated than that."

"No, easy. Why are you here? I thought — no contact. If the police —"

"It's not just the police now. It's Emniyet."

Mihai stopped, quiet.

"I thought you'd better know — where things are. It's not easy. It's complicated."

"So tell me."

There were no taxis waiting at the Koç yards, so they walked toward the Hasköy ferry stop, Leon talking, trying to put everything in order, like tidying a desk. Mihai said nothing, just listened. The ferry for Karaköy was docking when they got to the pier so they followed the crowd on and went out to the open stern to talk, everyone else huddling inside to stay warm. Mihai scanned the empty pier as the boat pulled away, spewing brown lignite smoke.

"No one behind," he said. "You're not be-

207

ing followed. They'll come and go. Now that they've made contact. It's a way they have. To make you think they're always there. You'll get used to it." He turned back, looking at Leon, as if he were still sifting through what had been said. "He's a killer of Jews," he said finally.

"But that's not all he is. I need papers."

"Not from me."

"Just an address. Who do you use." He waited. "We have to move him. You know that."

"Not Mossad. We can't. Not this man."

Leon nodded. "Not Mossad. Me."

"You. One man." Mihai thought for a minute. "Get out of this now. Or you'll never get out."

"Get out how? I've just been telling you —"

"A man like this? Give him back to the Russians. Then no one ever knows. Any of it. Just give them the address and it's over. He disappears." He stopped. "And we're safe."

"He'd be killed. You'd do that. Kill him."

"I wouldn't have to. They'll do it." He rubbed his palms, a washing.

"No," Leon said quietly.

Mihai looked away, not meeting his eye. "So. Make another knot. Tie yourself up. A

Houdini. How are you going to do it? Get him out?"

"First I get him papers."

Mihai took another minute. "You don't need me for that. You're Tommy now. You can make all the arrangements, right under the Americans' noses." A half smile. "While you investigate yourself."

The taxi to Bebek took half an hour. Leon talked to the nurses, so that their arrival would be noted, then went to Anna's room. She was dressed, sitting in a chair by the garden doors, a cardigan draped over her shoulders. Mihai took her hand and looked into her eyes.

"Hello, lovely," he said, then to Leon, "She blinked. She knows my voice."

"Maybe."

"We found a boat," Mihai said to her, his voice easy, making conversation. "Did Leon tell you? For four hundred. From the Greek. The one who sold us the *Ida,* remember? Ari says in pretty good shape. Panamanian flag. So we'll see. Mostly from Poland. From the camps. You know some went back to their homes and the Poles — pogroms, after the camps." He stopped. "But that's over. In Constancia now. So we have to hurry. When you get better, you'll see how much work. Bigger boats. In Italy they have one for two thousand. Imagine, two thousand at a time. The work, just to get them on board." He trailed off, looking at her, then got up. "It's always like this? No improvement?"

"But no regression. The doctor says that's the important thing."

Mihai stared at the garden. "Sometimes I think it's my fault. That work. I thought she was like me. But really only a young girl."

"It's nobody's fault."

"I know. If this hadn't happened, if that hadn't happened." He paused. "I knew girls like her. Everything for the family. The good dishes for Passover. My mother had a tablecloth — for once a year, special. She was like that. A daughter. That's why she did it, I think. Somewhere in her mind she was saving her parents. And then the night the children drowned — it started then. But not all at once, remember? A little at a time, like turning out the lights. Until the house is dark." He shrugged, his eyes suddenly moist. "No regression. What does that mean? From what, this? I remember when you came here. Both of you. The way you looked at her." He faced the garden again for another minute, the room silent. "And what happens to her? If anything happens to you?"

Leon said nothing, another knot being tied into place.

Mihai turned back. "For a killer of Jews."

"I knew they'd bring someone in," Ed Burke said, the pouches under his eyes pulled taut, anxious. "They think one of us did it."

"Nobody said that, Ed. They just asked me to go over the books."

"But they think it. Why not promote Phil?"

Leon shrugged.

"And why is Frank still here?"

"He's going back to Ankara. What's the problem, Ed? They didn't ask me to go over your books," Leon said slyly, almost a tease.

"Just Tommy's. All right, don't tell me."

"Ed, how long have you known me?"

"It's just a funny time for an audit." He looked down at the folder in Leon's hand. "The embargo list? That's during the war. How far back are you going?"

"Just getting to know the files. People have different systems. I still don't understand the expense claims. You don't have just one?"

"Depends who's authorizing the money. The consulate, use the white forms. If it's direct from Washington, they have to go by pouch. The yellow ones."

"But it all gets paid out of the same office here."

Ed nodded. "Welcome to the US Government."

Leon got up and went over to the wall of file cabinets, pulling out a few more folders.

"You think it's one of them? Somebody he turned down?"

"I don't think anything yet," Leon said, looking down at the file, then back up, a new thought. "Anyway, you said it was someone here."

"I said they thought so. Why else would the police be here?"

"Still?"

"All morning. Right through the consulate. 'Where were you — ?' Alibis."

"Did you have one?"

"Very funny."

"Come on, Ed. It's just routine. To talk to coworkers."

"It gives you the creeps. Thinking it's someone here. Walking down the hall or something, and you don't have any idea."

Leon looked at him, not saying anything.

An hour later, Frank called him into his office to meet Detective Gülün, a heavyset man in a gray suit, shiny at the cuffs, with what seemed to be a permanent five o'clock shadow. By that time Leon had had the filing system explained by Tommy's secretary and had gone through every drawer, looking for anything not officially connected to Commercial Corp. But Tommy had evidently taken that part of his cover seriously — his other work had never existed, at least on paper. There were only a few personal items in the desk drawers, a datebook, check stubs, the white expense chits, breath mints, anybody's desk. The bottom drawer was locked but shallow, just enough room for a bottle for an after-work drink. Would he keep records at home, vulnerable to theft? There had to be something. Maybe coded within the other files, memos that meant something else, trails that would take weeks to unravel. Money, however, was always accounted for. Tommy had paid his outside people. It had to come from somewhere.

"I told Detective Gülün that you were helping us."

Leon nodded. "Anything yet?" he asked Gülün, who seemed startled by the question, defensive. A murder in the European community, the last thing any policeman would want. Angry diplomats demanding answers, calls from Ankara, people you weren't supposed to intimidate. That was Altan's world, full of resources and foreigners. Gülün was the kind of policeman more comfortable with car thieves in Taksim.

"Some witnesses in the café."

"Witnesses?"

"The car only. Unfortunately too dark to identify."

"But a car, not a taxi?" Leon said. "That narrows it a little, doesn't it? Someone who can afford to run a car. With the gas shortages. I haven't taken mine out in months."

A diversion, Gülün eager to take it.

"As you say. Someone who can afford. Maybe black market connections." Taking it even further away.

"You've talked to people here?" Leon asked.

Gülün nodded. "Of course we have to check their stories." Hours wasted.

"But nothing suspicious?"

"No. But, you know, I didn't expect —" he said, a deference. "I apologize if it's inconvenient."

"No, no, you have a job to do. We want you to do it. If you think it's someone here —"

"As I said, I don't expect that. A matter of procedure only. The likely explanation is a robbery, but the difficulty is the money. Mr. King still having it."

"And nobody in the café saw anything? How many there were?"

"Just the car. It's possible there was only one. Scared off, perhaps, before he could take the money." Already preparing his Unsolved folder.

"But if it wasn't, then it's something more serious."

"More serious?" Gülün said.

Frank looked up, slightly alarmed, wondering where he was going.

"A thief, that's one thing." Leon stopped, hesitating, looking down at the folder in his hand. "What I keep wondering is, what if it wasn't accidental, what if there was a motive, some reason."

"Some reason," Gülün said, a monotone.

"It's just an idea I had," Leon said. "Do you know what Tommy actually did here?"

Frank raised his eyebrows.

"Commercial Corp. was set up by the Board of Economic Warfare." He glanced at Gülün, already lost in the bureaucratic chart. "His job was to buy up things so the Germans couldn't — chromium, mostly. A good thing for Turkey, by the way — he'd pay top dollar just to keep it out of German hands. And to steer American business to friendly firms. He could also embargo unfriendly ones," he said, dropping his voice.

"Embargo them," Gülün said, waiting.

"That's right. Stop doing business with them. If he thought they were too cozy with the Germans. That could be tricky — companies wanted to sell to both sides. Sometimes they had to, to keep going. An Allied embargo could put you out of business."

"Ruin you," Gülün said.

Leon nodded. "What occurred to me was, what if it's somebody Tommy put out of business, somebody with a grudge."

"I see," said Gülün, familiar with grudges.

"Or somebody he was going to —"

"But the war is over, Bauer Bey."

"But not all the embargoes have been lifted yet. And now, who else is there to sell to? Somebody's just getting by and Tommy wouldn't — well, it's just an idea."

"No, it's possible." Involving Turks, people Gülün was more comfortable investigating.

"If you like, I'll make a list for you." He held up the folder. "Any business that was affected. Might have a grudge. Or maybe would find it convenient to get Tommy out of the way. Would that be useful?"

"Very useful," Gülün said, dipping his head. "A kindness."

"Well, we want to find out who did this. Anything to help —"

For an instant, he felt ashamed of his own

216

smoothness. Gülün and his force grilling hapless businessmen, piling up reports. But not just any businessmen after all — German sympathizers, people who still deserved a little police scrutiny.

"I think we're getting someplace here," Frank said, a dismissal. "How long to put together a list?"

"Give me a day or two," Leon said to Gülün. "A preliminary anyway."

Gülün dipped his head again. He picked up his hat as Frank started for the door. "His files," he said to Leon. "They're for these businesses only? Nothing else?"

"Like what?"

Gülün took a second. "Personal business, perhaps. Some other business," he said, floundering.

Leon shook his head. "Just Commercial Corp. Tommy kept a very clean desk."

Gülün turned this over, then nodded and followed Frank out. Leon sat back on the edge of the desk, leafing through the folder. Export licenses. A political report on the company's owner, vague enough to be gossip. Tommy's cover work. An idle thought: did he favor businesses dealing with the Soviets? But he would have, then.

"That was good," Frank said, coming back. "The embargoes. That should keep him busy. Not poking around here."

"The Emniyet are already doing that. They talked to me. They know about — what's his name?"

"Jianu. Yes, we're cooperating with them." He looked up. "They're everywhere. They might actually get him."

"What makes you think they'd turn him over to us?"

"Politics," Frank said, sure of it. "They're afraid of the Russians. And they should be. Find anything, besides the embargoes?"

"There's nothing to find. Either Tommy played his cards pretty close to the vest or somebody's been cleaning house. Not even payment records."

"I have those," Frank said casually.

"You have them," Leon said. "I'm not supposed to see? What exactly do you want me to do here? Be like Gülün, spin my wheels?"

Frank adjusted his owl glasses. "Don't get excited. I didn't want things sitting around in Tommy's office. Somebody might take a look. I've got them all here."

"What's 'all'?"

"The other files. Operations." A half smile. "You come up once in a while."

"You've been through them."

Frank nodded. "But I don't always know

what I'm looking at. Who the people are."
He opened the desk drawer, pulling out
several folders. "Two sets. Regular Expenses, Special Funds. Some of those are in
code, so we may never know."

"Why would he do that? I mean, here. At
the consulate."

Frank turned. "Well, what occurred to me
was that he didn't trust people here. One of
them, anyway. That's why you're here, remember?"

They went through the expense books
together, Leon identifying names when he
could. Mehmet at the bar, Tommy no doubt
one of several paymasters. A Turk in the
Customs House. A few names from Robert
College. He stopped. F. Gülün.

"What's our detective's first name?"

"Farid. I know. I thought he'd have a
special interest. Try to get this wrapped up
before anyone got too far into the books."

"Several payments," Leon said, still looking at the sheet.

"You know what these people are like.
They're all on the take over here."

"No more than anywhere else," Leon said.
Beat cops in Chicago, aldermen in South
Boston, but only foreigners corrupt.

"No offense. I didn't know you'd gone
native," Frank said lightly, trying to ease

out of it. "Just part of the culture, isn't it? A little baksheesh?" A Groton drawl, rubbing his fingers together.

"And what about us? We're the ones paying."

Frank looked over his glasses. "Point is, he took it."

"All right, but what did he do for it?"

Frank shrugged. "Parking tickets. Maybe some off-duty surveillance. Who the hell knows? Ask him."

Leon shook his head. "He'll think he's a suspect. He's easier to play this way."

"If he thinks we don't know."

"He's in a spot. He knows what Tommy was doing — he worked for him. So he knows the embargo list is bullshit. But he's not going to say anything, just keep his head down. They don't like crooked cops over here, either, believe it or not. He'd be out."

Frank raised his head to say something, then let it go and turned back to the expense sheet. "Here's one of the codes. Twelve-two. A date?"

"No, the date's in the left column." Two hundred and fifty liras. Same cost as the boat he'd hired last September. Another look at the date. "It's me."

"Twelve-two?"

Leon looked at it, a crossword clue.

220

"L.B.," he said finally. "Twelve in the alphabet. Like a kids' game. Christ, Tommy. See if it works for the others."

"And then what?" Frank said. "The question is, who the fuck's J.M.? Or any of them?"

"Let me look at it," he said, tracing his finger down the column, looking for whoever had supplied Alexei's papers. Probably no more than a month ago. When had the operation started on the Romanian side? Somewhere between a hundred and two hundred dollars would be about right, in Turkish liras. He looked at the coded entry. Not initials he recognized, a delivery he'd made. How could he do this without the Jianu file?

"Where's the operation file on our guy?"

Frank looked at him, not saying anything.

"There must be one. Do you want me to do this or not? I need to check a date."

Frank waited another minute, then got up and went to his desk. "It stays here. You can take the others, but this stays here."

Leon opened it. All laid out. The contact number Tommy must have called when the storm hit. The army transport landing permit, with a routing from Istanbul to Casablanca, so no one in Greece had been involved, a plus. An address in Tophane for

Enver Manyas, photographer, presumably the forger, consistent dates.

"Are you going to read over my shoulder or let me do this?"

Frank moved away. "Who else knew Jianu was coming? That's what we're looking for."

And anything that might need to be taken out, references to twelve-two. But there weren't any, not here. Tommy was supposed to be the pickup. So why ask Leon? But then two people wouldn't have been dead, Leon's body what the police would need to close the case.

"And the codes," Frank said. "Just to keep things neat. So we know where we're spending our money."

Leon nodded. "I'll need the payout sheets. I'll bring them back."

"You understand, it's not that I don't —"

"One other thing? Some of the operations that went wrong."

"What do you mean?"

"Operations that didn't work out. This one didn't. I want to see if there's a pattern. Somebody who crops up."

Frank stared at him. "Somebody here," he said, a trace of excitement in his voice, the hunt that interested him. Suspecting everyone now, except Tommy.

Leon kept leafing through the file, hoping

for a match, but most of the initials stayed unclaimed, Tommy's secret. Manyas had been a lucky exception, mentioned because he'd already done work for the unit before Tommy arrived. Passports in several names. Leon memorized the address.

Messages from Bucharest sent by diplomatic cable, part of the chain that got Alexei to the coast for the handover to Tommy. Leon traced the route in his mind. Just as Alexei had said. Infinitely easier for the Russians to snatch him on the coast, if they had known. Which meant they hadn't. And impossible once he was on army transport. Istanbul would be the last chance.

There was a brief bio in the file, Alexei's time with Antonescu, juggling the Soviets after he was deposed, finally running and hiding, the first approaches to the Americans, the story Leon already knew. Nothing about Străuleşti, either still not known or scrubbed from the file, our butcher now.

Number 15 was the second shop down from the *hamam* near the Kiliç Ali Pasa Mosque in Tophane. The street was flat, behind the shipping terminals, and the shop was scarcely wide enough to fit a door and a display window. The dusty framed photographs covered the usual rituals of family life: soldiers stiff in new uniforms, secular weddings, solemn young circumcision boys in round hats and white satin cloaks. In some of the older pictures the men still wore fezzes, steamed and pressed for the camera, already artifacts. According to a small sign, Enver Manyas offered a choice of backdrops — a garden pavilion, Seraglio Point, Bosphorus views — but most of his customers seemed to have opted for less expensive plain canvas.

A bell tinkled when Leon opened the door, bringing out a short, round-shouldered man with wire-rimmed glasses. At first a look of surprise, then a guarded dip of his head.

"Efendi."

"Merhaba. Manyas Bey?"

The man nodded, still wary.

"I have some work for you. For Mr. King," Leon said in Turkish.

Manyas stared at him, keeping his face composed, noncommittal.

"We're alone?" Leon said.

Another nod, waiting. Leon reached into his pocket, pulling out Alexei's passport.

"Mr. King is dead," Manyas said.

"Yes. I've taken his place." He held out the papers. "Are you interested? Same price."

Manyas glanced at the passport. "He didn't use it."

"Change of plans."

"Romanian. Traveling through Turkey. You have a new picture?"

"Same picture. Now a Turk. Traveling to Greece."

Manyas looked up at him, putting this together, the man in the picture still here.

"How long will it take you?"

Manyas examined the picture, fingering the raised seal. "Still a Jew?"

"If that makes it easier for you."

"It's of no consequence to me. It's a matter of the spacing. The length of the name. A Turkish Jew. Barouh. Sayah," he said, offering names.

"Barouh," Leon said, ordering up an identity.

"First. Izidor. Nesim. Yusuf."

"Nesim, I guess."

"So. Nesim Barouh. Going to Greece. Same everything else?" He looked up. "Same man?"

"Same everything else," Leon said. "How long?"

"The seal has to be matched. On the photo."

"Tomorrow?"

"There is some hurry?"

225

"Half now? Half tomorrow?" Leon said, taking out his wallet.

"And the other one?" Manyas said, watching him count out the bills.

Leon looked up at him.

"Of course, I understand now it's not — But the work was done. You'll pay me for the work? Two hundred liras outstanding. If I hadn't done the work, but as it is —"

Leon waited.

"A moment," Manyas said, going to the back room and returning with an envelope. "I thought, you know, when I heard, there's no money now. But it's special paper for these, an expense. And the black market — it's not possible for this one. Not now."

Leon took the passport out of the envelope. American.

"You can see the engraving is excellent — no difference."

Leon opened it. Russell Brooks, born Pennsylvania, an engraved stamp over the man in the picture. Tommy. Leon stared at it, trying to keep his face blank. Something Tommy had ordered for himself. He could feel the quiet in the shop, suspended, like dust.

"Two hundred?" he said, to say something.

"It was agreed. No studio work, so a saving. Duplicate prints. If we hadn't been able

226

to use the same picture —"

"The same picture?"

"As the others. The other two."

"The other two," Leon said slowly, feeling his way. "Different names?"

"Yes, of course, different."

"Tommy had three passports?" Leon said, thinking out loud.

"It's useful, no?" Manyas said simply. "In his work."

Leon looked back at the passport. "Does he owe for them too?"

"No, no, that was last year. Just this one now. If you want — as a favor, no charge, since he's dead — I can change the picture. The passport is good work. A shame to waste —"

"I'll let you know," Leon said, putting it back in the envelope. "I'll bring the two hundred tomorrow. I don't have that much on me now. That all right?"

"Of course," Manyas said, bowing his head, his voice formally polite, like a dealer in the Bazaar. "And whom do I have the pleasure of serving now?"

"It's still Tommy. It's still his account."

He stood outside for a few minutes clearing his head. Why did anyone need another passport? To be someone else. To cross a border as someone else. But Tommy was going home, as himself. Unless something went wrong at Bebek. Prepare for the unexpected, an ace up your sleeve if you had to get out fast. As someone else. But he hadn't picked it up yet, so he'd have had to use one of the old ones. Which meant they were still around somewhere, more Tommys. Not in his office desk. At home, then, with Barbara? He wondered if she knew. But no passports had been made for Barbara. If Tommy had needed to bolt, get out of Turkey, he was planning to do it alone.

Leon took a taxi to his bank in Taksim and drew out enough money to cover Manyas and the trip to Edirne, then walked down Tarlabaşi Caddesi to a garage he'd used before. His car needed a tune-up. If he brought it in did they have another he could use for a day or two? Who had cars to spare these days? But somehow, for a fee, they could. He thought of Frank, smug, the land of baksheesh after all.

He walked back uphill to the consulate, feeling the passport in his breast pocket. Why an American passport, something conspicuous? But what else could Tommy be? A Bulgar in a fleece hat? Jianu could shift nationalities in a minute, a chameleon. Tommy could never be anything else. A hopeless defector, if it came to that. Where would he go, Russell Brooks?

At first, a jarring second, he thought it was Alexei leaning over Tommy's secretary's desk — the same cropped gray hair and straight military back, the jacket in fact a uniform, how Alexei must have dressed once. Voices pitched low, private. It was only when they heard him at the door and turned that Leon could see his face, fleshy, almost without definition, not like Alexei at all, except for the gray.

"Mr. Bauer," Dorothy said, jumping a little, flustered.

A closer look now, navy jacket filling out at the waist, too old for active duty, but evidently not for making a pass. Dorothy was in her thirties with glasses and hair rolled up on top, maybe glad of the attention.

"My husband," she said.

"Jack Wheeler," he said, offering a hand. "Didn't mean to — Just got in from Ankara so thought I'd stop by."

Leon nodded.

"Jack's Naval Attaché," Dorothy said, explaining.

"In Ankara?"

"I know," Wheeler said, a familiar question. "Not too many ships. But lots of admirals. You have to be where the orders are cut. But I get to go back and forth, so we pass in the night once in a while," he said, head toward Dorothy, who looked away at this, flustered again. "Navy wives. At least I'm not at sea. And once they wrap things up here at Commercial Corp. — how long's your brief?" What everyone in the consulate wanted to know.

"They didn't say."

"One thing when the war's on. You do your part. But now they'll be bringing new girls over, let the wives go home. You'll be in Ankara before you know it."

"Yes," Dorothy said evenly.

Wheeler smiled. "She says you might as well be in Omaha. But at least the streets are safe. Hell of a thing, a man getting shot like that. An American."

"Jack, I'll see you later," Dorothy said, picking up a pad.

"Isn't she something? All business. Well, that's right, I guess. Nice to meet you," he said, shaking hands again. "Sooner you wrap things up here, the better I'll like it. You take good care of my girl here."

"Jack —"

"We'll do our best."

"Hell of a thing, right in the streets. You knew him, I guess?" Wheeler said, looking at Leon.

"Just from around," Leon said. "Everybody knew Tommy."

Wheeler waited, expecting more, then nodded. "Well, I'll get out of your hair. Later," he said, a two-finger salute to Dorothy.

"I have the list you wanted," she said to Leon, barely nodding at Wheeler, shooing him out with her eyes. "I'm not sure what you meant, though, by Athens. Mr. King never called Athens."

"His embassy contact there."

"There was no embassy. Greece was occupied," she said. "Well, not now, of course."

"He had no contact there?" Someone for Alexei, once he was over the border.

"I can get the general number if you need to talk to somebody. Is that it?"

"I thought there'd be a liaison. To this office." Using the same cover.

"Not that I know of. We deal with Turkey, that's all. He went to Ankara, sometimes. Izmir, once, to look at companies. But not Greece. Not as long as I've been here." She paused, her hands fluttering, brushing back a stray hair. "Can I ask why you're asking? I mean, I'm not sure I understand what you're doing here. Everyone's nervous as a cat since the — since Mr. King died. The police asking questions and Mr. Bishop coming in and now —" She stopped.

"And now me. Have a seat. I'm not sure I know what I'm doing here, either. Snooping, I guess. That's what Frank wants anyway."

"On Mr. King? He was the victim."

"But not of a robbery. You know that. So I need to know anything that might —" He looked at her. "I need your help. You knew him better than anybody."

"What makes you think that?" she said suddenly, head flying up, so unguarded that for a moment their eyes met and he knew, both of them silent with surprise. They looked at each other, bargaining. Another piece of Tommy's secret life. Weekends somewhere? Here in the office? Tommy, of all people. Leon imagined her without her glasses, taking the pins out of her hair. Or did she regret it? Some moment of weakness that now threatened to blow up in her face. Shooing Wheeler away.

"Working with him, I mean," Leon said. Safe, between us.

She looked away.

"Both jobs."

"I don't know what you mean."

"Yes, you do. Your husband's on the embassy staff. He'd have security clearance.

So you'd be vetted too. It was a natural fit."

"I was an American wife with time on my hands. And I can type eighty words a minute."

He held up his hand before she could say more. "Don't. I worked for him too. Or did you already know that?"

They exchanged looks again, then she crossed her arms over her chest, a truce.

"You seem to think he — confided in me. It wasn't like that. I did the work, that's all. We didn't talk about it."

"Never?"

"Never," she said, meeting his glance, setting a boundary.

"But you wouldn't have to. Everything would go through you."

"Not everything. He kept some things to himself." A faint smile. "He was like that." She looked up, making a decision, a direct stare. "What do you want to know?"

"We were bringing someone out. You knew that?"

She hesitated, then nodded.

"Who else did?"

"I don't know. No one."

"But someone must have."

"Mr. Bishop took the operation file. You could look there."

"I did. How about an appointment book?"

A sly smile, almost conspiratorial. "He never asked for that."

"In my office, Turhan's got my whole life there. Day by day."

"I'll get it," she said, standing up.

"And a key for this by any chance?" he said, pointing down to the locked drawer.

She nodded then turned to go, taking off her glasses at the same time. Pleasant, no more, an ordinary woman, with enough sense to know better. Then Tommy had made her feel special. The mysteries of other people.

She came back with the calendar and a pink telephone slip.

"Mrs. King called," she said with a straight face. "Wants to set up a time. To go over his things."

"Okay."

"He never kept anything at home, you know," she said, slightly disapproving. "Said it was safer here."

Leon took the appointment book.

"We locked the files at night. So the cleaning staff — He was strict about that. I know he liked a drink, but he didn't talk, not even to me. Not about the work."

"What did he talk about," Leon said, leafing through pages. Hour after hour, all the scheduled appointments, but not random

234

meetings in the hall, or a late drink at the Park.

"What do you mean?"

"The war? Politics?" he said easily, an idle question.

"Politics?" she said. "Tommy? I don't even know whether he was Democrat or Republican. It never came up. You mean here? In Turkey? Well, it's just one party, isn't it, so there's not much to say. I don't think he cared about any of that. This office, you couldn't. You have to deal with all kinds."

"Mm." He moved his finger over the page, shaking his head. "Look at this. He knew everybody in the building."

"Well, the commercial department, you do," she said, smiling a little. "But that was him too, what he was like."

"The groom at every wedding."

"What?"

"An expression."

She started to turn away, suddenly at a loss. "Don't forget to call Mrs. King," she said, then handed him a key. "For the drawer." She waited while he opened it.

"As I thought," he said, bringing up a bottle. "He must have pouched this one in. You can't get it here, since the war."

"He brought it with him. I never saw him drink it, though. Too expensive. He was careful about money. His, anyway. Expense account — that was something else. I brought that too, by the way." She indicated another folder. "Mr. Bishop didn't ask for that, either. Maybe you'll find something there. Well, I'll get back to the phone." She fingered the expense folder, stalling. "You asked what we used to talk about? The house, sometimes. The one they were going to have when they got home. Him and Mrs. King. Big. With a powder room downstairs. He said it gave a house class, a powder room. You didn't have to go upstairs. That's what he used to talk about. To me."

Leon looked up, caught by the break in her voice.

"So I guess he was saving it up for that," she said, nodding at the bottle. "Anyway."

"What are these?" Leon pulled some folders from the back of the drawer.

Dorothy opened one. "So that's where he put them. I wondered. He didn't want them with the rest of the files."

"Why?" Leon said, rifling through. "Cross-refs to the Joint Distribution Committee? War Refugee Board?"

"He said one day they'd be history, but right now they were — not illegal exactly, just classified. He was proud of these. You know, people thought they knew what he was like." She looked over at him. "But there was more to him than that. The side he didn't let people see."

Leon raised his head.

"Mr. Hirschmann, from the War Refugee Board, brought a boatload of children out. Tommy got the transit visas for the train. Otherwise they wouldn't have been allowed to go. Strictly speaking, the ambassador wasn't supposed to ask for something like that, so Mr. Hirschmann got Tommy to do it. Three hundred dollars each. I never forgot that. Imagine, selling children. He helped them lease some Turkish ships too. That's how he knew about you. Your wife was working for one of the groups getting refugees out. Is she still doing that?"

"No."

"But that's how he heard. That you went to Ankara." She nodded again at the expense folder. "Good luck with this," she said, looking straight at him, her voice lower. "He wasn't always the most sensitive man in the world, but he had this side too. He didn't deserve to be killed."

Leon waited, feeling a burning in the tips of his ears, not sure how to answer. "Nobody does," he said finally.

"No, that's right. Nobody does."

He suddenly imagined her entering a jury

box, next to Barbara, next to Frank, all of them looking at him, taken in. The lies got easier, one leading to the next until you believed them yourself. The way it must have been for Tommy, lying to all of them too.

A few minutes later Frank came in, looking pleased.

"Take a look. Gülün actually came through with something. They've traced the other gun."

"What other gun?"

"Tommy had two on him. Now why the hell he needed two never made any sense."

"No," Leon said carefully, seeing Tommy plant them, one in Alexei's dead hand, one in his.

"And look. It turns out it's Romanian."

"The one he fired?"

"No. That was Turkish."

"Turkish? He didn't have his own?"

Frank nodded. "But a Turkish gun couldn't be traced back here. No American connection, if anything happened."

"Where did he get it?"

"Gülün says it's like buying a pack of cigarettes. Not this baby, though," Frank said, poking his finger at the police report. "Not so easy to pick up a Romanian gun."

He looked up. "Unless you happened to be meeting a Romanian."

"So you think it's Jianu's?"

"Don't you? Maybe Tommy frisks him — he should have — and, oh, look, maybe we'll just hold onto this until — Too bad, in a way. Meant Jianu was unarmed when the Russians got there. They plug Tommy and the guy hasn't got a chance."

Leon listened to him fill in the scenario in his head, detail by plausible detail.

"So where does that get us?"

"Not very far. But not wondering about two guns anymore, either. So one less thing." His eye caught the open folder on Leon's desk. "Oh, the kids," he said. "He kept copies? He wasn't supposed to."

"You can read upside down? Quite a talent."

"The letterhead. Hirschmann had his own." He picked up a sheet, glancing at it. "So now you know. Not that it matters anymore, I guess."

"Now I know what?"

"What you were carrying," Frank said easily. "Tommy always used you for the Hirschmann deals."

"These?" Leon said. "Why? Why not use the pouch?"

"He never explained? Distance the ambas-

239

sador. You send it by pouch, it's official. Logged in. Distributed. This way Steinhart could say he never knew. What did you think you were carrying? The Allied invasion plan?"

"No," Leon said, looking away, oddly embarrassed, remembering the train, alert in his compartment, feeling important. He picked up a folder. "War Refugee Board? He had to be distanced from that?"

"You have to remember what it was like last year. The Bulgarians, the Romanians — Hitler doesn't look like a winner anymore. Everybody wants some way to look good to the Allies, for after. You know even Eichmann approached us? Wanted to trade trucks for the Budapest Jews. That didn't go anywhere — sending war matériel to the Nazis?" He touched the folder, reminiscing. "But Hirschmann got a waiver from Morgenthau in Treasury. Otherwise, he'd be trading with the enemy — which is what it was, technically, you've got money changing hands. So he could make deals. He says he got fifteen thousand out. Maybe less, he likes to exaggerate. But we're not supposed to know. Nothing in the pouch. So Tommy sends you. No embassy connection, and if anybody finds out, well, you've got a wife in the business. It'd be natural, you being involved in this."

"For her," Leon said, trying to keep his voice neutral. Tommy using Anna too. "And if the Turks —"

"We would have protected you," Frank said. "What the hell, you were doing it for humanitarian reasons."

"Whether I knew it or not." He stared at the folders. "So that's all it ever was? What I did?"

"No," Frank said, looking at him. "Not all. But you were perfect for this, what with your wife —"

"He thought of everything," Leon said, brooding. "All this, just to cover Tommy's ass."

"Well, Steinhart's. The embassy couldn't go near this."

"Why not?"

"The Russians. As usual. The minute Steinhart talks to anybody on the Axis side, the Russians think we're trying to make a separate peace. Before they get there. Which is probably what Antonescu did want, but all we're asking is to let some kids out. Hirschmann, the Russians are suspicious because they always are, that's what they're like. So the grunt work, it's better if it's somebody they do know, who won't make them nervous." He opened his hand.

"Tommy. They know what he does and it's not negotiating peace."

"They know him? How?"

"When we first set up here, there was some crazy idea we'd exchange information, you know, ally to ally, but that turned out to be a one-way street, the way it usually does with them, so there wasn't a hell of a lot that got exchanged. But everybody kept pretending it did. Anyway, Tommy was our side. So they knew him."

Leon's cheek jumped, an involuntary tic. "He met with the Russians? On a regular basis?"

"At first. Then off and on, just to wave the flag, pretend we're all working together. He'd give them stuff. German minefield chart once, for Sulina harbor. That was a big deal. We got our hands on it and no use to us, so let's help the Russkies. Not that we ever got anything out of them."

"Tommy talked to the Russians," Leon said flatly, letting this sink in. Authorized, no need to meet in secret on a park bench or at a ferry railing, one eye looking back.

"Well, during the war. Now nobody talks to anybody. But it made him a good cover for Hirschmann. Hirschmann knew a lot of people in Washington. FDR even. The kind of guy puts the right word in somebody's

242

ear, and all of the sudden you get posted back stateside. I suppose I shouldn't say, I mean he's dead, but you know how Tommy always wanted Washington. So he probably thought Hirschmann was his ticket back. Was, too. Until the Russians got in the way the other night."

"There's a rumor around town they're still looking for Jianu," Leon said, floating it, something Frank was bound to hear anyway.

"There's a rumor about everything," Frank said, dismissive. "Smoke screen. They're good at that. They have him. I want the one they don't have. Who ratted Tommy out. He's here. I can feel it." Frank glanced at his watch. "I'm late for the consul. Walk with me."

In the hall, Leon couldn't let it go. "These meetings he had with the Russians. They keep minutes? What was said?" Some proof.

"Minutes?" Frank said, smiling. "This stuff? You had lunch maybe. A drink at the Pera. By accident. You didn't take *minutes*."

"But he'd tell you later. What was said."

"For what it was worth. He thought it was mostly a waste of time — well, we all did."

"Why Tommy? I mean, he volunteer for this?"

"When I asked him." Frank looked at him. "I'm point desk for the Soviets."

Leon stopped for a second, then caught up as they rounded the corner. "So Jianu — this was your operation?"

"I was briefed," Frank said, careful, another distancing.

"Anyone else in Ankara? Sometimes things get overheard."

"There was nothing to hear. All the details were up to Tommy. Time, drop-off. It's procedure. Safer for him. The fewer people know."

"No backup?"

"That would be for him to arrange."

"But he didn't," Leon said, turning this over. "So he'd be the only one who knew."

"But he wasn't, was he?" Frank said. "And you're not going to find him in there." He gestured to the file in Leon's hand. "Old war stories. He's not in Ankara, either. He's here." He stopped. "Katherine."

She was leaning against the desk, dressed for going out, high heels and a wide-brimmed hat, expecting sun, not Istanbul winter.

"There you are," she said. "And I thought I was late."

Frank looked at her blankly.

"For lunch?" she said, prompting. "The one you're taking me to?"

"To tell you the truth —"

244

"You forgot and now you're busy," she said, sliding down off the desk, her skirt hiked up for a second, a flash of white slip.

Leon looked at her. A gray jacket open to a white silk blouse, bright lipstick that made the reddish hair seem darker. Green eyes, not a trick of the light.

"And then you're back in Ankara and I'll never get out, unless Barbara takes me." She shuddered, for effect, then looked at Leon. "Why don't you join us? The two of you can talk, and I'll just sit there quiet as a mouse and nibble my cheese."

"Can't. Chained to my desk." He gave a small tip of his head toward Frank, now cast as overseer. "Besides, there's Lily's party. I don't want to run out of things to say."

"You won't. Not with Katherine," Frank said, unexpectedly playful. "These people giving the party, they're friends of yours? We have to be —"

"Lily runs Istanbul. The parties, anyway. Everybody'll be there."

"And no ambassadors," Kay said. "For a change. I won't have to be 'representing my country.' "

"You're always —" Frank started, about to be pompous, then caught himself. "Well, she's dying to go." He looked at her fondly. "You'd think it was your first party. All

245

right, lunch. Just let me see the consul first." He looked at his watch again. "Why don't we go next door?"

"To the Pera? I can do room service myself." She pulled a paper out of her purse. "Ginny gave me a list." She turned to Leon. "You must know all these places. Troika?"

"Somewhere near," Frank said.

Leon nodded. "Just a few blocks. Russian. You'll enjoy it."

"Fine, fine. Give me ten minutes," Frank said, leaving.

Kay leaned back against the desk, the room suddenly quiet enough to hear the wall clock. An awkward silence, Leon fingering the folder, just standing. When he looked back up, her presence like a tug on his arm, he found her staring at him again, the way she had at the Pera. Another moment, still not talking, and then she looked away, breaking it. "Russian," she said. "That's funny. Here, I mean."

"White Russian. Lots of them came in the twenties."

"Another thing I didn't know. More layers?"

"When you're there, take a look up at the balcony. Two ladies knitting. Another one's behind the cashier. They switch around. All

246

blondes. Well, used to be."

"They come every day?"

"To keep an eye on the place. It's theirs. They were dancers. Then friends of Atatürk's."

"Friends?" she said, looking back at him.

"Mistresses," he said, bowing.

"At the same time?"

He met her eyes, amused. "That I don't know. But when he got tired of them, he set them up with the restaurant. So they'd have something. Or so the story goes."

"Is that what they do here? I wonder if Frank would give me a restaurant when he gets tired of me."

"Maybe he won't."

"No?" she said, then backed away. "Well, that's lucky." She picked up her purse. "How dressy is the party? What does Lily usually wear?"

"Something floaty."

"Floaty."

"You know, long and — floaty. Like a sari. I don't know how else to describe it. She always seems to be floating through her parties."

"That's a help. So not the jersey. Maybe I'll get some roller skates and we can float around together."

Leon smiled. "You'll be fine in anything,"

he said, indicating the clothes she had on. "Whatever you like."

"Only a man would say that."

"Say what?" Frank said, coming back.

"That it doesn't matter what you wear," she said, suddenly jumpy, as if she'd been caught at something. "Ready?" She took his arm.

"It doesn't. You always look nice."

She rolled her eyes. "That's because you never look," she said, teasing.

"Be careful with the Chicken Kiev," Leon said. "The butter squirts."

She raised her eyebrows, not sure whether he was making a joke, holding his glance for a second, then led Frank away.

Leon watched her go, not floating, high heels clicking across the parquet floor, legs long and sleek, pitched forward by the heels. Don't ever wear skates. She must have once, a girl with freckles. Now it was high heels and soft blouses and a walk, something in the air. Marooned in Ankara, where Frank watched the Russians.

Leon looked down at the folder in his hand. A lot of trouble to go through to distance the ambassador. A Tommy he hadn't known, the best of him. How do you weigh all the sides of someone? What had the Russians offered him? Money, an idea?

But then there was also this, something he'd been proud of, according to Dorothy. The same man who'd tried to kill him at Bebek.

He took the folder back to his office and started reading through. What he'd been carrying on the train, history now. Still, why keep them locked away? The war was over. Or had Tommy simply forgotten about them? He read more, hoping to find something, but it was just what Dorothy and Frank had described, the Joint Committee, backdoor messengers, desperate trades.

He looked at the drawer. So why there? Why the bottle for that matter? Everyone knew Tommy liked a drink, hardly a secret. He opened the drawer. A few more files like the ones he'd read. He paged through. More of the same. He stared at the now empty drawer. Not the bottle, not the files, neither worth locking up. But nothing else there. He started closing the drawer. Maybe just another of Tommy's Hardy Boys games, a man who used alphabet code. He stopped. Who played at hiding things.

He pulled the drawer all the way out and tapped a few places on the bottom then stopped, feeling silly. False bottoms? Not even Tommy. He felt along the sides and lifted the drawer off its runners, pulling it all the way out, feeling behind, then tipping it over.

The envelope was taped near the back, away from the runners so that it would clear the bottom frame when the drawer was opened. He pried one piece of tape away, then yanked at the rest. A consulate envelope, not even sealed. He took out two passports. The same picture Enver Manyas had used. In one, Tommy was Donald Price, Rhode Island, in the other, Kenneth Riordan, Virginia. Turkish entry stamps, no doubt Manyas again, but nothing else. He'd never left the country.

In the back of each passport was a narrow slip of paper. More of Tommy's code, not alphabet this time. DZ2374, AK52330. Leon stared at them, trying to work out a key, but came up with nothing. It seemed absurd, all of it. He was sitting at a desk with a drawer turned upside down, staring at meaningless numbers. But they must have meant something to Tommy. A man with passports who didn't travel.

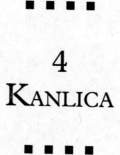

4
KANLICA

"I didn't think anybody was this rich anymore," Kay said, looking past the bow of the boat.

Ahead of them the jetty that fronted Lily's *yali* had been lined with hurricane lamps and the jalousied shutters left open, so that the whole house seemed to be shining with light, the white neoclassical facade bathed in it, throwing its mirror image back to the water. Lily had been lucky in the weather, a mild evening, more spring than winter, but even so it was cold on the water and Kay was hunched into a caracul coat, too curious to sit inside the cabin.

"The Vassilakos shipyards," Leon said.

"Her husband was Greek?"

"No, no, a Turk. A Cypriot. The original owner was Greek. Lily's husband bought him out during the population exchange. He kept the name, but he's the one who really built the company."

"What population exchange?"

"After the war with Greece. In 'twenty-three. Ethnic Greeks were sent home. Vice versa with Turks there. Whether anybody wanted to go or not. People who'd been here forever. It was a bad time. You go to Izmir, places like that, it's still an open wound. Anyway, it gave Refik a chance to buy."

Kay looked up, about to ask more, then turned back to the house, too excited to be dragged into the past.

"Here comes the return trip," she said as an empty launch approached. "And another. My god, how many boats has she got doing this?"

Lily's *yali* was on the Asian side, near Kanlica, where people went for yogurt, and she had provided a small fleet of motorboats to ferry guests across.

"This is how they used to do it," Leon said. "Everybody went by boat. See the *yali* next to hers? With the big overhang? The boats would just slip in underneath, the way they do in Venice."

"Not anymore, I guess," she said, looking at the dark house, half its timber fallen in. "What happened?"

"Fire. They're all wood, the old *yalis*. Heated by braziers. One hot coal and —

254

woof. It's a shame, that one. It's as old as the Köprülü, a really classic *yali*. They're all going, one by one. Arson sometimes, to collect the insurance. People can't afford to keep them up anymore."

"Except Lily," she said, looking at the house again. Houseboys in white jackets were helping people out of boats, lanterns flickering, the rippling water flashing back. She turned to Leon, her eyes catching the light. "Thank you. For bringing me."

He dipped his head in a mock bow. "Pleasure. No dancing, you know. Mostly just gossip. I hope you won't be bored."

"I've never been less bored in my life," she said, almost laughing. "I keep thinking a pumpkin's going to come and take me away."

He pretended to look at his watch. "Not yet. Remind me to show you the garden before we leave. It's famous."

"This time of year?"

"Well, you have to imagine it."

And suddenly he was seeing it, that first Bosphorus spring with Anna, everything in blossom, Judas trees and lilac and yellow laburnum, cherry and soft-green chestnut trees, pulling branches down to smell, dizzy with it. Years ago, when they'd been other people. He glanced over at Kay, still gawking at the house. As eager as Anna had been that day, bubbling over, catching his eye while Lily chattered away, a joke between them no one else heard. We talk about seasons, he thought, as if they repeated, came back, but they don't. That spring was gone, irretrievable, a picture in an album, faces smiling, unaware of what would happen to them.

"What?" Kay said.

"Nothing," he said, shaking the mood off. "You know the sultans used to light their garden parties with turtles? They'd put candles on their backs and let them wander around. Hundreds of them."

She looked at him. "The things you know."

He helped her out of the boat, handing her up to a houseboy, hand outstretched, the cabin passengers lining up behind them. He looked across the strait to Rumeli Hisari, just up the road from where Alexei had landed, not deserted tonight, busy with taxis dropping off people for Lily's party. While Alexei sat smoking in Laleli, listening for sounds in the hall, turning the chessboard around — unless he was checking exits again. How much longer before something happened? Get the papers from Manyas and go.

"You're right," Kay said, looking through

the open doors. "She does float."

Lily was greeting people near the fountain that splashed softly in the center of the reception hall, now talking to Georg Ritter and a burly man Leon didn't recognize. She was wearing a silk caftan with gold embroidery that billowed as she moved, her hair swept up, seemingly by the wind, in a high bun, held in place by two jeweled combs.

"Leon," she said, coming over as a boy took their coats. "How wonderful, you brought her. I'm so glad," she said to Kay, taking her hand. "How pretty you look. Such a lovely dress." She gave it an appraising look, which Leon followed, the first time he'd seen her without her coat. A long off-white dress with a deep V-neck, cinched at the waist by a silver cord, a simple butterfly pin near her shoulder, garnet he guessed, like a piece of red that had dropped out of her hair.

"Thank you for having me. Your house —" She broke off, suddenly awkward. "I've never seen a *yali*."

"It's not one of the old ones, though, you know. Just nineteenth century, when everyone was in love with France." She gestured toward the facade. "Now the one next door —"

"The one that burned?"

Lily nodded. "Poor Selim. Now that was the real thing. Tulip Period. And now it's gone. He says he's going to restore it, but they never do, do they? Just build something new. Do you know Dr. Ritter? He's at the university. An *éminence grise.*"

"Grise? Blanche," Georg said, pointing to his hair. He took Kay's hand. "But delighted. Leon, I was hoping you'd be here."

Now introductions were made, Georg bringing over the other man. "Ivan Melnikov," he said to everybody. "Mrs. Bishop. Leon Bauer."

"Melnikov?" Leon said involuntarily, hearing Alexei's voice.

"Yes, you know me?" he said, his voice direct, too blunt for the frothy room, someone who might bump into the furniture. A broad, weathered face, pitted, maybe scarred years ago by acne.

"No. The name seems familiar, that's all."

"It's common, the name. Mrs. Bishop. The Bishop at the embassy?"

"You see?" Lily said. "Everybody knows everybody in Istanbul."

"You know Frank?" Leon said, curious.

"We have met." He turned to Kay. "He's here?"

"No. Ankara. I'm visiting Istanbul for a few days."

258

"A beautiful woman alone in Istanbul," he said, shaking his head, a stage gesture, trying to be courtly. "No Russian would allow it."

"I've got a chaperone." She nodded at Leon.

"Him? A chaperone?" Georg said.

"You don't think I'm safe with him?" Kay said, looser now.

"Safe, yes. In the right hands, maybe not so much."

"Oo la," Lily said. "And who do you nominate? You?" She turned to Kay. "Of course he knows everything about Istanbul. But no reputation is safe with that one." A tease and a compliment to Georg, overweight and aging.

"Maybe I should offer myself to the highest bidder. Like the girl in *Oklahoma!*"

Leon could tell from the blank expressions that no one had really caught the reference, but Lily smiled anyway.

"Then you must choose Melnikov. A true pasha. He brought caviar. Imagine, in Istanbul, where no one can get it. For love or money. A whole tin." A sly glance at Leon. No one brought gifts to parties like this.

"For a gracious hostess."

"You must have some before they eat it all up," Lily said to Kay.

259

"And me," Georg said, offering Kay his arm. "Let's have caviar."

"Always gallant, when there's food," Lily said, taking her other arm. "Come, I'll protect you. Besides, I want to show you off. Such a prize, a new woman."

Leon looked at the room as they left. There were, in fact, only a few women, most of them European. In the old days they would have been in the other part of the house, having sherbet and coffee, watching the party through latticed grilles.

"You're working with Bishop now," Melnikov said, not bothering with small talk.

"News travels fast," Leon said, off guard.

"Maybe that's where you heard my name."

"Maybe."

"Or from Tommy King. Another friend of yours."

Leon looked at him for a second. "Everybody knows everybody in Istanbul," he said, glancing toward Lily.

"An old comrade. We met from time to time. During the war."

"Ah," Leon said, noncommittal. Those drinks at the Pera, more information exchanged than Frank imagined.

"To survive the war, then this." He shrugged. "Now of course you want to find the man who did it."

"Well, that's a police matter. Naturally we hope —"

"I want to find him too," he said, his voice low, almost a growl. "Georg has spoken to you about this."

Leon looked at him carefully. "That was you? Offering the reward?"

"You worked for Tommy. A man for hire. Why not for me? Avenge your friend's death. Perhaps you could use the money. In these difficult times." He paused. "The man belongs to us."

"And why would I turn him over to you? Assuming we found him."

"Self-interest. The Americans want him. We want him more. So we're willing to pay. Are they?"

"What makes you think —"

Melnikov waved this off. "You can put your flag away. A man like you."

Leon felt a flash of heat on his face. "I don't know where he is," he said, keeping his voice even.

"But you will. Now that you're inside. It's a bet to make anyway. Whoever's protecting him, it's not a stranger. Someone who's part of this business. You don't know yet? Here's an incentive for you, to find out. Enough money to take your wife back to America. It's a reasonable offer."

Leon stared at him. A hard face, lived-in, knowing eyes. Buying someone.

"Go to hell," he said.

Melnikov said nothing for a minute, then looked away. "So. Then take a message. You know how to do that. Be a messenger."

"What kind of message?"

"To whoever has him."

"I don't know —"

"It's important," Melnikov interrupted. "We are going to find our friend. And kill him." He looked directly at Leon. "And his protector. If he would give him to us — a different situation. But if not, both are dead. Tell him that. We'll kill both."

Leon waited for a second, trying not to react. The chill of a death sentence, like a hand on your shoulder, the air still. Melnikov held his gaze, emotionless. How many had he already killed?

"Is that a paid message?"

Melnikov nodded. "If you like. And not as expensive for us." He raised his eyebrows. "At first I thought it might be you. One of Tommy's men. The question was, why? To bargain for Jianu? Get a better price? Then Bishop brings you in to help. Not a foolish man. So, not you. Now we only have to pay you for a message."

"You won't have to pay for anything."

"Deliver it anyway," Melnikov said, his voice thick. "To the one who helps. You might save a life."

"From you? You'd kill him anyway. For the sport."

Melnikov's eyes clouded, as if he'd been offended, then darted over Leon's shoulder. "Here's Georg. Alone. He must have lost the bidding."

Georg, champagne flute in hand, was plodding toward them, feet heavy, older.

"You enjoyed the caviar?" Melnikov said.

Georg put his fingers to his lips in a kiss.

"Then I'd better hurry before it's gone," Melnikov said.

"The guest eats his own present?" Leon said.

"I'm not so polite. A simple soldier. I was never taught these things."

"Lily's very grateful," Georg said, evidently the point of the gift.

"An interesting conversation," Melnikov said, nodding to Leon, a leave-taking.

"Yes? What about?" Georg said.

Melnikov ignored him, beginning to move away, then turning. "Mr. Bauer, if it is you — take the money."

He started to walk again and Leon followed, his back to Georg.

"How about an answer? As a kind of down

263

payment?"

Melnikov stopped. "And the question?"

"Why did your Romanian friend shoot Tommy? If Tommy was there to —"

"Yes," Melnikov said, a movement to his lips, almost a smile. "How the Americans must want to know that."

"Don't you?"

"A speculation. Tommy found out."

"What?"

"That his information is worthless. Something wasn't right, so he became suspicious. He had a mind like that."

"Tommy?"

Melnikov nodded. "A suspicious man."

"Of you, maybe."

"Me, certainly. That was his job. And now of Jianu. The minute Jianu sees this, Tommy's dead. He's a fantasist, Jianu, but good at protecting himself."

"A fantasist. Of course, that's exactly what you'd want us to think."

"But you won't. You'll believe him. Whatever he says. A good thing for us, in fact. This has been discussed. Let the Americans have him — believe his lies."

"But you want him back."

"A question of discipline. In the end, more important. A man who betrays?" He shook his head. "He dies," he said flatly. "And he will."

"Still Stalingrad."

Melnikov peered at him, not expecting this, but decided not to respond. "So, is that an answer?" he said, walking away.

"What was that about?" Georg said, apprehensive. "Such talk. What, Stalingrad?"

Leon turned to him. "He shot his own men. The ones the Nazis didn't get."

"For defeatism. Disloyalty to the Party." An automatic response, then, avoiding Leon's eyes, "He was a hero in the war."

"So was Hitler. To millions. It depends where you sit. Christ, Georg. You brought him to Lily's?"

"She asked me to bring him."

"Someone like that?"

Georg shrugged. "She arranges meetings. That's what her parties are. So people can meet."

"And who wants to meet him?"

"I don't know. You give your old friend too much credit. Would they tell me?" He looked up, a faint smile, a peace offering. "Please, such things. You know where I sit. I'm a Marxist."

"He isn't. He's a thug. Or can't you tell the difference anymore?"

Georg took a step back. "You're upset. He

said something?"

"Do you know what he is? You must, running errands for him."

"Leon."

"Part of the dialectic, is that it?"

"To accept contradictions? Yes."

"He threatened to kill me. I'm your friend. How do you reconcile that one?"

"Threatened you?"

"He also seems to think I'll do anything if he waves a dollar bill in my face. Where'd he get that idea? You? Did you tell him he could buy me?"

"Buy. Some information comes to you. A piece of luck. Why shouldn't you profit from that?"

"My fucking four-leaf clover." He looked over. "Buy, Georg. You made the same offer. It must be what you think."

"He asked me to. Not such a nice character. As you say. So I did." For a second neither said anything, a willed slowing down.

"Why do you still do it?" Leon said finally. "People like that."

"He's nothing," Georg said. "But the war — I wanted to help." He looked up. "Didn't you?"

"Help who? That country in your head?"

Georg's face went slack.

266

"It's not Russia, the one up there," Leon said. "It's not real."

"Maybe to me," Georg said quietly.

"He is, though. And the people he's killed. That's what it is there now."

Georg stared at his drink. "Not here," he said, a finger to his temple. "You don't know how it was. How much we were going to do. You know I knew Rosa? Luxemburg? The current of history, that's what she said we had. We could sweep away —" He stopped. "Then they came, the Melnikovs. Maybe they were always there. I knew after Trotsky. But the idea, to keep that alive — So was it right? I don't know. But it's too late now. To find another one." He paused, then finished his glass. "Don't be offended. It's not personal."

"You were the first friend we had in Istanbul."

Georg put his hand on Leon's arm. "And I'm the only one who's changed?"

Leon said nothing, suddenly aware again of the voices around them, the Turkish musicians playing in one of the alcoves.

"It was different before," Georg said. "Everything was different. Now, what's the same? Maybe Anna. Only she's the same."

Leon moved his arm, the name like some physical intrusion, separating them. The noise of the party seemed to get louder.

"You should take her home," Georg said, his voice an echo of Melnikov's, the same bait, what they'd agreed.

Leon stared at him, white hair and apple cheeks, caught now too, everyone different, except Anna.

"Where would I get the money?" he said, still staring, until Georg looked away, embarrassed.

He walked across the big room to the garden entrance, a low-railed seating area with divans and an arched ceiling glowing with mother-of-pearl. Two men smoking a water pipe looked up, waiting until he passed before they started talking again.

The garden was colder than he expected. He lit a cigarette, looking back at the bright, busy house. People passing in and out of the dining room, standing with meze plates, servants with trays of glasses, flutes of champagne, fruit juices for the observant. One of Lily's parties. Where you could arrange an import license or plant a story in *Hürriyet* or hint at an arrangement outside official channels. They'd had a special excitement during the war, Germans across the room, drinking the same wine, British officers just in from Alexandria, Romanians who seemed to belong nowhere, buying and selling. He wondered who wanted to meet Melnikov, say something over a champagne glass that couldn't be said in an office, but Melnikov had disappeared, swallowed up in the crowd.

The old parties had seemed more frivolous, flashbulb occasions for the newspapers, but maybe they'd always been the same, little marketplaces, people bargaining, Leon too naïve to notice. Both of them naïve, relieved to be out of Germany, the flowers and soft Bosphorus night part of a larger happiness. Inside, a skirt rushed by one of the dining room windows, and he saw Anna's dress, the one she'd bought for that first party. "How do I look?" Pleased with herself, buoyant, thinking the dress was a success, when it was really the shiny skin, just being young.

"Everyone is so nice," she'd said, "don't you think?"

"They like a new face."

They were standing by an umbrella pine, the air heavy with fresh resin.

"And you? Not so new to you."

"No," he said, putting his hand up to her cheek, just brushing it.

She leaned into his hand, a cat's movement. "Oh, it's wrong to be so happy."

"No, it isn't."

"Think of my parents."

"They'll get out."

"Buying dresses. Going to parties. Champagne. Who gets to do these things now?"

"You do," he said, stroking her cheek.

"Isn't it terrible? I'm so happy." She looked up at him. "I don't want anything to change. And it will."

"What?"

"Things. Everything changes." She looked up, a smile. "Maybe not you. So stubborn. So that's lucky, yes?" she said, her voice throaty, a German inflection, something she would always have, like a fingerprint. She looked back toward the party. "How does she know so many people?"

"Her husband's rich. That makes you a lot of friends."

"No, they like her. You can tell."

Everyone charming then in their new eyes, the room dancing with light. Maybe they simply hadn't been aware of it, the quiet introductions, the plotting, any of it. Just the sound of dresses swishing, voices spilling out, lapping at the garden.

"It's really true? She was in the harem? To meet someone like that."

"You could be in a harem," he said, his face closer, already wanting to go home, those days when they couldn't get enough of each other.

"Oh, a dancing girl. With those pants you can see through. Me, a *hausfrau*." She looked at him, eyes shining. "Frau Bauer. What if you had never come to Germany?"

"You'd have found someone else."

"No. I'd have waited."

"Yes?"

She nodded. "I'd have waited."

For an instant, the memory was so real that he felt her breath on his face. He dropped the cigarette. Before all the luck had run out. But maybe it hadn't, not all of it. Isn't that what Georg called it, a piece of luck, meaning something else? Turn the board around. Tommy was gone and no one knew. One word, an address to Melnikov, and Alexei would disappear and no one would know that, either. Money in the bank, a fresh start, for a man not worth saving. A fresh start for Anna. Maybe a chance for her to come back. And Leon still lucky, in the clear, while Frank turned the consulate inside out, every trail getting colder. None of them leading to Leon. He moved the men around the board in his head, looking for the flaw. A straight play, no piece lurking on the side. Except Melnikov, who would know and use that to put Leon in check, another Georg, his man now, cheap at the price.

"A penny for your thoughts."

He turned to the house, his vision hazy, out of focus.

"All right, a Turkish lira," Kay said. She was leaning against the doorjamb, watching him, elbow tucked in, holding a cigarette, its smoke curling up past her face. "Two liras?"

He smiled, back now. "Not worth it. How long have you been there?"

"Where do you go? When you go off like that?"

"I was just thinking about Lily's parties. The way they used to be."

"They were different?" she said, walking over to him.

"Not really, I guess. They just seemed different."

"Everyone was younger," she said, a gentle tease.

He dipped his head. "That, and the way they spent. Buckets of caviar then."

"You could have fooled me," Kay said, glancing back at the party. "I had no idea she was down to her last nickel. I mean, my god, a fountain in the middle of the living room."

"*Sofa,*" he said then, seeing her expression, "the main hall." He nodded to a seating area. "I guess that's where we got the word.

Usually there'd be a brazier in the middle, for heat. Fountain out in the garden. Whoever built this was showing off. The layout's traditional, though. You'd be received in the *sofa.*" He gestured with his hand, a tour guide. "And mostly you stayed there. But if you were a favored guest, you'd go there, into the *selamlik,* the men's quarters."

"And the women?"

"The other side," he said, pointing. "Where the dining room is now. See the alcoves around the main room? That's where you sat. No furniture, not like this anyway. All the chairs. It's a hodgepodge now. Like Istanbul. It can't decide what it wants to be."

Kay stared at the house. "I used to feel that sometimes, didn't you?" She looked at him. "No, I guess not. Not you. Men. I used to hate it, when I was little. 'What do you want to be when you grow up?' "

"What did you say?"

"Oh, nurse, mostly. You had to say something or they wouldn't leave you alone."

"But what did you want?"

"What did I want?" she said. "To be married, I guess. I wanted to be safe."

"So you got what you wanted," he said, a question.

"Yes." She looked up at him. "And what

273

did you want to be?"

"I don't know. What do kids want? Something exciting." He looked over. "Not safe. Well, and safe at the same time."

"Yes." She drew on the cigarette, her eyes still on him, some conversation she was having with herself.

"You enjoying the party? Don't let Lily wear you out."

She shook her head. "I feel like it's someone else, not me. Everybody making a fuss."

"Somebody new."

"Meaning it won't last? I don't care. I have to go back anyway. Put away my new dress. Not that you noticed. Just like Frank. I wear a dress like this and you don't even notice."

"I noticed," he said, looking at the open neckline.

She turned her head away and dropped her cigarette. "I didn't mean like that." She hesitated. "Maybe I did," she said, looking back at him. "Anyway, you're not Frank, are you?"

"No."

"No," she repeated, still looking. "I can say things to you. I don't know why. And then I can't," she said, her voice running out.

"What?"

"Before. I was standing there and all I

could think —" She stopped, then took a breath and put her hand on his sleeve. "Do something for me." Her eyes green again in the light from the house, darting across his face.

He looked at her, waiting, aware of her hand, the warmth of her, then felt her reach up, pulling his face down to hers. Her mouth just brushed his, a soft pressing, testing, then opened to him, a sudden urgency, as if he were going to be taken away. He put his hand behind to draw her closer, surprised at his own response, alive to her, feeling her down the length of his body. When he started to move away, she held his face to hers again, lips still open, their mouths wet now, excited. They pulled away at the same time, out of breath, staring. Not just a kiss in the garden, neither of them talking, Leon hard.

He moved first, reaching for his handkerchief and slowly wiping the lipstick from his mouth, his eyes still on hers, some line crossed. No need to do it again, neck like kids. She reached over, taking the handkerchief, daubing a spot at the corner of his mouth, intimate, the way people were with each other after sex.

The noise of the party inside seemed farther away, the air in the garden still, broken only by night sounds, rustlings. He put away his handkerchief, glancing through the French windows. A few people passing, talking to one another, Dr. Obstbaum standing, looking straight at them. Leon felt the blood pulse through him, a rush of shame. Then Obstbaum turned away, even more embarrassed, as if he could tell, more than a kiss and now none of them safe.

"What is it?"

"Somebody I know."

"Did he see?"

"I think so."

"Well —" she said lightly, wanting it to pass, looking at him again.

"My wife's doctor."

"Oh," she said, physically backing away, some spill spreading toward them.

"I'm sorry," Leon said. "I mean, in public. To embarrass you like that."

"He doesn't know me. He knows you," she said. "Anyway." She came closer. "It was my idea."

"Still."

"Still," she said, looking at him, eyes brown now, only flecks of green.

"We'd better go in," he said.

"In a minute. Just stay for a minute." Letting the air settle around them, holding on.

"Look —" he started.

276

"I've never been unfaithful to Frank," she said, her voice flat, so that he wasn't sure what she meant, how to respond.

"There you are." Lily's voice from the steps. "Don't hide. Everyone wants to meet you."

"Everyone *has*," Kay said, smiling, a quicksilver moment, Leon a beat behind.

Lily came out toward them. "A tryst in the garden," she said, teasing. "Really, Leon. Like a play."

"My fault," Kay said. "I wanted a cigarette. You know how people are — a woman smoking."

"Mm, look at them," Lily said, turning her head to the party. "Stealing husbands. The silver too. Yes, you'd be surprised. But smoke and they're offended." She turned back to Leon. "*Am* I interrupting something?"

"Would that stop you?" he said, smiling, but still shaken. Do something for me.

"Of course not. If I am, then it's a reputation at stake," she said, having fun, watching them.

"Not yet," Kay said easily. "Just a cigarette."

"What happened to your Russian?" Leon said, moving somewhere else. "Bringer of caviar."

"Yes, I know, dreadful. But important now. Not very *distingué,* though, are they, the new ones? Remember the Germans? Of course, terrible people, but the consul was charming. Four languages. Not like the Japanese. You remember, Leon? Two of them. Never a word. Not one. Bowing only. Then like birds, picking at the food, making little sounds."

Kay laughed. "And how were the Americans?"

"Oh, serious. They're always serious."

"Always?" Leon said, half listening.

"Always. They want to save the world. You have to be serious for that."

"The Russians are serious," Leon said. "What do they want to do? Or didn't Melnikov say?"

Lily shot him a look. "Everybody knows what they want to do," she said, then turned to Kay, light again. "You see? Even Leon. Serious. I had such hopes."

Kay nodded, smiling. "But not as bad as they are in Ankara. Not yet," she said to Leon.

He glanced back. Something different in her voice, private. Could anyone else hear it?

"No," Lily was saying. "So why now at the consulate?" She poked his shoulder gently. "What does it mean?"

"Just filling in."

"Yes? They say you're a detective now."

"Who says?"

"On dit," Lily said, brushing this away. "And have you found him yet? The killer?"

"No."

"No suspects?"

"Your new guest is everybody's favorite," he said, motioning toward the dining room. "At the consulate anyway."

"But how could it be? He wasn't even in Istanbul that night."

"How do you know?"

"Oh, people say things. They think I don't hear. You know, at Yildiz — you learned to listen. Every sound. A long time ago, but it's a lesson you don't forget."

"What else are they saying?"

Lily waved her hand. "Gossip. That's why I ask you. But you don't tell me. So come. Before people talk. I don't care for myself. Refik can't hear anymore. But Mrs. Bishop —"

"Refik was your husband?" Kay said.

"Yes. And jealous too. *Ouf.* I think it amused him. Some men are like that. They think every man is —"

"Every man probably was," Leon said.

"But was I interested in them? Never. Of

course he knew that. Maybe he thought it flattered me. To be jealous."

"You were in love with him?" Kay said.

"What a question," Lily said, suddenly tentative, surprised at this. "Certainly. But love — it's not always so reliable, you know? It changes. But with us there was also a debt. I owed him everything, my life. How could there be anyone else? He rescued me."

"Literally?"

"Oh, a long story. Not for a party. Leon, you must know this, how Refik found me. After the harem."

"Only that he did."

"Tell me," Kay said. "Do you mind?"

Leon glanced at her, eager, wanting to know. A kiss he hadn't expected. He looked over her shoulder, unsettled. In the same garden. But not the same, just a few pines. The other trees pollarded, cut back for the winter, the laburnum and chestnuts only in his head, in the past.

"Mind?" Lily was saying, delighted to have an audience. "Well, everybody wants to know about the harem. What was it like? Something romantic. But it wasn't like that. The house in Yildiz, nothing to do. Games, with the other girls. What did we learn? How to act. How to dress. And what good was that when it was over? People don't ask that, what happened after. Nobody thought. After they sent Abdul Hamid to Salonica, there we were and no one knew what to do with us. Hundreds of girls, some children. So they took us to Topkapi. It was the first time I'd ever been there. So damp. At least Yildiz had been warm. And then they sent messengers to all the villages where we'd been born — come and get your daughters, take them home. And some did. Farmers, and their daughters are dressed like — well, you can imagine the kind of clothes you wore for the sultan, beautiful, and now they're going back to the farm. Useless for work. Some didn't want to go. What would happen? Make yogurt, be married off to some ox. So they'd cry, but of course they had to go. The fathers would sell their jewelry, and that's the last they'd see of Istanbul. Now the fields. If they were still virgin, maybe a marriage in the town, somebody who liked good manners. If not, not. Any marriage that could be arranged. The jewelry would make a bride price. And that was the end of the harem for them."

She stopped, catching herself. "I don't know, maybe some of the girls were happy to see their families again. There must have been some, yes? But I didn't see it. Just the crying. In *carts* sometimes, they drove away

281

in carts. In Istanbul. Behind veils, of course, but you could tell they were crying.

"And these, you know, were the lucky ones. Someone came for them. The rest of us, we'd think, why doesn't my family come? Maybe they moved from the village. Maybe they never heard the messengers. Maybe this, maybe that. But what you thought was, they don't want me. And now what? We couldn't stay at Topkapi forever. The government didn't want to keep us, the expense. What happens to a girl in Istanbul who knows — what? how to make herself attractive? Galata, one of those houses, what else? If you were a virgin, they could sell your first night. Money to them. After that, you were just in the house, one of the — well, you know what that was. That's what I thought would happen to me. They'd lock me up in one of those houses until they could sell my first night. And then the rest. Who knows what it's really like? Just things you hear. Maybe it's worse. And then I was rescued."

She looked up at Kay. "Not Refik, not yet. The first rescue was Nevber, one of the girls. Her parents had died but they had friends who came for her, to adopt her, and she said, please, would they take me too. I don't think they wanted to, one daughter was all they could afford, but Nevber said they should take me as a servant. I could do housework, whatever they liked. A servant, but I wouldn't be put out in the streets, and you know they were all right. A lot of work, but a place to live. This was in Izmir. Jews, so I always felt a debt to that," she said to Leon. "That's why I helped Anna, when she needed money for the boats. And when Nevber married and left the house, they kept me. Not a daughter, not a servant, something in between. But there wasn't money to arrange a marriage. So what future? And then, Refik. Some business and he comes to the house and he sees me. A Cypriot. What happens between people? Do we know? I don't."

"No," Kay said. "It just happens."

Leon looked at her, mouth slightly open, deep in the story. Do something for me. Reaching up to him.

"So it happens for him," Lily said. "Why, I don't know. And a few days later, he's back, and then back again and they tell me he wants to marry me. No bride price, no family, never mind. Not some arrangement, a girl in a room — they would never have agreed to that. Marriage. So my first night was with my husband, not some house in Galata." She moved her hand toward Kay.

"Love? Not then. But the debt began. And everything that happened after." She extended her arm to the *yali*. "The life we had. You know in the harem, you want to be *gözde,* one who's noticed. Abdul Hamid never did, I was too young. But Refik did. I was *gözde* to him. I sometimes think what would have happened if they'd kept the harem. Become a *kadive* to Abdul Hamid? An old, crazy man. Maybe now I'd even be *valide.*" She shook her head. "But never have this life. Never see Paris, anywhere. So it was lucky for me, Refik. Better than the sultan."

"*Gözde,*" Kay said, trying to pronounce it, still in the story.

"Yes. 'In the eye.' And it was true, I was. So later, when there were other women, I'd think, well, they're — women. But I'm the one in his eye."

"You didn't mind if —" Kay began.

"Yes, at first it's terrible. You think it's the end of the world. But you know, the world doesn't end. It just becomes something else. I remember when the Ottomans finally left — the last ones, the household, children, grandchildren — I went to Sirkeci to see it. I knew some of them from the old days, so I was curious. They put them on the Orient Express — one way — and this woman at the station, maybe a servant, tears and wailing. It's the end of the world. And this is 'twenty-four when Kemal Pasha is making a new Turkey. So, whose end? Well, listen to me. Who talks like this? Old women." She put her hand on Leon's upper arm, patting it. "Don't make trouble with my Russian. You know everyone comes to my house."

"When did he die? Your husband," Kay said.

"Before the war. A few months after Kemal. People said it broke his heart. They were so close."

"Kemal —"

"Atatürk," Leon said.

"Another lion," Lily said, without irony. "Now come. Have something to eat. Hacer has been cooking all day. Ah, there's Ivan."

Leon followed her glance through the doors to Melnikov, head bent in conversation with Colonel Altan.

"He's found a friend," Leon said. "Maybe he's a better mixer than we think."

"Oush," Lily said, a behave-yourself sound. "And now Georg. Always when he's not wanted."

She moved toward the doors, intercepting him before he could reach Melnikov, and led him to the dining room, gliding, a sequence of perfect dance steps. Why? So

285

Melnikov and Altan could talk? The meeting she'd arranged? Melnikov seemed to be doing most of the talking, Altan simply taking him in, barely nodding, his eye now over Melnikov's shoulder, catching Leon's, just a flicker, then back, everyone noted.

"What a story," Kay said. "Did you ever meet him, the husband?"

"Yes," Leon said, still trying to watch Melnikov.

"And was she? His *gözde?*"

"Mm. What she didn't say is that she was fourteen when she caught his eye. So you wonder what he was seeing."

"Fourteen?"

Leon nodded. "It takes some of the romance out of it, doesn't it? But Lily made it last. And now look. The rumor was that she caught Atatürk's eye too."

"And?" Kay said, intrigued.

"I doubt it. Refik lent the treasury a lot of money in the early days, and they really were friends."

"And he had his Russian dancers."

Leon smiled. "And then some. Of course, Lily loves to keep the rumor going. Part of her myth."

"It's all made up?"

"No, no, it's true. Refik was crazy about her."

"And a few others."

"No, only her. The others didn't matter."

"Do you think that's possible? An affair that doesn't matter?"

"I don't know."

She looked up, ready to joke, then met his eye. "I think it would have to, somehow," she said, her voice steady. "Unless both of them agreed that it wouldn't. Just be something that — happened. Something you could walk away from after. No harm to anybody."

He waited a minute. "You don't mean that."

"Why not? The good wife?" she said wryly.

"Aren't you?"

"Yes," she said, looking away. "So what am I doing? Why you? I don't even know that. How do people do this? Give a room number?" She shook her head. "I am a good wife. So say good-night, Kay, and thank you for the party." She stopped. "But I thought that. What would it be like?"

"With me."

She lowered her head. "God, look at your face. I know. I'm embarrassing you. Bored wife. Away from home. Lily's right, in the garden, like a play. No moon, though, at least give me that. I haven't gone completely corny."

He took her elbow, leaning closer. "Stop." Aware of her again, even a simple touch.

"Just pretend I had too much to drink, all right? And tomorrow I'll be myself again. Not say things like that." She looked up. "I never did before, for what that's worth. To anyone."

A silence, both of them just looking, night sounds behind, glasses tinkling.

"So," she said, moving her arm. "We'd better go inside. Before you say anything. Make it worse. There's that man who was talking to Frank yesterday," she said, spotting Altan. "He's always around." Talking, just to fill up space, then stopping, turning back to Leon. A small smile. "It wasn't all me, though, was it? Maybe we both wondered, a little."

"Mrs. Bishop," Altan said, leaving the terrace step. "Murat Altan. We met at the funeral."

Again the thin moustache until he stepped into the light.

"Yes, I remember," Kay said.

"Mr. Bauer," Altan said, nodding.

"I was just taking Mrs. Bishop in. It got chilly all of a sudden."

"The Bosphorus is like that," Altan said.

Which meant what? Did anything show in his face? Kay a little breathless, but that

288

could be the cold.

"You'll excuse me?" Altan was saying to her. "A quick word with Mr. Bauer?"

"I was just getting a wrap," she said, sounding relieved to get away.

"Mr. Bishop has gone back to Ankara?" Altan said to Leon, watching her go inside. "A courtesy, to escort her."

"Frank asked me to."

"Ah," Altan said, his eyes moving with some private amusement but his face blank. "Part of your new job?"

"No job. Just helping out until they send a replacement."

"It makes one wonder," Altan said, "what assignments they thought had prepared you for this."

"I think the biggest qualification was not having any. Frank wanted someone new. Outside the consulate."

"Put the cat with the pigeons. Well, an idea. Assuming he can rely on you." He glanced again toward Kay's back.

"Frank tells me we're working together. Emniyet, I mean."

"We cooperate with everybody. But yes, a special case this one. The elusive Mr. Jianu. So, my new colleague, what do you think?"

"Officially or personally?"

"They're not the same?"

"Personally, I think he's dead."

"You do? I doubt that."

"That he's dead?"

Altan nodded. "And that you think so."

"Why not dead?"

"By whose hand? His own? Jianu? Not, I think, the suicide type. The Russians? They would be the first to tell the world, a great feather in their caps. A spit in your eye — is that exact? And they are looking for him."

"Is that what Melnikov said? Is that why you wanted to talk to him?"

"Well, he talked. I listened. Not a subtle man. Would he pretend to look, if they had him?" He shook his head. "He would gloat. And the Americans? Making demands in Ankara. Extra men at the ports, at the border. Such expense. But of course we have to do it. So, not dead."

"Extra men?" he said, trying to keep his voice steady.

"You insist," Altan said, a waiter's nod.

"But you can't cover the whole coast."

"You think he would leave in a rowboat? It's possible, I suppose. Depending on who is helping him."

"Helping."

"He can't speak Turkish. Even Jianu would need help here."

"Any idea who?" Leon said carefully, feeling the familiar twitching at the back of his neck.

Altan gave a listless shrug. "He came to Turkey during the war. Perhaps someone he met then."

"He came here? Istanbul?"

"Not here. Ankara once. Edirne twice," Altan said, familiar with the records. "Government business. Or so his papers said. Only a day each time. A courier, perhaps," he said, glancing up at Leon. "So maybe a friend from the old days. We are checking the Romanians here. A long job, more men."

"But he can't go back to Romania."

"No. So where then? If he went east, it would have to be by train, easy to check. The drive is too long to risk. He would be seen. And Baghdad for Jianu? Not so attractive, I think. I would say Greece. He made trips to Edirne. The first stop coming from Romania, but also from Greece, so maybe some Greek business those trips, old colleagues. And in Greece he might be useful. The Greeks are fighting their own communists. He might have information he could sell to them — now that he's not selling it to you. It's true as you say, we can't control the whole coast, so many places. But where would the boat be going? One of the islands, then Piraeus most likely. Then it's my old friend Spiro's problem." He shook his head, pretending to be amused. "A man who works for the Germans and now for the Greeks — he must have something on everybody. Who better to find him?"

"Works for the Greeks how?"

"State security. I thought it best to alert them. If Jianu tries to cross the border — by road, train — we have him. But if he somehow manages it, the little boat, then Spiro. Personally, I hope he does. Let the Greeks have him."

As Altan spoke, Leon saw the border guards checking cars at Edirne. There'd be photographs now, the Emniyet forced to supply them, pressured by the embassy. Conductors, ticket offices, a net flung over Turkey. Greeks waiting on the other side. Watching the docks at Piraeus. Passenger lists from Rhodes, Chios. Even assuming that could be arranged. He hadn't imagined anything beyond a few hours' drive, sleepy Edirne guards glancing at Enver Manyas's new papers and waving them through. His chest tightened.

"There's something wrong?" Altan was saying, peering at him.

"Just thinking. But the Greeks would hand him back."

Altan sighed. "No doubt. The police here want him for murder. Why would the Greeks protect him? So, back. But then neither of you get him. We do."

"Melnikov wouldn't like that."

"Neither would your Mr. Bishop. And who's in the middle?" He looked at Leon. "Much better, you know, if one of you do find him. The police? They'd put him on trial and that is a trial no one will want to have. Consider the testimony. What it might be."

"But if we found him, we couldn't get him out now. Past your blocks."

Altan nodded. "You would have to consider an alternative solution," he said smoothly, polite conversation, only his eyes hard, making the point.

Leon stared back. "We don't do things that way."

Altan raised an eyebrow but said nothing.

"Melnikov would, though," Leon said. "If he finds him, your problems are over."

"But he won't find him."

"Why not?"

"He has no idea what to do. A simple man. It makes no sense to him. So he looks to Emniyet to do it."

"That's why the chat?"

"He's disappointed. Impossible for a man

293

to disappear. We must be working for the Americans. And so on," he said, idly waving his hand. "It's always a question of blame with them. It's the way they think. No human factor."

Leon looked at him, waiting.

"You don't find it's usually the case?" Altan said. "There's a logic and then someone upsets it. Why? A personal motive. Why did Jianu run? Why does someone help? To sell him? Old comrades, a loyalty? Something else. So you look for that. Melnikov doesn't. Things are this way. If not? A correction is needed, someone at fault. You talk to him, you see his character. A great believer in the rational." He shrugged. "But look how they live. They kill their own people — that makes sense to them. Better to bend a little." His lips turned up. "The Ottoman way. So we've promised to do our best."

"This what you wanted to tell me?"

"Not tell. Just to talk. Get to know your character. Not so easy as Melnikov." He took a card from his breast pocket. "And to give you this. You can reach me at this number if you need to meet. Not at the consulate. Melnikov would hear — so quick to take offense. Somewhere neutral. A hotel. A social gathering. Like this."

"Why would we need to meet like that?"

"Mr. Bauer, we are working together. If you do find him, you will need our help."

"To kill him?"

"To get him out. I thought that was the alternative you preferred. So, a cooperation. Of course, if Melnikov gets him, or Spiro, then my hands are tied. You will keep me informed? Your progress?"

"I thought you already knew everything that happens at the consulate."

"Not everything." Altan smiled. "You have a suspicious nature. Maybe Mr. Bishop was right in his choice." He nodded. "Use your home telephone, please. We may not be the only ones with ears at your consulate."

Leon stood for a few minutes looking down at the card, the noise of the party rising and falling at his back. A direct line to the Emniyet, something that would have seemed surreal a few days ago. He thought of the meeting he and Anna had had with the Gestapo before she had been allowed to leave, the usual summons to Prinz-Albrecht-Strasse, just a formality, all the exit papers in order, but his throat catching the whole time, feeling the sweat under his armpits. Now suddenly on that side of the desk, part of Atatürk's secret army. Working together. You will keep me informed?

He put the card back in his pocket, staring at the night garden, the main axis outlined with flickering candle lanterns, but the other paths dark. You had to squint to see them. He replayed the conversation to see how Altan had steered it, but it began to overlap with Melnikov's. We will find him. But he won't find him. Frank somewhere in the background too, all of them flailing, like the people in the water when the *Bratianu* sank, all reaching for him, he could see the hands outstretched, strong enough to pull him under. Protect yourself. Listen to what mattered: the border was being watched and the Greeks were waiting. Not Edirne. A new plan.

"Leon, it's too rude. Hiding out here. You're supposed to be meeting people." Lily standing behind him, holding two glasses, champagne the color of her hair.

"They seem to be finding me," he said, seeing Altan talking by the fountain.

"Yes," Lily said, following his look. "What's he like? Halit brought him. Old friends, apparently, I don't know how."

"Friendly," Leon said, taking the glass she held out to him. "A big improvement on your Russian anyway."

"So everyone says. I think one time only for him, it's enough. We'll have to find another Russian. Some *chargé d'affaires* who doesn't frighten people. So, my old friend," she said, shifting her voice lower and taking a sip. "What are you going to do now?"

A question that seemed part of the conversation in his head. "I don't know," he said to the air.

"You don't know?"

He looked out at the lanterns. Extra men at the border. "No," he said, then turned, realizing she meant something else, her eye to the dining room.

"She's talking to özmen from *Hürriyet.* You know what that means. She says one thing and he prints another and your consul's in a rage. Why did you say that? I was misquoted. It's always the same."

"The society column? The consul won't even notice."

"That's where you're wrong," Lily said, holding up a finger. "The front page, maybe not. But everyone reads özmen."

"I guess," Leon said, drinking. "All right."

"No, don't go. A minute. I never see you. Anyway, the damage is done."

"And maybe she's more careful than you think."

"Ooh la. With özmen. So tell me," she said, lowering her voice again. "What don't you know?"

"I was thinking before — the first time I

came here. Spring. Remember? A long time ago."

"Not so long."

"Long enough. I don't even look the same."

"Well, it doesn't matter for a man. They look — how they look. For women, it's something else." She reached up, grazing her fingers over his temple. "Some gray, but the same. I remember. So curious, both of you. So many questions. With Georg. He said you had good manners. For an American."

Leon smiled.

"A compliment, from him," Lily said. "Only the Germans had manners. And music. *Kultur.* I think he still believes that, even after everything. Anyway, men don't get old," she said, moving on. "So it's not that. Some other trouble. I know you a little. When you think I'm not looking, I see you're worried. This new work maybe."

"What do you mean, worried?" Reading his face like a map.

"*Inquiet.* The way people look when they're late."

"Running out of time," Leon said. Hours to the border, now closed. He caught himself, and made a forced grin. "There. Better? All the time in the world."

She smiled, indulgent, playing along, then looked at him. "And how much is that? If we knew. The Hindus think we come back as something else. A bug."

"If you're bad. You can also go up the scale."

"Well, up, down, what does it matter? All nonsense. No one comes back." She pointed up. "No garden in the sky, either. This one, that's all there is."

"Is that what you learned in the harem?" he said, teasing.

"No, from Refik," she said, serious. "Who knows how much time? Better to use it, no?"

He said nothing, waiting to see where she was going.

"You know what else they believe, the Hindus? *Seti.* The husband dies, the wife throws herself on his cremation fire. A lot to ask, don't you think? To follow the other one? Who would ask such a thing? Not Refik. Any of us." She looked at him. "So why are you out here? Are you waiting for her permission? To keep living?"

Leon stood silent, feeling heat rise in his face.

"You know, I thought once, it could be me. We're easy together. And you look. A woman always knows when a man does that. But it's this one, I think. There's something there." She touched his arm. "We're alike this way. When Refik was alive, there was only him. No one else. But life goes on."

Leon met her look. "Anna's not dead," he said.

She lowered her head, a retreat. "Well, as you like." She patted his arm. "Don't be angry. I didn't mean —"

"I know."

"Come. At least get her away from öz-men."

But neither of them moved, not quite finished.

"It's a kind of *seti*," Lily said. "What you're doing. You know that?"

He looked at her, a moment. Then another moment, so quiet that the sound of the crash inside seemed like an explosion. Glass breaking, splintering, voices stopping, then starting again all at once, like birds rushing to a tree.

"Oh god, the new boy. I told Mustafa he wasn't ready. And try to find good crystal now."

She held up her skirt to walk faster, Leon following. Voices louder, clustered around one of the serving tables in the dining room. Servants ran back and forth to the kitchen, and Leon thought of birds again, the whole room fluttering.

"Let me through, let me through." Dr. Obstbaum shouldered his way into the crowd.

The Turkish musicians, oddly, kept playing, an undertone to all the voices, until one of the servants rushed over to stop them.

"He was just standing here and all of the sudden he grabbed the table. That fast and he's down."

"Careful of the glass."

"Georg!" Lily cried, seeing him now.

He was on the ground, the edge of a tablecloth still clutched in one hand, Obstbaum leaning over, sweeping away shards of glass so he could kneel next to him, frantically opening his tie, Georg's face a bloodless white, the forehead shiny with sweat.

"Call an ambulance," Obstbaum said. "Give him some air." He swung his arm in an arc as a signal for people to step back, leaning closer to check Georg's breathing.

"What is it?" Leon said, kneeling with him, ignoring the glass.

"Heart. An ambulance!" Obstbaum said again to the crowd. Two people raced off, presumably to phone.

But now Georg was moving, shaking his head a little. *"Nein, nein,"* he said, barely audible, spittle in the corner of his mouth, then a rush of German. "Not here, on the Asian side. A German doctor."

"Yes, yes, a German doctor," Obstbaum said in German.

Georg had now opened his eyes halfway, his face still contorted with pain. "Leon," he said, grabbing his hand and squeezing. "A German doctor."

"*Ssh.* Be quiet. Everything's going to be all right." But how could it be? He turned to Obstbaum. "Can we get him to the clinic? Would he survive the boat?"

"I'm not a fortune teller," Obstbaum said, impatient, feeling the pulse in Georg's neck. "If he has another attack —"

"Bebek," Georg said, squeezing again.

Leon turned. "Lily, would you get a boat ready?"

She nodded, leaving, so that Kay suddenly came into view, her arms folded across her chest, as if she'd caught cold, her eyes fixed on him.

"Will he be all right?" Leon said to Obstbaum.

"I don't know. The breathing is better. He should be in the hospital. Here, there, what does it matter? I can go with him if he needs to hear German. Foolishness."

"No, Bebek," Georg said.

"Can I help?" Colonel Altan said, squatting next to them.

Leon shook his head. "When the ambulance gets here, we'll use the stretcher to get him in the boat."

"Can you make the water calm?" Obstbaum said to Altan. "A boat. It's a risk. He needs to lie quietly."

"It's his risk," Leon said, feeling Georg squeeze his hand again, a thank-you.

Altan took out a handkerchief and handed it to Obstbaum for Georg's forehead. "Shall I call the clinic for you? To have them prepare?"

"Yes, thank you," Obstbaum said, then turned to Leon. "I take no responsibility for this. He should go to the hospital here. A few minutes can make a difference."

"Georg?" Leon said.

"Please. The boat. I'll be all right." He tried a weak smile. "Sea air."

Leon looked at the face under the chalky skin, the one he'd always known, mischievous, hunched over his chess set, their first friend in Istanbul. What would happen to the dog? He heard his own voice earlier, baiting, hectoring. He took the handkerchief from Obstbaum and wiped Georg's forehead, drier now, and smiled. "You always get your way," he said.

"Ha."

"Has this happened before?" Obstbaum said.

Georg nodded.

"What medications?"

"Ask Kosterman. In Şişli."

"Do you know him?" Leon said to Obstbaum.

"Yes. I'll call. Keep him quiet, yes? No dramatics. We're not out of the woods with this."

"The boat's here," Lily said, coming up to them. "You want to telephone? Oh, your knee." She glanced down at a bloodstain from the broken glass.

Obstbaum waved this off. "When the stretcher comes — gently. Understand?" he said to Leon, then glanced over at Kay. "There's nothing to do now," he said in general, a kind of dismissal.

Two houseboys came over to sweep the glass so the crowd backed away, drifting across the room, talking again. Kay stood still, fixed on Leon.

"What's happened?" Melnikov, gruff, even the sound of his voice disruptive.

"Something with the heart," Lily said, intervening. "Oh, the ambulance. Please, we have to move."

Georg had heard the voice and now

clutched Leon's hand tighter, drawing him down closer to his face. "You think I'm not a friend to you," he said, almost a whisper.

"*Ssh.* Never mind about that. The ambulance is here."

"No. You have to know. In case —" Georg pulled him closer. "I am your friend."

"I know."

"I never told him. Melnikov."

"Told him what?"

"Sürmeli. The landlord in Laleli. He thanked me for referring you. He thought I sent you to him."

"Georg, later. The stretcher's here."

"No, now. In case. That's how you knew him, remember? He owned the office building. In Beyazit. So when you took the flat — I never told Melnikov. But I knew. Why would you take a flat? A woman, Sürmeli thinks. Not you, a woman in a flat. So I knew. But I never said. Your friend, you understand?" He opened his eyes wider. "I never said."

Leon looked at him, then nodded.

"We have to get him on the stretcher," one of the attendants said in Turkish.

"Georg? You ready?" Leon said.

"So it's safe," Georg said, still somewhere else. "I never said."

"Okay, here we go. Just hold on to me."

305

They lifted him, one smooth, fluid movement, and covered him with a blanket, placing an oxygen tube in his nose. The rest of the guests stood watching as the attendants moved out to the landing, Georg still grasping Leon's hand, Kay following. Obstbaum was waiting in the boat.

"Where's Lily? Here, take his hand," Leon said to Kay, slipping gently out of Georg's grip. "I'll be right back. Hold on to her," he said to Georg. "And behave yourself."

Georg smiled faintly. Obstbaum looked up, uncomfortable, Kay's presence some awkward test of loyalty.

Leon hurried back into the house. The party was now breaking up, people milling around the fountain. A houseboy pointed him to the telephone room, a small study in what had been the *selamlik*. The door was already open and he pushed it wider. Altan was hanging up the phone, turning to Lily, both voices low. Leon froze. Not just talking, intimate, their faces close. A couple. What's he like? she had said. Leon remembered her eyes at the Pera Palas, brushing past him. Now talking just to each other, the way people did in bed. Leon stepped back. How long?

He waited another minute, then knocked. "Lily?"

"Yes, yes, coming," she said, at the door in seconds.

"We're off. Oh —" Taking in Altan.

"These phones," Lily said. "But finally, the clinic. They'll meet you on the other side." Her voice easy, leading them out of the room, as smooth as the attendants lifting Georg. "How is he?"

"The same."

"You don't mind, I come with you?" Altan said as they walked. "There's room?"

"Yes, but now."

"I'll tell Halit," Lily said. "So he won't look for you."

"A pleasure, Madame Nadir. Thank you for the evening," he said politely, as if his face had never been close to hers. "I'm sorry that —"

"Yes, such a terrible thing. Leon, you'll call? Let me know how he is?"

They were at the landing now, being helped in, the boat rocking in the wake of some larger ship, so that everything, even her voice, seemed to be shifting, unsteady. He turned to her. A woman who arranged things. How much did Altan tell her? Faces close, whispering. His old friend, her hair golden in the lamplight. Before he could answer, the boat pulled out onto the dark water.

"Keep the tube in," Obstbaum was saying to Georg. "You need the oxygen."

"On the Bosphorus," Georg said, but closed his eyes, obeying.

The air, in fact, was sharp and fresh. The freighter's wake had passed and the water was calmer, their headlight slicing across the surface, the opposite shore twinkling.

"My father had an attack like this," Kay said, her hand still in Georg's. "He's getting his color back, see?"

"Leon," Georg said, motioning him closer again.

"Don't talk. You have to stay quiet."

"I didn't say," he whispered, his eyes closed. "I didn't say anything to Melnikov."

But he would, his mind filled with it now, brimming, maybe not intending to but letting it slip out.

"What does he mean?" Kay said.

"Nothing. *Ssh.*" Patting Georg's hand to quiet him. Not here. Not anywhere. What if he talked in his sleep, unaware, sedatives loosening the last restraint?

"You are old friends?" Altan said.

"Old. Like a son," Georg said, his voice faint, eyes moist. "I didn't say."

"*Ssh,*" Leon said, brushing the hair off his forehead, soothing a child, feeling Kay watching him.

308

"Kosterman says it's the second time," Obstbaum said, taking Georg's pulse again. "So it's dangerous."

"My father survived two," Kay said.

"But not the third," Obstbaum said, blunt, dismissing her presence.

And the landlord didn't talk only to Georg. A whole neighborhood of friends, eager for news, the sort of gossip Altan's men were bound to pick up. The *ferengi* renting a flat for his woman. Whom nobody had seen. Imagine the expense. A flat, not a hotel. Someone who couldn't be seen. He could almost hear the voices, a sibilant buzzing, Sürmeli smoking a water pipe, the center of interest. If Georg had heard, it would be just a matter of time before someone else did, whether Georg talked or not. Running out of time.

He looked at Kay holding Georg's hand, wisps of hair blowing across her face in the breeze, a nurse's calm. Obstbaum deliberately not looking at either of them. How could he bring her to the clinic, Anna down the hall? Georg was mumbling something again, too indistinct to be heard above the running engine.

"Good. They sent the ambulance," Obstbaum said, seeing it on the quay ahead.

Move Alexei, the sooner the better. Not a

hotel. Somewhere private. He thought of the house he and Anna had rented one month on Büyükada. Pine forests and empty coves, no one else in sight, afternoons just walking and looking at the Sea of Marmara. An easy exile — Trotsky had stayed there — but also a trap, no fast way off the island if someone found out. Better to hide in plain sight, even the Cihangir flat, the last place they'd expect. Unless someone was already watching it. He glanced over at Altan. His new colleague, expecting a report.

"Be careful," Obstbaum said, waiting for the driver to tie up before they lifted the stretcher.

"You think I'll break?" Georg said, then gave an involuntary moan as the stretcher jerked, the last heave up to the quay.

They loaded him into the back of the ambulance. Obstbaum opened the black bag an assistant had brought and took out a syringe, filling it from an ampoule.

"What's that?" Georg said. "Kosterman —"

"Prescribed it. This will pinch. But it'll feel better, the pain. Just keep calm. We'll need to monitor you at the clinic, your rhythm's still irregular."

"But Kosterman —"

"On his way. He'll meet us there." He looked up at Leon, standing at the door. "You coming?"

Kay started toward him, but Leon turned, stopping her. "No, don't wait. It could be all night. I'll just make sure his doctor gets here. Colonel Altan, will you see that she gets home? The Pera."

"But —" Kay started to protest.

"Really. You'd just be sitting in the waiting room." Down the hall. "There's no point. I'm sorry the evening had to —"

"Nobody's fault," she said vaguely, trying not to look wounded.

"I'll call tomorrow," he said. "Let you know how he is."

She looked at him, eyes still puzzled. "Not the best timing, was it?"

"Things just happen sometimes."

She nodded. "And sometimes they don't."

"Now, please," Obstbaum said from inside the van.

Leon climbed up, closing the door behind him. He looked back through the oval window as the ambulance pulled away, Kay in her party dress with Altan, boats bobbing behind them, and for a second he wanted to open the door and jump out, then Georg moaned and when he looked again she had got smaller, too far away.

At the clinic, Georg was put on a gurney and wheeled into one of the medical rooms where nurses attached electrodes to his chest from a bulky machine next to the bed.

"If it gets worse we'll have to move him to a hospital," Obstbaum said. "We're not equipped here —" He looked at his wristwatch. "So where's Kosterman? Şişli's fifteen minutes." He glanced up. "Maybe you'd better wait outside. The less talking the better. We need to keep him quiet."

Anna's room was dark, just the dim nightlight near the door and a thin strip of hall light underneath. She was asleep when he came in, so he tiptoed to the chair. Eyes still closed. Usually she was aware of movement, and he wondered whether they'd given her a sleeping pill, more rest after a day spent not quite awake. Outside the door, the hushed sounds of the clinic at night.

He sat for a few minutes watching the faint movement of her breathing. Did she dream? Melancholia, from the Greek, black bile, what they used to think it was, a gloom spreading through the body, addling the mind. Something you could drain away.

Georg's here, he said, the voice in his head, imagining her listening. A heart attack. Serious. We were at Lily's, at the *yali*.

You know what I thought about? The first time we went there, her garden party. I could hear you. Worried about your parents. You said it was wrong to be so happy. Those words. And I said no, and then — I couldn't remember any more. What we said. It just faded, your voice. It keeps getting harder to remember. Even your face — I see it and then it fades too. The way it looked then, I mean.

He touched his hair. Not just a little gray, Lily's flattery, older, someone else. No one stayed the same. But what happened when everything just stopped? The air still, memory suspended in it, getting fainter. In the garden earlier he'd felt he could hear his own pulse, his senses so alive they seemed to be outside his skin, touching, listening. Now he barely heard the voice in his head, a steady murmur that seemed as far away as that first party. What it must be like to be dead, when you couldn't even hear yourself. Then suddenly a louder voice came in over it, not really talking to Anna anymore, to anyone, just pouring out.

You were the only idea I ever had. To be with you. The way we were at the *yali.* That's all I wanted, to be like that. Not change. But it did. I still don't know why. The child. Then the war. Everything. Sometimes I blame you — and then it's worse. But Lily's right, we're both dying this way. And I don't want to. I see a woman, near Tünel. And it doesn't mean anything. How can something like that not mean anything? Like the lab frogs in school. You could make their muscles twitch, with electricity. Even after they were dead. It's like that. A jolt, but you don't feel anything. Then tonight. I did. I think so anyway.

He shrugged to himself, the voice taking a breath. So what did I do? I sent her away. So I could come here. Sit with you. That was right, wasn't it? The right thing. But I can't even remember your voice — a few minutes and then it goes. I'm not sure anymore what I'm holding on to.

The voice stopped, the sudden quiet a vacuum in his head. He looked over at the bed. Anna lay still, not moving, as if she were holding her breath, waiting. I'm sorry. Listen to me. One kiss and now all this. Like a kid. He paused. But it's true. It's getting harder to remember.

Outside, there were footsteps in the hall, a nurse hurrying past. Kosterman had probably arrived. Why sit here brooding? Check on Georg and leave. Move Alexei. Where? Georg wouldn't be going home to Nişantaşi. Just one night. But there'd be neighbors taking care of the dog — Georg never left her alone. Mihai had a cousin in Kuzguncuk, on the Asian side. A street with old wooden houses and plane trees, as quiet as an Anatolian village. And just as small — everyone would know in an hour. Much safer in an impersonal flat. A cheap hotel, no questions.

There were more steps outside, nurses' shoes, a hospital sound. How many times had he sat with Anna listening to rubber soles and swishing skirts? The sound echoed, back to the other hospital, Anna lying with her hair spread out on the white pillow, not crying, her face drained, facing it.

"We can have another," he'd said, not knowing what else to say.

"Don't give it a name," she'd said, her eyes far away for the first time, something he thought now he should have noticed, but didn't. "If you name it, we won't be able to forget." As if it had existed, had personality, a place in one's heart, all the things that can happen in the first seconds of life.

The hospital listed it as "baby," or "infant," he forgot which, the form tucked away in some box of papers where Anna wouldn't see it. You couldn't lose a child who'd never existed. But she'd known the sex, her boy, and here he was, years later, still in the room with them. All it took was the sound of nurses' shoes.

"You'd better come," Obstbaum said at the door. "He's had another attack." Not waiting for Leon, starting back, talking over his shoulder. "Kosterman's working on him, but he's not responding."

In the room a gray-haired man was pushing down on Georg's chest, kneading it, nurses around him, glancing nervously at a monitor.

"Nichts," he said, but kept pumping, somehow angry, as if Georg were being stubborn.

Another minute, then a quick knowing look from the nurse, and finally his hands stopped. He moved them away slowly, and shook his head.

"He's gone," Obstbaum said, needlessly.

Leon looked down at Georg's face, already different, empty. For a moment the room seemed motionless, stunned by the gravity of death, then nurses began to remove the electrodes, wheel a cart away, cover the body. Kosterman looked at his watch, noting the time, already preparing the certificate in his mind. Leon kept staring. Something you never got used to, no matter how many times you'd seen it, the stillness of a dead body. Not Georg anymore, irretrievable in a second. Not coming back, not in any life, whatever the Hindus imagined.

"There was nothing you could have done," Kosterman said to Obstbaum in German. "Like a bomb." He opened his fingers, mimicking an explosion. "I told him."

"Have you finished?" a nurse said to Leon, holding the sheet, waiting.

Leon nodded.

"There's no family," Obstbaum said to the doctor. He turned to Leon. "Did he ever say anything to you? What he wanted?"

Leon shook his head. "The dog. The neighbors must have her. Someone should make sure. And call Lily," he said, making a list, things to do, a way of not thinking about it. "She'll want to know. She can have someone tell the papers. An obituary — he knew a lot of people. I'll call Vogel at the university. He can arrange a memorial service later."

And then there seemed nothing more to say. Georg disposed of, gone. He wondered suddenly how easy his own death would be — a notice to the Reynolds office, an insurance claim for Anna, Mihai settling the apartment. Maybe a piece in *Hürriyet*. American businessman. Nothing about the trains to Ankara or Tommy or Alexei. Would Anna know he was gone? A paragraph would do it.

Two aides came to wheel the gurney away, and Leon felt people moving around him, busy. Why wasn't everyone standing still, letting it sink in? But they hadn't known him, hadn't just lost something. It was Georg who'd explained about the storks that Sunday when they went out to see the Byzantine walls, a picnic in the shade, looking up at them perched on their high rickety nests. "They migrate south, over Arabia, so the Muslims believe they make the pilgrimage to Mecca every year." Was it true? Did it matter? Anna delighted, smiling. Sandwiches in waxed paper. Beer. The wheeling stopped, the aides looking at him, in the way.

He thanked Obstbaum and started back to Anna's room, then stopped, his feet suddenly lead. Not another vigil, talking to himself about Georg, regretting their last conversation, sneering at his Marxist heaven. Then on the landing, still your friend. Maybe his own form of warning — the landlord was talking, it wasn't safe anymore. But where would be? Hotels with sleepy night clerks checking the *tezkere* Alexei didn't have? What would be open? The Muslim world went home at night, whole sections of the city blacked out in a medieval dark, streetlights like the old torches. Only the Greeks and Armenians and foreigners went out, drinking in noisy *mihanyes*. But eventually they closed too. Even the Taksim Casino went dark, forcing the streetwalkers to lurk by the late-night kebab stalls and the dim lights of the taxi ranks. He stopped.

A simple answer, the obvious overlooked. It wasn't too much to ask. And if it was, there was always Cihangir. But not Laleli anymore, Georg's warning like an omen now.

"What is it?" Alexei said when he opened the door. Dressed, the way he always was, maybe the way he slept, ready to get out in a hurry.

"I'm moving you."

"Something's —"

"No, a precaution. It's time."

"Good," Alexei said, putting out a cigarette and folding up the chess set. "Somewhere better, I hope. The Pera Palas?"

Leon looked up.

"A joke," Alexei said. "One minute. My razor, that's all," he said, heading toward the bathroom.

"I met your buddy Melnikov tonight," Leon said.

Alexei stopped. "Be careful with that one.

A friend of Beria's."

"Meaning?"

"He does what he likes. Kill first. He can afford to make mistakes. Is that why we're moving?"

"No. It's time, that's all. He's still trying to buy you back."

"How much am I worth now?" Alexei said, coming in with a Dopp kit. "Have I gone up?"

"I didn't ask. That everything?"

Alexei put on his jacket and woolen sailor's cap. "You go first," he said, suddenly in charge. "The street that goes to the big mosque. I'll use the back. Give me five minutes. If anything seems wrong, come back here. You forgot something."

"But you'll be out there."

Alexei shrugged. "How far is the car?"

"We're walking."

Alexei looked at him, then took out a gun and put it in his jacket pocket. "The lights," he said, nodding to the switch.

Outside, Leon headed past the high walls of the university grounds. He could hear his footsteps. No one else around. Two men in jellabas and skullcaps, lost in their own conversation. He slowed, giving Alexei time, forcing himself not to look back. You could see the great dome from here, a weak milky

320

light in the square facing the mosque. The night, so clear at Lily's, had turned misty, the cobblestones slick. Alexei would have left by now, slipping through the streets, some route he'd worked out when he should have been inside.

And then he was there, a shadow suddenly turned solid, walking with him, the mosque getting closer, filling the end of the street. Some voices in the square.

Leon felt the hand on his sleeve, Alexei looking back over his shoulder then jerking them off the street, wedging them into an arched doorway on the narrow side street, backs flat against the wood. He took the gun from his pocket and held it, waiting. Leon slowed his breath. No voices, a soft indistinct sound behind, maybe footsteps if you were listening for them. He glanced over at Alexei. His face was rigid, the wool cap covering his short, receding hair, so that the head seemed almost skeletal, like a death mask. As still as Georg had been, and just for a second Leon saw him the same way, already dead. Even if he got him out. Once he said whatever he had to say there'd only be some half existence, listening for sounds. Assuming he got there. Now he was breathing again, fear pumping life back, and Leon could feel his shoulder move and realized they were breathing together, the same adrenaline rushing through them.

Real footsteps now, then a shadow moving down the street, backlit by the streetlamps. It stopped at the side street, as if it were listening too, then started again, a shuffling sound, not trying to be quiet, the shadow weaving slightly. Maybe a drunk. But someone who'd been behind them. They waited, Alexei's gun close to his chest, following the footsteps down to the square until they were out of hearing. Another minute, nobody coming back up the hill to find where he'd lost them, then another to make sure, and Alexei nudged Leon toward the street.

They walked quickly, making up time, still not talking, but Leon felt shaken, the mask still in his mind. Contours of bone, the shape of a head, lifeless. Süleyman's Mosque and its outbuildings bulked up ahead, but all the details were lost in the dark. The old *medrese*, the cylinder burial *türbes*, the leafy courtyard — Leon's dream of Istanbul, where he used to come just to sit, listening to the hum of the prayers inside, now all in shadow, someone's hiding place. The way Alexei saw things. How he had begun to see them too.

He led them past Sinan's tomb and down

the steep streets of broken cobbles littered with clumps of garbage. On Galata Bridge a few fishermen were still tending rods.

"Where are we going?" Alexei said.

"You wanted the Pera. Not far from there."

The lighted cars of the funicular would be a risk, but Alexei was already winded and climbing the hill seemed worse. Leon looked at him on the platform. A man in a wool cap with a duffel, some sailor docked in Karaköy, out for a good time. No one followed them on top.

Marina opened the door in the silk kimono Leon thought she wore only for him.

"It's you," she said, a question.

"Are you alone?"

"It's late," she said, another question, noticing Alexei.

"I need a favor. A bed. For a friend. Just the bed."

She looked past him. "Who is he? He's trouble for me?"

"Just a customer. Who wants to spend the night. You have customers like that, don't you?"

She stared at him.

"I'll give you the going rate."

"What a bastard you are."

"I didn't mean it that way."

"No?"

"You have no idea who he is. He paid for the night, that's all. You can show the money. If anybody asks."

"Who? Police?"

Leon shook his head. "Anybody. But nobody will. One night." He paused. "A favor."

She looked at him, then opened the door. "Don't stand in the hall."

Alexei dumped the duffel bag inside, looking around the room, then at Marina. "Much better," he said.

"What's he done?" Marina said, lighting a cigarette.

"Nothing. He's a customer. That's all you know." He looked down at the kimono, her breasts half showing.

"And you? What have you done?"

"Nothing. I wasn't even here."

"If anyone asks," she finished.

"That's the favor."

She snorted, then turned to Alexei. "There," she said, pointing to the bedroom door.

"I appreciate this," Leon said. He took out his wallet. "How much?"

"I'll let you know," she said, waving the cigarette.

"Then here's fifty. On account." He held

out the bills.

"Fifty," she said, raising her eyebrows. "And it's not police."

"In case you need to show. That he paid."

"You think I'd do this for fifty?" she said, slipping the bills in her kimono pocket.

"Then how much —"

"No, this." She opened her hand to the room, the risk, everything.

He met her look. "Thank you."

Alexei was standing in the bedroom doorway smoking, his eyes half shut, fixed on her. He took off his cap, running his fingers through his flattened hair.

Marina put out her cigarette, then shrugged. "Does he speak Turkish?"

"No. German. A little English."

"All right. Anything special? What does he like?" Her voice wearily matter of fact, taunting him.

"Just the room. I'm not asking you to do that."

"No," she said, raising her eyes to him. "Other things."

The hall light operated on a timed switch but he ignored it, feeling his way instead toward the dim landing. In the dark, the usual wet plaster smell seemed even stronger, feline. He waited at the outside door for a few seconds to see if anyone was in the street, then turned left down the hill for a block and circled back up. No footsteps behind.

In Tünel Square the tram had been turned around and was waiting for the conductor to start, a few passengers slumped in their seats. The whole square seemed motionless in fact, opaque in the misty air, and for a moment Leon imagined them all dead too, the conductor's hand frozen on the controls, every face like Georg's and Alexei's, immobile. He felt his chest squeeze and forced himself to breathe out, a kind of protest. What would happen to him someday. When? Tommy surprised in a second, Georg clutching the table. Alexei jolting himself alert with fear, but already gone.

Leon started for the tram. What you thought about when you were exhausted. But in the doorway he and Alexei had been the same. Get on the tram and go back to Cihangir, watch the ferries, the room as quiet as the clinic. Lily's garden, seeing ghosts, talking to them, receding. Then real eyes, darting across his face. Do something for me, she'd said, then brought his head down.

The conductor rang the bell, waiting for his straggler. Leon grabbed the pole, about to swing up, then stopped, remembering the doorway again, Alexei's mask. He stepped away, waving the tram off, even the sleepy passengers now awake watching him. A scene, something noticed. Five minutes ago he'd been slinking around buildings. Now he walked through the lighted part of the square and into Sofyali Sok, still busy with late-night restaurants. Down to Meşturiyet, not looking behind, loud steps, nothing to hide. At the Pera, he went straight to the elevator. An American in a good suit, somebody who might be staying there. The elevator boy, in a pillbox hat and white gloves, took him up without a question. A birdcage lift, Parisian grillwork and red plush. He walked down the hall, not hesitating, a soft tap, then a louder one.

"Yes?" he heard from inside. A rustling sound, maybe belting a wrapper.

She opened the door, eyes widening. Her hair was down, brushed out, and she had taken off her makeup, her face still a little shiny from the cold cream, but flushing now, real color.

"You came," she said, surprised, then clutched the lapels of her bathrobe. "I didn't think you would come." Her voice slightly out of breath.

"Is that all right?"

She was still holding the door, and he felt

as if he might pitch forward, the momentum that had carried him from the square suddenly stalled.

"My hair —" she said, touching it nervously, a gesture so beside the point that he smiled.

"Your hair?"

She caught his eye but didn't smile back. "I don't know what to say."

"Say, come in." He paused. "Unless you don't —"

"No," she said, shaking her head and opening the door wider.

He stepped into the room. A small lamp by the bed, the lights of the Golden Horn through the window beyond.

"I was reading," she said, just to say something, closing the door and backing against it, as if he had pinned her there. "I've never done this before."

He kissed her, leaning his body into hers, warm. "No?" he said, kissing her again, hands on her now, feeling her body move against him.

"No," she said, breaking away for air.

"So why —" he started, but she had reached up, pulling him down again, her mouth on his, and his head filled with the taste of her, new, not like anybody else.

"I don't know," she said, the words in a

gasp, near his ear.

He leaned down and kissed her neck, smelling the last trace of perfume.

"Just something. When we met. I thought —"

"What?" he said, still kissing her.

"Maybe it's my last chance."

"For what?" he said, raising his head, caught by the words.

"I don't know." She stared at him for another second, then reached over and slid his jacket off his shoulders. "Ask me later."

Then they didn't say anything, kissing in a rush, their breathing louder, ragged, undoing his tie, buttons, still backed against the door, as if they were hiding in a closet, stealing the minutes. He slid off her robe, the shoulder straps of her nightgown, letting it fall from her breasts, then cupping them, bending down to kiss them. Not fleshy like Marina's, just filling his hand, but nipples hard already, all of her taut. One touch and you felt the skin move under your fingers, a string vibrating, little gasps of air over your head.

She pulled the nightgown the rest of the way down, crumpling the silk at her feet, and he reached behind, hands on her cheeks, pulling her toward him, kissing her mouth again, pulling the soft skin even closer, as if he could pull it inside of him. She moved a hand down between them, clutching at his prick, still in his pants, stroking the length of it until they both broke off, out of breath, and he threw off his shirt, starting on his belt, then kissing her again, backing her toward the bed, mouth still on hers, hands on her behind, and then laying her down, snapping off the light, shoes, socks, stepping out of his pants, standing next to the bed looking down at her, naked, just the light from the window. Her skin seemed to be rippling, not still, legs opening to the patch of hair, the lips beneath, already wet to the touch. He moved a finger over it, excited by the wet, some involuntary yielding, and then she reached up, grabbing him and pulling him to her, and he thought he might come then, her eagerness more erotic than anything Marina had ever done.

He moved onto the bed, his prick still in her hand, drawing him into her, not waiting, wanting to hurry too, moving her hand away so he could put the rest in all at once, the skin inside slick with sex, one sliding motion, then the warm softness closing around him. He stopped, dropping to his elbows and kissing her, not wanting to move inside, just feel her holding him, but her skin had begun to ripple again, moving against him, and he started moving too, finding her rhythm, then moving with her, only the movement familiar, the feeling something new, sex with her, not anyone else. She let out a sound, the most private thing there is, something nobody else ever heard, and he put his head near hers, wanting to hear more, the sounds urging him on, making everything go faster, so that he could feel the sweat now, the heat of it, and hear himself panting, his prick swelling with sensation, almost apart from him. When she cried out, he could feel her clenching then going loose, the string snapped, then more sounds in his ears, the wonderful abandon, not caring who heard, still moving with him, as if each thrust set off another release, then another, until finally he could feel it racing up in him, faster, then spurting out, an explosion of pleasure, helpless, leaving every part of him exposed.

He lay motionless for a second, and then he felt his weight on her, the sweat, and the world started seeping back. He rolled off onto his side, his heart still racing, then slowing down, waiting for the deflation that always came, embarrassed, back in himself. But she had turned to him, running her hand along his face, and it wasn't Marina, something else.

"Thank you," she said, so quietly that he thought he might have imagined it.

"No. You," he said, moving his hand now, calming each other, like animals. "I didn't mean to be so fast."

She smiled.

He leaned forward and kissed her, hand at the back of her head. "Next time we'll go slow."

She touched him below. "How much time do you need?"

"Keep doing that." Shifting slightly so that she could take all of him in her hand, hard again, then looking into her eyes. "Where did you come from?" he said, running his hand down her back, wanting to touch her everywhere, as if he could read her skin, know her with his fingers.

She made a little gasp, responding to his hand, a shivering as it crept lower, then fell back, letting him kiss her everywhere, her nipples, then moving below, everything slower this time, unhurried, his mouth moving so slowly that she shuddered when he reached her sex, teasing and kissing it until she was open to his mouth, moving against his tongue, and he went deeper, tasting the inside of her, smearing, until she made a sound, a muffled cry, and reached down with her hands to stop his head. "No, in me," she said, her voice shaking, and pulled him toward her, then in, and this time even that was slower, a rocking, so that when they came, both panting, it wasn't an explosion but an overflowing.

Afterward she lay with her head on his chest, both of them drowsy.

"A chance for what?" he said.

"Hm?"

"You said, ask me later."

She was quiet for a minute. "To have something different, I guess."

"Why me?"

"I liked you. The way you look. Your chin," she said, putting a finger on it.

"That's it?"

"And you're here," she said, leaving his chest, sitting up. "Not Ankara. No complications. Running into each other. Things like that." She got up and went over to the table and picked up a cigarette, the match like a small flashbulb lighting up her naked body. "It's funny, isn't it, how people talk after. No clothes. No secrets. I think I know everything about you. And I don't, really."

Leon said nothing, reaching for a cigarette of his own.

"Why didn't you want me to stay with you at the clinic?"

"There was nothing you could do there. He was — he died. Another attack. You didn't need to be there for that."

"Died?" she said, dismayed. "I'm sorry. You were fond of him."

"Yes."

"I could tell. The way you were with him. So that's one thing I know about you." She looked at him. "One layer." She walked over to the window. "Altan said it was because your wife's there." She exhaled some smoke. "What's wrong with her?" She waited a minute, then turned. "You don't want to talk about her?"

He looked at her bare skin, nothing covered. The way people talked after. He drew on his cigarette, hearing the silence in the room. "She went mad." Something he'd never said out loud before, admitted. Mad, not away.

"Oh," she said. "So what will you do?"

"Do? There's nothing to do. Wait, see if she gets better." He leaned over and stubbed out his cigarette. "So that's her. What else did Altan have to say?"

"He didn't tell me that — what was wrong. Just that she was there."

"Well, now you know."

"So you'll never leave her," she said, her voice neutral. "That makes it easier for me."

"What?"

"I told you, no complications." She was quiet for a minute. "You don't have to worry about that. About anything."

She came over to the bed, sitting next to him.

"So what did Altan talk about?" Leon said.

"Talk about? Frank. He's very interested in Frank. As if I would know anything. So it must be true, what he does. Secret work. He never says, and now a man like Altan asks, so what else could it be? And you, is that what he does with you? Secret work?"

"I'm just filling in for Tommy. At Commercial Corp."

"And that's an answer," she said, raising an eyebrow. "Never mind, I don't care." She reached up, brushing the side of his head. "But no secrets here, all right? I mean in this room. I don't care what you do at the consulate. But not here."

"Frank never says anything?"

"We don't talk like this. It's different." She stopped her hand, dropping it. "Do you want to know about us?"

"No."

"I was a secretary. Not his. When I was growing up, we never had any money, anything extra. And I thought, I won't have to worry about that. I'll be safe."

"And?"

"And I am. Safe." She looked at him. "And I'm here."

He touched her arm. "I should leave soon."

"You don't want to stay?"

"Someone might see."

"My reputation?" she said, amused. "Well. I never had to think about that before."

"Now you do."

"Like a farce? The maid comes in and — oops!" She covered herself with the sheet.

"Not so funny when it happens." He moved his hand to her shoulder, then ran it down to her breast. "You're an embassy wife."

"Not here. Not in Istanbul." She arched her back to the hand stroking her.

"No," he said, leaning his face close to hers.

"No complications here." She lowered her head. "There is, though. One. I didn't expect."

"What?" he said, kissing her ear.

"I said, we could just — walk away. But I don't want to," she said, her voice naked now too. "I thought I could. But I don't want to." She turned to him. "Do you?"

He looked at her, a feeling of pitching

forward, dizzy, then righting himself, sure-
footed. "No."

■ ■ ■ ■

5
ÜSKÜDAR

■ ■ ■ ■

Enver Manyas needed another day, an unexpected delay, but now Leon did too. He'd been awake half the night at the Pera making a new plan, Kay sleeping next to him, one hand on his chest, the reflected lights on the ceiling like plotting points on a map of Turkey. Edirne, the most likely crossing, would have extra border checks now, too risky even with good papers. A boat from Izmir would go where the Greek police expected it to go. Trains were easy to check, the Orient Express like traveling in a spotlight, the overnight to Ankara the wrong direction. Where she would be, a complication. He felt her breathing next to him, something he'd almost forgotten, the peace afterward. One more day. His eyes moved over the map on the ceiling.

In the morning, they were lazy with each other, sex a hotel luxury, like breakfast in bed. Then the moment of farce he'd predicted, the maid at the door, Leon hiding in the bathroom with his clothes. Later, please.

"When do you go back?" he said, in bed again.

"Tomorrow night."

"So we have today," he said, the plan already decided, most of the pieces worked out in his mind.

"Don't you have to work?"

"Yes." He kissed her shoulder. "But I have to eat too."

"Take me to your favorite place."

He shook his head. "Too far. It's up the Bosphorus."

"Second favorite then. Don't look at me — I mean like that, in the light. It's different at night."

"Mm. Harder to see. It's like milk," he said, stroking her belly.

"Tell me something about you."

"I'm a good driver," he said, his head still filled with cars, how to arrange one on the Asian side.

"No. Something about you."

He leaned over her. "Ask me later."

After Manyas, he went through the checklist he'd made during the night. An appearance at Reynolds to tell Turhan he might have to go to Ankara for a few days, the same story to Dorothy, not sure yet but don't be surprised. Some file requests to look busy, Tommy's payment reqs. Errands to run.

"Can you keep him another night?" he asked Marina.

"I have my Armenian. It's his other day."

"Put him off. I'll pay you."

"It's all right. He paid me." She nodded toward the bedroom.

Leon looked up at her.

"Maybe it means something to him. Pay his own way."

"Marina —" he said, suddenly awkward.

"When was the last time he had a woman?"

"I don't know." He hesitated, not sure how to ask. "Anything wrong?"

She shrugged. "He's hungry, that's all." A half smile. "The prisoner and his last meal."

"He's not a prisoner."

"Yet."

"What did he tell you?"

"Nothing. He doesn't have to say a word. There's a smell, when you run."

"What's going on?" Alexei said, coming out of the bedroom, dressed, neat and shaved, nothing rumpled.

"There's a hitch. One more day."

"Some trouble?"

"No. We just need a day." He turned to

343

Marina. "All right?"

"But tomorrow it's finished. I don't care —"

Leon nodded. "How much for the Armenian?"

She made a brushing motion with her hand. "It'll be all right. There's a room upstairs. He doesn't take long. What's wrong with you?" she said to Alexei, catching his expression.

"Nothing," he said, turning back to the bedroom.

"Where do you think you are?" Marina said to Alexei's back, her voice flat, a kind of apology. She watched him go into the bedroom. "They all want to think it's something else," she said. "Even with the money in their hands, they think it's something else."

Mihai was yelling into the phone in what Leon took to be Hebrew, getting nowhere. An eruption of words, then silence, finally a grunt.

"What?" he said to Leon, hanging up. "I thought you weren't coming here anymore."

"I wasn't followed."

"The expert."

"I need something. Two things."

"Two, why two? Why not seven? Four

344

hundred. See down there, by the Koç docks? Four hundred waiting. All with passports. End visas. Everything paid for. And the boat sits."

"What happened?"

"Quarantine. Suspicion of typhus."

"Is there?"

"My friend, do you think if there was typhus the Turks would keep them here? They would tow them to sea. Let them die out there. Anywhere. But not here."

"So what —"

"What is it always? Something for the harbormaster, the public health inspectors. Then a miracle recovery. We're still buying Jews out. Still. But I don't have so much here, so it has to come from Palestine. We wait. And meanwhile they're taking turns to go on deck, just to breathe. So how long before dysentery, a real disease? Bastards." He stopped, looking up. "What do you want?"

"A car. On the Asian side."

"What's wrong with yours?"

"I can't put it on the ferry. They might be watching."

Mihai grunted. "More games."

"Doesn't your cousin have one? In Kuzguncuk?"

"I don't involve family."

"He'll get it back. A few days."

"A few days? You're driving to Palestine maybe? Take a few of my Jews. The overland route."

"I'd pay him."

"Pay me. Ten thousand dollars, so I can get them out."

"That's what they want? Christ —"

"It's explained to me, a fair price. Twenty-five dollars a head. During the war it was more. Now practically a tip. A little baksheesh, to help speed things up. So much work to examine the ship." He made a noise in his throat. "When do you need it?"

"Tomorrow. Can you do it?"

"There's a garage in Üsküdar that maybe has a car. Not family. Nobody, in fact. No registration. If you get stopped, it's your problem, understood?"

Leon nodded.

"What's the second thing?"

"A contact in Antalya."

Mihai took a minute, turning this over. "You're going to drive all the way to Antalya," he said calmly. "Over the mountains. On those roads. And stay where on the way? The Ritz, maybe? Might I ask, what's in Antalya? Dates? This time of year? Oranges?"

"A boat to Cyprus."

"Cyprus. Where they send the Jews who don't make it to Palestine. Back to camps."

"I'm not trying to get to Palestine."

"With your passenger? No, not advisable. If you want him alive. What's in Cyprus?"

"The British, not the Greeks. I can pass him on there. You must know a boat in Antalya. You got people out there."

"From people like him."

"Any boat. That doesn't need a passenger list. We were never there. No one will know."

"And where were you all this time?"

"Ankara. On business. The embassy will say so, if anybody asks. They'll have to, if this works."

"If."

"Nobody's expecting it. Nobody here. Nobody on Cyprus. Nobody's looking for him there. Or in Antalya."

"No. Who makes such a trip? In winter?"

"He'll die if he stays here."

"That's nothing to me."

"Then don't do it."

Mihai looked over at him.

"I'll get another car."

"The element of surprise," Mihai said, dismissive. "An overrated strategy. A car's a valuable thing in Istanbul."

"You can have mine if I don't bring it back."

"And you'll be here to give it to me."

"I'd trust you with my life. You can trust me with a car."

"Oh, your life. When did I become such a person? That you'd do that?"

"When," Leon said, not worth answering. He waited. "It's just a car."

Mihai looked at him for a minute, then began writing something on a piece of paper. "Don't play that card too often," he said, writing. "It loses value, you do that."

"Not if it's life or death."

"His life."

Leon said nothing.

"You know Üsküdar? Halk Caddesi. The first big intersection up from the ferry, where the road splits. On the right after the post office. The garage is in the first block. If you reach the mosque you overshot it. Give them this. In Antalya, the old port. The café across from the boat basin, the big one. Ask for Selim. I'll make the call." He handed him the paper. "Don't ask again. For him. If he dies —" He waved his hand.

They looked at each other for a second, not saying anything.

"Take extra gas. In the mountains not so many pumps. Mules. If you get to the mountains. *Agh.*" He made a what's-the-use sound and walked over to the window.

"How long will they have to stay?" Leon said, looking over his shoulder to the ship.

"Until I can pay. Aciman sends food, so they don't starve, but the conditions — like vermin. We only have the ship till the end of the month. The lease. Then what? Tell them to go back to Europe? To that hell?"

"You don't own it?"

"Nobody sells ships since the war. And who has that kind of money? So you lease. Not so cheap, either. Fifty-five thousand pounds — Palestinian, not Turkish. Sterling."

"Then pay the bribe. Tell your people it's an emergency."

"Everything in Palestine is an emergency." He moved away from the window. "Well." He looked up. "The car's an old Horch. Don't stop in the villages. Everyone will want to look."

They had lunch at a fish restaurant underneath Galata Bridge, Kay facing the old city, the postcard view of slender minarets and domes behind a kite tail of circling birds. It was too cold to eat outside but they had got a window table, and Leon twisted in his seat to point out landmarks. The New Mosque, then Süleyman's farther up the hill. They were drinking coffee, lingering, hoping the sun would come out, the water in the Golden Horn steel gray.

"What else?" he said.

"Well, this," she said, indicating the bridge, low on the water. "How do boats get in and out?"

"They swing it open at night. Four a.m., something like that, when there's no traffic. All the boats pass through then."

For a second he imagined Mihai's ship, limping in from Constancia before dawn, some tender guiding it to a dock to rot and wait, not even a minaret visible in the dark. People who'd been in the camps. Slop buckets.

"What else?"

"Tell me about you."

"That again. First you. What was your name? Before Bishop."

"O'Hara."

"Scarlett."

She shook her head. "Bronx Irish, not even lace-curtain. My mother was a maid. But my father was a cop, so there's a step up, they thought. Until the war. The first one. He was killed a week after he landed. I think it broke her heart. Anyway, she had to go back to work. Stairs, all day. She said she never wanted to see another stair in her life. But she made sure I didn't, so I owe her for that. She paid for the school."

"Secretarial school."

"Well, it was that or the nuns. I didn't see myself as a nun."

He looked at her. "No."

"I meant the calling."

He smiled. "Ah."

"Stop," she said, but pleased, looking out again toward the water. "Tell me something. The truth. Did it matter it was me? Could it have been any — ?"

"It wasn't. What kind of question is that?"

She reached over, touching his fingers, barely meeting them on the tablecloth. "I mean, you can say. I would have anyway. I didn't expect —"

She stopped, looking past him, suddenly alert, her mouth open. A shadow moved over the table.

"Mr. Burke," she said, snatching her hand back, trying not to be noticed, like someone caught biting her nails.

"I thought it might be you," Ed said, disconcerted too, glancing at the hand. "Leon." He nodded at him. "Showing Mrs. Bishop the sights?"

"The Cook's tour. Frank's idea," Leon said, but all of them awkward now, Ed looking from one to the other. "You? Late lunch?"

"Galip," Ed said absently, his mind back a minute ago. "Exports. Once a month. I don't know why." He made a show of checking his watch. "I'd better be getting back, though." He looked at Leon. "I hear you've been requesting files," he said, nervous, unable to hold back.

Leon raised his eyes.

"I was just curious. You know, if anything's come up. Someone at the consulate. You know, what people say."

"I'm auditing payment reqs. Outside payments."

"Outside? Then you think —"

"Ed, I don't think anything. I'm just going through the books. Honestly."

"Well," Ed said, backing off, literally taking a step. "It'd be nice to know. Before Barbara leaves."

"She's leaving?"

"Next week. They got her a priority rating for a flight. She doesn't sleep." He turned to Kay. "Well, you can imagine. She says the sooner the better. We're giving a party at the club. If you can make it."

"I'm sorry. I'm going back tomorrow."

"Leon?"

"I'll try. I may be in Ankara."

"Ankara?" Ed said.

Kay looked over, not saying anything.

"Just for a few days."

"Oh," Ed said, wanting to ask more. "Well," he said, another minute, waiting. "I'll see you back at the shop then." A leave-taking nod. "Mrs. Bishop."

"Kay."

"Kay," he said, awkward again, a glance down at her hand, the coffee cups, as if the tablecloth were a rumpled sheet.

"Well, that was fun," she said, taking out a cigarette after he'd gone, her hand shaking a little. "Christ, what am I doing?"

"It's just Ed." He lit it for her. "We're having lunch. That's all."

"And that's what he thinks?"

"Nobody cares what Ed thinks."

"What was that about Ankara? I can't see you there."

"Why not?"

"I can't, that's all. Everybody'd know in five minutes."

"You can't keep coming here."

"No."

"So how did you think — ?"

"I didn't. If I were thinking, I wouldn't be here. Christ." She drew on the cigarette. "When did you decide to go to Ankara? Last night?"

"I'm not. I just want Ed to think I am."

"Why?"

353

"It's none of his business."

"Or mine?" She looked away. "Where are you going?"

"Somewhere else."

She was about to speak, then looked down. "When?" she said, a different question.

"Tomorrow."

"So we have today."

"What would you like to see? Haghia Sophia? The Grand Bazaar?"

"Somewhere where we won't run into anyone. I'm not good at this." She looked again at the water. "I promised myself I wouldn't think about what happens next and now it's all I can think about."

Leon reached for her hand. "I'll come to Ankara."

She moved it back, skittish. "And meet where? The Ankara Palas? With everybody and his uncle in the bar." She made a wry face. "It's funny. It's just what my mother said would happen. When I moved out. 'The next thing, you'll be meeting some man in a hotel room.' That was her idea of the worst thing that could happen to me. And here I am."

"Here you are."

She looked at him, then smiled. "And we have the day. You pick. Somewhere you like.

354

I don't care who sees."

They went up to the Eminönü piers and caught the ferry for Üsküdar, standing outside, her hair flying back in the breeze. At the landing, men in cloth caps drinking tea looked up at her, foreign women a rarer sight on this side. There were more headscarves, even veils, overcoats almost touching the ground, noisy motorbikes weaving around idling buses, the air heavy with diesel. A taxi took them out of the square, past the food market, and up the long hill.

"Where are we going?"

"The Çinili Camii, the Tiled Mosque. You'll like it."

"Can women go in?"

"Mm. Just cover your head. A woman built it. One of the great *valides* — she was mother to two sultans."

The gate to the courtyard was open, but the mosque itself was closed, so Leon went to the teahouse next door to find the caretaker. A small mosque, with a small adjacent *medrese,* the courtyard simple, just an ablutions fountain and a shade tree that seemed older than the buildings. Kay walked around the courtyard, the only sounds her own heels. When Leon finally came back he brought the imam, a bearded man in a long white robe carrying a heavy key ring, grumbling at being disturbed. He frowned, seeing Kay, then peered at her closely and smiled, turning to Leon with a stream of Turkish.

"What's he saying?"

"Your hair is the color of the red in the *mihrab* tiles. He's never seen it in hair before. He says I'm lucky. To have a wife like an Iznik tile."

Kay laughed. "That's a compliment, right?"

"From him? They were the most beautiful tiles ever made. Nobody knows how to duplicate the colors now. Leave your shoes out here."

The imam was fumbling with the key.

"It's freezing."

"There's a carpet."

Almost the entire floor, in fact, was covered with intricately designed carpets, but the eye scarcely took them in, drawn instead to the walls covered in turquoise and blue tiles, not one color but a series of shades, like a musical exercise in blue. In the *mihrab,* there were lines of green and the rust of Kay's hair, but everything else was blue and white, even the corners of the ceiling tiled.

"It's like being inside a jewel," Kay said, staring, shivering a little, the room cold despite the carpets.

"It's the size, partly. In the big mosques all you see is how big they are. Here you really see the tiles."

Kay stepped forward. "It's allowed?"

The imam bowed, extending his hand.

"Don't worry. I told him I'd like to make a donation. You can go up to the gallery too, it's okay."

Twisting narrow stairs, then a railed balcony barely wide enough to hold a single line, but the whole room visible now, vines and flowers and abstracted patterns, repeating themselves, flowing into each other, blue into blue. She smiled at the room, then at him. Downstairs the imam stood in a corner, pleased, as if someone had praised his children.

Afterward they sat on a wall under the courtyard tree in a small patch of winter sunlight.

"It's beautiful," she said.

"And no one ever comes here. That's what you wanted, wasn't it?"

"You do, though."

"Once in a while. When the weather's nice. Just to sit."

"Alone? I mean, you don't bring —"

"Anna? Not anymore."

She looked away, toward the fountain. "So

what do you think about, when you sit here?"

"Nothing. That's the whole idea. The patterns, on the tiles, you're supposed to get lost in them, let your mind drift. Not think."

"You? I thought there was always something going on in there."

He smiled. "Not when I'm here."

She was quiet for a while, scanning the courtyard. The imam appeared again on his way back to the teahouse, dipping his head to them as he passed.

"But it can never be yours," she said.

He turned to her.

"I mean, you probably know more about it than he does," she said, a nod toward the imam. "Who built it. Where everything comes from. All that. But it's not yours."

"What difference does that — ?"

"Oh, I know. It's wonderful." She waved her hand to the mosque. "But what about the rest? When do I take off my shoes? Cover my head? The looks people give you. It's not a real life here. I mean it is for them, but we're — just visiting." She paused. "I am, anyway."

"Give it some time. It takes a while."

"What?"

"To live here."

"But now that the war's over, you could —"

"Go home?" he said, looking around. "I can take care of her here. The clinic. I don't know if I could do that there. So I live here. It is home."

"Sorry, I didn't mean —"

"I know. You just want to know more about me. See if I'm the guy in the hotel. The one your mother warned you about."

She looked up, her eyes meeting his. "You are," she said. "You must be. When you said that I wanted to be there."

He felt the blood flow to his groin, as if she had touched him there.

"I should be ashamed, shouldn't I? For thinking that."

"Yes," he said, pulling her to her feet.

They caught the ferry back to Eminönü and wandered through the spice market like tourists, looking at the tall cones of ground spices and piles of dates. At a nougat stall he thought he saw Sürmeli, the landlord, tunic stretched tight across his back, so broad he blocked the aisle. Who gossiped to Georg, maybe to everyone. But then the man turned, eating candied pistachios, just another fat man, and Leon realized he'd been staring and looked away. They went out the side exit, past the bird market, cages noisy with song and fluttering.

"Look at the wicker ones," Kay said. "So elaborate. I'll bet they hate them anyway."

"We had a parakeet when I was a kid. We'd let it out and it would come right back."

"It didn't — ?" she started, looking at him, then cocked her head, smiling.

"What?"

"You as a boy. I'm trying to picture it."

"It was a while ago. Do you want to go up to the Grand Bazaar? You can't come to Istanbul and not —"

"Let's go back."

"To the hotel?"

She put her hand on his neck and his skin jumped, the talk irrelevant. The day no longer lazy, stretching out ahead of them, suddenly running out of time.

"We could stay in," she said. "Get room service."

On Frank's bill, the Pera Palas waiters winking at each other. Over her shoulder, the fat man was coming out of the market.

"I have a better idea," he said.

They took the tram up the hill and out to Laleli, not circling back from the stop as he usually did but heading straight for the flat, his arm around her shoulders. So fat Sürmeli could see them, watching at his usual window drinking apple tea, his suspicions finally confirmed, Leon with a woman, the reason he'd taken the flat. But there was no movement as they passed his building, no curtain twitching, maybe out collecting rents.

They were luckier at the flat itself. Two men carrying books came down the hall as Leon put the key in Alexei's door. Nods and muttered greetings, curious. A foreigner and a woman, something they'd remember. Not Alexei, quiet as a mouse.

"What is this place?" she said inside. "Is this where you bring your women?"

"It belongs to a friend. He asked me to keep an eye on it while he's away." Lies now to her, but harmless.

"*They* thought it was," she said, nodding her head back to the hall. "Did you see the way they looked at me?"

"Never mind."

"Somebody really lives here?" she said, looking around the almost empty room, not even the duffel bag to suggest a presence anymore, just the lingering smell of tobacco. Had anyone heard Alexei coughing?

"It's more a pied-à-terre. For when he's at the university." The story growing. He touched her arm.

"It's not like a hotel, is it?" she said,

mischievous, surprised at herself. "Somebody else's sheets." She looked at the bed. "Is there a woman who comes? To change them? I mean, what would your friend think?"

"I don't know," he said, pulling her to him. "Let's do it on top."

Afterward, adding more smoke to the stale air, they watched the light turn gray at the window.

"Now what?" she said, leaning over to stub out her cigarette, then noticed his face. "I don't mean it that way. I promised I wouldn't say that." She looked away. "I meant, really, now what. We can't stay here."

"Now we get dressed," he said, but pulling her down to him, her face resting against his chest. "And you go back to the hotel. After all the sightseeing. And tell the clerk how much you like Istanbul. Then have dinner in the dining room. So they'll all notice. Alone. Bring a book."

"And after?"

"I come and spend the night."

"And then what?"

"I don't know," he said quietly.

She got up and went over to the chair, picking up her blouse. "And what if I meet somebody I know in the dining room?"

"Good. More witnesses."

"For my alibi." She looked over at him. "Who thinks of these things? Bring a book. Do you see so many women like this?"

"No."

"You could. You'd be good at it. The stories. This place." She looked around. "So convenient to have a friend away."

"He's never come in handy before."

"Stop asking, you mean. So maybe that's a story too."

He got up from the bed, holding her by the shoulders. "I've never brought a woman here."

She looked away, then started stepping into her skirt. "What book? For my dinner."

"How about a guide to Istanbul. Read about what you've seen."

She nodded. "Every detail. And what will you be doing?"

"Working. So people won't think I'm out chasing somebody's wife."

"You didn't have to chase very hard," she said, pulling at the side zipper, then smoothing out the skirt. "Anyway, it's so important what people think?"

"It is for you."

She looked at him, half amused. "I never thought before. How useful it would be, secret work, for this. Knowing how to hide, make stories. Someone in that work, it'd be easy for him."

Leon picked up his pants, beginning to dress. "Why don't you stay longer?"

"I can't. Besides, you're going away. On a trip you don't talk about. So maybe it's better this way. What we always said. Just walk away. Oh, god," she said suddenly, sitting down on the bed, head bent. "Now what?"

He sat down next to her. "Stay."

She said nothing for a minute, looking down, then raised her head. "No, it's what we said." She turned to him. "Just come and stay the night."

In the street, he took the direct way again to the tram, one last chance to be noticed. This time Sürmeli must have been waiting at his window — stepping suddenly into the street, *merhaba,* had Leon heard about Georg, so sudden, a rush of mournful Turkish, but all the time looking at Kay, eyes wide with interest, the flat explained.

"Who was that?"

"Someone Georg knew at the university." Not quite right, bending the truth again, using her for cover.

"Does he know? About the heart attack?"

"That was all the Turkish. Life being so short."

She looked at him, not saying anything.

At Sirkeci they took separate taxis.

364

"See you," she said, door open, putting a hand on his arm. "What did I like best? For the desk clerk."

"Topkapi. The jewels."

She nodded, then held his arm tighter. "I eat an early dinner."

He grinned. "Don't get picked up in the bar."

In the taxi he went through the checklist in his head. Clothes, the papers from Manyas first thing tomorrow, then the car in Üsküdar. Safer to split up. Alexei could take the Haydarpaşa ferry, just a few streets away from the funicular, impossible to miss even if you didn't know the city. Avoid Haydarpaşa itself, the station full of eyes, and follow the quay on the right instead, toward Kadiköy, an easy pickup at the end, both of them on the Asian side without having crossed together, already on the road south. Even safer if they could leave tonight, in the dark, but there were the papers. And Kay. What did I like best? For the desk clerk. Get Alexei out first — keep things separate. But he realized the excitement of one had spilled over into the other, part of the same thing now, getting away with both, juggling balls faster in the air.

At the office, Turhan was getting ready to leave. The monthly figures were done. Mrs.

King had called again. A farewell party, time and place. Dorothy at the consulate wanting to know if he was expected back today. Frank Bishop.

"What did he want?"

"He just said he'd try again."

Checking in. Maybe checking up. But why would he? Someone Leon should feel awkward about and yet didn't. He could feel her hand on his arm again, the promise of later, not the little qualms that hid away in corners. Frank unaware at his desk in Ankara. Something else to think about later. I eat an early dinner.

By the time he left it was dark, Taksim bright with neon, Istanbul's Piccadilly. He glanced at the signs while he waited for the Istiklal tram. Persil soap. Pamuk, the Coke substitute. If he was early he could always have a drink at the bar, run into somebody from the consulate, say he was on his way home. Colgate. A cinema with running lights. The big branch of Denizbank.

On the tram, he stood near the back, seeing his reflection in the glass. Not smiling exactly, but his lips half curled up, expectant. Going somewhere. He thought of that first rainy night in Bebek, seeing himself in the mirror at home. Now feeling like this. Lighted storefronts, barely noticed. They were near the Flower Passage now, past the big sweets store with its blocks of lokum in the window, then a bookstore, an Akbank branch. He felt a nagging, as if he'd forgotten something, or seen something out of place. Akbank. A.K. Denizbank. He gripped the rail tighter, trying to remember. Maybe that was it, not a code.

He leaped off at the next stop and threaded his way down to Meşturiyet. Lights were still on at the consulate, telephone night staff, cleaning ladies slowly making their way through the building. The snappy Marine day guard had been replaced at night by a local watchman, who asked to see Leon's ID.

"People working late?" Leon said in Turkish while the guard examined the pass.

"Always," he said, surprised at the Turkish. "Americans, they like to work." He shrugged.

"It's the time difference. Their bosses are still —" Leon began, then gave it up as too complicated to explain. "I won't be long."

He didn't wait for the elevator, racing up the stairs instead. A woman was emptying wastebaskets in the hall.

"Mister," she said, bowing, surprised at someone on the stairs.

Leon nodded back, wondering if she sifted

through the baskets, one of Altan's eyes. Behind her several transoms still had lights coming through.

He switched on the overhead in the outer office, then went into Tommy's and got the passports from underneath the drawer. Slips inside. Yes, A.K., the other D.Z. — Denizbank? Not code, bank account numbers. Under different names. Manyas's flawless papers all the identification a bank would need. But Leon wasn't the man in the picture. He'd need a power of attorney or some equivalent paper Akbank would accept. Executor. He went out to Dorothy's desk and found some consular stationery. The wording wouldn't matter, as long as it looked official. He typed out two, one for each name, giving him authority to access the accounts. How much had Tommy stashed away?

He put the passports and letters in his jacket pocket, then hurried out of the office. The cleaning lady had disappeared and so had the watchman, maybe out back for a smoke or in the bathroom, but the front door wasn't locked so Leon just pushed through. Outside, the iron gates were open, a few cars still in the courtyard, so there was no need to ring for a guard. What if he'd been a burglar?

But wasn't he? Whose money would it be, technically? Barbara's? The government's? Not the Russians' anymore. Assuming money was there. But it had to be, or why have the accounts? How had it been arranged? Wire transfers, something traceable, finally proof? Or an envelope of cash, passed under the table at the Park or at one of those Allied meetings, Melnikov exchanging more than information. Tommy's thirty pieces of silver.

He looked down the street to the Pera, jumpy and elated at the same time. Withholding evidence, the police would say. But it had to be the link, a way to prove Tommy — Tucked away in his pocket, something only he knew, while he had a drink at the bar. Waiting to go upstairs.

He sensed that she was already awake, her back to him, maybe staring out the window at the drizzly morning. He lay still, watching the faint rise of her shoulder as she breathed, feeling the warmth, his body curved along hers. It had rained during the night, streaking the windows, making them snuggle under the covers, but now it had slowed to a fine mist, the skies finally exhausted. The roads through the mountains would be slick, slower to drive. Then

369

sun at the end, citrus trees. What time did the banks open? She pulled at the sheet, covering herself.

"What are you thinking?" he said quietly, a morning whisper.

She turned in the bed, facing him. "How it happens."

"What?"

"Standing in the street. After the funeral. And you gave me a cigarette. And I wondered. That's all. That's how it started. Then we talked at the reception. So one thing, then another. I was trying to trace it, in my mind, how that happens."

He put his hand to her face.

"I woke up and I could smell you," she said. "On my skin. I thought, I'm lying here and he's on my skin. So how did that happen?"

"One things leads to another," he said, a cued response.

She looked at him. "Well, until it doesn't."

"I'll come to Ankara. I go there on business. It's easy."

"For you," she said, sliding away, reaching for the robe on the floor.

"I'll arrange it. I'm good at that. You said so."

"But I'm not." She stood up, beginning to put on the robe.

370

"No, don't. Wait a minute. Just stand there. Like that."

She put her hand to her breast, covering herself. "What are you looking at?"

"Just looking."

He leaned up on one elbow, facing her. Her skin pale white with the window light behind.

She lowered her head. "I've never done this. Have somebody look at me. Naked."

"Never?"

She put her arm through the sleeve. "Anyway, it's cold."

"Keep it open," he said, getting out of bed and coming over to her. "I want to see you."

"So you can remember?"

He held her against him. "I'll arrange something."

For a second she didn't move, then let her arms hang loose and stepped over to the window. "You'd better get dressed. It's stopping."

"I don't have to leave yet. It's early."

"Yes, now. It's the right time." She turned to face him, trying a smile. "And I'll get back into bed for a while. Smell you on me." She stood there for a minute, then belted the robe. "Get dressed, okay?" she said softly, picking up a cigarette and lighting it.

He reached for his pants, watching her. "I

won't be away long. I'll come to Ankara after."

"And maybe we can all have dinner. Frank looking at us. And you looking at me and me avoiding you. And me sneaking around with Orhan, that's our driver, we have a car there and it would look funny if I took a cab anywhere. And then what? I pretend to go shopping and he waits and I run around the corner — to where? Some room you arranged? Maybe your friend here has one there too. For a quick one while I'm supposed to be shopping."

"It doesn't have to be like that."

"It is like that."

He stopped, letting his tie hang from his collar. "Kay —"

"So it's a mess." She ran the cigarette around the rim of the ashtray, tapping off ash. "My god, I'm the other woman, aren't I? In a hotel. My mother was right. Smoking. Half hanging out of my robe. Quite a sight."

"Utterly depraved."

She looked up, a small smile. "I'm glad you stayed the night. It makes it less like —"

"It's not."

"Then what is it?"

He finished his tie. "It's what we have."

She drew on the cigarette, looking at him, then stubbed it out. "All dressed. You'd better go. What do we say? I'm new at this."

He walked over and took her chin in his hand, kissing her on the forehead. "Say, I'll see you soon."

She met his eyes, then moved back, shoulders slightly drooped.

He picked up his jacket, not really looking, so that he grabbed it upside down, the breast pocket hanging over the floor. A quiet thump, Tommy's passports spilling out, then one of the consulate letters. He looked at the pile for a second, jarred, then scooped them back up. Nothing seen, no names, just the fact of them, obviously passports, more than one. Kay folded her arms across her chest, a protective reflex, then glanced up at him. He put on his jacket, sliding the passports back into the pocket.

"Don't ask," he said. "Remember?"

She kept looking at him. "What else don't you tell me, I wonder. Maybe it's the same. With us."

He adjusted his collar, not answering.

"Maybe you like it this way. Secret. Like your work. Seeing me like this. It's exciting for you."

He looked over. "There are two of us in this room."

She said nothing for a minute, then nodded. "All right. Yes. I like it too. I'm just not as good at it. I keep thinking it shows in my face."

He moved closer, putting his hand on her neck. "It does. But nobody else sees it."

She touched his breast pocket, not patting it, her hand still. "Whatever you're doing with these — it's safe?"

He nodded. "I'll come to Ankara," he said, and then before she could answer, "You can give Orhan the day off."

She looked up. "All the details."

The numbers turned out to be for safety deposit boxes, not accounts. No deposit slips, no transfers, no records at all.

"But you have the date when he took the box?"

"Yes, of course," the Denizbank manager said, and referred to an index card in his hand. "May 'forty-four. The nineteenth. There's some irregularity?"

"No, no, we need to audit his assets, that's all, so we can settle the estate."

"He's dead? I'm sorry," he said, Mr. Price clearly unknown to him. An American with a valid passport and money to pay for a box. "We would need to see a death certificate before we could release the contents. You understand."

"Yes, naturally. We don't want to close it out. We just need to know what's in it. Any papers. His wife thinks there may have been bonds — she can't find them at home. If you'd like to have someone from the bank present while I do the accounting —"

The manager brushed this aside. "Please. A consulate request. Is there anything you need? There's a desk in the room. Only a signature here. To confirm the grant of access."

"Do people sign every time they come in?"

The manager smiled. "No, not the box holders. One woman, you know, comes in every day. To look at her jewels. Imagine if we had to ask her." He looked up, hesitant. "This is not a police matter?"

"No, nothing like that. A simple audit."

Leon was shown into a vault room lined floor to ceiling with metal boxes. The manager drew one out and put it on the table, handing Leon a key. Leon put a notepad and pen next to it.

"Ergin will wait outside," the manager said. "Leave the key with him. Now if there's anything —"

"I can't thank you enough."

The manager bowed as he left, an embassy gesture.

Leon looked up as he turned the key. No Ergin, no mirrors, nobody watching. He raised the lid, half expecting the shine of gold, some treasure chest effect, but there was only the dull gray-green of currency, several bundles of it, no identifying bank bands or other papers, just money. He flipped the corners of one bundle, counting. One-hundred-dollar bills in stacks of fifty, five in all, twenty-five thousand dollars. He stared at it. In dollars, something the Russians usually hoarded. Why not pay in Turkish liras? Not a fortune, but a lot of money. What had Tommy actually done to earn it? Copy cables? Sell names? But not accumulated in bits over the years, the stacks crisp and of a piece, a single payout.

Leon counted all of it, just to be sure, then closed the box again and locked it. A big house in Chevy Chase with a powder room, the one he'd told Dorothy about. He wouldn't have to wire the money home, pay taxes, just carry it in his briefcase on the plane, nobody, not even Denizbank, the wiser. For what? Alexei might be worth twenty-five thousand dollars, a bounty hunter price. But the money had already been here when Tommy was killed, and it was unlikely the Russians would pay in advance. Anyway, why pay Tommy to kill

Alexei when they could easily have done it themselves. If they'd had the information.

The manager at Akbank was more scrupulous, insisting on staying in the room while Leon opened the box, his only concession a discreet turning away as Leon raised the lid. One-hundred-dollar bills, the same plain stacking bands, a duplicate of the first box. More than enough now for the house. Or maybe another life, lived on another passport, nothing to link Tommy to either box. If anything went wrong. But what would?

"No one else can open this box?" Leon asked. "His wife?"

"I'm sorry. There is no countersignature. Just Mr. Riordan." Again, someone clearly unknown. "Of course, if there were a court order the bank would be obliged —"

"Who could get that?"

"The police. The treasury. During the time of the wealth tax there were investigations. Undeclared assets. But Mr. Riordan is a foreign national. Not, I believe, subject to Turkish taxes?" His eyebrows rose with the question.

"No."

"Then it would not concern him. In any case, you know, the law was repealed. Mr. Riordan took out the box afterward."

"When exactly, do you know?"

The manager checked a card, similar to Denizbank's. "Last year. May."

"But technically the government could still get access?"

A good reason not to put everything in one account. Mr. Price. Mr. Riordan. Tommy spreading his bets again.

"Technically. But they have not done so. May I ask, is there some reason — ?"

"No, just curious. When the will is executed, I'll need to attest to the integrity of the assets. I just wanted to be sure that no one —"

"No one. Only Mr. Riordan." He dipped his head to Leon. "Now his executor. The estate will be responsible for the box fees? I'm sorry to ask, but —"

Outside Leon stood for a few minutes watching the traffic snaking through Taksim, the air hazy with bus exhaust, trying to make sense of the money. What was worth fifty thousand dollars to the Russians? Or had Tommy been acting as paymaster, using the deposit boxes the way he had his consulate accounts, funding two networks. With the same currency. Why would the Russians waste precious foreign reserves on an Istanbul payroll? They wouldn't. Maybe not even on Tommy. But there was the money, in AK and DZ, waiting for two Tommys to collect it.

A big ship had docked at the end of Enver Manyas's street, and the noise of winches and *hamals* shouting drowned out the ping of the shop bell.

"Manyas Bey?"

"Efendi," he said, slipping out from behind the curtain like a cat, his tail still behind. "You're early."

"Too early?"

"A minute."

Leon stared at the wall. Families posing stiffly against painted backdrops of Topkapi. Manyas came back with a passport and handed it over the counter.

"Nesim Barouh. Traveling to Greece."

Leon flipped through the pages. "The seal is good."

Manyas dipped his head. Leon took out an envelope. "And for what Mr. King owed you." Another dip.

Leon pocketed the passport, then pulled out the two from Tommy's desk. "I assume these were you?"

Manyas glanced at the inside covers. "Yes, last year."

"The airport arrival stamp — yours, too?"

"Yes, everything."

"Any others? For him, I mean."

"Just the new one you paid for." He turned the page. "No exit stamp. So he never used them?"

"Not for travel."

Manyas waited, then ran his hand over the page, his slender fingers almost stroking it. "A valuable thing, an American passport."

"Not if you're dead."

"As you say. Valuable to someone else then. The paper, it's very difficult to copy. A shame to waste." His eyes moved up. "Of no use to you now. Of course we would share. Like Mr. King."

Tommy's business partner. Something extra on the side. But how much could it have been? Windfall money, a few rounds for everybody at the bar. And suddenly for a second he was back at the Park, Tommy nostalgic for a room full of Manyases, everyone for sale. When Istanbul had been his playground, full of secrets like his own. Missing it already, as he planned to kill Leon.

"Tommy supplied you with passports? Real ones?"

"A few. Difficult to obtain. Sometimes one is lost, the consulate issues a replacement. You might perhaps have a similar source there?"

"Perhaps." Wanting to know now. "How much? Tommy's cut."

"Forty percent. The work, you understand, is mine."

"Changing the picture."

"Not as easy as you might think. Even for Turkish papers," he said, nodding to the passport in Leon's pocket. "And other services. Arranging the sale. Mr. King insisted on that. No involvement. No risk to you," he said, looking now at Leon.

Leon stared back at him. A simple negotiation, part of the culture, a moment over tea.

"Fifty percent," he said. "Tommy's cut."

Manyas said nothing for a minute, then nodded. "A worthy successor."

"And how do I know what price you get?"

A faint smile. "*Efendi*. A certain amount of trust is required in business. Mr. King never complained. May I?" he said, reaching for the passports.

"Later," Leon said, stopping them with his hand. "I need them for a little while."

"Need them? With his picture?"

"Don't worry, they're not going anywhere. You can start looking for customers. Who would that be, by the way?"

"An American passport? Many buyers. But the best prices? During the war, the Jews. What price do you put on your life?

Now still, I think. Still the best prices with them."

Leon felt his stomach move. "You and Tommy sold passports to Jews?"

Manyas looked at him. "Who needed them more?"

The ship was being unloaded and Leon, his head somewhere else, followed the noise down the street. Gears and cranes, people shouting over them. He watched a load swinging up out of the ship and over the pier, guided to its receiving area with furious hand signals, *hamals* rushing over to break it up. Some of it would simply disappear. Things had been falling off ships for thousands of years in Istanbul, heads turned, something slipped into the hand, as natural as breathing. Did Tommy skim the consulate accounts too? Fond of petty cash, payments to sources who were just initials. Doing business with Enver Manyas. Baksheesh was part of life here. A ship with missing cargo. Expense accounts with something added in. Everybody did it. And then drew their own personal lines. This, but not that. Where had Tommy drawn his? Fleecing Jews. The same desperate people who then crowded onto Anna's ships. How much could it have been worth, crossing that line? Making them pay for their lives. While he was arranging their rescue, the last person anyone in the consulate would suspect. But you didn't make fifty thousand dollars selling a few passports. What would he have done for that kind of money? If he'd already crossed a line for a few hundred. Something that valuable to the Russians. Leon frowned, watching another load being landed onto the pier, men carrying sacks away. Not just a piece of cargo. Fifty thousand. In dollars. Who had American dollars? Leon stopped, following the question, then not wanting to get there. Americans.

There were police cars in the consulate courtyard, as many as there'd been after Tommy had been found, drawing the same crowd of onlookers outside the gate.

"What's going on?" Leon said to the marine as he showed his ID.

"They got the cops here again."

"What, asking questions?"

"Yeah, they —"

"Corporal! They're coming down. Give us a hand here. On the double."

He waved Leon in and started running toward a group of people near the elevator, two full cars at least. Leon headed up the stairs instead, taking them two at a time. More questions about Tommy. Hours he didn't have to waste, Alexei waiting. Enver's papers in his pocket.

Upstairs there was an odd quiet, no typewriters clicking, as if everyone were on coffee break. Dorothy had stepped out too, all the lights on, a sweater draped over the back of her chair. Leon went through to Tommy's office, rummaging through the top drawer for Tommy's appointment books. May, last year. Donald Price had supposedly entered the country in April and needed, or knew he would need, the box in May. He flipped through the pages, mid-month, then further, then went back. Routine appointments. But the others would hardly be the sort of meetings he'd record. Look for the money instead. He opened the bottom drawer and pulled out the files he'd gone through before, looking for something else now. Mr. King was proud of these. Having it every which way, crossing the last line.

"Oh!" Dorothy stood in the door, her hand raised to her chest in a cartoon movement. "You're here. You gave me a turn. Thank heavens. The police have been asking."

"In a minute. I just want to see —"

"What?" she said, noticing the files.

"Last spring. Did Tommy take any trips?"

384

"Trips?" she said, the idea itself implausible.

"Out of the country."

"Last year? During the war? No. Mr. Bauer, the police. They're down in the conference room. You'd really better tell them you're here. They've been phoning the Reynolds office."

"Reynolds? Why?"

"You don't know?" She started fingering the button on her blouse. "It's Mr. Bishop. He's dead."

"Frank?" Leon said, not taking this in.

"Last night. Well, I suppose last night. That's what they're asking about anyway. Where everybody was last night."

"Asking here?" Leon said, still trying to make sense of this. "But he was in Ankara."

"No, here. In the consulate. They found him this morning. Poor Mary. Just opened the door and — They had to give her something. See a thing like that. No warning. The lights are on and she walks in and there he is. Blood, everything." She shuddered.

"He died — here?" Leon said, as if he were feeling his way along a wall in the dark.

"Why he'd want to do it here, I don't know. Think what it feels like for everybody."

"What?"

"Oh god, you don't know, do you?" she said, her voice breaking.

"Dorothy."

"He shot himself."

For a second he had no reaction at all, his mind blank, then a rush of pictures: Frank at Karpić's, taking an envelope, smoking a cigarette in Tünel Square, Kay's pale skin against the morning window, hand over her breast, Leon lying on his elbow, watching her. He felt blood leap to his face. Had Frank known? Where was Kay?

"Mr. Bauer —"

"Shot himself," he said dully. "In his office?" Maybe there when Leon had come for the passports, one of the lights pouring through the transoms into the hall. But how could he have been? "Mrs. Bishop?"

"She's downstairs. With the police."

Leon started for the door, a file still in his hand, just following his feet. Frank sitting at his desk with a gun. Writing a note?

"Mr. Bauer —"

Not hearing her, already walking down the hall. There were police photographers in Frank's office, flashbulbs lighting up the pushed-back chair, a small overnight bag, a few files in the outtray, no note on the blotter, no signs of any disturbance at all, except for the dark stain on the carpet where he'd bled. Two policemen with measuring tape and plastic bags were going through the rest of the room. Leon walked over to the desk. Personnel files, Frank hunting to the end, but leaving a clean desk, tidying up loose ends before he picked up the gun. Had he called the Pera Palas?

"Don't touch anything," one of the policemen said in Turkish.

Leon moved his hand back.

"No one's allowed here," the policeman said, cocking his head to the door.

Leon looked at the chair again, trying to imagine it. Had he slumped over on the desk or been thrown back against the chair? Did it matter? A policeman wearing gloves. Kay downstairs.

There were a few consulate people waiting in chairs outside the conference room talking in low voices. Leon brushed past the police guards, barely noticing them.

"Mr. Bauer." Gülün, the burly policeman who'd been on Tommy's payroll, looked up from the table, a stenographer next to him, one of the consulate secretaries being questioned across from him. "A late start this morning." His cheeks dark with stubble, maybe called out too early to shave.

Kay was at the end of the table, a coffee cup in front of her, face white and vague, like someone who's been sick.

"I just heard," Leon said.

"You can go," Gülün said to the secretary. "Mr. Bauer —"

But Leon was looking down the table. Kay winced, her dazed expression now filled with something else, the guilty apprehension of someone about to be punished.

"Dorothy said he —" Kay looked away. "Shot himself," he finished to Gülün. "Is that right?"

"He was shot, yes," Gülün said, officious, enjoying himself. "By whom is another matter."

"What do you mean?"

"I mean that is not yet determined. There are things to consider — the angle of the shot, technical matters."

"He means that suicide is not likely. In fact, not possible." A voice from behind. Colonel Altan got up from a chair and walked toward them. "You can be frank with Mr. Bauer," he said to Gülün. "He was Mr. Bishop's colleague. Both, you know, were cooperating with us. On another matter." He turned to Leon. "Lieutenant Gülün thinks it best for the staff not to be alarmed. So, a simple suicide for now. Nevertheless, he asks questions," he said with irony, but in English, an effect Gülün would not pick up. "He wants to eliminate possibilities."

Leon looked at Gülün. "Someone killed him?"

"I'm trying to establish the facts," Gülün said, a strut in his voice. "Please." He opened his palm and indicated a chair.

Leon sat, glancing again at Kay, head down, fingering her ring.

"When did you see Mr. Bishop yesterday? An approximate time," Gülün said with a small wave.

"I didn't. I thought he was in Ankara."

"But he called your office. Your secretary says."

"You talked to Turhan?"

"It's important to be thorough. A man's death. So, he called —"

"I thought from Ankara."

"No. A local call. According to your secretary."

"She never told me that. I had no idea he was here." Looking at Kay, talking to both of them.

"Ah. And yet you went from your office to the consulate. Not to meet him?"

"No, I had some work to finish up."

"Saydam, the night guard, said you came here about seven, is that correct?"

"Yes, about that."

"But he did not see you leave."

"He wasn't at the door. I don't know where he was. Maybe having a pee."

"He said he was always there."

"Well, he would, wouldn't he? Look —"

Gülün waved this off. "So we don't know. An hour? More? How long were you here?"

"Not long. Twenty minutes, maybe half an hour."

"And then?"

"Then I went to the Pera Palas." He glanced down at Kay. "For a drink."

"You were seen at the bar?"

"I don't know. Ask the bartender. Why? Are you suggesting I killed him?"

Gülün made a calming gesture with his thick hands. "And after?"

"After? After I went home," he said, looking at Gülün.

Gülün held his gaze for a second. "Not according to Mr. Cicek. It's correct, yes? Cicek? The *bekçi* at your building?"

"You've had a busy morning," Leon said.

"Lieutenant Gülün is methodical," Altan said quietly. "It's correct?"

"That he's the *bekçi*, yes. That he knows where I am night and day? No. Look, what is this? I was at the consulate half an hour at the most. Say till seven thirty. When was Frank shot? Didn't anybody hear it? A shot?"

"Unfortunately the police cannot be accurate about the time of death," Altan said. "Mr. Bishop had been dead for some time when his body was found. The police doctor says yesterday evening — early, not so early, it's impossible to say which exactly. Maybe when the cleaning staff is running the vacuum, maybe the guard thinks he heard a sound in the street. We don't know."

"But we do know he was shot," Gülün said. "And we know you were here. So we must account for your time. So, the Pera bar. And after?" Another steady gaze.

"I went home. Mr. Cicek must not have heard me."

"No. He heard your telephone. Ringing. Until the caller gave up. Do you often do that, not answer your phone?"

A standoff minute, Leon facing him down.

"He couldn't," Kay said. "He was with me."

Leon shot her a look, a slight shake of his head. Don't.

"Madame?" Gülün said, surprised.

Altan sat up, eyes moving from one to the other.

"He wasn't at home. He was with me. All night. I can swear to it." Her voice getting fainter.

"Let me understand. You spent the night

with Mr. Bauer."

"Yes," she said to Leon.

"Your husband's colleague." He paused. "You are lovers?"

"We spent the night," she said, looking down.

Gülün glanced at the stenographer, embarrassed, and stood up. "Your husband knew this?"

"No, of course not."

"But he comes to Istanbul. A sudden trip. So perhaps a surprise. For the lovers."

"He called Mr. Bauer," Altan said calmly.

Gülün looked at Kay, then at Leon, not sure what to do with this.

"A moment, please," Altan said to Gülün, drawing him toward the door. "You will excuse us? More coffee?"

Kay shook her head. The stenographer got up and went over to the window, as if she were leaving the room too, out of earshot.

"Why did you say that?" Leon said quietly when they'd gone.

"Why not? It's true, isn't it?" she said, her voice flat. She pushed the cup away. "A surprise for the lovers," she said with Gülün's inflection. "It would have been, wouldn't it? Quite a surprise."

"Kay —"

"The nuns had it right," she said to

herself. "You pay one way or the other. Maybe not this way, though. Even they wouldn't think of this."

"Are you all right?"

"I was still in bed. When the phone rang. Could I come down? There's been an accident. Accident. So I wouldn't become hysterical, I suppose. And I've got the smell of you on me." She got up, hands on the table. "Not that they'd know that."

"They do now. Why did —"

"Do you know what they asked me? Did he have any enemies? And I thought, I don't know. I don't know that. My husband, and I don't know anything about him. So maybe you do. Did he? Have enemies?"

"He must have had one."

She looked down, then put her hand up to cover her eyes. "Imagine not knowing that." Not crying, but quiet now, receding.

Leon went over and touched her shoulder, but she swung away, out of reach.

"An accident," she said, taking out a handkerchief and blowing her nose. " 'What kind of accident?' Then this. 'Last night,' they said. So he must have been lying there, dead, while we —"

"Kay," he said.

"I had to make the identification. 'Is this your husband?' 'Yes.' And all the time I'm thinking, I don't know this man. A man who gets shot. He had some other life to do that. Like you," she said, lifting her head. "I don't know you, either."

"Yes you do."

He took the handkerchief and wiped the corner of her eye.

"And they were asking for you. I thought maybe they knew. About us. But you weren't here. And I thought, why not? You left me and then what? Where were you?"

He said nothing, finishing with the handkerchief.

"Tell me!" she said, her hands suddenly on his chest. "I hate this. 'Don't ask.' 'I can't say.' First Frank and now you. And now look."

"I had some errands."

"Errands," she said, not believing him, her voice rising, caught up in it. "What errands? 'Don't ask.' Tell me!" Hitting his chest.

He took her arms. "I went to the bank," he said, looking straight at her, breaking whatever spell had taken her, so that she almost laughed at the simple unexpectedness of it, then lowered her head onto his chest, not sobbing, just letting go, her body limp against him.

"Kay, listen to me," he said into her ear so that the stenographer could only hear whispers. "We need to be careful. Calling Turhan. Mr. Cicek. They're going to a lot of trouble to prove I was here. Could have been here."

"But I told them. You were with me."

He nodded. "And now they have a motive."

"What motive?"

"You."

Her eyes clouded. "I'm sorry. I didn't mean —"

"I know."

"They'd think that?" she said brooding. "Then why not me. The unfaithful wife."

"They don't think anything yet. We have to be careful, that's all. It's not just police. Altan's Emniyet."

"But he was at Lily's party," she said, a reaction so off the point that he didn't know how to respond.

She turned away, holding her arm. "This place. Who knows who anybody is?" She stopped, shivering a little, then looked up, reading his face. "Tell me one thing. The truth. You had nothing to do with this. Tell me that. I couldn't live with myself if —"

"Nothing," he said.

A quiet second.

"My god, and I believe you. Just like that. You say it and I believe you," she said, lowering her head again to his chest.

"Mrs. Bishop," Altan said, coming through the door. "You're not well?"

Kay jumped. Gülün shuffled behind, his face in a kind of pout, watching them.

"She's had a rough morning," Leon said, still holding her. "She ought to rest." He looked at Gülün. "Do you need her much longer?"

Gülün waved his hand, too annoyed to bother with words, and went over to his place, scooping up his notes. "Another time," he said to her. "You'll be staying on in Istanbul?"

"I hadn't really thought —" Kay said, moving away from Leon.

"It would be advisable. You too, Mr. Bauer."

"Until when? I may have to go to Ankara."

Altan looked up at this, but Gülün was busying himself with his papers.

"I'm asking this of everyone who was here last night," he said, then looked over at Kay. "Do you need someone to take you to the hotel? For your rest." The last said with a sting he couldn't resist.

Kay shook her head. "Are there things I'm supposed to do here? What do widows do? I mean, I don't know —"

"Dorothy can help you," Leon said. "With

the arrangements."

"We can't release the body yet," Gülün said. "The law requires an autopsy."

"Yes," Kay said vaguely. "The body. He'll have to be buried somewhere, won't he? All that."

"Would you call extension sixty-two?" Leon said to the stenographer. "Ask Dorothy to come down?" He turned to Kay. "You don't have to do this now. Dorothy can get the paperwork ready."

"No. I can't just sit. Do nothing. I'd go —"

Altan nodded. "It's difficult, a sudden death. The shock," he said, his voice knowing, personal.

"One more question?" Gülün said, not looking at Altan. "Your husband. He didn't call yesterday to say he was coming?"

"No."

"This was usual? He liked surprises?"

"I don't know. No, not really."

"Yet he flies here —"

"He flew? But he hated to fly. I just assumed he took the train," Kay said, genuinely surprised at this.

"No. So something urgent, something that couldn't wait." He paused. "A surprise. No message to the hotel. You were out during the day?"

"Sightseeing."

"Alone?"

"No. With —" She nodded to Leon.

"Ah," Gülün said, as if some point had been made. He turned to the stenographer. "We're finished for the day." A sly look at Altan as he filled his briefcase. "By the way, Mr. Bauer, we spoke to Saydam. The guard. There may have been a cigarette, some time away from the door."

"Yes."

"Unfortunately no one else was there, either. So anything is possible." He glanced over at Kay. "People coming in. People going out."

Dorothy appeared and everybody began moving toward the door, relieved to be leaving.

"Don't mind Gülün," Altan said to Leon, bringing up the rear. "Your embassy in Ankara has been making calls. Two men killed now. Of course they blame the Russians, but it's our police who get the calls. What arrests? So a difficult time for him."

"What about the gun? Any prints?"

"Only Mr. Bishop's."

"It was Frank's gun?"

"No."

"But you're sure he didn't —"

398

"Sure. He was shot in the back of the head."

"Then why wipe the gun? To make it look —"

Altan shrugged. "The head wound was large. Maybe he thought no one would look too closely. Examine the angle. But Lieutenant Gülün has a fondness for that. So, no, not a suicide."

"Were there prints anywhere else?"

"Everywhere. A busy office, people in and out. Gülün will have to compile a list, see if there's a match with someone who was here last night. A long job. There was one curiosity about the prints, though."

"What's that?" Leon said, stopping, letting the others move out through the door.

"They found prints everywhere except one filing cabinet. Evidently wiped, like the gun. Personnel files."

"Like the ones in his outtray."

Altan looked up, pleased. "Excellent. Gülün has not yet made that connection."

"And you think someone took a file and wiped his prints off the drawer?"

"No, I think someone put a file back. Which Mr. Bishop had taken out. Not something you want to go missing, your file. Then it might be noticed. Something you want to have back with all the others. That

399

Mr. Bishop had never taken out."

"Somebody working here then."

Altan nodded. "It would have to be. Poor Saydam's not a very good guard but still, it's unlikely a stranger could come in off the street, shoot Mr. Bishop, and then go back out again. Not even a wife," he said, looking up. "Gülün likes magazine stories. European women, a fascination. They behave differently. A Turkish man goes to a whore, not to a hotel with someone's wife. It would be unthinkable. You'll forgive me, I'm making a point only."

"What point?"

"That Gülün could conceive such a woman slipping into the consulate to shoot her husband. An exciting solution for him. But of course it was more likely someone who belongs here, whose coming or going wouldn't be noticed."

"Like me."

"Oh, you. And then down the street for a night of love? No." He shook his head. "Anyway, you don't have a file. You're from outside. Brought in after Mr. King was shot. Mr. Bishop always said it was a traitor. In the consulate. You, I think, didn't believe him, I was never sure why." He glanced over at Leon, as if considering it again, then let it go. "But now you see he was right. There was a traitor and Mr. Bishop found him. So he had to be killed."

"How do you know?"

"Because he called you. Think for a minute. Don't be Gülün. The angry husband? No, I don't think he ever suspected." He looked over. "A small relief for your conscience."

"You have no —"

Altan waved him silent. "Apologies. So he packs a bag and takes a plane — no time to lose — and where does he go? The hotel? No, straight to the consulate. And who does he call? His wife? No, he calls you. Gülün doesn't appreciate this point. He called you. And who are you to him? The other man? No, his partner, the man he brought in. He calls you because he has news on the case. He was right. He's found the leak." Altan paused. "A pity you weren't there to take the call. Instead of — sightseeing." The others were still standing outside the door. "You left something, I think," he said, picking up the file and handing it to Leon, his eyes skimming over the tab. "And how is your work going? Any ideas yet?"

"Just a question. The Romanian. You said he'd never been to Istanbul. But he did come to Turkey. You had the dates. I assume you got this from passport control?"

"Why do you ask?"

"Because he must have someone here who's helping. Whom he knew before. Where did he go? Do you know?"

"Ankara and Edirne."

"What was he doing in Edirne?" Leon said, looking at the file, as if he were thinking out loud.

"A visa signed by Antonescu. So, government business."

"Government business? Last year? What kind of business would they have?"

Altan shrugged. "Maybe asking for peace. A way out. A day visa, it's usually for a courier. Not long enough, I think, to make a friend here. Who helps."

In the hall the group had begun to break up, Gülün rescheduling the people still waiting, Kay farther off talking to Dorothy.

"By the way," Altan said. "Why are you going to Ankara?"

"Business." He caught Altan's raised eyebrow. "Tobacco business."

"You'll spread yourself too thin."

"I didn't ask to do this," Leon said, opening a hand to indicate the consulate. "Frank asked me."

"And now he's gone. So naturally you feel an obligation. To help. That's what I told Gülün. We are allies in this."

"There he is!" A voice in Turkish down the hall. "He can tell you. He's the one who promised me the money."

A man in a rough jacket, holding a cap in his hand, shaved but grizzled, as if the razor hadn't been sharp enough. He was walking fast toward Leon now, one of the consulate clerks following. Leon looked up, at first not recognizing him. People were turning to the commotion, Gülün stopping in midsentence, Altan stepping aside as the man pushed forward, everything happening as fast as a shot.

"Tell him," the man said to Leon. "The extra day, because of the weather. You said I'd be paid for it."

Leon stood there for a second, still not reacting, then went over to the fisherman, blocking him from Gülün's line of sight. "Yes, yes," he said in Turkish, low, trying not to be overheard. "You'll be paid. Right away, if you calm down. Don't make such a racket."

The fisherman pointed to the clerk. "He didn't believe me. He kept asking for a name. I don't know, I said. How would I know a name? Work like that. They don't give you names." He turned to the clerk. "You see, I told you. He was there. He can vouch for me. It wasn't my fault it rained."

"I'll take care of this," Leon said quickly to the clerk, moving the man away by the elbow, feeling everyone still watching. "Dorothy, take him up to the office. Go up with her. We'll get you the money."

"Two hundred," the fisherman said. "I still had the expense of the boat. Keeping him."

A frantic look to Dorothy to get him away. He turned to the others. "Excuse me, I'd better go up." A routine matter, nothing wrong. "I'll be back in a minute," he said to Kay, who was looking lost, the Turkish a mystery to her.

But it wouldn't be to Gülün. Leon turned back, avoiding him. What had anyone heard? The clerk still seemed puzzled. Not a visa applicant, someone whose presence he understood. Work like that. They don't give you names. Just get him out of here, before he could say anything else. Leon started for the stairs.

"A moment, Mr. Bauer," Altan said. He looked at the fisherman. "Go," he said sharply, cocking his head to the stairs, expecting to be obeyed, a cop's authority. The fisherman bent his head, and started backing away. "Please," Altan said to Leon, heading back to the conference room.

"I'll be right up," Leon said to Dorothy. "Just keep him there."

Altan closed the door, then slammed Leon back against it, hand on his throat. "What do you think you're doing?" he said, his voice rough, the way he'd talked to the fisherman. "Is it possible you think I'm Gülün?"

Leon said nothing, too shocked to respond, Altan's hand like a vise.

"Someone else you can trick? 'What was he doing in Edirne?' " Now using Leon's voice. "Somebody he knew before." He dropped his hand, Leon now gulping air. "What was the point of that little charade?"

"Not a charade," Leon said, breathing heavily. "I wanted to know. About Edirne."

"Then why not ask Jianu?" He jerked his head toward the conversation outside. "Since you picked him up."

Leon touched his throat. "Is this how Emniyet does it?"

"My friend, if this were an Emniyet inquiry you'd know. A fit of temper only. Much deserved. Lying to me. How many sides do you work for? Maybe none. Just you." He made a sound in his throat, a hint of disgust. "What does it matter? It's over soon. How much time do you think you have left for these games?"

Leon said nothing.

"Do you think I can protect you again?"

405

He shook his head. "Gülün is a fool, but not a complete fool. He is interested in you. And people talk. A strange little scene just now and he'll think about that too. The minute he understands, the minute he puts you on the quay that night, he acts."

"What do —"

"Don't," Altan said, cutting him off. "There's no time. You met the boat — he has a witness now. You were there. Mr. King was killed. Now another colleague killed. The man investigating the first crime. And you're even sleeping with his wife. Gülün makes the connection. So will any jury. I can't protect you from that." He took a breath. "And why would I want to? A murder solved. Two. Your ambassador will be grateful. Justice served."

"I didn't kill Frank."

"I believe you," Altan said easily. "But no one else will. You'll hang."

"Unless?"

"Unless we can save Gülün from himself. Change the story."

"And why would you do that?"

"Because I don't care about justice being served. Gülün hears the fisherman, he hears one thing. I hear another. You were there? Then you have our friend. Or you know where he is."

"And I tell you or you let me hang?"

"A generous offer. Considering."

"So you can shop him."

"Mr. Bauer, what do you care? Scruples at such a time? Lily said you were like that. I think maybe to criticize me a little. But maybe you just don't know the world. No matter. You're running out of time."

Leon stared at him.

"How long?" Altan said. "I don't know. Hours? You can run upstairs, pay off your fisherman and get him out of Istanbul before Gülün thinks to question him. But such men aren't hard to find. This one leaves a loud trail. So you buy a little time only. To do what? Leave the country? Gülün would have you stopped at the border. Appeal to your ambassador? Who won't believe you, either. So what do you do with this time? Run? Wait for Gülün to come? Maybe the Pera. A tender farewell scene."

"You're so sure I'm going to hang for something I didn't do."

"Aren't you? It's a chance I wouldn't want to take. Turkish justice. Sometimes not as perfect as one would like."

"No. And people get beaten too. By Emniyet. They say. Is that next? Try to beat it out of me?"

"I could. And worse. But the Americans

407

don't understand these things." He looked over. "And it's possible you're — the martyr type. A long job. Anyway, not necessary. People make mistakes when they're running. It's hard to think. You'll make them too. And I'll be there." He looked up, meeting Leon's eyes. "But I don't protect you then. That's your choice."

"Why not just call Gülün in now?"

"You haven't made the mistakes yet. I don't have Jianu. And it seems you don't want to tell me. So Gülün will come in his own time." He cocked his head. "And maybe it's a little for the sport, a head start to give Gülün the chase." He paused. "Before you trip. That's what you want? To trade your life for a man like Jianu?"

"I haven't traded it yet."

Altan stared at him for a second, then reached for the door. "Not yet." He turned the knob, opening it. "Your fisherman's waiting. Better hurry," Altan said, now to Leon's back. "The clock is running."

On the stair landing, stopping to catch his breath, he felt he could hear an actual ticking. How long? He looked up the steps. Think for a minute. Down the corridor a police photographer was probably still taking pictures. A crime scene. And the man

408

who could link him to it waiting in his office. First deal with him. Then what? The car in Üsküdar. Alexei on the ferry to Haydarpaşa. The mountain road. But all that seemed impossible now, the drive endless, exposed. Something else. Think. People make mistakes when they're running. He tried to slow his breathing. How long before Gülün put things together? Not a complete fool. There would be roadblocks. A car that might be traced back to Mihai, no matter what he said. But how else? Somewhere they'd never look. He felt himself turning to the steps then stopping, his feet refusing to move. He couldn't count on more than today, Altan's head start. I believe you, but no one else will.

"Oh, Mr. Bauer, I was just coming down." Dorothy on the stairs. "What am I supposed to do with him?"

Somewhere they'd never look.

"Coming," he said, his feet moving now. "Do we have Turkish liras?"

"Petty cash would. I'd need a voucher."

The fisherman was sitting in the outer office, fiddling with his cap, impatient.

"My secretary is going to get your money," Leon said, signing the form Dorothy had put in front of him. "Two hundred, right?"

"I didn't know there would be police," he

said, still uneasy about Altan. "Now they've seen me."

"Don't worry. It's not about this. Something else." He handed the voucher to Dorothy, then waited until she'd left. "Sorry about the delay with the money."

"Well, you did say —"

"The man who used to arrange the money died. So things got lost."

"Died? The one they said was shot?" Alert now.

"Yes."

"And now it's you," he said, looking at Leon.

Leon glanced toward the door. "Tell me something. Do you have your boat?"

The fisherman nodded.

"You interested in another job?"

"What, another one from Romania?"

"No, here. One night. Five hundred."

The fisherman's eyes widened. "To the Black Sea?"

"I'll tell you tonight. Not far."

"But five hundred." Suspicious.

"There could be police." He waited while this sank in. "Like last time."

The fisherman thought for a minute. "Well, that's always the risk, isn't it? That's what you pay for."

"And you're good at it. One night. Five

hundred."

"In advance?"

"On the boat. All of it."

He twisted his hat, thinking. "Where?"

Well, where? Not in town.

"The same place," he said. "You remember?"

The fisherman nodded.

"As soon as you get the money here, go to the boat and take it out on the Bosphorus. Anybody asks, you're going home. Go right up, Sariyer, anywhere up there, and put in until tonight." He took out his wallet and handed him a hundred liras. "Extra. For dinner. No raki. Then come back and pick me up. The same place as before."

"I'm taking you?"

"Two of us. Then you drop us and go home. One night."

"What time?"

"Late." Leon did a mental calculation. "Say, eleven. Okay?"

"Five hundred?"

"On the boat."

The fisherman looked at him, then nodded. "Five hundred." A verbal handshake.

"Good. Here's Dorothy with the money. Count it, make sure it's right."

"Mr. Woods wasn't thrilled about this. It's a lot of petty cash."

"I'll talk to him. All there? Good, I'll walk you down." He started to lead him out, turning to Dorothy. "I'm going to take Mrs. Bishop to the hotel. I'll be back later."

"Why are they asking questions?" she said, blurting it out to catch him on the run. "If he did it himself?"

Leon stopped.

"He didn't, did he? It's just like Tommy. Two now. It gives you the willies. Here. Down the hall." She caught herself, then glanced over at the fisherman. "How do you want this charged? The petty cash req. We have to charge it somewhere."

"It's one of Tommy's. The payment accounts with the initials. I'll do a memo when I get back."

"Oh," she said, interested, the fisherman part of Tommy's world.

Tommy, who still had to be explained. If Leon got the chance.

"That reminds me," he said, taking a file out of the desk drawer and putting it in a briefcase with the others. "Look," he said to Dorothy, "if it bothers you — about Frank — go home. I'll be out most of the day anyway."

"You'd think there's nowhere safer, wouldn't you? Marines and gates and everything. And now look. In his office. And you

412

know the way people talk."

"What way?"

"Well, Tommy, now Mr. Bishop. And you knowing both of them."

"So I did it?" he said easily, dismissing it. "Dorothy."

"I didn't mean — But you were here?" Troubled, wanting to know. "Mr. Burke asked if you were still here. When I left. He thought I'd been with you."

"You were here late?"

"Not here. Jack's office. You know, my husband. He has to go back to Ankara. So I waited around."

With access to the files. Already in the building.

"Well, I was probably long gone." He looked at her. "Don't start imagining things, okay? We've got too much to do."

Keep moving.

"By the way, when Hirschmann was here, when they were getting people out, how did they pay?"

Dorothy looked blank for a second, dazed by the quick switch. "To hire the ships, you mean?" she said, feeling her way. "Liras if they could. If they were paying Turks. Otherwise gold. Gold sovereigns."

"Not dollars."

"Not the ship owners," she said, still

413

uncertain what was being asked. "They'd have problems explaining where they got it. Government agents, it didn't matter. They had foreign currency reserves. So if we were sending a ship to Burgas, we'd probably have to pay the charter in gold."

"But the Bulgarians on the other end in dollars? And the Romanians?"

"Sometimes. Antonescu got paid in dollars. Why are you asking this?"

"I think some of it may have gone missing."

"No, Tommy would have said. He was very careful about money. You had to be. You couldn't trust the Romanians. They'd take the money and not send the people. You'd have to arrange it like that — part on delivery."

Leon stared at her, his mind racing ahead, his stomach dropping. Not the Russians. Something worse.

"Is that what you wanted to know?" Dorothy said, tentative, really asking why.

Tommy's secretary. More. Had they talked in bed? Never about this. How could you live with yourself knowing? But Tommy could. Planning powder rooms.

Outside, the fisherman kept his face down as they passed the police cars still idling in the courtyard. Leon hadn't bothered introducing Kay, still stunned, her face empty, off somewhere.

"Take a taxi," Leon said. "Go straight to the boat."

Efendi. Tolerant, almost amused. "Me? In a taxi?" He dipped his head to Kay, awkward. "At eleven," he said to Leon. "Perhaps something in advance?"

"On the boat."

And then, like some trick in a vanishing act, he slid away between two parked cars.

"What was he saying?" Kay asked.

"He was thanking me."

"No he wasn't."

"You feel okay?" he said, not answering.

"I don't know," she said, half to herself. "I don't know what I'm supposed to feel. To see somebody like that. The blood. You want to wipe it off and then you don't want to touch it. And then you think, it's my fault."

"It wasn't."

"You think it, though." She lowered her head. "You think it."

He took her arm to lead her into the hotel, but she shied away, an involuntary reaction. "You want to come up? Now?"

"And then leave. I want them to think I'm there. I have some things to do."

"What things?"

"Do you think I killed Frank?"

"What?"

"Well, they do. Or they're going to."

"But you were with me. I said."

"There's something else. I have to get out. I don't want you to get involved in this. Just go up the elevator with me so they think I'm with you."

"Get out. Of Istanbul? If you do that, they *will* think —"

"I can explain it somewhere else. Not here."

"Explain what?"

"Look, if you don't want to do this, I'll go. Maybe that would be the right thing anyway. But we can't just stand here."

"You're so sure somebody's watching."

"It's Istanbul." He took a breath. "If you don't want to, it's okay. I'll figure something out."

"That's right. That's what you do. You and Frank." She looked up, alarmed. "Whoever did it, he's going to try to kill you too? The same work —"

"No," he said quickly, then stopped, disconcerted. What if he'd taken Frank's call, knew what file he was going to pull? He'd be a threat, the next target. Move. "He won't have to if the police get me. They think I did it. Kay, I can't stay —"

She slid her hand through his arm. "Now

416

this," she said, to herself again, her lips grim.

They were quiet in the lift, eyes forward on the art nouveau grillwork, then aware of the elevator boy watching them go down the hall.

"What are we supposed to be doing?" she said inside. "Going to bed? With Frank there? Is that what they think of us?"

"Maybe. Or we're going over our stories, making sure they match." He looked over. "Or we're wondering how this happened. What's next."

She lit a cigarette, quiet. "That's something to think about, isn't it?"

He opened the briefcase, starting to riffle through the Hirschmann file.

"You brought work?" she said, thrown.

"I just want to check something. To be sure."

She drew on the cigarette, thoughtful. "You're really going away? Where?"

He looked up at her, not saying anything.

"You think I'd give you up to the police?"

"If you don't know, you won't have to."

"For how long?"

"Not long."

"And what's your plan for me? What do I do? Wait? While you run from the police? My god, I never even *talked* to the police until now."

He touched her arm. "I'll be back."

"If the police don't get you."

He looked at his watch. "Stay in for a few hours, okay?"

"With my lover," she said.

"That's right."

"Who tells me nothing."

He looked at her. "I'll be back." He turned the knob.

"What if they're already here?" Her voice like a hand, trying to stop him.

"They'll be in the lobby watching the elevator. The stairs. Having coffee. Some dates, this time of year. They won't be on the fire stairs."

They weren't. He took a backstreet down the Kasim Paşa side of the hill, then circled up, avoiding Tünel. Marina was in her kimono, putting on nail polish.

"It's about time. You said one more night only," she said, holding her fingers out to the air.

"We're leaving?" Alexei said, ready.

"Not yet."

"Yes, one night only," Marina said. "You'll make trouble for me."

"Don't worry. I'll get him out today."

"You think it's a hotel here."

"No, better," Alexei said, looking at her.

"Better for you," Marina said.

"Had any visits?" Leon asked. "From our friend?"

She shook her head, blowing on her fingers. "The landlord comes tonight."

"We'll be gone."

Leon took out Alexei's new passport and handed it to him.

"Barouh," Alexei said, looking at it. "What kind of name is that?"

"A Jew," Marina said, blowing on her nails again.

Alexei grunted, shrugging this off.

Leon brought out one of Tommy's passports. "Recognize him?"

Alexei looked at it carefully. "It's a different name."

"Remember the real one?"

"King. Like King Carol. They use that for a name in English."

Leon took a breath, his stomach dropping again, finally there. "Tell me about the meeting in Edirne."

Alexei peered at him, not sure where this was going. "You know that? How?"

"Twice, right?"

Alexei nodded.

"The first time he had Hirschmann with him."

"I never knew the other one's name."

"Big guy. From the Jewish Committee.

You were making a deal for Antonescu. Selling Jews. How many?"

"Three hundred. A few more. From the Transnistria camp."

"How much," Leon said flatly.

"Three hundred dollars a head," Alexei said. Merchandise. "We had used this price before. We delivered them to Constancia. The Jews had to pick them up. The mines, any German ship, that was their risk."

"They give you money at the first meeting?"

Alexei nodded. "Half. That was the purpose of the meeting. The arrangements had been made. Why are you asking this?"

"Tell me about the second meeting."

"Only King this time," Alexei said, then stopped, waiting.

"Let me guess. He was supposed to bring the other half, fifty thousand dollars, but he didn't. Why not? Did he say?"

"Your government stopped the exchange. They said the money was supporting the enemy. Of course this was foolishness, the money was for Antonescu only. He was like Carol, he wanted to take the treasury with him. So, Jews for dollars, why not? The American Jews would pay. But you stopped it."

"No," Leon said quietly, "he said you did.

420

Took the money and then betrayed him. What happened to the people?"

"They were sent back to the camp. No one was coming now to pick them up. There was no deal."

"Or any others after that," Leon said, running his hand over the top of the briefcase. "They stopped. No more exchanges."

"Without the money? He was not, you know, humanitarian, Antonescu. And anyway now the Russians were there. He didn't have time."

"But these people would have been saved. He would have made good on that."

"They were already in Constancia." He looked down again at the passport. "You're looking for him? That's why you're asking this?"

"No, he's dead. He was the man we shot on the pier. You would have recognized him. You knew about him. The only one who did." He looked down again at the briefcase, seeing Tommy's pink face. Not just one ship. All the others that didn't follow. "To do something like this. For fifty thousand dollars."

"You're surprised? People do worse for less."

Leon looked up. "Not worse."

"And they believed him? This story?"

"It was easy to believe. The Romanians? Look what you'd already done."

Alexei tapped Tommy's passport, then handed it over to Leon. "And you."

There was no one following on the tram back to Taksim, but to make sure Leon got off just before the French Consulate and used side streets to approach Denizbank from behind. The same manager, still eager to help, not surprised by Leon's explanation of a mix-up in his notes. Ergin again waited outside the door. Leon hesitated for a second, staring at the neat stacks in the box. He glanced up to see if anyone was watching. No one. He snatched up the bills in batches, slipping them into his briefcase. Another second, looking at the empty box, then he closed it, taking a deep breath. Now robbery, a criminal act. But stealing from whom? Blood money.

He called Ergin and watched him turn the key to lock the box. Would the weight of it feel different? When he thanked the bank manager, he felt his briefcase somehow glowing, the stolen money like a light inside that everyone could see, waiting to set off an alarm at the door. He imagined tellers with their hands in the air, getaway cars, police waiting. But no one in the street seemed to notice him, know that a crime had taken place. He took a taxi from a hotel rank.

He turned and looked out the back window as they left the square, down the sweeping curve of Aya Paşa. The usual traffic. How much time did he have? He had to get Alexei out of Marina's by nightfall. And stash him where? Now past the Park Hotel, the old German Consulate, the island of plane trees curving toward the Cihangir Apartments where Mr. Cicek listened to ringing phones. He thought of his picture window, the water view, and wondered suddenly if he would see it again. Something he hadn't imagined before, not being able to come back, the door closed behind him. Was anyone watching? Some car across the street with a bored policeman, smoking? Not even looking twice at the taxi, a man in back with twenty-five thousand dollars in his lap. Crossing another line.

■ ■ ■ ■

6
BÜYÜKADA

■ ■ ■

Mihai was out of the office, down at the Hasköy docks, but Leon had kept the taxi and they were there in minutes.

"Just wait. I shouldn't be long."

"With the meter? You'd be better off with an all-day rate." A higher fare.

"All right," Leon said, not wanting to argue, someone with money in his pockets. He looked down the street. No cars idling. Unless the taxi itself were the tail, now tracking his every movement. But it had been a random pickup, hadn't it? What it felt like, always looking over your shoulder.

There were health quarantine signs posted, but no barriers. The *Victorei,* listing slightly, was eerily quiet, as if everyone on board really was sick or some ghost ship had drifted into the Golden Horn. There were patches of rust on the hull and makeshift clotheslines strung up across the top deck, laundry flapping like ragged sails.

"It's not permitted." A harbor policeman, coming from behind. "Passengers are not permitted —"

"I'm not a passenger," Leon said, flashing the front of Tommy's passport. "Captain's expecting me."

The magic of an American passport. The guard nodded to the gangplank. Leon started up, noticing the garbage in the lapping water alongside, peels and eggshells that hadn't yet flushed away. There were sounds now, ropes creaking and voices from inside the ship, a baby, but still subdued, saving strength, the lassitude of a hospital ward. Up top, people wrapped in shawls and blankets were huddled on benches, facing the weak winter sun. There was a flutter of interest when they saw Leon, someone from the outside, maybe news. Sitting up, but their posture still wary, people who knew everything, who had been in the camps. Sallow skin, drained and skeletal, the faces Anna used to see.

Mihai was with the captain and a boy volunteered to get him. While he waited, Leon walked across the deck. Low murmurs in a language he didn't know, presumably Polish, open stares. On the other side of the water, Süleyman's Mosque rose up the hill in a cluster of swelling domes, the old

428

picture-book city a kind of mirage. The end of the Black Sea crossing, everything foreign now, home gone for good.

"So. What's so important you risk typhus?" Mihai said.

"They look all right," Leon said, nodding to the passengers.

"You should see down below. We send them up in shifts, so everyone gets some air. Down there it's — so never mind. What do you want?"

"Is there somewhere we can go?"

"What, here?" Mihai said, looking at the deck. "For a *kaffeeklatsch?* Find a square inch." He checked his watch. "They go back down in fifteen minutes. Just try moving them early."

"I'm serious. Off the ship, then."

"All right, come on," Mihai said, leading him toward the bridge. "What's the occasion? What happened at the consulate? You didn't shoot him, I hope." Airy, but looking at Leon from the side.

"You heard?"

"Everybody's heard. It's Istanbul. Anything to do with your Romanian friend?"

"In a way."

"What way?"

"It's a long story. I'll tell you later. I see the quarantine signs are still up."

"Bastards. A few more days we really will have typhus. Living like this —" He peered at him. "I thought you were making a trip. A little drive to the country."

"I changed my mind."

"Just like that?"

"I'll tell you that later too."

"Everything later. And the boat in Antalya?"

"Who is he?" one of the passengers asked Mihai in Romanian. "A British? He wants to stop us here?"

"American. A friend."

The man snorted. "Whose? Ours? So when do we leave?"

"Soon."

The man waved his hand down in disgust.

"They're all afraid of being sent back," Mihai said as they walked away. "We should have been there by now."

Leon looked again across the Horn, the pincushion of minarets. "What do they think it's going to be like? Like Poland?"

"That one lost his whole family. The pogrom in Jassy. Big open grave. He thinks it's going to be better than that, that's all."

In the bridge cabin, a man was leaning over a chart spread across the table, the Sea of Marmara, the thin bottleneck of the Dardanelles, then the open water, filled here

430

with numbers and channel markers, the orange trees somewhere in the imaginary distance.

"Ah," he said, looking up, "the new rations. Finally. Did you have any trouble with the harbor police? Unloading? We had to pay extra for the water."

"No," Mihai said, shaking his head, "not the rations yet. A friend. David, our captain."

"Oh," David said, ignoring Leon, disappointed. "When? Mihai —"

"I know. The truck will be here. Aciman promised." He nodded to Leon. "A social visit. We can have a few minutes?"

David hesitated, then realized he was being asked to leave, and nodded awkwardly. He moved away from the map. "You heard there was more trouble with Pilcer, the rabbi? The one suitcase allowance. He wants an exception, for the synagogue. How can he leave the menorah? You know. Like before."

"Tell him to throw his clothes over then. One suitcase. The extra fits another child. He can get new once we get there."

"He says it's special to them."

"One suitcase."

The captain shrugged, leaving. "He says that's what the Nazis said, for the train."

"And he's the one who survives. Tell him he calls me a Nazi again, I'll personally throw him over. And the menorah." He flicked his hand, a gesture of contempt. "The Orthodox." He turned to Leon as the captain left. "Just what Palestine needs. More Torah scrolls. Haganah asks for young people and who do they send? Make a soldier out of that. They want to bring Europe with them. What Europe? The ovens? A bullet in the head? My father was the same. And my uncle. Every day, in shul, hours, and outside you could see what was happening. Come with me, I said, get out now. No. We're too old to make a new life." He paused. "So they lost the old one. My sister at least listened. Now, Haifa. She helps meet the boats. Pull people out of the water before the patrols get them. And he wants to bring menorahs." He looked up, aware that he had been rambling. "So what's so important? What do you want?"

"To help get you out of here."

"Oh, Moses. You want to part Galata Bridge?"

"No," Leon said, opening the briefcase. "Go out when they raise it this morning. Now that everyone's feeling better." He handed over two stacks. "Ten thousand dollars. That's what you said, wasn't it?"

Mihai lifted the money, as if he were weighing it, then looked at Leon. "Where did you get it?"

"Who's going to ask? The harbormaster? The health officials? You can go tonight."

"I'm asking."

"Don't."

"Another long story?"

"It was money to help Jews. Now it will."

"But not the same ones."

"Use it," Leon said, looking directly at him. "No one knows. Leave tonight. Before they ask for more."

"An overnight recovery. From typhus."

"Insist. You can't stay here much longer. How long would it take? To pay them off."

"Not long."

"When do they raise the bridge?"

"Three thirty, something like that."

"Not sooner?" Leon said, thinking.

Mihai peered at him. "What do you want?"

"Nothing," Leon said.

"Ten thousand dollars for nothing."

"They were going to buy Jews out with it," Leon said. "So buy them out now. No strings." He reached for another stack.

"And that?"

"Two places. On the boat. Five thousand dollars. However you want to use it."

"There are no places on the boat."

"Standing room."

"So," Mihai said. "Money to help the Jews." He lifted a stack. "And money to help a killer of Jews?" Raising his eyebrow toward the other stack. "That's who it is? Two places? Who's the other one?"

"Me."

"You," Mihai said slowly. "You want to take the butcher to Palestine. On this boat."

"Just hitch a ride. For part of the way."

"And you think I would do this?" He held out the money. "There are no places."

Leon shook his head. "The money's yours. It's not a condition."

"No, an obligation. What made you think I would take this?"

"I thought you'd want to get them out of here."

"Not for this price."

"Hear me out. One minute. You leave tonight. There might be an inspection, so we won't leave with you. He's traveling as a Turk. All the boats come out of the Horn at once, it's busy. When you're out of the city, past the Princes' Islands, you pick us up. I have a boat arranged. The other passengers don't have to know who. Two more. We'll stand if we have to. Near Cyprus, the boat from Antalya picks us up. We're gone. As far

434

as you're concerned we were never here." He stopped. "It's the last place they would ever look."

"For him? Yes," Mihai said. "And you were never here. Is that how you arrange things for your conscience these days? Pretend they never happen?" He put the money on the table, then looked up at Leon. "Why are you doing this?" he said, his voice softer. "Do you know anymore? For your country? The one you don't live in?"

"Why do you?" Leon said, nodding to the boat.

"A house is burning, someone jumps out. What do you do? Keep walking? Not try to help?"

"Then help them."

Mihai looked down at the money. "The devil bargains this way."

"The devil."

"You don't see yourself. Come to this side of the table."

"I have to get him out."

"And that makes it all right."

"He'll die."

"Well, people do," Mihai said, his voice hard. He went over to the window. "Millions. No deals." He looked down at the deck. "These people," he said, waving his hand, brooding. "Who knows what they did

435

to survive? *Sonderkommandos* maybe, some of them. You don't ask. If you weren't there, you have no right. The Romanian you met? On the deck? He told me what they did at Jassy. People like your friend. They tortured families together, to find the others. They didn't beat you, they beat your wife. Made you watch. If you'd like us to stop — like that. They raped a girl, in front of her father. A mistake. He never told them anything — he went mad. So a waste. Except for whatever pleasure they took." He looked away, toward the deck. "They all have stories like this. So who knows what bargains they made? And all you want me to do is take some money. I keep my soul. But I help the butcher. That's your idea?"

"Jianu doesn't matter anymore. They do."

"And what happens after you get him out? He tells your people things about the Russians. Maybe even true. So they know something for a while. So the Russians change them. And the game goes on. But he's out of it. He goes free. And you want me to help. That's the business you're in now? And what do I get? A boat so old maybe it sinks. But maybe it gets them there." He stopped, looking down on the deck, the flapping laundry, quiet for a few minutes. "So I answer myself. To get these

436

people to Palestine — what would I do? Is it even my choice?" He picked up the money, absentmindedly flipping the corners, then looked up at Leon. "But I don't forget you did this. Arranged such a bargain for me. The debt's canceled. We're quits."

"What debt?"

"Whatever debt there was between us. It's paid." He put the money in his pocket and reached over for the other stack. "How far past the Princes' Islands?"

Leon didn't say anything for a second, dismissed. Mihai waited, the silence a kind of prodding.

"Off Büyükada. We'll signal. The other ships will be heading for the main channel. Harbor police too. Just have the captain go slow."

"Don't worry, that's the only speed he can go. If you're not there, we won't wait, understood? Your friend's a Turk now?"

"A Turkish Jew."

Mihai looked up. "You think of everything. I'm assuming the deal is we get him there alive. That's why you're going? The body-guard?"

"No, I have to leave too. The police are looking for me."

Mihai went still. "Why?"

"They think I shot Frank."

"Why would they think that?" Mihai said quietly.

"And Tommy," Leon said, looking at him. "The boat at Bebek? The fisherman turned up. They saw him. He can identify me, put me there that night. So they add two and two and get five."

"He can identify everyone there that night."

"But there wasn't anyone else," Leon said, meeting his stare. "Just me." He took one more stack out of his briefcase.

"What's that?"

"I can explain what happened to Washington. I'm bringing them a witness they'll believe. My house present. I'm not so sure about the Turkish police. Once they have an idea, they don't like to be wrong. Especially when our people say they are. So I may not be able to come back. If not, this is for Anna. I'll make arrangements to move her, but you'll need this — to handle things."

Mihai said nothing for a minute. "Why didn't you tell me this before?" he said finally. "That it was for you?"

"It's for both. I need him."

"You have another witness."

"No. There was no one else there. I'll swear to it."

Another second, not talking.

"It's interesting how you do this," Mihai said, looking away. "Draw these lines. This is acceptable, not that. Do you argue with yourself? You should study Talmud. You'd be good at it. You can find anything there. Though maybe not why you should save the butcher."

"No one else. Or you'd never work here again."

Mihai looked back, then nodded, accepting this. "And your fisherman? Will he swear too?"

"If it comes to it. He likes the work. It's easy money. He'd want to do what we say."

"And when his job's over?"

"There's another one. He's bringing me tonight. Make yourself scarce, so he doesn't spot you. Trigger any memories."

"You hired him?"

"This way I know where he is. If he's with me, he's not with the police. And if he is someday, the job puts him in a spot. He's accusing me, but helping me to escape? For pay? How do you build a case around that? And then there's all the other work, things he'd rather not talk about."

"In Turkey they don't need to build a case."

Leon nodded. "Then let's not get caught." He handed over the stack for Anna. "You

439

may not need this. The ambassador makes the right calls, I could be back in no time. In good standing. But just in case. You'll take care of her?"

Mihai pocketed the money, an answer. He looked at the briefcase. "Is that it or does the money keep coming? Like a magic hat."

"Just a little pocket change. Traveling expenses." He touched Mihai's upper arm. "Thank you."

"Listen to me," Mihai said, gruff, but not removing the hand. "Any police, David puts you off. Orders. It's understood? It's not for you, this ship. It's for them."

"There won't be any trouble. It's the last place they'd look."

"Yes." Mihai shook his head and turned away. "The last place. Who else has to do such things, just to live? Survive the ovens and — then help the killers. And maybe it's not even the worst before we're finished with this." His mouth turned up slightly, a wry tic.

"What?" Leon said, catching his expression.

"Rabbi Pilcer. If he knew. What I'm taking instead of his menorah."

He told the cab to take him back to the Pera but then, a hunch, asked to pull up instead to a pay phone near the Koç shipyards.

"Thank God you called," Kay said.

"The police are there?"

"No. I mean, they may be, I don't know, but Gülün called, asking for you."

"And?"

"I told him you made sure I was okay and then went back to the consulate."

"He buy it?"

"I don't know. He wants you to call him. He has a few questions. Polite. Well, for him."

"I can't come back, then. He must have men there." And probably at the consulate, the Reynolds office, Cihangir, the door really closing now.

"Where are you? I'll meet you."

He looked through the glass at the taxi waiting by the curb, the stretch of empty road by the docks, some cranes moving silently in the distance. Out in the open.

"Kay —"

"You can't just go. Not like this. Just go. I have to see you. Do you know what it's like, sitting here? Like a wake. Like his casket's in the room."

"Kay. They'll put a tail on you. I won't be gone long."

"Come up the back then. Like before. Don't just go."

441

"I can't go to the Pera."

"Somewhere else then. Please. Just tell me." Her voice catching, some nerve finally snapping.

He glanced again at the taxi. Not Laleli. Georg's in Nişantaşi? A story for the neighbors, a photograph Georg wanted him to have, and how was the dog? Assuming they had a key. Wondering who the lady was. The whole maze of Istanbul and nowhere to hide.

"Leon —"

"I'm thinking." A movie, anonymity in the dark. But not where a new widow would go. Somewhere in plain sight. That would make sense to them. Outside, the cabbie flicked away the end of a cigarette. Leon followed its arc, a few sparks, to the gutter. "Okay," he said quickly. "Go to the concierge." Methodical now, as if he were laying down cards. "Ask him to recommend a good shop in the Bazaar. For copper, silver work. He'll know one, they all do. Then take a taxi to the Beyazit Gate. There'll be a lot of gold shops just inside. Keep going straight. I'll find you."

She was quiet for a second. "I'm going shopping? Leon —"

"For an urn. For Frank's ashes. Be sure to tell the concierge that. They'll ask him what you wanted."

"My god," she said, her voice squeamish.

"I know. But it's something you'll have to do, sooner or later. They might even give you a little room, out of respect. I doubt it, but they'll still want to keep their distance. And it's something you wouldn't be doing with me."

"No."

"So they won't be looking for that. Give me fifteen minutes, then go downstairs."

"Why the Bazaar? Why not somewhere over here?"

"Because it's easy to get lost in the Bazaar. Everybody does. So they won't be surprised when they lose you."

Leon waited in a stall a few doors down from the entrance, back half turned, fingering necklaces, while the salesman scurried around the shop, bringing out more trays. Every inch of wall space seemed to be covered in gold, dangling and shiny. Who bought it all? The line of stores stretched for at least a mile, all crammed with jewelry, shimmering with reflected light. In a few hours the market would be locked, only night guards in the empty shuttered streets, but now it hummed, the noise of a thousand voices rising up to the domed ceiling.

443

When Kay came through the gate she stopped for a minute, dazzled, trying to get her bearings. A winter coat and hat, the western clothes like a magnet to the shopkeepers, inviting her in as she walked down the passage. Leon waited a few more minutes, watching the people. The salesman brought out another tray. And then Leon spotted him, a man in a suit who could have passed for a relative of Gülün, maybe actually was. Stubbly cheeks, eyes fixed ahead, keeping Kay in sight. Two more minutes. No one else. Not a team. Leon left the shop and began to follow, tracking Kay's hat in the stream of bobbing heads. She passed Feraceciler Sok, the first big cross street, and then began to loiter, gazing into shop windows, waiting for Leon to appear. The policeman stopped too, turning away slightly.

Leon went over to one of the tea boys who darted through the market like mice, appearing around corners with trays and vanishing behind rolled carpets. He handed him a coin. The woman in the hat, say my name and lead her toward the Iç Bedesten, then take the first left, the coin disappearing into a pocket, the boy gone almost as quickly, something out of *Ali Baba*. Leon watched as the boy approached Kay, just brushing by, but she turned after him, not looking back. The policeman picked up speed. Leon took a parallel street, circling. In this part of the Bazaar the streets were a grid, easier to plot. Curios and souvenirs now, inlaid boxes. He stepped into a doorway just after where she would turn and handed the shopkeeper a ten-lira note, then stood to the side, a screen nearby. Any minute, around the corner.

"Kay."

She started for the shop.

"Don't come in, just look at the window. He'll have to stop."

She raised her eyebrows, who?

"You'll see him. He looks like Gülün. Probably a cousin. Go up two streets, then left and duck into a stall. Wait till he passes and then come out. Now he'll be looking for you. When he sees that you're behind him, he'll have to keep going. Stay behind. Let him get a street or two ahead, then take a quick right. There'll be a lot of leather shops. Bags and things. Just follow the street. Ready?"

She began walking. Leon stood out of sight until the policeman went by.

The shopkeeper looked at Leon. *"Efendi?"*

"Her husband," Leon said.

The shopkeeper's eyes widened, an unexpected drama. Leon handed him another note.

"If he comes back, you never saw her."

The shopkeeper dipped his head, the note gone as quickly as the boy's coin.

Leon hurried toward the narrower streets with leather and clothing, everything hanging on hooks in tiers, almost blocking the light. Where he'd told her to turn. A few minutes, people offering him wallets and belts, then finally a glimpse of the hat.

"This way. Did he turn back?"

"I don't know." Flushed, slightly out of breath.

They took the curved passage back toward Beyazit Gate, a circling the policeman wouldn't expect as he wandered through the aisles looking for her.

Outside, they crossed into the square, scattering pigeons, and went through a plain door that opened onto a cloistered courtyard with a marble fountain in the middle.

"What's this?"

"A library. He probably doesn't even know it's here. It was an inn for the mosque. See the doors? That's where people stayed."

Kay exhaled, as if she'd been holding her breath. "Can we sit down? It's okay?"

Leon led them to one of the low walls surrounding the courtyard. After the Bazaar

446

the air seemed eerily quiet, the only sounds a few birds drinking at the fountain pool. The last of the afternoon sun. He thought of the crowded benches on the *Victorei* deck, people wrapped in blankets.

"We don't have much time."

"Will he keep looking?"

"For a while."

"All this just to see you. It's serious now, isn't it? How long can you do this? Before —" She looked at him. "I had the feeling, at the hotel, I might not see you again."

"No," he said, brushing her cheek with his hand. "What's wrong? You look —"

She smiled a little. "Makeup never works when you need it, does it? Am I all blotchy?"

He shook his head.

"Don't be nice," she said, taking out a handkerchief. "I'm probably a mess. Well, it's the right day for it. It's not as if I didn't have feelings for him. I mean, I married him." She blew her nose, nodding to some question. "And cheated on him. Not a very good wife, was I? So maybe it's not just for him. Maybe me. Everything." She wiped the corners of her eyes. "You think crazy things." She took a minute, looking over toward the market. "What happens when I don't bring an urn back?"

"You were overwhelmed. You couldn't go

through with it. Not today."

She looked down. "Another one of your stories. You like it," she said, cocking her head back to the Bazaar. "The cat and mouse. It's easy for you."

"Losing someone's easy. The rest isn't."

"But you enjoy it."

"Sometimes," he said, turning it over. "It's seeing if you can stay up there." He pointed to some imaginary balance beam. "Not fall. Anyway," he said, taking a breath. "We can't stay long."

"One more minute." She touched his hand, then moved hers back. "It's like a church, this place. If somebody sees —" She twisted her ring. "Are you leaving soon?"

"Tonight."

"What I was thinking —"

He waited.

"At the hotel. The police. Maybe you can't come back." She looked up. "Take me with you."

"What?"

"Just as we are. You don't have to — The way we are. I don't care what people think."

"I can't."

"Can't? Why? Where are you going? At least tell me that. I won't get in the way. If they follow. And you're good at this."

"I can't," he said, stopping her. "It's not

448

just me." He paused. "You're safer here."

"Safer," she said.

"I'll be back in a day or two."

"Maybe. Or maybe shot, like Frank. In your cat and mouse. And then what's my life?"

"Kay —"

"Well, it's possible, isn't it? So tell me what to say when they ask. He went to Ankara? Why? I don't know. And make up a story for me. What happens. If you don't come back."

"I will."

"And then what?"

"Then we'll see."

She was quiet for a minute. "We'll see. It's not much, is it?" She stood up, folding her arms across her chest. "My god, look at me. Ready to run away with you. Where? I don't know. Like criminals. And Frank not even buried. What kind of woman does that?" She held up a hand before he could answer. "I know. You can't. So now what. Buy an urn. When I'm feeling better." She pulled a piece of paper from her pocket. "The concierge said this one was the best." She looked over at him. "What did you mean, it's not just you going?"

"Somebody's going with me."

"Who?"

"Kay —"

"And that's why it's not safe?"

He nodded, then looked at his watch. "We have to go."

"Walk away," she said quietly. "All day, at the hotel, I kept thinking. What if it's the end?" She looked at him as if she were trying to memorize his face. "Like Frank. It could be. The same work. Secrets. And now he's dead. For what? His country?" She turned her head. "Whatever it was to make someone do that. It's funny, what people will do for their country. Things they would never do for each other. So what if it's like Frank? He's not coming back."

"I'm not dead."

She walked over to him, putting a hand on his shoulder. "No. But maybe not coming back, either." She took a breath. "So. When I leave here —" She left it dangling.

"Go out past the mosque to the taxi rank. If he spots you, he'll just think you wandered off and he's picked up the trail again. I'll wait here. Go back to the Pera. Talk to the concierge."

"Tell him I couldn't go through with it. And what's the rest?" she said idly. "Dinner in my room? Or downstairs, with a book. So they can see I'm not waiting?"

He looked at her.

"Never mind. It's all right," she said, moving her hand up to the side of his head, a tentative touch, then brushing his hair back. "I just wanted to see you. In case. Do you know the awful thing? I'm not sorry. Isn't that terrible?" Her voice breaking a little at the end. "To say that today?"

Leon got up, taking her by the arms.

"No," Kay said, patting his chest. "No good-byes. Just come back."

He nodded.

"And then we'll see," she said, then suddenly reached forward, putting her arms around him, head next to his. "But for a second. Nobody's here."

He felt her tight against him, hands tugging at his coat.

"Just for a second," she said.

The creak of an opening door.

"Oh," she said, startled, breaking away.

A woman in a headscarf, looking like a nun in the cloistered walkway.

Kay stepped back, her eyes anxious, as if a platform whistle had just blown, then lowered her head and started walking to the door, leaving it ajar for the Turkish woman, only a quick last glance over her shoulder, then into the square. Where Gülün's cousin would see her. Willing to run away with him. And then what's my life? Her hands pulling

451

at him. For a minute he stood still, a ticking in his ear, feeling suspended up on a high rope with his arms held out. Too far away from the edge now to go back. Everyone below looking up, waiting.

Marina didn't want any more money.

"Just get him out of here, before it's trouble."

Alexei had gone into the bedroom to get his duffel, packed and ready, everything as trim as his short hair.

"You're so rich?" Leon said.

"No. But you're nice to me. Not so many are. So maybe it's thanks for that."

"Nice?" Leon said, thinking of sweaty sheets.

"Call it what you like. You like to think the best. Not like him. He thinks the worst. Of everybody."

"Maybe he's right."

She looked up at him. "He'll be trouble for you. Someone like that."

"He talk to you?"

"He didn't have to. You take someone's clothes off, you know things."

He smiled, nodding at her kimono. "Do you ever get dressed?" A life in silk, lying on beds, a painter's idea of a harem.

"Yes. Like a lady, very nice. Shoes, hat.

Sometimes like a Turkish lady, with the scarf. My old friend Kemal comes with me. An escort. So I can go places."

"Like where?" Leon said, intrigued.

"Here and there. Shops. You're surprised? You think I live in bed? Waiting for you?"

"No."

"Yes, you're surprised. What would you do? If you saw me on the Rue de Pera? Walking there. In a dress."

"Say hello."

"No. You're with somebody maybe. Or you don't see. You know why? Because you don't expect it, to see me. You know what I do sometimes? Kemal takes me to the bar at the Park. And I see men who come here. And them? They don't see it's me. They don't expect to see me there, so they don't."

"Maybe they think you're working," Alexei said, coming out of the bedroom. "The hotel bar."

"Ha," Marina said, annoyed. "You think I go looking for business?"

"Not in the streets," Alexei said, volleying. "Not yet."

"Go fuck yourself. That's the language you use with him," she said to Leon. "What he understands." She turned to Alexei. "So you're ready? What are you waiting for?"

"Thanks for everything," Alexei said, playing with her.

She waved this off. "I don't do it for you."

Alexei bowed. "So now I've met one. With the heart of gold."

She said something in Armenian that Leon couldn't understand, presumably a curse, spitting it out. "I hope they catch you. You deserve it."

Alexei moved closer to her, putting his hand to her throat, so quickly it seemed to have already been there. "Just don't help them."

"Hey," Leon said, surprised.

"You wouldn't do that, would you?" Alexei said, waiting for her to shake her head before he took his hand away.

"Pig."

"For Christ's sake —" Leon started.

"Don't waste your breath. She'd sell you out too. How much, I wonder," he said, looking at her.

"For you?" she said. "Not much."

"All right," Leon said, ending it. "You ready?"

Alexei made a thank-you flourish to Marina and went out to the hall.

"What was that all about?" Leon said to her.

"He wanted it for free. After he ran out of money. For a man like that? Don't think the best of that one. Get rid of him."

"But you wouldn't take the money be-fore?"

"To hide him? Then it's a crime. They ask, I say no, I never helped. Just money to fuck me. How did I know who he was?" She looked up. "I still don't."

Leon leaned over and kissed her on the cheek. "Thank you."

She flinched. "Don't think the best of me, either. I took what he paid. Go," she said, shooing him out. "Before the landlord." She paused. "Maybe you'll come see me again. Like before. When it's over with him."

"I'll buy you a drink at the Park."

She raised an eyebrow, then smiled. "Go," she said, closing the door.

They walked single file down the stairs, just the sound of their footsteps and the faint dripping of water, the familiar cat smell. At the door, Leon looked out, then steered Alexei left, around the hill.

"That was a hell of a thing to say," Leon said. "A girl saves your life."

"She's a whore."

"And what does that make you?"

Alexei said nothing, following him. They passed the Dervish Lodge, then the church where Tommy's funeral service had been. Kay sitting ahead, face hidden by her hat.

"So this business with your Mr. King. Who kept the money. He's just a thief. That's your thinking? Not with the Russians?"

"No."

"So it's safe, the consulate?"

"Not exactly. Somebody was shot there last night."

Alexei stopped for a second, looking over at him. "One of your people?"

"From Ankara. Head of the Soviet desk."

"But he's killed in Istanbul. So there is someone here," he said, beginning to walk again, thinking. "But why? The embassy, yes, they'd want someone inside. But a consulate? Passports?"

"You can pick up a lot here. Tommy's group was here, don't forget."

Alexei shook his head. "The war, it was different. The cable traffic's in Ankara. That's where you want your people. How many can they have? Americans are hard for them to recruit. Usually locals. So maybe a local here too."

Saydam the guard, gone for a smoke.

"Or maybe to make you *look* here. Not in Ankara. Your man was here alone? No one came with him?"

"Just his wife. A few days ago."

Alexei grunted. "His wife. Well, not her."

456

"No."

"It's something a Romanian might think of. Not the Russians. Not Melnikov."

"They're not all Melnikovs."

"Yes, all. They think with this," Alexei said, making a fist, then smiled a little, amusing himself. "But think how perfect for her. To have the Russian desk in bed."

Lying side by side on pillows. Some other face, not hers. But they must have.

"These hills," Alexei said, a little winded.

They had come downslope from Galatasaray, but were now climbing again past the Italian hospital.

"And the police?"

"They think I did it."

"You?" Alexei said, surprised. "Why?"

"I was there." Leon paused. Why not say? Even Gülün knew. "I'm sleeping with his wife."

Alexei peered at him, at a loss, then grunted. "You should have told me before. Now they're after both of us? That's twice the risk."

"Only for a few hours. Then we're gone."

"And where now? Another flat?"

"No. I figured you could use a bath. After all the exercise."

They stopped at a wooden door with a list of services posted alongside.

"A public place?" Alexei said.

"You can sit here for hours and nobody'll even notice you. Just a man in a towel."

The *hamam* wasn't old, probably turn of the century, but it had been modeled on the historic baths in Sultanahmet, the entrance hall a large rotunda with a fountain where men sat drinking tea, cooling off from the steam in the hot room. They were given towels and slippers and changed in the cubicles surrounding the courtyard, then went through the temperate room, Alexei adjusting the towel around his waist. A tight, wiry body with dark scars on one side that Leon realized might be bullet wounds, little flecks elsewhere. Knives? Nine lives, eight of them gone.

They walked into a wall of steam in the *hararet* and for a second Leon's eyes started to water, stung by the heat. He could feel the wet air pushing down into his lungs, a searing, like standing too close to a fire. A man was being kneaded by a masseur on the marble slab in the center and attendants were scraping a few others with coarse mitts, but everyone else just sat lazing on benches with their eyes half closed, like lizards in the sun. They took in Leon and Alexei, then went back to the heat, chests glistening. Leon looked around the room once, scanning faces, indistinct in the steam, then joined Alexei leaning back against the wall.

"Of course, sometimes it's a matter of opportunity," Alexei said, brooding, back in the earlier conversation. "You don't have to plant someone — he's already there." He was quiet for a minute. "And then he has to protect himself. You're lucky."

"You think so," Leon said, offhand.

"You're looking for him, yes? He must know. But he shoots the Russian desk first."

"Maybe Frank found him. I haven't. That's not why I'm there, remember? I'm supposed to find who killed Tommy. I'm looking for myself."

Tangling again, like the calligraphy in the tiles around them.

Alexei smiled. "An interesting board. But how do you win it?"

"You're going to win it for me. I just have to get you out alive."

"With the Russians looking. Now police. Not just me anymore. You. Easier to identify." He closed his eyes again. "Someone who sleeps with the wife." He shook his head, then sighed out loud, giving in to the steam. "It feels good, the heat. Women. Turkish baths. I should have come to the Americans sooner."

"But you were busy."

Alexei lifted an eyelid. "That's right. Busy."

He wiped sweat off his upper arms then got up and went over to the basin, pouring water over his head and chest. The man getting the massage moaned. Everything hidden in the steam, the street outside miles away.

"How did you get that?" Leon said, nodding to the scar on Alexei's side.

He sat down again. "Stalingrad. I was lucky. If it had been deeper — sepsis. No field hospital. You died right away or you died later."

"You were at the front? I thought intelligence —"

"Antonescu liked to put us in the forward units. To make sure. No deserters, no defeatist talk. The Russians did it too."

"He'd risk intelligence officers that way?"

"Think how many he killed himself. Why not let the Russians do it." He wiped his forehead. "You're surprised? It's what they are, these men. Look at Stalin. Never safe. Sooner or later, everybody goes. So the trick is to go later."

"If you're lucky," Leon said, imagining the field littered with bodies. "You were hit twice?"

"This?" Alexei said, pointing to the smaller scar. "No, this was a woman. In Bucharest. You don't expect it from a woman."

"She shot you?"

Alexei shrugged. "She was a little bit —" He touched his temple. "Again, lucky. Not a good shot."

"And the others?" Leon said, pointing, curious now.

"Shrapnel. Also Stalingrad." He ran his hand down his side. "Like a war map, no? Except for Ilena. A crazy temper. But a good fuck. Like that one back there," he said, jerking his head toward Marina's flat. "Well, you know. She said you're a regular. A good fuck." Something between them, easy, locker-room friends.

Leon said nothing.

"But these days," Alexei said. "You never know if it's your last. So they're all good. The Russian desk? How's that?"

Leon stood up and went over to the basin, sluicing himself. Why couldn't everything wash off like sweat? Selling Jews for Antonescu. Sending them back. Străuleşti. Fucking Marina. They're all good now. He rubbed a soapy mitt over his chest, scouring it, as if he were wiping away Alexei's hands, touching him. The same woman. More water.

When he turned back, the whole room seemed to be behind gauze, not quite clear. Bodies shiny with fat, hairy, leaning over with their heads down or sitting back, faces raised to the star-shaped pinpricks of light coming through the dome, the fleshy democracy of the baths, everyone just a body. Who were they all? Shopkeepers and rug salesmen, maybe a policeman off duty, a dockworker, not real in the steam, bodies to hide behind. He looked at Alexei, smaller somehow in his towel, paler, the war map of scars just little bruises from this distance, skin beginning to sag, the inevitable gravity. Before Leon had seen a fighter in military trim, but now the body was older, as slack as all the others, the same tired face Leon had seen when they walked out of Laleli. You never know if it's your last. Not a monster, a man in a towel. Both.

"You weren't in the war?" Alexei said when Leon came back, his voice drowsy.

"No. My eyes."

"In Romania they take you even if you're blind."

"I tried. I was too old for the draft but I went anyway and I couldn't get past the eye test. All they'd have let me do was hold down a desk somewhere. I was already doing that here." Explaining himself, some

462

point of honor.

"And that's why you started doing this work?"

"I guess. It came up, that's all."

"No eye tests for this. And now it's over, the war? You want to fight the next one?" He snorted. "A soldier. You think you know what it's like. What you have to do." He went quiet for a minute, private. "The first time, it's difficult. But then it's easier."

"What? To kill somebody?"

"No, betray them. You think you can't do it. It closes up." He put his hand to his throat, a choking gesture. "That's how it was for me anyway. I couldn't breathe. But you have to do it, so you do. And after that it's easier. You'll see," he said, facing Leon.

Alexei turned back, closing his eyes again, drifting with the steam.

"Do you know what I remember about the war? The cold. No mountains there, just wind. I thought I would never be warm again. And now look. Sweating. Maybe they'll send me somewhere where it's warm, when they're finished with me. We never discussed that. What should I ask for? Where is it warm in America?"

"I don't know. Florida."

"Florida," Alexei said, pronouncing it in syllables.

"Just go wherever they can hide you."

"You think it's like Trotsky? I'm so valuable the Russians send out assassins?" He shook his head. "Once I say what I have to say, they don't care." He paused. "Neither will you." He stretched a little, enjoying the heat. "They have nice women in Florida?"

"Jews."

Alexei opened his eyes, looking over at him. "Always that with you." He leaned back again. "Ilena was a Jew."

Leon was quiet, trying to imagine what the story had been, what she'd known. Or maybe it had been before Străuleşti, a lovers' quarrel. Angry enough to shoot. And then miss. His sixth life, or seventh.

"You've paid for a massage?" Alexei said, looking toward the masseur. "It's okay?"

Leon nodded.

"What's the word?"

"*Uğma.* But just lie down. He'll know."

Leon watched Alexei flop on the warm marble, the *tellak* kneeling over him, hands already working his shoulders. A full-body massage, lying out there in plain view. He squinted at the other men in the room, none of whom were watching, lost in their own worlds. Moustaches and stomach folds. Bodies. The women's baths would be the same, not Corot's pink nymphs, but drooping

464

breasts and doughy thighs, little boys pretending not to look as towels came unwrapped. Kay naked in the hotel window, self-conscious, an alabaster light. Then he saw her again in bed with Frank, just talking, murmuring, in bed with the Russian desk. Think how perfect. Well, not the wife.

But what if Frank had called the hotel? You don't expect it from a woman. Standing behind him at his desk, an easy shot. Facing down Gülün. He was with me. Each other's alibi. But Leon hadn't been, not all the time. Not while he'd been in Tommy's office, the unreliable Saydam gone somewhere else. Somebody in Ankara. It was Frank who thought there was a plant in the consulate. Who had killed Tommy. Except he hadn't. Leon had.

His mind, idling in what-ifs, began racing now. Everything she had ever said to him. Hating secrets, his. Tell me. Or maybe something simpler, like Ilena picking up a gun in a Bucharest hotel, doing it for love, not missing this time. Coming up to him at Lily's. Do something for me. What did he know about her really? Everything. His mind stopped, so still now that he felt the trickle of sweat on his chest and then he felt it on hers, brushing it with the back of his hand. How do you know? Because you do, the rest all steam and circles, fever dreams. Not like Alexei, suspecting everybody, the only life he knew. How long did it take for that to happen? You think you know what it's like. In bed now, his skin still slick, but not with Kay, Marina, Alexei on her other side, leaning over, winking at him, sharing.

He opened his eyes, panting, not sure where he was. Smoke. No, steam, hot in his throat as he gulped it down. The bath, awake again, but the room still insubstantial, wispy. How long had he been out? Crazy dreams, with Alexei in them now, in his head. But not here. He looked again at the marble slab, empty, a Turk being pummeled near the edge. He stood up. Don't panic. He wouldn't have been taken without a fight, some noisy struggle. Unless he had walked out by himself, waiting for his babysitter to nod off, a plan of his own.

Leon went over to the basin and poured water over his head, as if he still hadn't completely awakened. Don't draw attention. He looked around the room. The same interchangeable bodies, no Alexei. Not on the benches, in the alcoves. Gone. Check the cubicles. See if his clothes are still here.

He hurried through the temperate room, back to the big rotunda, and stopped short. Alexei was drinking tea by the fountain, a new towel wrapped around his waist. Leon breathed out, a relief that was almost a physical shudder.

"What's wrong?" Alexei said.

"I didn't know where you were," Leon said, hearing himself, a parent who'd lost a child in a store.

"You should drink some tea. Replace the sweat." Unconcerned, only Leon rattled, aware suddenly that Alexei had become his lifeline, that without him everything would go wrong.

He picked up a towel and started to dry himself, catching a flicker of movement over Alexei's shoulder, a newspaper page being turned. *Hürriyet.* Where Özmen had his column, picking things up at parties, then passing them on to the Emniyet, they said. Altan's ears everywhere. Lily more than a friend. Like Topkapi with its peepholes and listeners, still the same Istanbul. Another impatient turning, the man probably looking for the sports section. Then the paper dropped a little and Leon saw his face. Enver Manyas. Not looking back at Leon, eyes fixed on the page, maybe willing them there. The paper went up again.

"Now what?" Alexei said.

Leon sat down, keeping his voice low. "The man behind, with the newspaper. He knows us."

"Us?"

"He made your passport. He had your picture. His place isn't far from here. Maybe a coincidence. Just a bath."

Alexei took this in, then nodded. "Change your clothes. Now. The big street below? There was a café on the corner. Wait there fifteen, twenty minutes. If I don't come, then go the rest of the way down the hill. There was a mosque. I'll find you there." In control, as if he were reading from some map in his head.

"He may not be —"

"Go change. Now."

Alexei got up, heading for the toilet, not looking behind.

Leon sat for a second more, glancing at the row of men in towels. What if there were others? Or none? Why not just walk back to Enver and say hello, get a reaction. But the only way to really know would be to see if he followed. Either of them. Go change. Orders.

Outside the air felt cold after the warm bathhouse. He started down. A café he'd never even noticed, but already on Alexei's escape route, like the stairs to the roof in Laleli. He ordered tea and sat with his back to the wall looking out the window. Not as many people out now, just a few heading down to the trams, and never the same one twice. He ran his fingers nervously over the tulip glass. What if Alexei didn't come, snatched at the door? A few days ago Leon had wanted him to disappear, the easy solution. Now there was no end to it without him, nothing anyone would believe. The room was quiet, just the click of dominoes, a smoker's cough. He should be here by now. Leon imagined a gang of men leaping out of the shadows at Enver's nod.

And then there he was, stopping for a second at the window to make sure Leon had seen, then heading down toward the Bosphorus. Leon threw some change on the saucer.

"It's all right," Alexei said on the street, but still moving quickly, Leon catching up. "If they're out here, they have to wait for him. They won't know which one I am."

"But if he's right behind you —"

"No. He slipped in the toilet. You have to be careful there. The wet floor."

A second before this registered.

"Slipped —"

"If he's still inside, then so am I. They'll wait. We're all right."

"You killed him?" Leon said, a tightening in his chest. "You don't know if —"

"I don't believe in concidences."

"And if he was? And they find him?"

"We have a head start. It's all you can ask for sometimes. A little time," he said, his voice cool, discussing logistics.

Leon stopped, taking a breath. "You killed him?" An echo.

"You can get another forger. Anyway, I knew. When he followed me to the toilet."

"You knew," Leon said, almost spitting. "How could you know? You didn't know."

"But I'm safe. So are you, by the way." He took a minute. "He knew my face."

Leon glared at him, still not moving.

"Don't worry," Alexei said. "They'll think it's a fall. It's easy to twist your neck. If you fall that way. No marks." The only thing that concerned him.

"It's murder," Leon said.

"Well, self-defense." He looked at Leon. "Like your Mr. King."

A cold streak, like real ice, ran down Leon's back.

"And meanwhile we're standing here in the street. By this time, someone else uses the toilet and everyone's shouting. And you want to talk about it? This is what we do. Where now?"

"The tram," Leon said, a vacant sound.

"Again public?"

"A taxi might remember. A tram won't. Keep your head down."

They got a seat in the back. Leon expected a rush of police cars and sirens heading toward the *hamam* but the street was quiet, the water twinkling with boat lights in the distance. At Findikli the tram bell announced the stop, and he was back in Manyas's shop, the ping of the bell over the door, the dusty pictures of boys in white circumcision cloaks. Careful eyes, hooded. A life could turn in a second, just the drop of a newspaper, a glimpse of a face. Leon stared out the window, seeing Alexei's head in the reflection. No marks. After a while they passed the swirls and arches of Dolmabahçe Palace. Not even time's going to help it. Anna's voice. Laughing as she said it. Life turned in a second — the drop of a newspaper, a hand slipping from yours in the water. Neither one coming back.

"I've been thinking," Alexei said. "What if you had been alone back there."

Leon turned to him.

"You know Washington?"

"To visit," Leon said, not sure what was being asked.

"I've been thinking," Alexei said again. "After it's over, the talks. I could be useful. Somebody has to train people. It's dangerous, amateurs. Before, it was something new to you. And Donovan was a crazy man — dropping people in, no one comes back, and then the civilians pay too. But now —"

"They're closing it down. A few people to State, that's it. War's over."

Alexei shook his head. "The turtle goes back in the shell? No. Not now. Why do they want to talk to me? And somebody will have to train you."

"To be like you? Twist heads?"

Alexei caught the edge in his voice and looked at him, slightly puzzled.

"What do you think this is?"

Past Yildiz, then the cluster of lighted streets in Ortaköy.

"Get off here," Leon said. "We have to eat something."

"There's no food later?"

"No," Leon said, seeing the hollow faces on the *Victorei* waiting for rations.

They bought kebabs from one of the outdoor stalls and ate them in the square on the water, pulling up their collars against the breeze.

"A drink would be nice," Alexei said.

"Better keep moving. We still have a while. Anyway, a walk would do us good. It'll be cramped on the boat."

"We're going by boat?" Alexei said, jerking his head up. "Why a boat?"

Leon looked at him, surprised.

"I don't like boats."

"This one'll get you out."

Alexei looked away, toward the water. "Another boat. At least a better night this time."

Sharp and clear, with enough moon to see the road after they left the town. A stretch now without a quay, just a shoulder, no other pedestrians, but cars seemed to stream past without noticing them. Then they were in Arnavutköy, a line of waterside *yalis* with elaborate fretwork, and streets behind to wind through, a maze for anyone following.

"Do you have a sense for it now?" Leon said, curious. "When anybody's tailing you?"

"No. I use my eyes. We're all right. How much longer?"

Leon checked his watch. "We're still early." He looked up. "One quick stop."

They kept to village streets, then circled back to the shore promenade, empty except for a few night fishermen, too late now for couples. In Bebek, they turned off just before the khedive's palace, familiar streets, the back way to the clinic. No one behind. They went in through the garden gate.

"What is this place?"

473

Leon raised his hand, a signal to be quiet. They went off the path, stopping at the tree outside Anna's room. Just the usual night-light, like a hovering ghost. Leon started for the French windows, then stopped. No need to go in, risk being seen. He could say good-bye from here. No one would hear him anyway. The room utterly still, a tomb's quiet. And suddenly, disconcerted, he realized that this visit, all his visits, were really trips to a cemetery, paying respects at the grave, the way they had visited his father's, flowers in hand, his mother solemn, Leon bored and uncomfortable, not knowing, as he did now, that she wasn't visiting his father but some younger part of herself, what she used to be. He stood for a second, looking through the window, expecting the faint light to grow dimmer until the room was finally dark. Instead there was a quick shaft of light as the door opened, a nurse coming to check, behind her a man sitting on a chair in the hall reading a newspaper, another Manyas. Leon ducked behind the tree. Keeping watch. Anywhere he might go, even here, Gülün taking no chances. Kay's hotel. Cihangir. Hunting for him. But not in the garden or he wouldn't still be standing here. A car out front? The nurse smoothed out the blanket and left, taking the light with her.

He motioned Alexei toward the gate. "Police," he whispered. "Careful." A follow-me gesture.

Down the backstreets to the shore road. Still too early for the boat, the quay wide open, anybody waiting visible in the moonlight. They passed the steep road up to Robert College, and he thought of Tommy, barreling down, sure how things would go. They went into the café where he'd called Tommy the first rainy night, the same old men smoking. Come to the Park, Mehmet's martinis.

"Finally a drink," Alexei said when his raki arrived. He took a sip. "So what was that place."

"Where my wife is."

Alexei peered at him, but said nothing.

"A clinic."

Another look, oddly sympathetic. "So, the good-byes." He poured more water into the glass, watching the liquid cloud.

Leon shook his head. "She's in a coma." Not quite the truth, but just as good.

Alexei looked closely at him again. "And police there. It's no good, you doing something like that. Save the good-byes for later. When we're gone." He sipped more raki. "So now it's the Russian desk?"

Leon looked away, not answering. The Russian desk. The pale light of the window behind her. Something to think about. Another chance — maybe the only one he'd have. But what kind of life, once they left the hotel room?

He glanced toward the wall, looking for the clock, the ticking, but it seemed to be in his head. There was no time in a café, hours to dawdle. The ferry to the islands from Eminönü used to take an hour and a half, two to reach Büyükada. The fisherman wouldn't be any faster. At least an hour to get to Eminönü, another hour as a cushion for any delays. They should be all right. But they had to be — the *Victorei* wouldn't wait, a promise. How fast was the fisherman's boat?

If they were early, idling off Büyükada wouldn't be a problem this time of year, the crowded port nearly empty, hotels shuttered. In the summer it was different, carriages and donkey rides and hikes to sandy coves in the south. They'd rented the house for August, on a spur off the road up to the monastery, looking down through the woods to the sea. At night the pines and wild roses and jasmine carried on the breeze. Before the war.

"You're very quiet," Alexei said.

"I'm thinking."

Alexei grunted.

"I don't think you were right about Manyas," Leon said, to say something.

"Who?"

"The forger."

"Take that chance with your life, not mine," Alexei said. He signaled for another raki. "Anyway, what does it matter? A man in that work, something always happens."

Leon looked at him, not saying anything. But it must have mattered to him once, before life had become this cheap, before the stacks of corpses. He'd had a wife, parents. Now dreaming of Florida. The ticking was louder, intolerable. Maybe the boat had come early. He pushed back his chair.

"It's time?" Alexei said, then tossed back the rest of the raki, wincing.

They crossed the road onto the quay, the empty space outlined in police chalk marks in his mind — Rumeli Hisari looming up ahead, Alexei's duffel being lifted out, Tommy's car squealing in, Mihai and Leon pinned flat on the pavement. Now they stood waiting quietly near the edge, the water slapping, looking at a single light coming toward them out of the dark. Almost there.

They were on board before the fisherman

could even tie up.

"It's the same man?" Alexei said to Leon. "He works for — ?"

"Me. A private deal."

Immediately discussed. The Princes' Islands were too far.

"It's longer than you said."

"No, it isn't," Leon said, his mouth thin, frustrated, all of them still at the quay.

"Efendi." Beginning to haggle.

"How much?"

Alexei stepped between them. *"Derhal!"* he said, almost growling.

The fisherman stepped back, cowering, then retreated to the motor. Leon glanced over. Alexei's eyes steady, capable of anything.

They stayed close to the shore, away from the cargo ships in the channel, retracing the walk from Ortaköy. The Bosphorus was calm except for the wakes of the freighters, and they made good time, passing the charred ruins of the Çirağan where Abdul Aziz had committed suicide, if he had, and Murat V had been locked away, the sort of things Georg used to tell them.

When there was a break in the cargo traffic, they crossed over to the Asian side, heading past Leander's Tower, the lights of the city around them now on all sides. Only

478

the usual water traffic, ferries and fishermen, no police boats. Haydarpaşa's Teutonic facade, where the trains left for Ankara. Nobody else came with him? Just the wife.

Kadiköy, Fenerbahçe, then the open sea to the islands, shore lights fewer now, the water dark. Alexei kept hold of the side, looking front and back, his knit hat over his ears against the chill. When they pulled farther away from the shore, he went over to the steering cabin and grabbed the signal light. The fisherman yelled at him in Turkish.

"What are you doing?" Leon said. "He needs that to signal the ship."

"Not yet." He put it between his feet. "When he does, it's here."

Another wail from the fisherman, Leon mollifying him.

"For Christ's sake," he said to Alexei.

"How well do you know him?"

"He's working for us."

"He cheats at cards." A long rainy night in some Black Sea hut, hurricane lamps.

"So now what? Do we break his neck?"

Alexei ignored this, focusing on the narrow funnel of light in front. Finally some window lights in the distance.

"Is that it?"

"Not yet."

The boat chugged past Kinaliada, then headed south between Heybeliada and Büyükada, finally idling near the lower tip of the island where the *Victorei* would pass.

"Tell him to kill the light," Alexei said, still alert, looking in both directions. No houses behind them, the empty stretch of the Marmara in front, city lights far in the distance, the boat hidden now in its own patch of watery darkness, rocking slightly with the waves.

"How much longer?" Alexei said.

"The bridge opens around three. Depends where they are in line." A convoy pouring out of the Golden Horn, most of them hugging the European shore, then sailing straight for the Dardanelles, only the *Victorei* veering off toward the islands.

"Another fishing boat?"

Leon shook his head. "A freighter. Was, anyway. Romanian."

"And now?"

"Now it's taking Jews to Palestine."

Alexei looked at him for a long minute, his face moving from one thought to another. "We're going to Palestine?"

"Cyprus. They're dropping us."

"Jews to Palestine," Alexei said, turning it over. "No one will think of that." Raising his eyes, a compliment.

"No," Leon said, feeling pleased, then embarrassed to have felt it.

Alexei snorted, a kind of laugh with himself. "Jews to Palestine."

The boat dipped, then rocked harder, the wind picking up. Alexei clutched the gunwale.

"What's wrong?" Leon said.

"Nothing. I don't like boats, I told you." Almost a child pouting, vulnerable, something Leon hadn't seen before.

And then they waited. The fisherman had cut the motor, so there were only sounds of buoys now, soft tinkles, and the wind blowing things on deck. The Byzantines had exiled people here, where they couldn't be heard. He thought of the whistles and screams when Anna's boat had gone down, sirens on the shore, his own rescue boat blowing horns, the air shaking with noise. Closer to the city, just past Yaniköy, which should have made it easier and in the end didn't matter. Children without life jackets, panicking, taking water every time they shouted, clutching. An endless night. A few even saved, the others slipping under, so close they could see the shore. And then the awful questions after — had the harbor boats come fast enough, had they wanted to come at all?

"There," the fisherman said.

Leon looked out. A bright beam slicing across the water, then the glow of the bridge, followed by a thin string of mast lights, hung like flags. The portholes dark, the boat moving like a shadow, no faster than a ferry. Leon imagined the engine below, creaking and hissing, but turning, getting them there. A miracle, bought with Tommy's money.

The fisherman waited a few more minutes then started up the boat, signaling the ship. The waves were rougher now, Alexei pale. From the water, the *Victorei*'s deck seemed stories high.

"Efendi," the fisherman said to Leon, rubbing his fingers.

Leon gave him the envelope with the money, watching him tuck it into his shirt.

"You're not going to count it?"

"I trust you," the fisherman said, smiling. "And now it's quick. Here." He handed Leon a grappling hook.

They pulled alongside. A rope ladder was dropped, and Leon tried to hook it, bringing the fishing boat up against the *Victorei* and holding it steady in the rocking waves.

"Leon?" Mihai's voice through a primitive megaphone, shining down a light.

Leon waved.

"Can you reach?" he said to Alexei. "I've got it hooked. Jump for it."

Alexei looked at him, whiter.

"I'll be right behind."

"Some trouble?" the fisherman said, a sneer he couldn't resist.

"How do you say, go to hell?" Alexei asked Leon.

"Cehennèm ol," Leon said.

Alexei cocked his head to it, not repeating it, and lunged for the bottom rung, grunting as he pulled himself up, grabbing on to the next, another, then finally a foothold.

"Let's go," Mihai shouted from on deck. The engines had idled, but the ship was still moving, drifting, pulling the fishing boat with it.

"Hold this," Leon said, handing the fisherman the hook. "Go back tonight. Not a word, right? And thanks."

The fisherman looked away, embarrassed.

Leon lifted his arms. Not quite high enough. "Steady," he said to the fisherman, then bounced, grabbing the step, slick with cold water, his arms straining as he pulled himself up to the next, and again, until his feet could take his weight. "You okay?" he shouted up at Alexei, who didn't answer, clinging to the ladder.

The fishing boat slid out from the hull,

then sputtered and roared away while they were still on the ladder, nothing below now but water.

Mihai and another man hauled them over the top, Alexei landing like a flapping fish, winded, trying to pick himself up.

"Tell David to start," Mihai said, then turned to Leon. "You made it." Not looking at Alexei, someone not there.

"Any trouble?" Leon said.

"After the dollars? No. A leap into health. Now it's just the engine to worry about. But at least we're moving."

Büyükada, however, seemed just where it had been, any change of speed unnoticeable. A long night.

"Over here," Mihai said. "It's out of the wind." Looking at Alexei now, his face deliberately blank, indicating a short bench near the bridge.

"Where is everybody?" Leon said, expecting to see people lining the rails, jubilant.

"Sleeping. If they can."

Or hunkering in blankets on benches, the way they'd been before, indifferent to Istanbul, saving their strength, heads drooping on shoulders next to them, the few still awake staring at Alexei and Leon, wondering, but more interested in the uneven throb of the engines below.

"Thank you," Alexei said.

"Thank him," Mihai said, brusque.

"There's a boat," David said, coming out of the bridge.

"Signaling?"

"No. Maybe putting into Büyükada. But we're just sitting here. Go see what's happening down below, will you? We'd make better time rowing."

A sudden wave rolled the boat, pitching Mihai forward, onto Alexei's chest. He pulled away.

"Right back," he said to Leon. "Stay over there."

"Your Romanian friend," Alexei said.

"You never saw him."

"I never see anybody." He grabbed on to a rail, the boat rocking again with a wave. "It's getting rough."

They sat in the niche by the bridge.

"He's the one told you about Strǎuleşti."

Leon nodded.

"So why does he take me?"

"I paid him."

"That one? No. Something else. Maybe it's a trap."

"He's not doing it for you. Get some sleep."

"In this?" He opened his hand to the wind. The boat had begun to creak.

One of the blanketed figures shuffled over, a man with a shaved head, and said something in what Leon took to be Polish, answered with an I-don't-understand hands up. Another language, probably Yiddish. Finally, German.

"Who are you, that they stop the ship for you?"

"Nobody," Leon said. "We were late."

"No. People are late on the dock, not out here. Haganah? You're Haganah, yes? What else? An honor," he said, extending his hand. Alexei shook it, Leon watching, his eyes fixed on the numbers inked on the man's forearm.

The man made a lips-sealed gesture and started back to his bench.

A sudden thud below, then a grinding, the whole frame of the boat shuddering, but moving again, the few lights on Büyükada beginning to recede.

"Maybe your friend's pushing," Alexei said, sitting back, enjoying himself, the movement of the boat like a promise. In a few hours, the Aegean.

"You never saw him before. You understand?"

"I heard you the first time." He opened his eyes. "Why?"

"He's not part of this."

Alexei looked at him, then around the deck, the glance its own comment. The boat lurched again. Faint noises came from below, groans. There would be crammed bunks, slop buckets spilling over.

A woman staggered out of the door to the hold, hand over her mouth, and ran to the railing, stretching as far as she could, hoping her vomit would clear the side, disappear in the water. A painful heaving, loud, the people on the bench unconsciously moving away from her. Sputtering, then more retching, only thin streams of bile now. The first of many, if the water stayed rough. She wiped her mouth with the end of her shawl, eyes toward the benches, too sick to apologize, her breath taken now by a hacking cough. Another woman got up and held her by the shoulders, steadying her until the coughing stopped. Some words, probably a thank-you, carried off by the wind. She nodded, gulping air, then started back, looking over toward Leon and Alexei. A frozen moment, silent, too stunned to speak.

"Voi," she said finally, to herself, trying to make sense of what she was seeing, walking now in a kind of determined stagger, through water, a waking dream.

"Voi." Closer now, making sure, then

trembling. *"Măcelar!"* A sudden scream, heads lifting on the benches. *"Călău! Călău!"* People getting up, her finger pointing to Alexei now, then a scream, piercing, people coming up behind her.

Alexei said something in Romanian, the tone of a denial.

Another scream, her whole body vibrating, about to explode. *"Măcelar!"* The language now part of the nightmare, the people on the benches not sure what was being said, responding to pure sound.

"Butcher," someone yelled, explaining.

Another stream of Romanian, the force of hysteria, someone murmuring "her sister" in the background, the finger again. *"Călău! Călău!"* And then she lunged for him, her fingernails on his face, reaching for his eyes, feral. Alexei grabbed her arms, trying to hold her away, but she had the strength of the mad, scratching and pulling at him, hands turned to claws. Alexei gasped with pain, pushing himself off the bench, so that she now had to reach up to rake his face, still screaming, the people behind her excited, their shouts swirling around Leon's head in a frenzied Babel, everything happening in a second.

"Stop!" He grabbed her arms from behind, amazed at her strength as she yanked away, everyone around them shouting, the whole ship seeming to have come awake, the feel of people moving below. Ruining everything.

Alexei shielded his face with his arms, still trying to quiet her in Romanian, duck away, but they were surrounded now, the crowd surging like a mob.

"Stop!" Leon tried holding her again.

She'd break down soon, the rage turning to uncontrollable sobbing, draining her strength away. But not before she could lunge at him one more time, tearing at his skin, hate spilling out of her.

"*Călău!*"

"Executioner," someone echoed, translating.

People coming closer, a wave of them, then something slicing through.

"What's going on?" Mihai shouted, breathless, grabbing the hands that had broken away from Leon.

A gush of Romanian from the woman, Mihai looking pained, a quick glance at Leon, people around them still shouting. "What is it?" "He's a Nazi." "How could he be a Nazi?" "A Romanian Nazi." People coming up from below, the air crackling like radio static. More Romanian. "He put them on a *hook*." Mumbling, then yells, the woman finally breaking down the way Leon had imagined, wailing that scraped on the nerves, not stopping. "Mihai! What's going on here? We have a right —"

"Yes, yes. Calm, please. You want to have a riot before we're safe?"

"He's a Nazi? On this ship? Are you crazy?"

"Get him to the bridge," Mihai hissed at Leon, his eyes sharp knives of reproach.

"Not so fast!" The man with the shaved head. "What's going on? He's not Haganah?"

More Romanian. "They hung them like meat," someone translated.

A second of quiet, taking this in. Alexei said something in Romanian, another denial, "It wasn't me," Leon guessed, then the woman shrieked back. The crowd now got louder, splashes of words, unsettled. Leon moved in front of Alexei.

"Enough!" Mihai said, barking it.

"So who is he? What's going on?"

"He's cargo on this boat. For Cyprus. Not Palestine."

"Cargo? What do you mean, cargo?"

"Everybody go back. Sit down. I'll explain later."

The Romanian woman crumpled into a heap, crying, pulling at the air, as if she were rending it, a grief too large to contain.

"No. Now!" someone shouted. "It's a trick! Maybe he warns the British. Not until the last Jew —"

Mihai raised his hands. "Please. This is crazy talk. He's a help to us."

"A help? How?"

The woman lifted her head and yelled something at Alexei, a curse with a raised fist. Again, a denial. Leon glanced at him. What was he saying? I wasn't there? I wasn't part of it? I couldn't stop it? Some version of what he'd said to Leon. But was it true? Did the sister know? Had anybody actually seen him? And for a fleeting second, his stomach sinking with the dip of the boat, he didn't want it to be true, wanted Alexei not to have been there at all, wanted him at least to claim the fragile innocence of those who just let it happen.

Mihai was speaking Romanian to the woman, gathering her up, his arm around her.

"Go back," he said to the others. "It's a mistake." The woman didn't hear this, inside herself now, only Leon catching his eye, dismayed. Lying for him. But what was the alternative? No right thing to do. He steered Alexei toward the bridge, the crowd still milling on the deck, confused.

"How a mistake? How could she make such a mistake?"

But they had all been on the long marches, crammed in refugee trucks, and they knew how minds finally snapped, pointing out of windows at everybody because everybody had done it.

Mihai handed the Romanian woman over to another woman, then turned to the crowd. "Go back now. There's no time for this."

"Who are these men? You stop the boat for them, so who?"

"Nobody. Cargo. I told you —" The rest drowned out by the siren, so loud it cut through everything — the people shouting on deck, the lumbering motor, tarps flapping in the wind — a giant *whoop,* meant to startle. A loudspeaker rasped something garbled in Turkish. The crowd rushed over to the railing. A police boat approaching the side, signal lamps flashing, searchlights sweeping up toward the railing.

"We have to stop," David yelled from the bridge. "They're signaling."

Mihai said nothing, looking down.

"They can shoot if we don't."

Guns already drawn on the police boat. But how did they know? Lurking in shadows since Bebek? But not in the broad stretches where they would have had to be seen. The deal made with Mihai, no one else. Blood money.

Mihai nodded to David, then looked at Leon, face strained.

"Prepare to board." The loudspeaker, still in Turkish, so the passengers, already rattled, began to panic.

Mihai held his hands up to them for quiet, then leaned over the side with a megaphone. "What do you want? We're the *Victorei*. Our papers are in order."

Leon leaned forward to hear, keeping his face out of the light. Maybe a routine check, another bribe, not given away after all.

"Police. Your new passengers."

A quick turn of his head, Mihai meeting Leon's eyes. Any police, David puts you off. It's understood? It's not for you, this ship. Endgame. And for an instant Leon felt an odd light-headed release, the clock stopping. Mihai looked from Leon to Alexei, then turned back to the rail.

"What new passengers? We are only ourselves."

"Yes, yes." A cocky gravelly sound on the loudspeaker. Gülün. "All right. Passenger search. A ladder?" A second's pause, Gülün drawing his gun. "Now."

Mihai nodded to two sailors to lower the

ladder, then turned to the crowd again. "Listen to me. Do you want to go to Palestine?"

A shocked nod of heads.

"Then do what I say. Go back. Say nothing. Nothing."

"But what —"

"Nothing! Or I leave this ship. They'll take me away." He waited.

A silence, only the police boat still shrieking.

"Do you understand? You saw nothing. No one. Take her down below," he said, looking at the Romanian woman. "Give her something. The rest, tell them to stay in their bunks."

"Ladder's down," the sailor shouted, a kind of alert.

"They'll send us back," Mihai said. "Understand?"

People began to move.

"And then maybe you'll explain —"

"You can take over this ship any time you want," Mihai said, then held out the megaphone.

The man looked down, then turned and headed for the stairs.

"Anyone else?" Mihai said.

Leon looked at him. Confronting everybody, spending what was left in his account, no reserves.

"Good." He glanced over the rail. "Get ready," he said, waving people back to their places, then went over to Leon and Alexei, suddenly at a loss, as if he'd forgotten about them. Shouts from the water, climbing feet banging against the hull.

"I'll take him below," Leon said, almost afraid to look at Mihai, the debt too great now.

"No. People know. Or they will. They'll kill him. I don't know how long I —"

"You want to give us up?" Leon said.

Mihai flicked his hand, brushing this off, then glanced around the deck, breathing in sharp intakes, finally beginning to panic.

"Is there another ladder? The other side?" Alexei said, thinking out loud.

"Ladder to what? There's no boat."

"To hide. We'll hang on. Nobody's going to look outside the boat."

Mihai looked up at him, a kind of reluctant salute, then nodded.

They hurried across the deck, heads following them, and lifted the clump of ladder and flung it over the side, the anchor ropes barely noticeable in the coiled piles near the railings. The lifeboats, refuge for stowaways, were overhead, a different search area. From the other side of the ship, a shrill whistle,

495

some signal to the search party that triggered involuntary cries on deck, the sound of roundups, whistles and boots. A woman started crying, burying her face in a man's shoulder.

"I won't sacrifice the ship," Mihai said to Leon. "These people deserve —"

"I know."

"Just pull us back up when it's over," Alexei said, a gruff familiarity.

Mihai stared at him. More noise from the police party, almost at the top, like a wake-up hand on his shoulder. "Quick," he said, turning, putting his body between them and the police.

Alexei looked at the rope, then at Leon, suddenly nervous again.

"All right," Leon said, going first.

He climbed over the railing and started backing down the rope steps, feeling for them, his last sight of the deck a row of heads watching him. One signal was all Gülün would need, one finger pointing. But the row didn't move, huddling into itself, turning to Mihai now. Leon looked up. Nobody.

"Come on!"

Then a foot, another, working their way down until Alexei's head was below the rail too, both of them dangling on the side of the ship, the wind slapping the bottom of the ladder against the hull. Leon kept going, past a row of portholes, his weight steadying the ladder. If this were a building he could make his way along the ledge to the window, climb in out of sight. To people who'd be waiting for them, the story everywhere now. Some rag in the mouth to muffle the sound, everything quick, no noise, then the splash of water, maybe not even heard on deck, another wave.

"Where are you going?" Alexei whispered, his hands gripping the rope.

"Out of sight."

"Where, in the water?"

"A little further. Okay, here. Hang on." The rough sisal began cutting into his palms. He shifted more weight to his legs, feeling the wind press into his back.

He could hear loud voices up top. Gülün bullying, eyes peering at him from under cap brims and shawls. Just one. But no one spoke. Do you want to go to Palestine? Worth everything.

A wave broke against the hull sending jets of spray upward, wetting the bottom of his pants, spattering drops on his neck, hands. A sudden light from the porthole to his right, maybe a flashlight going through the hold. Seeing the bodies stacked in bunks, a photograph from the war. Would the police ask them to get down, look behind everyone, or hurry through, anxious to get out of the smell before any hands could touch them. A baby started crying, wakened by the light.

Another wave sprayed icy water as the ship listed slightly. The rope ladder swung out from the hull. Leon looked down, a black void, then braced for the swing back, making his shoes take most of the impact. How long could they hang here, wet hands clutching rope? He shifted his weight again, feeling the strain in his arms. Not thinking anymore, not having to decide anything, just holding on. He had even stopped wondering what they were saying on deck, what Mihai would do if Gülün ordered the ship to turn around. But why would he? Unless he was sure Leon was on board. Not any ship, this ship. He thought of the *hamam,* the tram ride, but no one had been hovering behind, not even in his imagining. What had he said to Kay? More voices, closer to this side of the ship.

At first, he felt it was more spray from below and then he felt the drops on his head, random but steady. When he raised his face there were more, coming faster. He flattened himself against the rope, hunching his shoulders to keep the rain from dripping down his collar. Cold, seeping into his wool jacket. He heard Alexei swear to himself. But maybe it would make Gülün hurry, decide his tip had been wrong. If it had been a tip.

More flashlights sweeping through the sleeping quarters, bunk by bunk. At least they were dry there, not soaking on deck like the others. Another whistle signal, maybe calling the searchers back up top. How long before they gave up? You couldn't get everybody in a roundup. People hid beneath floorboards, squeezed behind stairs. The wind came up again, blowing rain against the ship, and Leon shivered, his hands stiff with cold, clothes heavier, pulling at him.

Then a loud crash, a lifeboat being lowered off its davits.

"There's some mistake. These people are refugees." Mihai's voice, closer now, the search party moving to this side.

"Take the cover off." A policeman, not Gülün, the rest of his Turkish cut off by a freighter's moaning foghorn, not too far off, the rain like a light curtain, making everything blurry.

The whistle blew again in the hold, lights moving away. Just the deck now and the lifeboats, hiding places exhausted. They were going to make it, hanging like bats in the dark.

The ship lurched in the wake of the passing freighter, the ladder swinging out again, farther this time, then crashing back to the hull, their shoes banging the metal, knuckles scraping. Alexei moaned. Then another swing, pushed by the momentum of the first, shoes hitting the side again.

A light appeared on top, someone shouting in Turkish.

"Nothing," Leon heard Mihai say.

A bright shaft pointed downward, flashing, then fixed on where they had just been, the curve of the hull keeping them just out of its beams, stopping short, not strong enough to reach all the way to the water. Frantic shouts, Leon holding his breath, then a sudden burst of gunfire, an automatic spitting bullets.

"Stop!"

Leon flattened himself against the ladder, head tucked in. Maybe just a warning shot. Wouldn't Gülün want them alive, a prize catch? Unless it didn't matter to him, Leon guilty, Gülün commended either way. The hull was smooth, nothing to grab on to if the ladder swung again. Another burst. Leon could actually hear the shots hitting the water, feel a quick thud on the rope.

They must be spraying bullets into the dark, just to see if there was anything to hit. And there would be, a matter of minutes before the ladder swung out again into the light.

"Idiot!" Gülün screaming now, the sound of running on deck, passengers whimpering in the background, the gunfire loud as bombs to them. Leon's muscles locked still, waiting. "Don't shoot! Alive, you idiot!" Wanting his day in court after all.

Leon glanced down. Black, nowhere to go, his body getting heavier in the wet clothes. He felt more drops on his hands, then looked at them. Not icy, warm, thicker. He moved his head to taste. Blood. Alexei dripping on him.

"Are you hit?"

"A scratch," Alexei said, but panting, in trouble.

"Haul them up," Gülün was yelling. "Get the searchlight."

Alexei gave a stifled cry with the first jerk of the ladder. No winch, just hands heaving it up. They felt the ladder rise then stop again, bouncing, one of Alexei's feet slipping from the rung, so that his hands took more weight. Leon looked up to see Alexei's leg poking at the air, trying to find a footing again, then a new light, almost blinding. The police yanked the ladder again, shaking it, and Alexei's other foot slipped, his body sliding down toward Leon, feet dangling, just his hands now, one of them dripping blood.

"There they are!" One of the policemen, pointing his gun into the light.

"Don't shoot. Just get them up here. Help with the rope."

Another pair of hands, a heave, this time with real force, just as a swell rolled the boat, the ladder swinging out as it rose, the jerk upward finally stronger than Alexei's grip. His feet smashed into Leon's head, then the rest of him, a rock slide, Leon's hands leaving the rope without his being aware of it, just rolling into an endless fall, Alexei clinging to his jacket, dragging him, and then not there, only the shock of icy water.

For a second he was too stunned by the cold to register anything, almost unconscious, then all the sounds came, the shouts from up top, the ladder flapping back, the frantic splashing, Alexei spitting and gulping water. Leon moved toward him, suddenly followed by the light, which had picked them up. Alexei was flailing, slapping the water at random and gasping for air. I don't like boats. Leon swam over, his clothes like weights. He tried to approach

502

from behind, cup Alexei's chin above water, lift him up to a float, something he could tow, everything he'd been taught. Boys who couldn't swim would clutch at you, make things worse.

"Alexei. I've got you." Meant to reassure, take away some of the panic. "Lie back."

Gurgling, not hearing, just seeing Leon and grabbing on, a desperate clinging, his head slipping under, pushing himself back up again on Leon's shoulders, wheezing for air. More shouts from the ship, the *thwack* of a life preserver hitting the water somewhere near, then nothing, the muffled quiet of underwater, Leon sinking under Alexei's weight. He forced himself up, bobbing.

"Let go. I've got you. We'll both —"

Then under again, swallowing water this time, Alexei on top, trying to climb on him, a human raft. Leon tried to move away but only managed to wriggle in place, as if he were wrapped in chains, and now he was sinking again and he realized, an ice pick of fear, that he could die. Saving Alexei. A man who'd do anything to survive, Leon nothing more than driftwood, something handy. His lungs began to burn, churning the same used air. And for a crazy second he thought of where he was, that he might drown somewhere in the view from Cihangir,

Alexei's hands still gripping his coat, taking him down too.

A hint of light-headedness, no time now. Get up. He turned his head, his mouth near Alexei's hand, and bit down sharply. Only a second of release before the hand started clutching again, but enough for Leon to duck away, then surface, sucking air, Alexei still grasping his other hand. He looked over, their eyes locking, Alexei's glassy with terror, and Leon saw what Alexei must have seen in the others, his victims, the terrible last moment when they knew they would die, a kind of animal bewilderment. Now his turn. All Leon had to do was let go of his hand, not responsible for any of it. An easier death, except for the frantic eyes, how the child must have looked, slipping from Anna's grasp. And what if she had held on, pushed under by the thrashing, the child not even aware that Anna was taking water, sinking? He let his hand grow slack, making Alexei struggle to keep it, and he saw how it must have been, even the same dark water, Anna letting the hand slide away to save herself, not knowing the child would take her under either way.

Alexei made a noise, flinging his mouth back for air, arms flailing again, then his head dipped, as if he were being pulled under, and Leon imagined hands at his feet, Străuleşti hands clawing at his cuffs, proof of the rightness of things. Except things were never made right. They passed, that's all.

He swam closer, pulling Alexei up, then holding him under the chin, keeping his head above water. "Listen to me." His voice rough hoarse.

Alexei's hands came up again, grasping. Leon smashed down on them, pulling free, then caught Alexei's coat as he was going under, twisting his body around so that Leon was behind as he yanked him back up, hand under his chin again. A violent sputtering.

"Fucking listen to me," he said into Alexei's ear. "I've got you. Do you understand? You'll be okay if you do what I say. Do you understand?"

Alexei nodded, making an indistinct sound, his breath a ragged gurgling, his hands still punching the water.

"Stop," Leon said. "Try to float." A meaningless term, Alexei's legs still scissoring beneath them. More sounds. "Stop, or I'll let you go. I'll let you go." A muffled squeal, then the feet stopped, now rigid, a new deadweight, even heavier. "Relax. Let the water do the work. It'll hold you."

Another noise from Alexei's throat, a yelp of disbelief. Weren't there pools in Bucharest, lakes in the mountains? Why hadn't he learned to swim? He tried to imagine Alexei as a boy, a kid in the streets, but no picture would come and he realized that he knew nothing about his life, that he was just a stranger who'd dropped in at the end of it, like the life preserver thrown from the deck. "I'm here," he said.

Alexei stopped thrashing, so quiet that for a second Leon thought he was gone, but that would have made him stiffen and Leon felt instead his body growing limp, a giving in. He moved closer, the back of Alexei's head resting against his chest, another breath, not as ragged, his body looser, moving with Leon's as a wave lifted them, entirely in his hands. No escape hatch to the roof, gun drawn at the door, only Leon.

Leon looked up past the misty halo of the bright light, the deck railing crowded now, people yelling and waving their hands, seeing a different drama, a sea rescue. Mihai was motioning him left. He glanced over — the life preserver, bright white against the water. He paddled toward it.

"It's okay, I've got you." Afraid any movement would startle him now.

On the deck, there were more whistles,

instructions, a new rumbling from the passengers. Leon heard Gülün ordering the police boat to pick them up. In a few minutes they'd be caught, netted up like fish. Saving Alexei for what? Saving himself. To be a murderer, the running itself evidence against him. He grabbed on to the bobbing ring.

"Here, hold this," he said, but Alexei didn't reach for it, safe where he was, and Leon saw that his arm was bloody, stanched only a little by the cold water and now starting again to leak through his matted sleeve.

He thought for a moment of putting the ring over Alexei's head, but he'd never manage to work his arms through, not the bleeding one, so he just hung on, keeping Alexei's head up against him.

"They're coming?" Alexei said.

"Yes."

"So we didn't make it."

"We're alive."

"For the Russians," Alexei said, his voice low.

"Hang on!" Mihai yelled through the megaphone. Around him, people were looking down through the light rain.

Leon's arm began to cramp on the lifesaver, feeling the cold. Think what to say to Gülün.

A minute later, he could hear the boat coming around the bow, another light shining toward them. Alexei turned his head.

"They're coming," he said.

"Just hold on," Leon said, missing his tone.

"Let me go." And then, before Leon could react, he twisted his head free of Leon's hand and dropped away, pushing against Leon's chest.

Leon stared for a second at the water, the empty space where Alexei had been, before he realized what had happened.

"No," he said, as if they were having a conversation, then "no" again, this time to himself.

He ducked under. The lights, so bright above the surface, stopped after a few inches, everything black. But he couldn't have gone far, a few feet. Leon dived down, then started back up where Alexei had gone under, reaching for anything, hands stretched out, water running through his fingers. He broke the surface, gulping. Nothing.

"Leon!" Mihai shouting from above.

He dived again, deeper this time, hearing a motor now, the boat closer. He moved his arms, sweeping across the space in front of him. Water. Then a piece of something, cloth, not seaweed. He snatched at it, using it to pull himself closer, then brought up his other hand, more cloth, a jacket, holding it now with both hands, kicking, pushing them up. When they hit the air, Alexei started coughing, too weak now to fight back when Leon grabbed his collar from behind. The boat light swept in an arc, followed by a sudden shot, Leon not sure whether to duck again, a helpless target.

"Stay where you are," a loudspeaker said in Turkish, evidently a warning shot, fired when they disappeared. More yelling from the deck.

"Let me go," Alexei said, barely audible.

"Hang on. I've got you," Leon said, ignoring this, holding him up.

Alexei stared at him, eyes suddenly wide, undefended, taking him in as if Leon were the last thing he would ever see. "Why?"

"Almost there," Leon said, reaching for the lifesaver.

Alexei coughed, choking on some water. "I'm tired."

"Almost there," Leon said again.

"No, tired. It's enough."

Leon glanced over. Alexei's head had begun to loll. How much blood had he lost?

"Not yet," he said, "I need you," Alexei looking up at this.

A rope hit the water near them, more lights.

"Grab hold!"

Leon looked at it, winded, still holding Alexei. A second to get his strength back.

"Move!" Another shot fired into the air, like a whip cracking, then sharp cries from the ship, oddly like dogs.

"Tell him to go to hell," Alexei said, barely lifting his head.

"You can't stay in the water. We'll freeze."

"I don't feel it."

"That's worse. You should."

"Yes?" Alexei said, looking up. "Ah."

He took Leon's hand, smiling faintly, an awkward clutching, not a shake, not expecting to be towed by it, just making contact. Leon looked back, surprised, a camera shutter opening, seeing him now, the kid in the street, just a glimpse before he could run away again.

"All right," Alexei said, nodding, his eyes going to the boat. "It's your move." His voice faint, running out of air, part of the quiet that was filling Leon's head, the clock finally stopping, at an end.

Gülün's boat was rocking nearby, the motor still churning, policemen shouting and pointing to the rope, all distant noises, background sounds where the ticking had been. There was no next move, just an automatic reach for the lifesaver, then a hook to drag them in, check. And the *Victorei* in Gülün's hands, all the anxious people on deck pawns again. His idea, somewhere they'd never look.

"Take the rope!"

Leon saw it floating on the surface, a lifeline, a noose. Your move.

The boat ran its siren again, a screaming alarm, loud enough to fill the quiet in Leon's head, a rush of prickly feeling in his numb hands. No, not the siren, a different horn, behind them, a new light flashing over the water. Leon glanced around, trying to make out the shape past the blinding light. Smaller than the police boat, gunwales of polished wood, the kind of boat you saw tied up in front of a *yali,* fast just for the pleasure of it. Bearing down on them now with another siren *whoop.* A shot was fired from the police boat, presumably into the air, like a sentry. A loudspeaker crackled.

"Hold your fire! Idiot!"

The speedboat on them now, fishtailing to idle next to Gülün's, like a skier at the end of a run.

"Are you crazy? Shooting at me?" Altan, furious.

There was an exchange Leon couldn't

hear over the sputtering engines, then another ring thrown to him, this one from the speedboat. More yelling between the boats, Altan taking over. In the lights, Leon could see Gülün's face, flustered and petulant.

"And them?" he said, jerking a thumb back to the *Victorei.*

"Let them go," Leon said, close to the side now. "They didn't —"

"You, my friend, are in no position to ask for anything," Altan said. "Hold on to that. Get them into the boat," he said to someone on board.

"No," Alexei said suddenly. "When we see the ship leave."

Altan blinked, stopped by this. "Don't be ridiculous. You'll freeze."

"Then hurry," Alexei said, eyes level, as if Altan were the fisherman, someone else to stare down. He turned to Leon. "It's what you want, yes?"

Leon nodded.

"So."

Altan, annoyed, yelled across to Gülün, then turned back to them. "He says his men are already off the boat. Get in."

"Then signal it to leave. You came for me? So there's the price. Or I take this one with me." Fierce, no indication at all that it was

512

Leon supporting him, a bluff as smooth as a swimmer's stroke.

Altan stood still for a second, stymied.

"They don't pay for me," Alexei said, jaw clenched against the cold. "Signal."

Altan turned toward Gülün's boat. Another exchange, argumentative, then a bark in Altan's voice, giving orders, Gülün's shoulders rearing back then sagging. Leon felt the water lapping at his chin, waiting, feet no longer there, just part of the cold. A series of lights flashed up to the *Victorei*, followed by a policeman shouting into the loudspeaker. A second's lag for the translation, then a roar of voices from the ship, the sound of a goal scored. Leon saw people slapping Mihai on the back as he stood frowning, staring down at Leon, not sure what to do. Leon lifted his hand a little and waved him off. There was a shuddering grind in the engines as the boat started up again. More cheers. Now Mihai waved back, barely raising his hand, still troubled, leaving someone behind.

"Get in," Altan said, nodding to the rope.

"When it leaves," Alexei said, still making his improbable bargain.

The ship had begun to slide away, its wake lifting the smaller boats.

He turned to Leon. "It's all right?"

Leon looked at him, a wordless thank-you, more, trying to see behind his eyes again.

"Always something for the Jews with you," Alexei said, trying to be wry, closing the shutter, but his voice trailed off, his eyes drooping.

Leon shook him, wetting Alexei's face to see the eyes open again, someone trying to nap, then paddled with one arm to Altan's life preserver. A long pole with a hook snagged the ring and started pulling them. Then there were hands lifting them up, Alexei not letting go of Leon until he was pried away, both of them wrapped in blankets. It was only then, with the first hint of warmth, that Leon started shivering.

"He's bleeding. They shot him."

"I can see that," Altan said, motioning for one of his men to look at the wound. He shouted something to Gülün who then ordered the police boat to pull away. "He's disappointed," Altan said to Leon. "Such good work too." Gülün, sullen, was saluting.

Behind the police boat, the *Victorei* was becoming a string of lights on the Marmara. Tommy's money and the butcher's price, whatever it took. Leon pulled the blanket tighter.

"He's out," one of Altan's men said, holding Alexei.

"He lost a lot of blood," Leon said.

"So did Enver," Altan said smoothly, looking at him. He turned to the driver. "Let's get going."

The boat recoiled, a shotgun effect, as the engine kicked in, throwing everyone against the sides. It swung around, heading back for the Bosphorus. Polished wood, a rich man's boat.

"What are you doing here?" Leon said, his head getting fuzzy. "Gülün —"

"You prefer his boat?"

"He works for you."

Altan shrugged. "In a way. But he doesn't always know what to do."

"No?" Leon said, making a sound, too tired to talk, then noticed the driver, a familiar face above a serving tray. "Lily's boat," he said finally.

"A courtesy."

"Gülün found us."

"No, I told him. A good idea, by the way. Clever. A ship of Jews."

"I bribed them. They had nothing to do —" Leon started, but Altan waved this off.

"How far were you going?"

"Cyprus," Leon said, voice flat.

Altan tilted his head slightly, calculating, then nodded. "I never thought of that," he said, an appreciation.

"But you knew about the ship," Leon said slowly, trying to think, what mattered.

"Not until the end."

"How?" Leon said dully. "How did you — ?" Wanting to know, then dreading it.

"The fisherman," Altan said. "I paid him. More."

A second to react, then Leon started to smile. An Istanbul answer, not Kay, not Mihai, complicated betrayals, just a market price.

"He's still out," the man with Alexei said.

"Radio ahead to have a doctor at Lily's."

"We're going to Lily's?" Leon said, confused.

"Would you rather the police?"

"Why Lily's?"

"So we can talk."

"Talk," Leon said, his voice distant.

"Make plans."

Leon tried to get hold of this, then let it go. "What you said before, about Enver. He was — ?"

"I hope that wasn't you. He had a family."

Leon said nothing.

"No, it would have to be him," Altan said, looking at Alexei, slumped under his blanket. "Don't forget what kind of man he is."

Leon looked up, not understanding.

"Then it's easier."

"What?"

"What the Americans want."

"The Americans," Leon repeated, his mind wispy, fogging up, like the faint drizzle around them.

Altan nodded.

"Oh," Leon said, with a faint snort. "You're working for us now."

"I work for Turkey," Altan said, his voice quick, some nerve touched. "Only Turkey." He relaxed his shoulders. "But right now I'm in a position to — offer a favor. To friends."

"What favor?" Shuddering again, the wind colder.

Altan opened his hand toward Alexei.

"You're giving him to us?"

Altan caught Leon's expression. "I know. So much work. So clever. You surprised me. But it's just as well," he said, his hand now taking in the absent *Victorei,* the night. "The Americans don't want him in Cyprus. They want him in Istanbul."

Leon tried to follow, a riddle he couldn't solve now, but drifted into the pocket of warmth under the blanket, the boat thudding against the waves, making spray, not resisting the pull anymore, going under.

■ ■ ■ ■

7
GALATA BRIDGE

■ ■ ■ ■

He awoke with sun in his face, the soft rustling of slippers in the hall, quiet as brushstrokes. Anna's room, some other hospital. But the comforter over him was satin and the light against the far wall glowed in colors, streaming through bits of stained glass. Lily's, one of the rooms in the old *selamlik,* the smell of coffee brewing. A shape near the door moved, becoming a woman.

"I'll tell Madame," she said, out the door before Leon could answer.

He sat up, the comforter sliding off his bare skin, so that he had to catch it, hold it to his chest. He noticed a brazier in the corner, bright with coals. He moved his toes, a test, recovered from the icy water.

"I thought you'd sleep longer," Lily said, followed by a woman carrying a pile of clothes. "All dry. Such a time getting off the wet ones. How do you feel?"

"Where's Alexei?"

"The Romanian? Eating breakfast. Well, lunch, this hour. Already making eyes at Ayşe and last night he was half dead. Men, *c'est incroyable.*"

"Why here?"

"I help Murat sometimes." She looked up at him. "So now that's our secret, yes?" She nodded to the maid to put the clothes on the bed. "I'll let you dress. We're in the garden room." She started to go, then turned, smiling to herself. "So now I know."

"What?"

"What you'd look like in the morning. I always wondered. Your hair, the way it sticks out. *Un petit garçon. Adorable.*"

"I don't feel *adorable.*"

"Ouf," she said, waving her hand, then dropped it, all business. "Hurry. Murat's waiting."

But only Alexei was at the table, his face bland and cheerful, as if waking up in luxury was simply part of the natural order of things, the next turn of the wheel.

"What is this place?" he said, motioning to the maid to bring more coffee.

"A friend."

"Friends like this in Istanbul. Imagine what America must be like." Almost winking, enjoying himself. He looked at Leon.

"You're all right?"

"What time is it?"

Alexei looked up at the sky, a peasant's clock. "Almost noon."

"They patched you up?" Leon said, nodding to the bandage on Alexei's arm.

Alexei nodded. "But no more tennis," he said. Then when Leon didn't react, "A joke." A few hours earlier, dragging Leon into the water.

"Ah, both of you. Good," Altan said, coming in.

Alexei stiffened, wary.

"Everyone feeling better?" Altan said.

"What are we doing here?" Alexei said.

"Recovering. Staying out of sight. The police won't bother you now, but let's not tempt them." He looked at Alexei. "You want to get to the Americans in one piece."

"And who's taking me? You?"

"No. Leon. That's his job."

Alexei accepted this with a grunt. "When?"

"As soon as they get here. Meanwhile, enjoy the day. It's always good after a rain, isn't it? Everything so clear."

An unintended irony, Leon's head still muddled.

"Get here from where?" he said. "The consulate?"

"No, Ankara," Altan said, not elaborating.

"Then why the ship?" Alexei said, suspicious. "All the arrangements —"

"Compromised," Altan said. "Once we knew that, we had to get you off."

Leon stared at him, trying to make sense of this.

"Compromised?" Alexei said.

"A word to the police. Luckily, intercepted," Altan said, almost breezy. "Someone, I think, didn't like you very much."

No sense at all now.

"But the ship got out," Leon said, alarmed. "You didn't have it stopped later."

"We made an agreement," Altan said, indicating Alexei. He checked his wristwatch. "They should be there tonight."

"In Palestine," Leon said, an odd sense of relief, at least one thing gone right.

"More likely with the British Mediterranean Fleet. Back to Cyprus after all. But that's not in our control, is it?" This to Alexei. "Now it's up to them."

Alexei nodded, watching him.

"I wonder if you would do something for me. While we're waiting."

Alexei said nothing.

"You knew Melnikov. A prominent figure here now. Very interested in Turkey. It would be so useful — a matter of dates. When you

524

knew him. After Stalingrad, I know, but when exactly?"

"Useful to whom?"

"To Turkey."

"I'm not working for Turkey."

"No, the Americans. But we have an arrangement with the Americans."

"Then let them ask."

"They will. But maybe not so soon. A small matter to them. But something more to us. Nothing, I think, to you." He paused. "A persuasive man, Melnikov. There was a Turk — well, born in Kars, a Turkish mother, you would think a source of loyalty, but a Russian father, so Russian during the war. When Melnikov persuaded him. To do some work. Against Turkey. We know what happened to him — Norilsk, not the reward he expected. But there was another man, and him —"

"I don't know."

"By name, no. If you did, an easy job for us. Just a name. But if we had the dates. We could match the dates. A matter of elimination. Where was Melnikov? When? Not so difficult. The Americans will ask anyway. So, an exercise for you. Since you're here."

Alexei glanced at Leon.

And why not? A little something for Altan, the *Victorei* well away now. Leon blinked

525

his eyes, a kind of nod.

"Exactly, it's not possible," Alexei said.

"Well, do the best you can," Altan said casually. "General movements. There's some paper over there. I find it helps, putting things down. One thing, then another one comes. More coffee? Ayşe? I'm going to steal Leon for a few minutes. Arrangements for later. You'll be all right here."

Alexei looked up, a tiny flicker of anxiety, as if he were still clutching to Leon's jacket in the water.

"There's the garden, if you get restless," Altan said, "but no further, please. We don't want to take any chances. Disappoint the Americans."

He took Leon through the *sofa* and out onto the terrace facing the Bosphorus, busy with boats. A few geraniums in pots had been brought outside to sit in the sun.

"Shall we start?" Altan said, half to himself.

"Enver," Leon said, the first thing that came to mind. "You knew all the passports."

"When a man wants to be someone else, it's always interesting," Altan said, then stopped. "You want to know about Enver? He's of no importance. So unnecessary, to do that. A madman, that one." He cocked his head back toward the garden room.

"Two children. And now I have to arrange a pension for the widow. Who gives me the money for that?"

"Maybe your new American friends," Leon said, trying it out. "Aren't they paying you for him?" Another look back toward Alexei.

"Paying? I don't think you understand how it is."

"Then how is it."

Altan looked over, almost a reprimand. "Calm yourself, Mr. Bauer. Leon. We're working together now, you know."

"How did that happen?"

"Your ambassador. And your Mr. Barksdale."

"Who?"

Altan smiled. "New to me too. From Washington. He came especially. A military plane."

"Especially for what?"

"Mr. Bishop worked for him. So there was a concern."

"And you thought you'd give him a ring and see if there was anything you could do for him."

"No. He called me. He asked for my help. There were, you know, liaisons during the war. Official channels."

"But this was unofficial."

Altan nodded. "As you say."

"So how much did you ask for Alexei?"

Altan glared at him, trying to decide whether to be offended or move on.

"Why not?" Leon said. "The Russians are paying. Why should you work for free?"

Altan took out a cigarette, lighting it with a hand cupped against the breeze, a minute's stalling.

"Let me explain something to you. We need the Americans now. So we help them. There's no price for that. How can there be? Without them, we'd be —" He opened his hand to the air, letting the phrase finish itself, then turned to Leon. "We can't be neutral anymore."

"What happened to the balancing act? Between us and the bear."

Altan smiled a little. "I know you better now. Colleagues. We don't have to pretend. The bear wants to eat us. You don't. Which would you choose?"

"So we get Alexei. And what do you get?"

Altan drew on the cigarette, looking back to the Bosphorus, taking another minute to frame an answer.

"Very beautiful, isn't it?"

"Not last night."

"No. But now look. It's always beautiful to me. Asia, Europe." He gestured back and forth. "And Istanbul the bridge. You say. Not us, you. A bridge to what? Some storybook in your head maybe. Byzantines. Ottomans. Not the Occupation, the British ships there." He nodded toward the water. "The shame. Soldiers coming back. In rags. No, all dancing girls and sherbets. Stories. You're in love with the past. Well, maybe all of us, a little." He turned to face Leon. "We don't think we're a bridge. We think we're the center. The world used to spread out from here, in every direction. For years. But then it began to shrink. Piece by piece, then all at once. And now there's only us. Turkey. So we have to keep that. The bear would eat us, he's always wanted to eat us. An easy job now. No more empire. This city? A backwater. Yes." He held up his hand, no objections. "They think so. So do you. Only Turks here now, and who cares about them? So we have to make you care. Make you our friends. Comrades. Hah. Against the comrades." He flicked the cigarette toward the water, pleased with his wordplay. "So we do what we can. For our friends. A small price to pay." He looked over. "You see why it was so important to find him. Even use Gülün. A matter of state," he said. "But you kept running. And clever." He shook his head. "Palestine. Not Greece."

Leon looked away, unexpectedly pleased. "I thought you would give him to the Russians."

"Leon," Altan said, his tone puzzled, as if Leon hadn't been listening. "We are giving him to the Russians."

Leon turned, the air around him suddenly still. Nothing moved, boats, waves, everything stopped in place.

"I told you last night," Altan said. "The Americans don't want him. Not now. Not if they can use him to trade."

"To trade," Leon repeated flatly, no sound at all now, not even birds. In the garden room, Alexei would be writing down dates, asking Ayşe for more coffee. "Trade for what?"

"Their man in the consulate. A much bigger fish now than our Romanian. Killing Mr. Bishop. Who next? Maybe you. Jianu's information, you know, is — how old? Months at least, maybe years. Useful, but not so important as someone still operating inside."

Leon saw Alexei back in Laleli, extending his hand, squeezing an invisible lemon.

"If he is inside," Leon said, his voice plodding, one thought, then another. "It could have been —"

"Well, that's what you'll find out."

"Me."

"Yes, of course. You make the bargain with Melnikov. Who else? I can't be seen as interfering. Even now, we should be indoors. Who knows if someone is watching?"

Involuntarily, Leon looked out at the water.

"He's there," Altan said. "And now another man dead. They have to act. That's why Barksdale called. Can you help. And of course I knew you must have Jianu. So everything could be arranged. If I got to you in time. And I did." He turned his hand up, then lowered his voice. "Jianu's not so important now. This one is."

"Then why would the Russians trade him for Alexei?"

"No one defects. A matter of principle with them — emotions, even," he said, correcting himself. "You remember Melnikov at the party? Don't worry, they'll trade. They can't afford to let him go, set an example. The one inside? It's just a question of time now, before the Americans get him. They have to. But such a mess — looking here, looking there, turning everything upside down. Much easier to have him delivered. Worth throwing Jianu back to get him."

"Then what was that charade before?"

Leon glanced toward the house. "People flying in from Ankara."

"Leon. Would you rather have him believe that you're taking him to the Russians?"

Animals were herded through gates, the lining up itself meant to reassure, pacify them, make the rest easier. Something every butcher knew.

"But not before you got a few dates out of him." Squeezing harder, only pulp left.

Altan shrugged.

Leon looked down suddenly at the wooden slats of the terrace, feeling them about to open, the jolt of a trapdoor, his whole body poised for a second in midair.

"Leon."

No louder than a faint echo, all sound pulled into some vacuum. On the Bosphorus, a swirl of silent birds were diving for something he couldn't make out, a fish, something hapless flailing on the surface until it slipped under.

"They'll kill him."

"Eventually."

The birds were regrouping, swooping up, then diving again.

He turned to Altan. "I won't do it." His breath ragged, the way it had been holding on to the life preserver.

Altan looked at him, surprised. "Won't do what?"

"Give him to the Russians."

"Do you think you are working for yourself? You're part of this. It's been decided." He peered at Leon. "You don't believe me? I'll phone. You can ask Barksdale yourself. It's what they want."

And suddenly his stomach, fluttering, began to cramp, knowing that he didn't have to call, that it was true. You're part of this.

"They'll kill him," he said again.

"This is a concern to you? No such tears for Enver, I notice."

"I didn't kill him."

"You're not killing this one, either. Who are you working for? Him? The Americans want a trade."

"You do it then."

Altan shook his head. "Why would I go to Melnikov to suggest this? The man in the consulate is nothing to us — the Americans' problem. Melnikov will believe you. He already thinks you work for them. And now it turns out — he's right." He looked over at Leon. "Isn't he?"

The logic of it encircling him, the slats holding.

"I was just supposed to pick him up,"

Leon said quietly, talking to himself.

"We all think that at the beginning. That it's easy. So you learn. You can't be sentimental. About him? You have to think what's important to you." He waited. "It's been decided." Another moment, staring at Leon now. "I've explained you to Barksdale. Bebek, all that business. They trust you to do this."

Leon stared back, saying nothing. I've explained you. And then it was too late. His silence had answered for him.

"Good," Altan said. "Now, the arrangements. You meet with Melnikov. Let him decide the place for the exchange. Then he won't be suspicious. But somewhere public. You bring Jianu, he brings their man — interesting to think what Melnikov will tell him, no?"

Lining them up in a stall.

"Make sure it's somewhere you can have your people waiting. You don't want to make a spectacle. He'll be armed no matter what you say, so you too, agree to that. But not his man — or Jianu. No dramatics. They like a formal exchange — start here, you there, a meeting in the middle. Like a duel. Always afraid of tricks. They think everyone's like them." He held up a finger. "But soon — today, if possible. I don't want to keep Jianu here. Anyway, it's better for them too. Before their man can suspect." He looked up. "A place where he can't run, when he sees your people."

"My people," Leon said.

Altan opened his hand, an offering gesture.

"But you can't be involved."

"Gülün's men don't always wear uniforms. But you see them at the door and you know there's no way out. Melnikov's men — you won't even have to guess. Cossacks. Out to here." He indicated burly shoulders. "Nothing ever fits. A place with exits would be good. Haghia Sophia, somewhere like that. But let him pick. A guarantee for him, that he's not walking into a trap. They like that."

"And if they start shooting?"

"They won't. That would ruin it for the next time."

Leon looked up.

"One of their men in Washington, I think. You'll talk to him another time about that trade."

"A man in Washington," Leon said, feeling his stomach clench again.

"Well, there always is. More than one. So for a while he's not sure who you mean, and they all lie low — a good thing for you.

If not, he'll like you thinking there is. But there must be. It's always safe to play that card. What's the matter?" he said, taking in Leon's face. "Ah, did our friend already play it? Always make them think you have more. Leon. How would he know? Do you think they would tell him that?"

Leon looked at the water. People hear things, sometimes by chance. And people lie. He saw the flat in Laleli again, tidy, duffel packed, ready to go, Alexei hunched over the board, plotting moves.

"So, your first meeting. Somewhere neutral. Where Emniyet wouldn't notice," Altan said, smiling. "Right under my nose, an innocent encounter."

"The bar at the Park."

"Like during the war? Easy days for us. All of you watching each other. No," he said, thinking. "The Pera. Mrs. Bishop. You're with her in the bar. Melnikov comes in, says hello — he met her here, at the party — you invite him to sit, she has to go. An errand. Or however you want to arrange that." He looked over. "You're good at those things. Try not to leave the hotel with him. When he's there, we can keep an eye on you. Afterward —" He made a brushing motion with his hand. "He'd know we were following. Even us."

"What about me? Won't he have me —"

"Naturally. So after, take a ferry to Üskü-dar. There'll be a taxi — don't worry, it'll know you. His people will have a longer time getting one. And the Asian side, it's confusing for them." He looked at his watch. "You'll be back in time for tea."

"All worked out," Leon said.

"No, not all," Altan said, preoccupied, not hearing anything in Leon's voice. "Now the phone call. Let's go over that. How did you get the number? His private number. He'll expect all their consulate phones to be tapped."

"Are they?"

"Mm. So is this one. But how did you get it? Not something he hands out."

"Georg," Leon said, not even thinking. "Georg gave it to me."

Altan looked over. "Good." He nodded, pleased. "Georg. Good."

Leon took up the part. "I found the man Georg said you were looking for."

"What man?" Altan said, lowering his voice, playing too.

"The translator. Fluent in Romanian, Russian. Some German. Hard to find, but I did."

Altan was quiet for a minute, running the conversation through his mind, then smiled a little. "So you did."

A French door opened behind them.

"*Domnul* Jianu," Altan said, the Romanian word a courtesy. "You're finished with your lunch?"

"Do you have a cigarette?" he asked Leon, then to Altan, "American cigarettes. You get spoiled."

"That's all they have in America," Altan said, pleasant.

Leon handed the pack to Jianu, keeping his hand steady. What did his face look like, some telltale blush, giving him away? But maybe people only saw what they were looking for, a magic mirror effect, the smooth, reassuring look of someone you thought you knew.

"It's arranged?" Alexei said, lighting the cigarette.

"Almost. A phone call," Altan said.

Alexei looked up.

"They want to hear from me personally," Leon said. "Make sure." Not even a catch in his throat, his voice smooth too, someone else.

Alexei nodded, accepting this.

"Let's see if the line's open now," Altan said, beginning to move. "Better stay inside." This to Alexei, with a look to the house. "Boats have eyes too."

"But you'd be the ones watching," Alexei said. "I thought."

Altan met his stare. "Not only." He made an ushering gesture toward the house. "Leon," he said, heading inside.

Leon stood rooted to the deck, waiting for Alexei, who drew on the cigarette, watching Altan go.

"Be careful of that one," Alexei said, his voice intimate, something between them. "I don't trust him."

Leon looked at the water, afraid of his face again. "He's right, though. You never know."

"No," Alexei said and started for the door, putting his hand on Leon's shoulder as he passed.

Leon kept staring out. The birds had gone away. Was anyone in fact watching? What would they see? The long white terrace, motorboats tied to mooring poles, the flash of the sun on the French windows. Pretty, placid, as calm as the water where the fish had been.

"How am I supposed to act?" Kay said, touching her hair, nervous.

"Like someone having tea."

"Tea. Mata Hari used to stay here. It says in the brochure. I'll bet she never had tea."

"At this hour she did."

There were only a few people in the Pera bar this early, the winter sun still warming the apricot walls. Lamps with fringe, velvet-covered cushions, the fussy luxury of an Orient Express car.

"I don't think I could have done it."

"What?"

"Sleep with generals. Steal things out of their pockets."

"I don't think that's how it's done now," Leon said, a half smile.

"No?" she said quickly, another pat to her hair. "How is it done?"

"You drink that and look happy to see me."

"And disappear when he gets here."

Leon nodded.

"Go to my room and not know what this is about, either." She looked down at her cup. "Happy to see you. It scares me how happy I was. I thought I wouldn't."

"I said I'd —"

"I know. And you did." She looked up. "For how long?"

"One last thing. And then it's over."

"Until the next time."

"No. Over."

"Really?" she said, then started picking at her finger. "Does it work that way? Just quit? I thought it was like the army." She took out a cigarette, something to put in her hand. "When did you decide this?"

"Today."

"What happened today?" she said, looking up.

He shook his head. "Nothing."

"Nothing," she said back, lighting the cigarette. "At least you didn't say it's because of me. I'd have probably believed it too." She shook the match out. "I'm an easy lay."

"Only at first."

She raised her eyebrows, then smiled.

"That's it. You're supposed to be happy to see me."

"Better?" she said, a full smile now, then looked down. "Will you come later?"

He nodded. "Wait for me."

"Do you know, I actually felt that. A jump. Here." She moved a hand down to her stomach. "Just hearing that." She knocked off some ash, fidgeting, glancing around the room. "Who's watching anyway?"

"I don't know," he said, following her glance.

"I mean, who's supposed to be watching?"

Who would be? Altan must have someone. Would Melnikov risk a meeting alone? Barksdale, still not sure of him? The barman? The waiter? The Turkish woman with the hat?

"I don't know," he said again, hearing himself this time, the absurdity of it. "Everybody. All the time. If you keep doing it. Someone always is. That's what it's like. All the time." A conversation with himself now. You're part of this.

"You're going to bend that spoon."

He looked down at his hands, his thumbs pressing against the thin neck of polished steel.

"You do that. There's nothing in your face, and then I hear a snap and I see something's been going on all the time."

He dropped the spoon, looking away, someone caught.

"Tell me what you were thinking. Just now. Don't make something up. What you were really thinking."

He picked up the spoon again, staring at it.

"Tell me."

"What do you do," he said, still looking down, as if he were reading, "when there's no right thing to do. Just the wrong thing. Either way."

She said nothing for a minute, not expecting this.

"And you can't avoid it anymore. Doing

something." He looked up. "What do you do?" Not really a question, not even to himself.

"I don't know," she said, stalling, then met his eyes. "Are you talking about me?"

"What? No," he said, moving his hands over, catching a spill. "I didn't mean —" He stopped. "Not you," he said softly.

"Oh," she said, just a sound, her face flushing, surprised again. She reached over, covering his hands. "Then what?"

Drawing him in, as if they were in bed, no secrets.

He looked at her for another second, then shook his head. "Nothing."

"We could get up, right now, and walk out of here," she said, still clutching his hand, her eyes fixed on him. "Just keep going. Before there's anything more. We could do that."

Through the doors, past one of Gülün's men, on Altan's leash, past the consulate. I've explained you. Altan waiting.

"I can't," he said, moving his hand away.

She kept hers on the table. "Why not? One last thing. What last thing?"

Well, what?

"We can find out who killed Frank."

"Frank?" she said, thrown, pulling her hand back. "How? What do you mean?

That's what he's coming here for?"

"No."

"Are you doing this for me? Don't. What does it matter who? Somebody, that's all. It doesn't change anything."

"And next time it'll be somebody else. Maybe me."

Her eyes flashed, then looked away, a backing off. She drew on her cigarette to calm down.

"You think a Russian did it," she said.

"Not this Russian. Smile again. He's here."

Over her shoulder, he could see Melnikov hesitate at the door, an entrance, then head straight for them. He did everything he was expcted to do — his surprise at seeing them, remembering Kay from Lily's party, not wanting to intrude but persuaded to stay — but all of it done so clumsily that only his awkwardness made it seem authentic. Leon thought of Lily, gliding through her guests. Melnikov ordered vodka. Then, having exhausted his script, he sat waiting for Leon, a silence anyone in the room would notice.

"I'll be right back," Kay said. "Powder room. You'll excuse me?"

Melnikov stood as she left, formal, then turned to Leon. "Where is he?"

"Safe. We can do it this afternoon."

"How much do you want?" Blunt, not the playful ritual of the Bazaar.

"A trade. Your man in the consulate."

"What man?"

"The one who killed Frank."

"There is no such man."

"Yes there is. Frank found him, that's why he's dead. So will we. Now that we know he's there. But we'd like to speed things up. They're both damaged goods now. An even trade."

Melnikov thought about this. "How do I know you have him?"

"You'll see him. I bring mine, you bring yours. Don't come empty-handed. It's a onetime offer. Pick the place."

"And no money. Not even a tip for you."

"Maybe next time."

Melnikov stared at him, not sure how to take this.

"This isn't hard. Take it or leave it."

"And if I leave it?"

"Then we get both of them. Bad arithmetic for you."

Melnikov shrugged. "But he's already talked."

"Only to me. Or he'd be in Washington now. He likes to wait for the right move — a chess player. But you know that. He said

you were a little slow. So I guess his information's still good."

Melnikov sat back, annoyed.

"We're wasting time. You'll want guarantees. So do we. Can you bring him today?"

Melnikov hesitated, running the tip of his
tongue between his lips, a wolf's anticipation.

"I think you may be surprised," he said
finally.

Leon looked at him. Done. A life dis-
carded in a second. Enver slipping in the
bath.

"Only if you don't show up."

Melnikov snorted, then picked up his
glass, draining it.

"You pick the place," Leon said again.

"Well, goodness, here you are, big as life.
I've been wondering. I thought maybe you'd
gone *home*." Barbara King, Ed Burke trailing behind.

Leon stood, kissing the cheek she offered.

"I hope you're coming to my party. I left
about a hundred messages."

Now turning to be introduced to Melnikov, Ed hanging back, as if the physical
presence of a Russian was upsetting, the
bogeyman real.

"Isn't it a little early?" Barbara said, noticing the glass. Then Kay was coming back.

"Kay," she said, stretching the syllable. "I've been meaning to call. Those first few days, I know what it's like."

And suddenly it was the crowd outside Sirkeci, everyone in motion, trying to get out of each other's way. Melnikov wary, suspecting tricks. But about what? Kay slightly panicky, someone who'd left her post for a second and now saw people rushing through the gate. Ed flustered for no reason at all, embarrassed maybe for Leon, his interrupted tryst. Only Barbara blithely enjoying herself, eyeing Kay's dress, taking the confusion for some kind of evidence, a vindicated house detective.

"Ed, have you met Ivan Melnikov?"

Ed now reluctant, barely managing to get through a handshake, Melnikov just as publicly diffident so that for a second Leon wondered if in fact they already knew each other. Melnikov's face a mask, giving nothing away. I think you may be surprised.

Leon looked at the other tables, people talking to each other, or pretending to. Try not to leave the hotel, Altan had said. But how could they stay now?

"Not even one drink?" Barbara was saying. "A *citron pressé?* I never see you."

"I'm late already," Kay said, fluttering.

"But can't it wait? Ten minutes."

Leon could see her thinking, a movement in the back of her eyes.

"Not the hairdresser," she said.

"Women and their hair," Melnikov said, indulgent, as if nothing more could be said.

"And us. I'm sorry," Leon said.

"You're going to the hairdresser too?" Barbara said, playing.

"The consulate." He turned to Melnikov. "I promised we'd be there by —"

"To meet the new guy?" Ed said, interested now. "They say — but you must have seen him. First thing. I mean he'd want —" He stopped. "What's he like?"

Melnikov looked at Leon. Presumably his new boss, someone Leon would know.

"He's from Washington, Ed," Leon said, trying to be light. "You know. I think they even get their suits from the same place."

And then they were in the lobby, Ed and Barbara left in the bar but still looking at them, everything a question mark.

"Well, now I'd better have it done," Kay said, brushing the back of her hair.

"Mrs. Bishop," Melnikov said, taking her hand. "A pleasure."

Not lingering, someone keeping an appointment. He moved back so Leon could say good-bye.

"Thanks for the tea," Kay said, one eye to the bar.

Leon took her hand. "We'll do it again," he said, something for Melnikov and the bellhops. Then low, only to her, "Wait for me."

She shuddered, as if a draft had just swept through the door.

"What?"

Her eyes wide, then darting across his face. "I just had the strangest feeling." She put her hand on his arm, holding him in place.

"What?"

She glanced toward the door, Melnikov waiting. "I don't know," she said, her fingers still gripping him. "Just a feeling."

Leon looked back over his shoulder. "He's watching."

She dropped her hand. "All right," she said, then caught his sleeve. "Wait. I know. What you said before. Two wrong things. They're not the same. They can't be. You have to decide."

"It's not like that."

"You wonder," she said, not listening to him, "did I do the right thing? But at least you made the choice." Her voice intense, as if no one else were in the room. Then she lowered her head. "Well, listen to me." She

549

let go his sleeve. "Did I do the right thing?"

"Kay —"

"I still don't know. You'd better go," she said, glancing to Melnikov again.

Leon looked at her, disconcerted, wanting to touch her, the room full of eyes, the clock beginning to tick again. "Wait for me," he said, code for everything else.

"An attractive woman," Melnikov said in the street. "No, this way." Up to Tünel, the route already picked out. "And now a widow."

"Yes."

"You were close to him?"

"Not particularly."

"I knew him. A careful man. But not with our friend Jianu. I never understood that. We didn't know — I admit that to you. It should have been easy for you. So what happened? A man so careful."

"He trusted the wrong people."

"But it was you he trusted," Melnikov said, the way it made sense to him. "And with his wife. Twice wrong, I think. And now you ask me to trust you."

"You won't come alone. Neither will I. We can trust each other that much. Like a time-out."

"Time —"

"When you stop the game. A little truce.

To make the trade. Then it starts again."

"But no money," Melnikov said, still brooding. "I thought you were keeping him for that."

"Maybe he's more valuable to us this way."

"Us. And how is it more valuable to you?" He looked at Leon. "A man of many loyalties, our Jianu. And you?"

"Only one," Leon said, not biting.

"Stars and Stripes," Melnikov said, still looking, skeptical, his voice almost a sneer.

And what was that? A *Saturday Evening Post* cover. But that was before. Now it was someone ordering a trade.

"You've tried this already. With Georg. I don't want any money."

"So it was something else. To make you give up your prize." Noting it, filing it away for the future. But not Leon's, almost out of it. Just play out the hand.

"Maybe he isn't worth as much as we thought."

Melnikov looked at him for a moment, calculating again, then started walking, almost at the square now, the scraping sound of a tram being turned around.

"You don't know how to talk to him," he said flatly.

"But you do."

"Yes. He'll talk to us."

Leon looked at the square, sunny, a break in the clouds, and felt the chill of a dripping basement. There'd be screams. Everybody screamed finally. Everybody talked.

People were pouring out of the funicular station.

"Just in time," Melnikov said.

"Where are you going? We need to —"

"Have you noticed? People always take it coming up. A *jeton?* A small price, to avoid the hill. But down? So mostly empty. Private."

The few people boarding were heading to the front car to be off first.

"You see?" Melnikov said, getting into the last car. "No one. A good place to talk. No ears."

Except the man who just then got in, standing by the window until he caught Melnikov's eye and backed out again, going to the next car, an almost slapstick retreat. One of Melnikov's own, too eager, or just somebody off the street? The buzzer rang, doors sliding shut, and they started down through the tunnel, old concrete and bare bulbs, what the way to Melnikov's basement might look like. Just the two of them.

"Now it's safe," Melnikov said. "How many men will you bring?"

All business, negotiating a contract, as if

552

they were in one of the banks on Voyvoda Caddesi at the foot of the hill. Guarantees. Procedures. Handing over someone to be killed. Meeting the funicular cars going up, at the halfway point, then swallowed up again by the narrow passage, Melnikov's eyes never leaving him, someone who'd killed his own men. Means to an end. But what was the end now?

At the bottom, he stopped himself from rushing out, waiting for the doors to slide all the way open.

"Six o'clock then," Melnikov said.

And it was done, over, the claustrophobic ride, Melnikov's eyes. They crossed Tersane, dodging cars, suddenly back in real life, everything opening up before him, the smells of the Karaköy market, the amateur fishermen dangling poles off the bridge, trams and cars and peddlers and the minarets beyond, the scene he'd known a thousand times before, but bathed in an unnatural light now, the city wonderful again because it was done.

"You have not said where," Melnikov said.

"You pick."

Melnikov spread his hand, turning the choice back to Leon. "Somewhere with people," he said.

Leon flipped through mental postcards.

Not Haghia Sophia, gloom and frescoes. Taksim, cars waiting close by? A tram was coming across from Eminönü, another from this side, like seconds marking out paces, crowds streaming by, oblivious. He stopped, almost laughing at the obvious.

"Here," he said, pointing. "Galata Bridge."

They left early, Alexei in a life vest this time.

"More boats," he said, but not the creaky fishing trawler, one of Lily's motorboats, sleek with wood trim.

"I hope you're not afraid of flying too," Altan said.

The story was a drive to the airport, army transport out, what should have happened days ago.

"Then why the boat?"

"The airport's on the European side," Leon said. "We can't risk the car ferry. They watch it." Keeping him safe. "Relax."

Alexei made a resigned grimace, the boat slapping hard against whitecaps, pitching up and down.

After they passed the Dolmabahçe Mosque, Leon looked up the hill, trying to find his window. There'd be mail waiting, curious Mr. Cicek, wondering what the police had wanted. Alexei was taking everything in, his first real look at the city, spill-

554

ing over its hills in the weak afternoon light. Leon checked his watch. Almost dark, but at this time of year a lingering dusk, light enough for Melnikov to see them on the bridge.

They swung into the Golden Horn, then idled just far enough away from the bridge to keep it in sight, the cranes and drydocks of the shipyards ahead.

"They won't expect us to come down the Horn," Altan said, indicating the factories and oily water farther along. He was scanning the bridge through binoculars.

"Who?" Alexei said. "The Americans?"

"No," Altan said, catching himself. "Anybody. Force of habit." So feeble that it passed as an excuse.

"There's no one on the bridge now," Alexei said, not meaning the crowds.

"How do you know?"

"I looked. When we passed under. You don't need those if you know how to look. They say a lion can sit, looking at grass, and then for one second something's not right, a movement, one second, and he knows."

Altan made a face. *"Aslan,"* he said wryly. Lion.

Leon looked at the bridge. Could anyone really see that way? A second's movement in a place perpetually in motion? The iron arches, the pontoons at their feet, people crowding onto the jetties from the ferries, the lower level of fish restaurants and stalls, trams sliding overhead, the sprawling market — all the same to him, nothing out of place. How much longer now? He turned and gazed toward the docks, trying not to look at Alexei. Around the curve was Kasim Paşa and then the yards where the *Victorei* had waited in quarantine.

"Any news of the ship?" he asked Altan.

It took Altan a minute. "Oh, the Jews. No. How would I hear? We don't follow them to Palestine."

"I'd like to know," Leon said, a request.

"You know it was said there was typhus?"

Leon nodded. "A miracle recovery. It cost ten thousand dollars. Turkish medicine."

Altan stared at him, more embarrassed than offended.

"How many? On the ship," Alexei asked.

"Four hundred," Leon said. "A few more."

"You saved four hundred Jews," Altan said to Alexei, an ironic taunting in his voice.

"And I only owed you one life," Alexei said to Leon.

"You don't owe me anything," Leon said quickly.

Alexei put his hand to his chest, an abbreviated salaam. *"Bereket versin."*

"You know Turkish?" Altan said, surprised.

"A few words. You pick things up." He looked at Altan. *"Aslan."*

Altan turned back to the bridge.

"Why are we here?" Alexei said to Leon. "What happens now?"

"It's not time yet. There'll be a car," Leon said, nodding to the Eminönü side. Where Melnikov must be waiting, in the big square filled with buses and stalls frying mackerel from the boats tied up alongside. "I'll walk you over. And then we're done."

Alexei kept looking at him, not saying anything.

"Nothing to it," Leon said, uneasy.

"Then why did you bring a gun?" Alexei said, looking to Leon's pocket.

"In case," Leon said vaguely.

"In case I run?" Alexei said. "So careful, the Americans. Where would I go? In Washington let's hope they're not so careful. A long job, if they don't believe me."

"Skip the Soviets' man there, then," Leon said, trying it. "If you want to build some trust. Or was he just for me? Keep me interested."

Alexei turned to the bridge, not answering.

"In high places," Leon said. "The one

nobody knows. Who isn't there. Is he?"

Alexei was quiet for a moment. "He must be," he said finally, "don't you think? Someone must be. A safe move." He turned back to Leon. "To keep me valuable, that's all."

He pulled up the collar of his jacket, hunkering down. "What does he think he'll find?" he said, looking at Altan in the front of the boat, still scanning the bridge.

Leon joined him on the seat, their jackets touching.

"Ten minutes," Altan said over his shoulder. "Get ready."

Alexei pulled the duffel bag closer. "Well, then it's good-bye," he said to Leon. He looked down, oddly hesitant. "You know that job — training your people — the one I talked about? If you could mention it to someone. If you think it would help. A word from you —"

Leon nodded, cutting him off, each word like a tug on his sleeve.

He got up, leaning against the gunwale, as if there were something to see in the water. "Tell me. It can't matter to you now. I mean, we're here. So what I think doesn't —"

Alexei lifted an eyebrow.

"What did you do at Străuleşti?"

"Why do you ask this?" Alexei said.

Leon looked at him, waiting. Make it easier for me.

"It's not enough, your ship?"

"I want to know."

A long silence, Alexei looking at his hands.

"What you told me —" Leon said.

"What? I don't even remember anymore. What I said. But you have to know. Something that happened —" He looked out toward the old city. "In another world." Quiet again, then turning back to Leon. "Outside. Only outside. I never went in. Didn't I say that? It's the truth. The meat stamps, the hooks — I wasn't part of that. Craziness. I was outside." He stopped. "Like a guard. Of what, I don't know. Outside." He looked up. "But I could hear. Is that what you want to know, what I heard?"

"No."

"No, it's better. Don't listen. Someday maybe somebody asks you," he said, looking at Leon, "and what do you say? I had to do it? All you can say is, I was there. But outside. I was outside." He stopped. "Do you think it would have made any difference? If I hadn't been there?"

Leon said nothing.

"None. Maybe a difference to me," he said, his voice lower. "Not to hear it. But not to them." He took a breath. "So. Now

559

stop asking me this. Wait a few years, when you see what things are like. Then ask."

"And that's the truth."

"Didn't I say so?"

Leon nodded. "Everyone else is dead."

"That's right. There's only me to say. Everyone's dead. Not just them. Everyone. People I knew."

"But you weren't standing outside then."

"You want to blame me for this? There has to be somebody? So it makes sense?" He waved his hand. "Go ahead. And will that make any difference, either?" He shook his head. "They're dead. You want justice for them? Not in this world."

"All right, let's go," Altan said, motioning the driver to pull up to the jetty. "Careful of the step."

Alexei stared at Leon. "That's what things were like, that time. It's different now."

Leon looked back. No squeals this time. Nothing to hear. A simple exchange, people passing by.

"Good luck," Altan said, taking Alexei's hand to steady him for the climb out of the boat. Friendly, helping him along.

Alexei made it in two steps, the duffel following.

"Gülün and his men will be at the top of the stairs," Altan said to Leon, glancing

560

toward the bridge. "Don't look for him or the *aslan* will know," he said, sarcastic. "Just the two of you. Until it's too late. Then bring Melnikov's man back. Let's hope he's not a Turk. After all this."

Leon stood, not moving, eyes fixed on Altan's upper lip. No moustache.

"All right?"

All right. A matter of minutes, that's all. Something Alexei had done — how many times? What he wanted to do in Washington, handing over names, already had done for Altan at Lily's. It gets easier. But just then, lifting himself out of the boat, the minutes felt endless. Altan waved and pulled away.

They made their way to the bridge through the Karaköy market, sidestepping pools of melted ice streaked with fish blood, strands of wilted greens. Cats lurked behind the stalls, waiting for scraps. There was more food near the steps of the bridge, stuffed mussels and braziers with chestnuts.

They stopped for a minute on top, catching a breath before they waded into the crowd. Don't look for Gülün, anybody, just start walking. Meet in the middle, no advantage on either side. Not too fast, as formally paced as a gunfight, except in a Western there'd be no one else in the streets, the townspeople cowering and

561

Melnikov dressed in black, to make everything clear. Instead there were water salesmen with silver canisters strapped to their backs and *hamals* wheeling carts and a *simit* peddler with a tray of bread rings balanced on his head.

Leon felt the gun in his pocket. Not something you'd want to use in a crowd, just in case. In case what? They had to shoot their way back? Altan had never said, but now that they were here Leon knew. Alexei would recognize Melnikov, not a stranger, and might have to be persuaded to keep going, prodded forward. Maybe even shot if he tried to bolt. In the foot, a knee, somewhere to keep him alive for Melnikov. The gun was for Alexei.

And Melnikov would have his own, ready to use on the other side, his man unsuspecting too until the final minute. Maybe until he recognized Leon. Someone who'd killed Frank and would kill again, meanwhile betraying them all to the Soviets. There were two people in this trade, not just Alexei. A frontier justice, maybe the only kind there ever was. Think of it as bringing someone to trial.

"What kind of car?" Alexei said. "American?"

"I don't know. They didn't say. In front of

562

the mosque, that's all."

Each step a foot closer. His eyes darted over the fishermen lining the rail, waiting for one of them to turn his head as they passed, not a fisherman. What it must feel like hunting, preparing to kill, a lion watching the grass.

They were on the Horn side of the bridge, traffic coming from behind. Maybe a burst of gunfire from a passing car. The Russians were capable of anything, any deceit. But all he saw were taxis on their way to Sirkeci. Don't look back, Alexei sure to notice. So far not even wary, trusting the car to be there, trusting Leon. Everything as planned. Then why the dismay, this constriction in his chest, Leon feeling that it was he who was being brought to trial. Betraying, Alexei had said, gets easier. Leon glanced over. Now eager, almost boyish, what he must have looked like in Bucharest.

Leon scanned the crowd up ahead. Maybe a quarter of the way across now, Melnikov here soon. I think you may be surprised. Some teenage boys ran out of the stairway from the restaurant level below. Where he and Kay had had lunch, looking at minarets, Ed embarrassed to stumble on them. Years ago.

How many times had he walked across

this bridge, feeling lucky to be here? Now, a shiver, he sensed everything was about to change. Even in this half-light things seemed sharper, as if they knew he'd have to remember them, be asked about them one day. And what would he say? I was outside. Listening. He glanced over at Alexei again. A head snapped on a bathroom floor because it was in the way. I'm not you. A wave of panic rose in his throat, like bile. I'm not you. But everything now set in motion, Melnikov already somewhere in the sea of heads coming toward them. The *simit* man was back, partly blocking the view. Leon leaned a little to his left.

And saw the hat. The same floppy brim she'd worn at Tommy's service, just in from Ankara. Not sure if it was proper to smoke in the street. Later, shy against the window light. Walking now with Melnikov. No. He kept moving. Kay raised her head, looking into the crowd. Looking for him? Or for some story Melnikov had made up to put her at ease? Part of him visible now, just over her right shoulder, as if she were a kind of shield to use before he threw her away. Someone in Ankara. The Russian desk. No. Leon hearing her voice, not the traffic, everything she had ever said, almost dizzy with it. Any of it real? None of it? Still coming toward them.

"What is it?" Alexei said, alert, a scent in the wind.

"Nothing," Leon said, his voice hollow, emptied out.

Nothing. Wrong about everything. Walking, unable to stop. A life can change in a second and never be the same. A hand sliding away in the water. A shot fired on a quay. More voices, then Altan's on the terrace. You have to think what's important to you. Meaning something else. But what was? Not even a second, less, and everything changed forever. One more, and he would be them. Not an accidental killer. One of them. Twisting necks, throwing people away. Maybe he already was, the second already passed. Alexei not seeing them yet, wondering what kind of car it would be.

"No," Leon said out loud, not even bothering to lower his voice.

Alexei turned to him, all attention, head up. A twig snapping in the woods.

"Don't. Don't look. Listen." Quick, his mind racing. The others still coming. "It's a trap. See the stairs?" Just ahead, no more than a minute at this pace. He took out the gun and slipped it into Alexei's pocket, a thief's movement. "Give me the duffel." One hand over the other, then only Leon's.

"When I say, head for the stairs. After that —"

"Run," Alexei said, finishing it.

"I'm sorry," Leon said, the word not big enough.

"And you?"

But there was no time, not for an answer, anything. Almost at the stairs.

"Ready?" Leon said, lifting the bag. "Now."

He pushed into the *simit* peddler, a shove with the duffel. The man pitched forward, teetering, the tray sliding off and spilling *simits* into the crowd, away from the stairs. Noises of surprise, everyone looking, then rushing to help the man, a general swarming. Leon looked up, Kay seeing him now, Melnikov coming from behind, his gaze to Leon's right, past the commotion to the blur of Alexei running away. Alexei stopped, recognizing him, then looked back to Leon, mouth open, moving pieces. A second, just long enough for Melnikov to raise his gun and fire. A sharp, clanging noise, the bullet hitting iron, then shrieks, sounds of panic, the *simits* scattered again as people ran for cover. Another shot as Alexei disappeared down the stairs. Melnikov started running, pushing Kay aside, everyone scattering, ducking against the bridge railing. When he

566

reached the stairs, he glanced over at Leon, panting, his face almost a snarl, before he plunged down.

From below Leon could hear screams, shouts of protest, people being shoved. He remembered the crowds shopping, lined up for the restaurants. Another trap. Why had he sent him there? But where else could he have gone? A head start, at least, a minute to save himself.

Melnikov's men raced after him to the stairs. Leon swiveled his head. Gülün's men, invisible before, were rushing down from the Karaköy side. Bottling him up. Leon imagined downstairs, women crouching, men yelling, Alexei running toward the freedom of Eminönü, seeing Melnikov's men coming down. Frantic, back and forth, the stalls a maze. Batteries and shoes and toys, knocked to the floor as people were crushed against them. Another shot, the sound different.

The bridge was still emptying, people hurrying to the ends, afraid now of being caught in any cross fire. A tram, unaware, had begun to lumber across and a few people ran over to it, hanging onto the side. Kay stood, still looking at Leon, her face bewildered, jumping when she heard the shot below. What was she seeing now?

Before? Wrong about everything.

She looked behind her, a quick check, then moved toward Leon, another woman following, not a Turk, western dress. Someone Leon knew but couldn't recognize, out of place. And then, even more confused, he did. Dorothy Wheeler. Who knew where all the files were, what Frank must have found. Who'd been walking behind Kay, next to Melnikov. I think you may be surprised. More shots from below, coming from both ends, as if they were firing at each other.

Then suddenly Alexei was at the top of the far stairs, a backtracking maneuver, his head poking up like a rabbit out of its hole, no, a fox, eyes desperate and calculating, trying to outrun the hunt. He looked around, the road almost empty, traffic stopped at either end, and started back to Karaköy, sprinting, wiry arms pumping as he came toward them. Leon could almost feel the surge of adrenaline, faster. Not far, a minute of luck, that's all. But the fox never won. Leon saw that the bridge was like a broad open field without cover, an illusion of escape. He hadn't saved Alexei, he'd only given him a head start to be killed. But at least running, all anyone could really hope for, a running start.

"Leon." Kay, heading toward him too.

Dorothy had disappeared. "Thank God."

"*Stoi!* Jianu!"

The blast of a shot, Melnikov firing from the top of the stairs, more screams from the railing. Alexei turned, looking back over his shoulder, catching a second shot in his chest. The force of it almost spun him around, his body slumping over, then forcing itself back up, the last ninth life, just enough strength to lift his gun. Hand shaking, trying to keep the shot from going wild. Leon pushed Kay to the ground, covering her.

"Stay down." Sounding like someone else, hoarse.

Another crack in the air from his right. He heard Melnikov grunt, then yelp, surprised, and looked up. The eerie quiet of a moment of elastic time. Melnikov slowly dropped to his knees, a forest trunk falling, holding his side, Alexei still bent over, but starting to move, awkward steps, staggering to some invisible finish line. Then Melnikov fired, a miss this time, but the sound speeding everything up again. Alexei tried to run faster, but his feet splayed, tripping over themselves, until they finally stopped and he crumpled onto the road, the gun clattering away from him.

"Don't move," Leon said to Kay, then got

up and ran to Alexei, blind to everything around him, Kay's voice behind, men rushing toward him, the fishermen at the rail lifting their heads to watch.

"Jianu!" Melnikov called again, weaker this time.

On the stairs there was a clomping of feet, Gülün barking out some order.

Leon dropped next to Alexei. He was gulping for air, blood pouring across his upper chest.

"The gun," he said, raspy, moving his eyes to the side. "Get the gun."

Leon picked it up.

"Jianu!"

Leon looked behind. Melnikov getting up, holding his stomach.

"So," Alexei said, still breathing in gasps.

"Hold on. We'll get an ambulance for you," Leon said. But who wanted him?

Alexei shook his head, then blinked at the gun.

"You do it. Not them."

Leon froze, the gun suddenly cold in his hand.

Alexei nodded. "It's time."

Leon stared at him.

"My friend." His eyes locked on Leon now. "Not them."

Leon heard the scrape of a shoe on the

road, Melnikov moving.

"What are you doing?" Kay said to Melnikov, somewhere in the distance.

"Do it," Alexei said, another blink, some awful permission. He moved his hand, limp, covered with blood, to touch Leon's arm, his eyes sure, so wide that Leon thought he could see to the back of them, who he was. "Please," he said, his voice fainter.

Leon knelt, paralyzed. One second. Alexei looking at him as if there was no one else on the bridge. Please. Leon fired. Alexei's body jerked, an electric jolt, his eyes even wider, then everything settled, quiet.

"Are you crazy?" Melnikov was yelling, close now, the bridge noisy again with men running.

Leon turned, as if he were protecting Alexei, already dead, with his own body. But Melnikov wasn't aiming at Alexei, his other hand still clutching his side, bleeding, eyes rabid with fury.

"Durak," he said, spitting it.

When the gun went off, Leon was too surprised to duck. Here? Like this? Why now? What was the point? Shooting him no more to Melnikov than stamping his foot. Then the fire exploded in his chest, literally the heat of flames, and some force, like a hand in his face, pushed him back, falling over.

"No!" Kay yelled, hitting Melnikov, but he was pointing the gun again, feet planted apart, rooted. She reached for it, trying to force it up from the ground. Melnikov knocked her away.

"Durak," he said again to Leon, then looked up as more feet approached and raised the gun, a reflex. Some shouts in Turkish and then an explosion, so loud Leon thought it came from behind his ear. This time Melnikov didn't make a sound, just looked down at the new hole in his tunic and dropped. Leon could make out Gülün kneeling by the body, gun in his hand. Something garbled in Turkish, orders.

"Leon," Kay said, her face over him, her voice high-pitched, almost a keening. Kay only a shield. Dorothy. But what could she have known? Passed on? Why do it? Money? Maybe like Georg, lost in an idea she couldn't let go. Now there'd be questions. Months of them, squeezing. A trial, if that was useful. Housecleaning. Protecting flanks. And then a new Melnikov would plant a new Dorothy and it would start again. Dorothy traded away. All Alexei was worth at the end. Leon heard more voices in the road, loud, then fainter, receding, the dusk suddenly getting darker.

And in some part of him, aware of what was happening, he was curious. Would it really be a white light, appearing from the end of a tunnel and enveloping him until he was part of it? What Alexei must just have seen. But it wasn't light, it was faces. Hazy, like underexposed film, but moving closer, until they were right next to him. Phil in his cockpit, waving. Georg walking his dog in Yildiz. Mihai at a boat rail, the faint suggestion of a smile. And then Anna. In Lily's garden that first spring, worried because they were happy. Before anything happened. Her face so close now he felt he could touch it. All the faces of his life. Then they went away.

"Finally," a voice said. "I'll get the nurse."

Light. Not that light, the enveloping one, just daylight. White walls.

"Leon?"

A face. Mihai. Leon tried to speak, his tongue stuck. "Some water."

"Yes, yes."

A plastic straw, a stream of cool liquid soaking into his dry throat.

"They said you'd be dehydrated, even with the drip."

Mihai's face now in focus, concerned.

"Where is this?"

"Obstbaum's. I had you moved. The hospital, there's a risk of infection. Even Kleinman said. After an operation."

"An operation."

"He had to take a piece of your lung. Where the bullet hit. Take a breath. See? A little less. No more smoking, so maybe a good thing. Not so good for your business, though. Considering."

Leon tried to smile, then wet his cracked lips with the straw.

"You're lucky, you know that? A matter of inches, he said, and then — And now look. The man of the hour. Watch, they'll give you a medal. Something. What for? Being lucky." He shrugged. "But that's what they're always for, isn't it?"

Leon tried to follow this, still catching up. "How are you here? You were —"

"How? The train. From Aleppo. Like always."

"That's days."

"Two. You've been out. Maybe Rabbi Pilcer prayed for you. He has a direct line," he said, pointing a finger up. "So he thinks. Somebody must have. You almost died."

"Yes."

"Yes? You knew?"

"It doesn't feel like anything," Leon said

to the ceiling, then looked back. "I saw you."

Mihai stopped, thrown by this, then took the water away. "Wonderful. With wings? This is what happens? A little disappointing."

Leon reached over the sheet to cover Mihai's hand, resting it there. Mihai looked up, surprised, not sure how to respond.

"The ship?"

Mihai nodded. "All safe. Four hundred new citizens. So thank you for that."

Leon shook his head. "Him. Jianu. He made them let you go."

"Why? For his sins? You think he feels something? Not that one."

"How do you know?"

"A man tries to cut your throat, you know everything about him."

Leon was quiet, looking toward the window, everything else too complicated.

"You don't forget what that's like. Ever," Mihai said, touching his neck, as if a knife had actually been there. He looked away. "Anyway, it's finished now. He pays. It's what I said from the first. The first night."

"That's not why I killed him."

"Why you killed him," Mihai said slowly, looking at Leon. "No? Why?"

"He asked me."

Mihai didn't say anything to this.

"He wanted me to do it."

"Leon," Mihai said gently, "maybe it's a little fast, all this. So much talk." He paused. "Altan said, the Russians. People saw them. It's still a little confusing, maybe. All the drugs —"

"Not the last shot," Leon said. "That was me." He lay back. As if it made any difference now. Altan already shaping the way it happened. You couldn't fight the next war until you'd lied about the last one.

"Yes?" Mihai said, humoring him.

"It was the right thing to do," Leon said, his voice trailing off, vague.

"Maybe you should rest now. I'll tell the nurse —"

"No," Leon said, gripping his hand. "Talk. I want to know. Tell me —"

"What?"

"Durak," Leon said, the first thing that came into his mind. "You know Russian? What does *durak* mean?"

"Fool."

Leon smiled. "Yes. That makes sense. He would think that."

"Who?"

"Melnikov. He said it before he shot me. And I was. But not then. Before." He lifted his hand slightly, brushing the air. "Wrong about Tommy. Everything. *Durak.*" He raised his eyes. "I'm glad about the ship. So that's one thing. That's why you came back? There's another? You can get more out?"

"Not from Istanbul. It's not so easy now. Italy."

"More typhus?" Leon said.

"No. Getting out of Romania. It's safer from the west. Through Vienna, away from the Russians. Istanbul's finished for us. The office — I don't know how long."

"You're going to Italy?"

"No. Palestine. Home." He looked up, tentative, his voice casual. "You too. Why not?"

"To do what? Grow oranges?"

"Fight. The British are going to make a mess. The Arabs hate us. Like the Poles. There'll be —"

"Another war," Leon finished.

"But this one we don't lose. You like all this so much." He waved his hand over Leon's bandages. "Come to Palestine."

"With one lung."

"We're not so picky. We take anyone who's with us." He took a breath. "There are other ways to fight."

Leon turned. "I'm not with anybody."

"And that's why you buy the *Victorei* out. And now who do you see when you die?" A joke to keep a door open, an exit if he needed it.

"I saw Phil too."

Mihai cocked his head.

"My brother. Who was shot down. I used to think, sometimes, I was doing this for him. Helping. Working for Tommy. But that's just something you tell yourself. To make it okay." He turned to face Mihai. "How do you help somebody who's dead? So who would I be helping this time? Anna?"

Mihai looked away, uncomfortable. "No. Four hundred, still alive. And more coming." He hesitated. "It could be useful with the British. Not being a Jew." Another pause. "What's here for you?"

"I can't take her there," Leon said quietly. "Do you want me to leave her? Is that what you'd do?"

Mihai sat back, at a loss, then got up and walked over to the window. "Me? No." He looked out. "You'd better sleep." The room confining now.

"I'm awake."

Mihai started fingering some plants on the windowsill, restless. "So who is this woman. She comes every day."

"Kay? She was Frank's —"

"I know who she is. Who is she to you?"

Leon said nothing. We'll see.

"She knows about Anna?"

Leon nodded.

"Not just a friend, I think." He held up his hand before Leon could say anything.

"She's here?"

Mihai looked at his watch. "Soon. Every day." He made a half smile. "Shifts. Me, then her." He looked up. "She was afraid she'd miss you. That you wouldn't wake up. Before she left."

"Before she —" Seeing her walking across the bridge in her hat, Melnikov's shield, not stopping this time, leaving. "When?" All he could say.

"I don't know. She has a priority. They arranged it."

They. Trying to think, his mind fuzzy, sorting this out.

"So tell me. What's what." Mihai looked over. "I don't judge."

But what was there to tell? Nothing decided. And then it was.

"When is she here?" Beginning to move, one hand on the sheet.

"Relax," Mihai said, coming over to stop him. "You've got tubes coming and going. You'll knock this over." He nodded to the drip. "Let me see. This probably isn't good for you, you know. The commotion, I mean. Head back. Come on. I don't leave until I see — okay, better."

So much better that Leon felt his eyes begin to close, seeing Mihai leave in a narrow strip, like watching someone through a venetian blind.

There was a voice in the back of his head, anxious, then another farther away, a man's voice, German.

"Only a few minutes, yes? He goes in and out. If you see that, let him go. He needs the sleep."

"All right." Kay's voice, the smell of her perfume.

"He may not know you."

"Mihai said —"

"Mihai. Now Mossad is giving out medical degrees."

At the door, heads bent toward each other, but Kay restless, shifting her feet, looking back at the bed. The way she had been that first morning in Tünel, having her cigarette, jumpy, not sure of things.

"Kay," Leon said, the sound sticking a little in his throat.

"You see," she said to Obstbaum, hurrying over to the bed. "He does."

Obstbaum nodded, tapping his wristwatch at her, and left.

"Thank God," she said to Leon, taking

his hand. "I've been so worried."

"You're leaving," he said, the scratchiness clearing.

She took her hand away. "Mihai told you. He said. I wanted to tell you myself."

"Altan's making you go."

"Why would he do that?"

"No witnesses. He's making up some story. Not what happened."

"Leon," she said, soothing. "People were there. On the bridge. It was — public."

"He got you a priority." Trying to put things one after the other, assemble them. "He wants to get you out of the country. Did you give them a statement?"

She looked at him, disconcerted. "Don't. Please. You almost died on the bridge. And you're still —" She stopped. "It was me. I want to go."

"Why?"

"I can't stay here," she said, picking at the sheet. "I had time to think — while you were out. I never did before. It was always — later, let's talk about it later. But then I did." She grazed his hand. "I want to go home."

"But you can't —"

"I'll stay with my sister for a while," she said, ignoring him. "Until we drive each other crazy. The way we always do. And then

— something. Frank's insurance isn't going to go very far." She looked up. "This isn't what you want to know, is it?"

"No."

She went over to the night table, busying herself. "I've been thinking how to say this and now —" She handed him a glass with a straw. "Here. You're supposed to keep drinking."

He took some water, then watched her as she circled the bed. "You're all dressed." A suit with an open-neck blouse, a silver pin on the lapel. Lipstick.

"A seat opened up today. I wasn't going to take it if you were still —"

"Today?" He tried to prop himself up against the pillow.

She adjusted it for him. "I wouldn't go without saying good-bye," she said, then stopped fluffing the pillow and sat next to him, running her hand across his forehead. "Oh god, how do I do this?"

"Don't. Don't go."

"No, stay. There's still so much to see," she said, using a guide's vioice, then stopped. "Except I don't want to see it anymore. I don't want to worry about drinking the water. And wonder what people are saying. All that screeching over the loudspeakers. How many times a day do

582

people have to pray anyway?"

"Five," he said quietly.

"Okay," she said, nodding. "It's not any of that. It's — I woke up. On the bridge. Do you know what that was like for me? Watching you die?"

"Why were you there? What did Melnikov tell you?" Still wanting to know.

"That you asked for me. That you —" She waved her hand. "Oh, what does it matter? He got me there so you'd go through with it, I guess. I didn't really *ask* him." She looked down. "I should have known. You wouldn't do that — ask for me." She lifted her head. "And then everything started. The guns. People *killed*." She looked at him. "They said none of that was supposed to happen, the guns. It was just a trade. Until you —" She hesitated. "Why did you?"

"It wasn't a trade," he said, throat still dry.

"But they said —"

"We knew what they were going to do to him. After they were finished with him." He stopped, the words still far back, pulling them. "That's not even — standing outside. Inside. Putting them on hooks."

"Inside?" she said, trying to follow.

He closed his eyes, too weak to unravel any more. "He trusted me," he said.

She looked at him, a minute's delay, as if she were translating. "So you helped him. And they shot you too," she said finally. "I thought you were dead. Everything just — stopped. Stopped. But you were still breathing. Eyes open. And you said something. I thought, maybe it's the last time. Do you remember? What you said?"

He shook his head, waiting.

"You said her name. You called her. You were looking right at me, eyes open, and you were calling her."

"Kay."

"No, it's all right. It's just — when I heard it, I knew. Like somebody shaking me awake. She was the love of your life. Is." She stopped. "Is. I was — something else." She bit her lip. "I went to see her. Down the hall. I wanted to see what she looked like." She nodded, answering an unspoken question. "If she was prettier than me. And then I didn't go in. Get close enough to tell. I didn't want to know. What if she isn't? It's better if I think she is."

"Don't."

She reached over, stroking his forehead again. "I know. It's just the way it is. It's not something you can —" She stopped, moving her hand away. "It's just, I'd like that too. To have that. So maybe I'll find him

584

back home. Not so exciting," she said, twisting her mouth, spreading her hand to take in the city outside. "Maybe somebody who plays golf and takes the train. But still — the love of my life. Like her."

She leaned over and kissed his forehead. "Anyway, I have to think there is one." She looked into his eyes, her face soft. "I hope it wasn't you. That would be so unfair, wouldn't it? Only a few days. While you were asleep I was thinking about that, how many there were, and then I thought, don't count. What if it's two, three, just a few, and it seems like —" She stopped. "So better not."

He reached up, putting his hand against her cheek, the IV line dangling, as if it were part of a string he was trying to hold.

"And, you know, maybe it's enough like this. To have a taste. Stop before —" She looked away. "You don't see it at the beginning. I don't know why not. How else would it end? What did I think this was. What did you think it was."

She moved his hand back to the bed and stood up.

"So. Before that. While we still feel —" She moved to the chair, picking up a hat and purse. "You know at least it makes it easier. You like this." She nodded to the

585

hospital bed. "With all those things in your arm. So you have to stay there. Otherwise. You know what it would be like. You'd get up and hold me and then how could I go?" Her eyes filling now. "Because I'd think it was you. The one."

She came back to the bed and leaned down, kissing him on the forehead, a good-bye kiss, then his arms went up around her, pulling her closer, and the kiss became something else, a secret, until he felt moisture in the cracks of his lips, smeared with her.

"Listen to me," she said. "Later, you'll think different things about me." She put her fingers to his mouth before he could say anything. "You will. I just want you to remember. This part was true. Will you remember that?"

He said nothing, afraid she would remove the fingers, actually go.

"Your car's here." Obstbaum in the doorway, Kay's head jerking back.

"Coming," she said, barely getting it out.

Obstbaum lingered at the door so she just squeezed Leon's hand, a different good-bye. Still caring about how it must look to him. She cocked her head toward the hall, the quiet room at the end. "I hope she comes back. Think how she'd feel. Knowing you waited for her."

She turned to go, Leon's hand resting on the bed but in his mind's eye stretching out and then, seeing Obstbaum, dropping back. By the time she reached the door, Obstbaum had disappeared, but it was too late to reach her now, and his body was sinking into the sheets, the way it had felt on the bridge, when he thought he was dying.

"But would you do something for me?" Kay said, turning, eyes brimming.

He looked up, not having to nod, knowing she could sense it.

"Don't tell her. About us."

He waited.

"She wouldn't like it. But that's not it. It's something for me. I want to be the one you can't talk about. I want that much."

They took the catheter out that afternoon and gave him broth, his first food. It was important to move, not lie in bed, so he was walked around the room, baby steps, wheeling the IV rack with him, a nurse at his side. Not too much at once, to the door, then back, a rest in the chair. By the end of the day, he could go to the bathroom by himself. Altan came just as it was getting dark.

"Out of bed already? That's a good sign," he said, flipping on the overhead light.

Leon looked up from the visitor's chair, where he'd been staring at the floor.

"A little gloomy, sitting like this in the dark." Altan pulled up another chair, a bustling motion, settling a briefcase by his side. "And you so lucky. The last man standing — that's the expression, yes?"

"What are you going to say happened?"

"Say? What did happen."

"No you won't. It was a mess. And Jianu's dead. Nobody got him. So what are you going to say?" His voice still weak, a slight croaking.

"Well, as to that." Altan crossed his leg and sat back, so that his face went partly in shadow, the phantom moustache flickering back and forth on his lip. "Everybody's dead. Except you. So it's your story." He looked at Leon. "How they killed each other."

"And Gülün finally gets his medal."

"No, that wouldn't be convenient," he said, drawing out a cigarette and lighting it. "A Turkish officer shooting a Russian? People would be upset. Oh," he said, noticing Leon's face, "it's not allowed?" He looked at the cigarette. "Maybe this once. Something between us."

"So who shot him?"

"Jianu. They shot each other. Unfortunately, some innocents got in the way." He nodded at Leon. "Fortunately, they recovered."

"And they'll believe that."

"Why wouldn't they? It's what everybody wants. What suits. Jianu's dead, which is what the Russians wanted. And you know, I think they'll be grateful Melnikov's dead too. A brutal man, even for them. You heard about Stalingrad? His own men? Think what a relief to have him gone. Of course, they can't say this." He drew on the cigarette. "The Americans avenge their Mr. Bishop. And we? We get to protest to both. Guns in the streets. Endangering Turkish citizens. Apologies have been demanded. Even the Russians are embarrassed. An excess. They should learn from the Ottomans. The silk cord. No noise. No *pop, pop.* But very effective. Of course, they won't learn that. It's not in their nature." He looked up. "But at least this way, an acceptable story."

"And who shot me? If they killed each other."

"Jianu. Before. If we say a Russian, there's no end to this. Official protests. Swords waving. Everybody a *gazi.* It's enough now. Jianu was that kind of man." He looked straight at Leon. "First Mr. King. Poor Enver. Now Melnikov. And you."

"Anybody else you can think of while you're at it? Some unsolved cases you can throw in the file? Christ. Alexei killed everybody. That's what I'm supposed to say?"

"You already have," Altan said, lifting the briefcase. "You think only Emniyet does this? Arranges things?" He patted the case. "We have the statements. Gülün confirms yours. No medal this time, but a different reward, for his discretion." He paused, taking in Leon's expression. "You think it's corrupt. The old empire. My friend, everybody changes the story. The Russians? They've believed their own lies for so long that —" He let the thought finish itself. "And now the Americans. You're just learning how to live in the world." He looked over at Leon. "They shot each other. You recovered. It's the convenient story."

"But there were witnesses. Not everybody's Gülün. So you got rid of her. You sent her home."

"Who? Oh, the faithful Mrs. Bishop."

"You couldn't take any chances with her. You got her a priority."

"Leon, she didn't need anyone to do that for her. All she had to do —" He stopped. "You still don't know? She didn't tell you?"

Leon said nothing, feeling for the armrest.

Altan made a kind of sigh through his nose. "That she leaves to me." He put out the cigarette. "So foolish, the Americans, using the wife. His idea too, I'm told. Why? To save money? She has time on her hands, why not put her to use? To get what? What people say at parties in Ankara? Amateurs." Alexei's assessment too, a professional shake of the head. "And what happens? Complications," he said, rolling an eye at Leon. "Emotions. There's no place for that. She wanted the trade. Her husband's killer." He glanced away. "Maybe she felt — well, whatever reason. I told Barksdale it wasn't necessary. Don't give up Jianu. It's just a matter of time. But no. They listened to her. An amateur."

Leon was listening now too. Just a trade, she'd said, until you — Why did you?

"Always a mistake, using a wife. Think of the risk, the one can be used against the other."

"But they weren't," Leon said dully, leading him, wanting to know, his voice sounding like an echo.

"Still, a risk. Two. It compromises any operation."

"No. She never said a word."

"Of course not. You were the operation."

He felt the chill on his back, air coming

through the open hospital gown. Then the weight again, his body sinking into the chair.

"Not that it did much good," Altan was saying. "You didn't give her anything. I thought, now she's got him. But she didn't."

"No," Leon said, another echo.

"You never gave Jianu away. Not even to her," he said, oddly admiring.

"I couldn't," Leon said, his voice still far away.

"Leon?"

He looked up, aware now that Altan had been talking. "I was supposed to keep him safe. That's what it was all for. Everything that happened. To keep him alive." His mouth began to turn up, as if he had heard a joke, back where his voice was. "Keep him alive."

Altan raised his eyebrows, a nurse watching a patient.

"You all wanted him," Leon said. "Everybody. Then nobody did."

Altan shifted in his chair. "In my opinion, a waste. What can he do for anybody now? Dead."

"Nothing. That's what he wanted."

Altan looked at him, not sure how to take this.

"All this to get Dorothy," Leon said, the idea still implausible.

"No."

"No?"

"A very devious man, Melnikov," Altan said, sitting back, settling in. "I don't think he trusted you. Your mistress, a little insurance to keep your gun in your pocket. Mrs. Wheeler to distract you. While the real one is taken away. Of course eventually you would realize the mistake. All those questions with no answers. But by then too late. He's gone."

"Who?" Leon said, only half listening.

"Mr. Wheeler. Naval attaché. An expert on the Black Sea. And much else, it seems."

Leon raised his head. Another joke, off somewhere. "Alexei always said he'd be in Ankara," he said.

"Yes. The logical place."

"She knew?"

Altan shook his head. "The Soviets would never use a husband and wife. They're too experienced for that," he said, making a point. "She knew nothing. Which, of course, came out. An odd marriage. But maybe not. What do any of us know? But suspicions, yes. A woman who noticed things. So maybe she knew and she didn't know. Both. It's possible, don't you think?"

"Yes."

"Anyway, we detained Mr. Wheeler before

he could go, so not such an ordeal for her. Polite questions, I understand."

"You detained him?"

"The Black Sea was an Ottoman lake. Once. When the bear takes an interest — we like to know why. A few questions. But now the Americans have him." He opened his hand. "They paid for him. You paid for him."

A face he couldn't even remember, leaning over Dorothy's desk.

"He went along with this? Setting her up?"

"Leon," Altan said, a mock patience. "What would be the sense of telling him? You never know how people are going to react. Of course he was in no position to object. They were getting him out. Maybe later he could send for her. Maybe she refuses. They often do, I'm told. Given what it's like there. But we got to him first."

He leaned back again, pleased, as if he had tied a bow that had come out right, like the statements in his briefcase. Dorothy would have to make one too. What she knew and didn't know. Left behind.

Leon looked up from the chair. "You're all bastards, aren't you? All of you. Tommy and —" He stopped, too tired to follow his own thought. "Bastards."

Altan stared at him for a minute, then

nodded slowly, humoring him. "But in a good cause," he said, getting up and walking to the window, then turning to Leon. "What did you think this was?"

Another echo, her voice again. What did you think this was? In the beginning. Maybe not thinking at all.

"Good cause," Leon said, his voice rough with scorn. "What cause?"

Altan's body went still, not rising to this. He took out another cigarette.

"Do you know how long we have been doing this? The empire should have been finished two hundred years ago, more. From then on, there were only bad choices. Good for someone else, maybe, but bad for us. How much money to borrow? How much land to give up. All bad choices. But we survived. We found a balance between. The Ottoman solution," he said ironically. "I like to think it's a kind of wisdom. Life is like that, don't you think? Mostly bad choices. All you can do is keep your balance between them."

"You lost the empire," Leon said flatly.

Altan peered at him through the smoke, annoyed. "And we learned from that too. Sometimes one bad choice is worse than the other. *Ferengi* who want to use us to fight each other. So we keep our eyes open now. We have to know how things are. It's the only way to protect ourselves, to know."

"No matter what you have to do. Who gets killed."

Altan shrugged. "It's not a perfect world. For whom are you in mourning?"

Leon looked away. "No one."

Everyone disposable, as he'd been, Tommy's gun firing at him.

"Good," Altan said, coming back from the window. "It's important in this work — to keep a clear head." He picked up the briefcase and put it on the table to open it. "It's been interesting, watching you. I didn't think you could do it. So many complications. But no, good instincts. You are — resourceful. Impossible to train someone for that. My only concern was this weakness — it's a mistake to form a personal attachment. Trusting a man like Jianu. Of course he'd take advantage, try to escape. That was sloppy. But in the end you did what you had to do. So you learn from that."

Leon looked up, another story.

"You know I killed him."

"So Gülün said. I confess, I was relieved. I didn't know if you were hard enough to —"

"That's not why."

"No? Well, it comes to the same thing."

He pulled out a paper. "For the Americans."

"What's that?"

"Your statement. How they killed each other."

"Why are you doing this? What difference does it make to you?"

"If the Americans knew, how it really was, they'd never trust you again. This way, who knows, they might give you a medal."

"I don't want a medal."

Altan nodded. "Or a job, either. They'll offer you one, I think. Here, sign. But you're finished with all that. Reasons of health, maybe," he said, touching his chest.

"Finished?" Leon said, waiting for the rest.

"You can't serve two masters. You might be tempted to play them off against each other."

"Two."

"I need to trust my people."

"Your people."

"People who work for me. I think it'll be good, the two of us." He held out a pen. "Sign it."

Leon stared at him, the soft click of a lock turning in his head. "And if I don't?"

"My friend, you don't want to put that gun in your hand. Everything changes. For you. It starts all over again. On both sides. And this time, you're Jianu. We have better things to do." He gestured again with the pen.

"What makes you think I'd ever do that? Work for you?"

"Leon, the best warriors the Ottomans ever had were the Janissaries. All foreign born. All loyal. They served the empire." He looked over. "And the empire served them."

"They were slaves."

"Only in a manner of speaking. Chains of self-interest would describe it better. Golden chains. You are the perfect Janissary."

"I don't want anything from you."

"No? There are other statements here," he said, reaching in and pulling out some papers. "For another file, I thought. Somewhere safe. The fisherman's. What happened at Bebek? Jianu can no longer tell us. Now there's only you. If a judge believes you." He pulled out more paper. "Gülün's other statement. So puzzling. What reason could you possibly have for shooting Jianu? Self-defense? A man lying there, without a gun? Of course other statements can be arranged. From people on the bridge. So there's no doubt. Now two men killed. Bebek, the bridge. Think how many stories we could make up to link them. Perhaps you have one of your own. But the facts will be that you were there, both places, and killed both men." He stopped. "Leon. Even with bad choices, there are worse choices."

Leon stared down at the paper, the one that said he hadn't done anything at all, a story of good intentions.

"I'm not a traitor."

"Yes, I know. The good patriot. Leon, we want the Americans to protect us. I don't ask you to work against them."

"Just what people say at parties?" Leon said, sarcastic.

"Well, the foreign community. It's true, we like to have ears there. But they're leaving Istanbul. The war's over. We're not —" A second, looking for the word. "Strategic anymore. If only the Russians would go too. But no, so we need other ears. Their Turkish friends. Some of them you already know. Friends of Georg. What do they say to them? A foreigner who speaks Turkish — a valuable asset. An American working for me? No Turk would ever suspect. And resourceful. Think of it this way. It's what you would do for the Americans. Except you do it for me. Unofficial. The way you like to work." He paused, the air still. "For me. But not against them. You have my word."

"Your word," Leon said, almost laughing.

"Yes, my word," Altan said, nodding to the papers. "Not Gülün's. Not the fisherman's. None of them. Mine. You have that. So you see. What a perfect Janissary arrangement it will be. We will have an obligation to each other. Sign, please."

Leon took the pen.

"And now you should rest," Altan said, glancing at his watch, then at Leon as he wrote, a hasty scribble, his head down, as if he didn't want anyone to see. "Obstbaum will be angry with me. Would you like help? To the bed?"

"No."

Altan put the statement in the briefcase. "So. We understand each other? You know, I'm looking forward to this." He began moving to the door. "One thing," he said, stopping. "You don't mind? A personal curiosity. Who did shoot Mr. King?"

Leon said nothing for a second. How long ago had it been? Then he met Altan's eyes.

"I did."

Altan tilted his head a little, surprised. "You," he said. "But why?"

"Self-defense."

Altan started to smile, as if Leon had said something clever, then rolled his eyes, a genial salute. "Of course. Self-defense." He nodded, leaving. "It's as Lily says. An Istanbullu."

■ ■ ■ ■

Later, lying in bed, he looked for a wall clock and realized he had entered Anna's timeless world. There were no hours at the clinic, no days, each the same as before, all continuous. Thoughts came out of sequence, at random, with no purpose beyond themselves, unless you tried to follow them. He had been thinking of the blue tiles at the Çinili Camii, the way they shaded into turquoise and gray, and he wondered if he was really thinking about Kay, or just the perfect peace of the courtyard that day, sitting near the fountain, Kay telling him he could never really belong here. Asking questions. For Frank. But at some point she had stopped. Maybe even that day. He would have known, felt it when they'd gone back to Laleli. It was important to remember, that she had stopped.

Maybe the night of the party, when things changed, watching him with Georg. He saw the round face again, shiny with sweat and fear, apologizing. The last thing he did in his life, too late to change. But did anyone? Even given the chance? He saw other faces, Barbara and Ed, touched by death and going on as before, and he saw how it would

601

be for him, back to days at the office, furtive Thursdays with Marina, drinks at the
Park, the nightly brandy at Cihangir with
his war memorial of photographs, all the
same, except for the meetings with Altan,
the deceit that would give an edge to all the
rest, then eat away at it until nothing else
was left. Visits to Anna with nothing to say
because everything in his life was now
secret, even from her.

He swung out of bed, backing against it
until he was no longer dizzy, then took hold
of the IV rack and moved it with him. In
the hall, just the dim night-lights and soft,
sibilant Turkish coming from the nurses'
station, something about the supervisor
changing their shifts, ordinary life. He had
put on slippers and now slid quietly over
the waxed linoleum. At the end, Anna's
room had the usual light near the floor,
some moon coming through. She opened
her eyes when he touched her hand.

"Don't be frightened. I know it's late. I
couldn't come before."

Now that she had registered the disturbance, the hand touching her, she retreated,
eyes blank. Thinking what? Maybe everyone
at Obstbaum's had the same mental life,
stray thoughts, out of order.

"I'm down the hall," he said. "Are you

surprised? I never thought I'd be here, did you?"

He stopped. Like talking to a child. Not what he'd come for, what they could do anymore. Ed and Barbara going on as before. But it wasn't before.

"I'm going to sit down," he said. "I get tired." He pulled the chair nearer to the bed. "There's so much to tell. I'm not sure where to start."

He sat for a minute, staring, trying to find a narrative, then gave it up.

"The funny thing is," he said slowly, sitting back, "I thought I was doing the right thing. Each time. When I helped him in the water, I never even thought about it. How could you do anything else? And then when I shot him. Each time. I thought it was the right thing to do. But it couldn't have been, could it? Both." He looked up, as if she had said something, then nodded. "He asked. I was the only one he had left. To ask. So what does that make me? Not that anybody cares. He wasn't —"

What? He thought of him in the *hamam*, showing his scars, his face in the doorway on the way down from Laleli, already a death mask.

"A good man," he finished. "The opposite. The opposite." Repeating it, convincing himself. "Still. I used to think I was. But who gets to say? I've been thinking about that, who gets to say?"

He rubbed the bandage over the IV on the back of his hand, the thought circling.

"During the war it's okay, killing people. Then it's not. Can you turn it off, just like that? Like some switch in people's heads. Once you start."

He looked up again, but she hadn't moved, her face smooth, not a line.

"Anyway, it's done. You don't get to do it over." His eyes went to the window. "Any of it, I guess. Everything you've done." Drifting, thoughts out of sequence again. "I met somebody."

He pulled back, hearing Kay's voice. She wouldn't like it.

"I thought that was right too. And stealing the money. Everything. And now —" Another minute, the silence like sleep. "It just happened, meeting her. I didn't plan it." He made a face. "She did, I guess. I don't know. But then — she didn't expect — Anyway, she said so."

This thought getting away too, his mind wandering out to the garden. Where he and Alexei had stood watching the dark room, saying good-bye. But there was something else, important.

"Do you believe someone can lie," he said, "and still tell the truth?" His face still turned to the window. "Lie about things. But not the two of you. What happens between you, that has to be the truth, doesn't it? Or we wouldn't have anything. Even for a while."

He stopped, aware that he was talking out loud, that she might actually have heard. Something she couldn't hear. He turned back to her, covering it.

"The rest I don't know. That's a funny thing too. I wanted Tommy to give me a job and now I've got it. But not for him." He leaned forward. "We need to think about what to do. Work for Altan — it's not illegal exactly, but it's something. And it won't stay that way, whatever he says. He wants me to think I can get away with it, everything, but the minute he's finished with me —" Alexei's lemon now. "They're all bastards. All of them. They throw people away. Our side too." He looked up. "But even so." He thought of Phil, kneeling with the ground crew.

"We have to leave Istanbul," he said, his voice firmer, planning. "He thinks I'm trapped, but he doesn't know about the money. The rest of it, just sitting there. Nobody knows. We can use it to get out.

There are ways — that's what I've been do-ing. I can do it. I'm resourceful," he said, a rueful joke to himself. "We could go to Italy. Help Mihai with his boats again. Anywhere. We could go home."

He leaned over, but her eyes were just as still as before and looking at them he saw that there wasn't any home, just where they already were, in-between.

"It wouldn't be hard to do if you came back," he said. "For me to arrange things. Altan wouldn't suspect. And what could he do, once we were gone. You can't want to stay there, wherever you are. And I'd be with you. I'd never leave you. You know that. She knew that. She knew that about me. We could —"

And then he was suddenly out of breath, leaning back against the chair, knowing that none of it was going to happen, that all the plans were just a last defiant wriggle before Altan's chains settled around him.

"I thought it was all for the best. Some-thing I could do," he said quietly. "For the war. No. Not just that. Exciting. I thought it would be exciting. Be one of those people at the Park."

Feeling a tightening around his chest, not fear, something staring at him, implacable, his new life. There wouldn't be any starting over, no new evenings together in Cihangir. What would there be to say? Both of them locked in silence for their own reasons. Even here, having to be careful everywhere. Anna lost to him now too. Then, for only a second, he thought he saw her finger move, maybe sensing it, feeling it with him, the way it would be, and he reached over and covered her hand.

"It's going to be all right, really," he said quickly, reassuring. "This is the best place for you and when you're better — Don't worry about Altan, I can handle him. He's no worse than the rest. Look at Tommy. I just have to keep him interested. You learn these things. And actually, I'm good at this. That's why he — I don't want you to worry about anything." Holding her hand tighter, his voice bright, making conversation, keeping everything from her now, not just Kay, everything he'd have to do. "You always liked it here. And you know, a Janissary, if he played his cards right, could become an important man. Wouldn't that be a kick in the head? The last thing we expected but —" Bubbling, keeping her spirits up, away from the rest. "And we'd still have the money if we need it. So there's nothing to worry about. We'll be fine." He stroked her hand. "You know, on the bridge, when I saw your face, you looked just the way you did when we first met. So that must mean something, don't you think? Nothing's changed." He paused. "Not for you." He looked away, out to the garden. "It'll be spring soon." In a month the Judas trees outside would start to blossom all along the Bosphorus. "You could come back for that," he said.

He waited a minute for an answer, and then nobody said anything at all.

AUTHOR'S NOTE

The horrors of Străuleşti, the sinking of the *Struma,* Ira Hirschmann's heroic work for the War Refugee Board rescuing European Jews, and the tireless efforts of Mossad le Aliyah Bet (Committee for Illegal Immigration) are all matters of historical record and appear here only as background. The events and people in *Istanbul Passage* are fiction.

Much has changed in Istanbul since 1945. The city now sprawls beyond its hills to accommodate an estimated eleven million more people. Old tram lines have been discontinued. The fabled Park Hotel was torn down to build a parking garage (with the same fabled view). Robert College is now Bosphorus University. Street names have changed: the old Rue de Pera had already become the Istiklal Caddesi, but now Aya Paşa Caddesi, where Leon lived, is Ismet Inönü Caddesi, etc. Word spellings, in a country that has used a western alphabet only since 1928, keep taking new forms. Haghia Sophia or Aya Sofya? Abdülhammit or Abdul Hamid? *Meyhanes* or *mihanyes?* Alternative spellings extend into the Balkans too. The Black Sea port may be Constancia or Constanța, and its country Romania, Rumania, or Roumania.

Given all this, my hope was to use only those place names and word forms current in 1945, but source materials show the same variants and inconsistencies, so in the end the usage here is whatever I felt would be most familiar to the reader or, sometimes, just personal preference. Of course, as any grateful visitor to Istanbul knows, much has not changed. Sinan's beautiful buildings still give the city its timeless profile and the fishermen and *simit* sellers still line Galata Bridge.

ABOUT THE AUTHOR

Joseph Kanon is the author of five other novels, *Los Alamos, The Prodigal Spy, The Good German, Alibi,* and *Stardust.* A winner of both the Edgar Award and the Hammett Prize, he lives in New York City. Visit him online at www.JosephKanon.com.

The employees of Thorndike Press hope you have enjoyed this Large Print book. All our Thorndike, Wheeler, and Kennebec Large Print titles are designed for easy reading, and all our books are made to last. Other Thorndike Press Large Print books are available at your library, through selected bookstores, or directly from us.

For information about titles, please call:
   (800) 223-1244

or visit our Web site at:
   http://gale.cengage.com/thorndike

To share your comments, please write:
   Publisher
   Thorndike Press
   10 Water St., Suite 310
   Waterville, ME 04901

ASHE COUNTY PUBLIC LIBRARY
148 Library Drive
West Jefferson, NC 28694-9793